D0717056

Books should be returned or renewed by the last date above. Renew by phone **03000 41 31 31** or online *www.kent.gov.uk/libs*

Fresh Fiction

House Rules
'Rising star Neill has made the learning curve for her gutsy heroine, Merit, quite steep, which means the journey is all the more spellbinding'
Romantic Times

Biting Bad
'As always there is heart-pounding danger, high-stakes drama, and excitement'
Romantic Times

C333719933

Blood Games

'One of my all-time-favourite vampire series . . . It's witty, it's adventurous, there's political intrigue, murder, magic, and so much more'

USA Today

Also by Chloe Neill

Chicagoland Vampires series

Some Girls Bite

Friday Night Bites

Twice Bitten

Hard Bitten

Drink Deep

Biting Cold

House Rules

Biting Bad

Wild Things

Blood Games

Howling for You (eBook only novella)

Lucky Break (eBook only novella)

Dark Elite series

Firespell

Hexbound

Charmfall

A Chicagoland Vampires Novel

DARK DEBT

CHLOE NEILL

First published in Great Britain in 2015 by
Gollancz
An imprint of the Orion Publishing Group
Orion House, 5 Upper St Martin's Lane, London WC2H 9EA
An Hachette UK Company

1 3 5 7 9 10 8 6 4 2

A CIP catalogue record for this book is available
from the British Library

ISBN 978 1 473 20849 0

Printed in Great Britain by Clays Ltd, plc

The Orion Publishing Group's policy is to use papers that are
natural, renewable and recyclable products and made from wood
grown in sustainable forests. The logging and manufacturing
processes are expected to conform to the environmental regulations
of the country of origin.

www.chloeneill.com
www.orionbooks.co.uk
www.gollancz.co.uk

Thanks to Jocelyn Bourbonniere
for assistance with French phrases.

Neither a borrower nor a lender be. . . .

—*William Shakespeare*

DARK DEBT

❖ ❖

CHAPTER ONE

CLEVER GIRL

Early April
Chicago, Illinois

There were two seasons in Chicago: winter and construction. If it wasn't snowing, orange cones narrowed the Dan Ryan, or lower Wacker was closed. Snow and traffic defined our lives as Chicagoans.

Nested within those seasons were the other activities that defined life for many in Chicago. During baseball season, it was Cubs versus Sox. During tourist season, you served them, you screamed at them, or, if you worked at Billy Goat's, both. During summer, the beaches were open. And for a few spare weeks, the water of Lake Michigan was even warm enough for a dip.

Not that I'd had much occasion to sunbathe or swim recently. They didn't make sunscreen strong enough for vampires.

But when spring rolled around and construction cones popped onto asphalt like neon flowers, even vampires shook off winter.

We exchanged quilted jackets, electric blankets, heavy boots, and balaclavas for tanks, sandals, and nights in the warm spring air.

Tonight, we sat on a blanket on the grass at Milton Lee Olive Park, an expanse of green and fountains near Navy Pier honoring a soldier who'd given his life to save others, and won a Medal of Honor for his sacrifice. A burst of spring air had warmed the city, and we'd taken advantage, finding a quiet spot for a picnic to celebrate the end of a long, cold winter. At two o'clock in the morning, the park was definitely quiet.

Ethan Sullivan, Master of Cadogan House and now one of twelve members of the newly established Assembly of American Masters, sat beside me on a piecework quilt, one knee bent, one leg extended, his hand at the small of my back, rubbing small circles as we watched the lights of Chicago blink across the skyline in front of us.

He had a tall and rangy body of hard planes and sculpted muscle, and golden blond hair that just reached his shoulders and surrounded honed cheekbones, a straight nose, deep-set green eyes, and imperious eyebrows. I was his Novitiate and the Cadogan's Sentinel, and I was utterly relieved that winter had finally weakened its grip on the city.

"This is not a bad way to spend an evening," said the girl on the blanket beside ours, her striking blue hair drawn in a complicated braid that lay across her shoulder. Her Cupid's bow mouth was drawn into a smile, her hand clasped in the long fingers of her boyfriend's. He was well built and shaved-headed, with piercing green eyes and a generous mouth. And, like her, he was a sorcerer. He had a thing for snarky T-shirts, and tonight's gem was black, with KEEP CALM AND FIREBALL in clean white text across the front.

Mallory Carmichael was my oldest friend, and Catcher Bell

was her live-in beau. Catcher worked for my grandfather Chuck Merit, the city's Supernatural Ombudsman.

"No, it's not," I agreed. "This was a very good idea." I sipped from a bottle of Sweet Summer Blood4You, a blend of blood and lemonade that I enjoyed against my own better judgment. The drink was good, and the air was sweet with spring and the scent of white flowers that drifted down from the trees like snow, forming constellations on the new grass. Ethan's hand warmed the skin on my back. This was as close to a day at the beach as I was ever likely to get. And it was a pretty good substitute.

"I thought some fresh air could do us good," Mallory said. "It's been a long winter."

That was the understatement of all understatements. There'd been murder, magic, mayhem, and too much mourning to go around, including episodes that had put Mallory in the hands of a serial killer and nearly cost Ethan his life. He was fine and she was recovering, and the incident had seemed to bring her and Catcher even closer together.

Even the vacation Ethan and I had just taken—a trip to the Rocky Mountains of Colorado that should have been filled with relaxation, elk watching, and plenty of sex—had been interrupted by a century-old feud between vampires and shape-shifters.

We'd needed a break from our break, so we'd sipped and snacked with Mallory and Catcher on the goodies Margot, the House chef, had packed. Grapes, cheese (both regular and almost preternaturally stinky), thin crackers, and small cookies coated in lemony powdered sugar with just the right balance of sweet and pucker.

"You've been eyeing that last lemon cookie for seven minutes."

I glanced back at Ethan, gave him a dour look. "I have not."

"Seven minutes and forty-three seconds," Catcher said, glancing at his watch. "I'd grab it for you, but I'm afraid I'd lose a finger."

"Stop torturing her," Mallory said, carefully picking up the cookie, handing it gingerly to me, then dusting powdered sugar from her hands. "She can't help her obsession."

I started to argue, but by then my mouth was full of cookie. "Not an obsession," I said when I was done. "Fast metabolism and rigorous training schedule. Luc has us on two-a-days now that Ethan's been upgraded."

"Ooh, Ethan two-point-oh," Mallory said.

"I think technically we're now at Ethan four-point-oh," Catcher pointed out. "Human, vampire, resurrected vampire, AAM member."

Ethan snorted, but even he didn't argue with the timeline. "I prefer to think of it as a promotion."

"You get a raise out of it?" Catcher asked.

"In a manner of speaking. I'll nearly be able to afford to keep Merit in the culinary style to which she'd like to become accustomed."

"You're the one with the expensive taste." I gestured to the bottle of wine. "Do I even want to know how much that cost?"

Ethan opened his mouth, closed it again. "Likely not."

"And there you go."

"A vampire cannot survive on Italian hot beefs and Mallocakes alone."

"Speak for yourself, fancy pants."

"I'm not fancy," Ethan said imperiously. "I'm particular. Which is actually a compliment to you."

"He did pick you after four hundred years of wild-oat sowing," Catcher said, earning an elbow from Mallory. He grunted, but he was smiling when he lay back on the blanket, hands crossed behind his head.

"You make it sound like Ethan picked her up at a farmers' market," Mallory complained.

"That would require Merit to eat vegetables," Ethan said, grinning at me. "Could you differentiate between a rutabaga and rhubarb?"

"Yes, but only because my grandmother made the best strawberry-rhubarb pie I've ever tasted."

"I don't think that counts."

"Oh, it counts," I said with a nod. "That pie was sublime. I've got solid culinary chops."

"My culinarily chopped vampire missed a spot of powdered sugar," Ethan said, leaning forward, swiping his thumb across my lips just slowly enough to heat my blood.

"Get a room," Catcher groused. He was grouchy but loyal, and had followed Mallory through her stint as a Maleficent wannabe and on to the other side. He was also unfailingly dedicated to my much-beloved grandfather, which gave him points in my book.

But I still gave him the much-deserved stink eye. "Do you know how many times I've seen you naked? You and Mallory considered the entire house your personal love shack." Mallory and I had been roommates once upon a time, before Catcher had moved into the town house we'd shared, and I'd moved into Cadogan House to escape the nudity.

"Your"—I waved my hand at his body—"rod and tackle touched pretty much everything in the place."

"My body is a wonderland" was his only response.

"Be that as it may," Ethan said, "Merit is not your Alice. I'll thank you to keep your rod and tackle away from her."

"Nowhere near my agenda," Catcher assured him.

Ethan's phone beeped, and he pulled it out quickly, checked the screen.

"Just a media inquiry," he said, tucking it away again.

Every phone call put us on high alert, because a ghost—or someone pretending to be one—had staked a claim on our lives. That ghost was Balthasar, the vampire who, on a battlefield nearly four hundred years ago, had made Ethan immortal and nearly turned him into a monster in his own image. Ethan had escaped his maker, made a new life for himself, and believed Balthasar had died shortly after he had escaped. Ethan hadn't yet told me the details, but he hadn't indicated any doubts about Balthasar's death.

And yet, three weeks ago, a note had been left in our top-floor apartments in Cadogan House. A note purporting to be from Balthasar, who was alive and excited to see Ethan again.

A note . . . and then nothing.

He'd made no contact since then, and we'd found no evidence he was alive, much less in Chicago and waiting for an opportunity to wreak havoc, to wage war, to exert control over Ethan once again.

So we waited. Every phone call could be *the* call, the one that would change the life we'd begun to make together. And there were so many more calls these days. The AAM was still working out the operational details, but that hadn't kept vampires from lining up outside Cadogan House like vassals, seeking protection, requesting Ethan's intervention in some city dispute, or offering fealty.

And vampires weren't the only ones interested. Chicago was home to twenty-five percent of the country's AAM members, and humans' fascination with Ethan, Scott Grey, and Morgan Greer, who headed Grey House and Navarre House, had ballooned again.

It was a strange new world.

"So, not to interrupt the mirth making," Mallory said, "but there's actually a reason we asked you guys to come out tonight."

"Who says 'mirth making'?" Catcher asked.

"I do, Sarcastasaurus." She elbowed him, with a grin. "And we're here for a reason?"

"Okay, okay," he said. "But I'm going to need that on a T-shirt."

"I was just thinking that," I said. "And you're making me nervous. What's going on?"

Catcher nodded. "Well, as it turns out—"

As it turned out, Catcher was interrupted by an explosion of noise, our phones beeping wildly in obvious warning.

I got to mine first, saw Luc's number, switched it to speaker. "Merit."

Luc's nose loomed on the screen. "Sorry to interrupt date night."

I grimaced at the image. "Step back from the camera. We don't need to see your sinuses."

"Sorry," he said, leaning back so his nose moved back into proper perspective, right in the middle of his very charming face, which was surrounded by tousled blond-brown curls. "You're alone?"

"We're with Catcher and Mallory," I said, then glanced around to ensure that no curious humans were eavesdropping. "We can talk. What's going on?"

"Media vans at the House. Four of them. Mess of reporters, all gathered at the gate, ready and waiting." Luc's pause, matched with his drawn expression, made me nervous. "They're asking questions about Balthasar."

We went quiet enough to hear the strains of a lone saxophone being played near the pier, probably a song being sold for tourists' cash.

"What questions?" Ethan asked.

"They're asking about a supposed reunion," Luc said. The answer made T. S. Eliot echo alarmingly in my head. *This is the way the world ends*.

Ethan's reaction was as hot and fast as Luc's had been cautious.

"Double the guards on the gate," Ethan said. "We're on our way."

I wanted to argue with him, to tell him he'd be safer staying put than running toward whatever reunion this Balthasar had planned. But Ethan was a stubborn and careful man. He wouldn't leave the House to face danger without him, and certainly not when the danger was a monster from Ethan's own past. Ethan still hadn't forgotten the things he'd done when he was with Balthasar, or forgiven himself for his own complicity. He was still looking for redemption. And he'd meet that opportunity head-on.

We said our good-byes, and I tucked the phone into my pocket again, tried to mentally prepare myself for what we might face— what Ethan might have to face, and the emotional storm that might rip through both of us.

And then I looked at Mallory and Catcher, remembering they'd been on the verge of making their own announcement.

"Go," Catcher said, even as Mallory began stuffing food back into the picnic basket. She was playing the trouper, but I could see the frustration in her eyes. "You want us with you?"

Ethan shook his head. "There's no point in dragging you into this debacle. Balthasar is dead; this is someone else's ploy for attention."

Catcher nodded. "I'll tell Chuck, put him on alert just in case."

"Be careful," Mallory said, and squeezed me into a hug.

"I will," I said, searching her gaze for answers, and finding none. "You're okay?"

"I'm fine. We can talk about this later. Take care of your House first. *Go*," she said when I hadn't moved, and turned me toward the street.

We went, jogging back toward Grand and the tall man with blond hair who waited for us in front of a glossy black Range Rover with a license plate that read CADOGAN. He wore a trim black suit and a sleek black tie, hands clasped in front of him.

"Sire," he said, bowing his head. Brody was a Cadogan House guard who'd been appointed Ethan's official driver. Luc had outfitted Ethan with all the necessary perks, including the car, which was equipped with a complete security system, a small arsenal, and a comm center.

"Luc called," Brody said, pivoting smoothly to open the door, one hand on his tie as he waited for Ethan and me to climb into the backseat. He closed the door with a solid thud, then rounded the car and slid inside onto the driver's seat.

The car was comfortable, and I appreciated that Ethan had extra security, but I missed Moneypenny, my vintage Mercedes convertible. She was currently parked in the basement of Cadogan House, weeping from neglect. I missed the freedom, the quiet, the solitude of a good long drive—as most drives anywhere in Chicago tended to be.

Unless Brody was driving.

"May I?" he asked, meeting Ethan's gaze in the rearview mirror, not doing a very good job of fighting back a smile. Brody had been a new guard, and he was still pink around the edges. But he did have one particularly enviable skill.

The boy could handle a car.

He was Chicago's version of the Transporter—master of the smooth ride, but equally adept at weaving and dodging through Chicago's gnarly traffic. Luc had given Brody a dressing-down the first time he'd ridden with him. But when the time came to assign Ethan a driver, he turned to Brody first.

"If you can get us there in one piece," Ethan said, and managed not to flinch when Brody dashed into traffic like a cheetah in pursuit.

Brody just avoided nicking a cab, then slipped smoothly into a gap in the other lane.

I'm not sure when I'm going to get used to this, Ethan said silently, using the telepathic connection between us.

You're just irritated you aren't the one driving.

I have a Ferrari for just such occasions. And speaking of occasions, what was Mallory's and Catcher's production about? She'd looked upset.

I'm not sure, I admitted. *But if it was really bad news, I don't think she'd have arranged a picnic.* There were plenty of milestones that might merit a picnic, but I wasn't sure they'd put that look on her face.

I'll call her, I promised, *and ferret out the truth. But for now, let's deal with vampires.*

CHAPTER TWO

——◄•══•►——

DEAD SPIN

Fifteen minutes later, a miraculous amount of time for Chicago, Brody turned off Woodlawn, tires squealing as he veered toward the House, its white stone glowing beneath heavy moonlight.

Media vans clustered outside the tall iron fence that bounded the House's large grounds, their antennas extended, reporters and cameramen on the sidewalk with equipment in hand.

The gate in the fence was closed—something I'd rarely seen—the black-clad human guards we hired out to protect the House staring down the reporters with open malice that made me appreciate them even more.

Our wealthy Hyde Park neighbors stood on their stoops or porches and stared grimly at the activity, probably already composing their letters to the editor—or to Ethan—protesting late-night vampiric shenanigans.

I sent Luc a message, advising him we'd reached our destination, as Brody pulled the car to a stop beside the nearest van.

Ethan was out of the car before we could stop him. As I followed him, scabbarded katana in hand, a red bus with VAMPIRE TOURS OF CHICAGO in white letters across the side rolled slowly down the street, tourists gawking out of windows, the driver's narration ringing through the darkness.

". . . Cadogan House, the city's second-oldest House, behind Navarre. And, ladies and gentlemen, grab your cameras, because that's Ethan Sullivan and Merit right there on the street!"

I waved politely for the camera flashes and shouts from tourists—no point in making things worse—but muttered a curse as soon as my back was turned. "Keep the bus moving," I told Brody when he met me on the sidewalk. "Let's not drag the tourists into whatever this is."

Brody nodded, jogged toward the bus, and directed it down the street.

The reporters ignored the onlookers—they were too busy with Ethan. Like sharks in the water, they'd scented blood, begun to circle.

"Ethan! Ethan! Who is Balthasar? What's he to you?"

"Is he in Chicago to cause trouble? Is Cadogan House in danger? Or Hyde Park?"

"Tell us about the reunion he has planned!"

Ethan, eyes silver with emotion, focused his dangerous gaze on the reporter closest to him. There was nothing kind in his expression, and very little that was human. "What did you say?"

I had to give the reporter credit. The smell of his fear soured the air, but he kept his knees locked and his eyes on Ethan, and didn't step back even beneath Ethan's withering glare. And what's worse, he must have seen something in Ethan's eyes, some hint of dismay that triggered his own instincts. His lips turned up in a hungry smile.

"Who is Balthasar?"

"Why do you ask?"

"Why are you avoiding the question?"

Ethan took another step forward, magic rising in an invisible cloud behind him. Dread settled low in my belly, both at the fiasco someone had arranged, and Ethan's potentially explosive reaction to it.

I positioned myself behind Ethan.

I caught sight of movement to my left, found Brody, Luc, and Lindsey (Luc's girlfriend, one of the House's guards, and my best House buddy) moving cautiously toward us.

"I am not avoiding the question," Ethan said quietly, every word bathed in rage. "I'm wondering why so many members of the media have come to my home and are disrupting the neighborhood with inquiries about a vampire who's been dead for centuries."

"Dead?" the reporter asked, his gaze searching Ethan's as if for weak spots. "That's not the information we've received."

Ethan's lip curled, and I took a careful step forward, just in case I needed to haul him back.

"Balthasar is dead. Any information you received to the contrary is mistaken."

All heads turned when a sleek black limousine raced up the street and pulled to a stop outside the House. While the reporters redirected their cameras, a liveried driver climbed out and opened the back door.

As I unsheathed my katana, a vampire stepped out.

Ethan had kept a miniature portrait in a drawer in his office, an oval painting barely two inches across, its frame delicately gilded. The man in the frame had straight dark hair, pale skin, almost preternaturally symmetrical features. Straight, long nose, dark eyes, lips pulled into a near smirk.

Then, the man in the portrait had worn a white cravat and a

vest and coat in regal crimson, and his hair had been straight and dark, pulled into a queue at the back of his neck.

Now his hair was different—shorter around the sides and back, longer in front, so dark locks fell dramatically across his face. He'd exchanged the period clothing for black pants and a long coat, and there were scars across his neck, a web of crisscrossing lines that rose just above the coat's mandarin collar and told of something harsh and ugly . . . but something he'd clearly survived.

He was attractive, undeniably so, with the look and bearing of a dark prince, a man used to having the attention of men and women, and reveling in it. And he was undeniably the same vampire as the one in Ethan's portrait.

The entire crowd around us—reporters, cameramen, guards, vampires—went eerily silent as he stepped onto the sidewalk in front of Ethan. A mourning dove cooed from a nearby rooftop—once, twice, three times, as if calling a warning. A cold sweat inched down my spine, despite the chill in the new spring air.

The vampire let his gaze drift from Luc, to me, before settling on Ethan. There was much in his expression—anger, regret, fear. All of that tempered with hope.

For a long moment, they stared at each other, evaluating, watching, preparing.

I took cautious steps forward, one after another, until I stood beside Ethan with my katana extended, ready to strike.

The vampire's eyes suddenly changed. They narrowed, darkness peeking through them like a demon at the door. The color turned, blue, darkening and shifting to swimming quicksilver.

And then his magic—warm, heady, and spicy; whiskey spiked with cloves—burst through the air like lightning. He bared his fangs, longer than any I'd seen, thin and dangerous as needles, and that trickle of sweat became a cold slick that matched the wave that rolled through my abdomen.

Ethan's eyes widened with amazement, with horror.

My first instinct was to move, to protect. But magic had thickened the air like molasses; merely lifting a hand through it brought beads of sweat to my brow. I glanced around, found the other vampires around us similarly still.

Once upon a time, vampire glamour had been a crucial skill for luring and seducing humans. Master vampires also used the psychic skill to call the vampires they'd turned, to psychically pull them to the Master's side. By stroke of luck, or the unusual circumstances of my turning, I could feel glamour, but I was largely immune to the effects. So why was this magic affecting me?

Hold, Ethan said silently, the word heavy and lumbering as if he'd had to force it out through a syrup of magic.

And then Ethan uttered one word aloud. A word that would change everything.

"Balthasar."

Ethan said the name with utter conviction, equal to his previous certainty that Balthasar had been dead. I wanted to demand this vampire produce his bona fides. But Ethan seemed to need no further convincing.

The word was like a charm, a key that unlocked the viscous magic. In the space of a blink, it dissipated, pouring across us like a northern wind. And just as quickly, now freed of our magical bonds, the world erupted with movement, with noise. Reporters, apparently unaware of the delay, rushed forward, shouted questions, microphones and cameras pointed like weapons.

Ethan took a step backward, shock etched in his face, in his eyes.

I lifted my sword, moved between them, putting my body and blade between Ethan and the vampire he now stared at. The vampire he apparently believed was the one who had made him.

Luc, Brody, and Lindsey moved behind us, katanas drawn, a steel shield against the horde of reporters.

Balthasar cast a mild glance at me and my sword before shifting his gaze to Ethan again.

"It has been a long time," he said, his accent faintly French, his words softly lyrical. But that demon still lurked behind his eyes. He was a Master from a different time, a man who demanded loyalty, who defined the world for his vampires.

Ethan's internal struggle was clear on his face—he was torn between biological loyalty to the vampire who'd made him and hatred of the monster he'd been and tried to make of Ethan.

"A very long time," Ethan cautiously agreed.

"There is much to say."

"So it appears," Ethan said. He gestured toward the reporters around him. "You arranged all this?"

"I believed it was the only way to secure an audience with you."

"For what purpose?"

"To give voice to long-unspoken things. To make amends. There is"—Balthasar paused, obviously selecting his words carefully—"a void when one of your children is separated from you, as we have been for so long. At this time in my life, I find that void more painful."

Ethan just watched him, as one predator might watch another, with careful consideration. "We have been apart for a very long time. I believed you were dead."

"And there is a very long story to tell." He let his gaze slip back to the House. "Perhaps we can discuss it?"

Another long moment passed as Ethan looked at Balthasar, his expression blank but his energy suddenly hot, as if centuries of anger and frustration had finally ignited.

Step back, Merit. Ethan's order was contrary to my mission. But before I could argue, he repeated it again.

Step back, Sentinel.

The second I moved, Ethan's fist was up. With a sickening crunch of cartilage, he slammed it into Balthasar's face, and the scent of blood filled the air.

The crowd erupted again, magic flaring from the Cadogan vampires. I stepped closer to Ethan, and Luc did the same, both of us ready to move should Balthasar attempt a response.

Slowly, he shifted his gaze back to Ethan, pressed the back of a hand to his nose. His eyes sparked with obvious shock that someone would dare to challenge him, much less a vampire to whom he'd gifted immortality.

"Comme tu as changé, mon ami."

"Oui, c'est vrai. La vie m'a changé," Ethan said, in perfect French I hadn't known he spoke. His voice was low and threatening, and utterly Masterly.

Balthasar pulled a handkerchief from his pocket and dabbed genteelly at the cut. *"Ça va. Je comprends."*

"And let us be clear," Ethan continued in English. "I am no longer a human, nor a boy, nor the child you once knew. Don't *ever* call me again."

Luc stepped forward, put a hand on Ethan's arm. "Perhaps we should take this inside, away from the paparazzi? I think we've given them enough for one night."

Is it safe to let him in the House? I asked Ethan silently.

And where else would we put him, Sentinel? I'd rather have him under watch than roaming the city.

"Get everyone inside," Ethan said as camera shutters winked open and closed around us. "Take him to my office."

I knew Ethan was right, but couldn't help thinking of the fox in our proverbial henhouse.

Luc nodded, gestured Balthasar toward the House. Balthasar nodded regally, as if he were being shown to the king's own chambers, and stepped forward as the guards opened the gate.

I slid my katana back in its scabbard and stood quietly with Ethan in the rain of flashes.

He sighed, ran his hands through his hair. "Of all the gin joints in all the world."

"And he walks into yours," I finished for him.

Ethan glanced back at me, and I saw the dread in his eyes. He'd confessed to me some of the things he'd done, the way he and Balthasar had worked their way across Europe, the women and blood they'd taken, until Balthasar had finally gone too far. But it had taken time for him to tell me. He'd been concerned my feelings would change if I knew who he'd been and what he'd done.

But didn't that make him *more*? The fact that he could have continued to follow Balthasar, to debauch his way across Europe, and hadn't. That he'd worked to free himself from a vampire whose psychic powers were undeniably strong. That he'd become a different kind of vampire, a true Master.

I couldn't change the fact that Balthasar waited inside the House. But I could give him comfort. A reminder. So as cameras flashed around us, I took his hand.

He is your past, I said silently, and nodded toward the House that glowed warmly beyond the gate. *We are your present and future. Face him on your territory, and let the reckoning take place there. And if he gets out of line, use that right cross and lay him out.*

Ethan smiled with obvious reluctance. "It may get ugly. Likely will before all is said and done."

I squeezed his hand. "Unfortunately, I think that's guaranteed. But if things get too ugly, I'll lay you both out."

Ethan's office was spacious and as beautifully decorated as the rest of the House. There was a desk on one side, a sitting area across from it, and a conference table that spanned the back wall.

Balthasar stood in the middle of the room, taking in the furniture, décor, mementos of Ethan's life. Was he evaluating what he'd lost in Ethan's revolution, or what he stood to gain if he could bring Ethan into the fold once again?

Luc stood in the sitting area, arms crossed and expression suspicious, beside Malik, Ethan's second-in-command.

Malik was tall and lean, with thoughtful pale green eyes that set off dark skin. His stance mirrored Luc's, and he was the only one in the room who wore the official Cadogan House uniform— slim-cut black suit, white button-down shirt. A silver teardrop, the Cadogan House medal, was suspended at the base of his throat.

Malik was protective of Ethan and the House, and his gaze drilled into Balthasar, eyes tracking across Balthasar's face as if committing his visage to memory. All the better for Malik to double-check his bona fides later, I thought.

As I closed the door, Malik shifted his attention to Ethan, to gauge his mood, his magic, and his emotion as only a confidant and colleague could do.

When he was satisfied, he looked at me, a question in his eyes—Was this man who he seemed to be?

I gave Malik a quick nod, shifting my gaze to Ethan. He seemed to believe, and that was the only thing that mattered now. But that only created more questions: How had Ethan been

wrong about Balthasar's death? Where had he been in the intervening years? And, most important, what did he want from
Ethan?

Balthasar dabbed at his mouth and, when he was satisfied the
wound had closed—the benefits of vampire healing—tucked the
handkerchief away again. "You have a lovely home, *mon ami*."

Ethan ignored the compliment and the intimacy, walked to
the sitting area, took a seat on the leather sofa, and spread his arms
across the back, staking his position, his authority. I stood at attention beside him, ready to jump forward should the need arise.

"We enjoy it. You should begin."

Balthasar quirked an eyebrow at the order—I wondered if
Ethan had unconsciously picked up the affectation from him. "I
will tell you my story, and you will reach your own conclusions."

"Tell your tale," Ethan said. "And we'll see what comes next."

Balthasar took a seat across from Ethan, fingers steepled in his
lap.

"I was in London," he began. "Three men walked into the
house with crosses and stakes. They were the relatives of some
girl or other, convinced I was evil, the devil incarnate."

Not just some girl, Ethan said to me, his irritation obvious even
telepathically. *Persephone.*

Ethan had loved her. Balthasar knew that, and had seduced
and killed her in order to taunt Ethan. That selfish and violent act
had been Balthasar's final blow, prompting Ethan's separation.

These men had been members of her family? I asked.

Yes was all Ethan said.

"I was the only one in the house," Balthasar continued. "You'd
just left, and I'd sent Nicole, as you call her now, on an errand."

"To find me and bring me back," Ethan said flatly, and Balthasar lifted his gaze to Ethan again, amusement in this eyes.

"Alive, if that was an option," Balthasar agreed. "And if it was not . . . Well, it was a different time."

"She did not find me," Ethan said. "But I went back anyway." A shadow crossed his eyes, as if he watched a memory play back. After a moment, he refocused on Balthasar.

"I heard about the mob. I went back, and saw you through the window. Bloodied. Almost decapitated."

That explained why Ethan had believed Balthasar dead. A vampire could heal most wounds, but once the head was severed, the game was up. That was too much for even vampire genetics to mend. And the fact that Balthasar hadn't contacted Ethan in the interim would only have reinforced what Ethan had seen. Still . . . there was doubt in Ethan's voice now, put there by the vampire now sitting across from us.

I inched closer to the sofa, just enough for my hip to brush Ethan's shoulder, a quick brush of contact I hoped would remind him that I was there. Balthasar saw the gesture, his gaze snapping like a cobra's hood to notice the intimacy. There was something old and icy in his eyes. The utter absence of empathy, as if I was nothing more than a few brushstrokes on the canvas of his very long life.

I wanted to shrink away, but I forced my shoulders back, my chin up. I was Sentinel, and this was my House.

"*Nearly* decapitated," Balthasar clarified, shifting his gaze to Ethan again. "The men initially decided to do away with me, and the gang of them, at least a dozen, made a very good first effort. That, I suspect, is what you saw. They'd decided burning at the stake would serve as a proper warning to those who would dare defile their daughters, and they left to prepare the bonfire. But that was not to be. One of the men, who had his own peculiar interests, decided he could use me for his own purposes. He was a member of a cult; they called themselves the Memento Mori."

Remember, you will die, I translated roughly, trying to remember my Latin.

"They believed vampires had the power to unlock the secrets of omnipotence and immortality, that we could traverse the gap between life and death. The man took me from the house before my torturers came back, bandaged me. Let me heal. And then began his work." Balthasar gestured to the scars along his neck. "He believed having a piece of me, quite literally, would give him strength. They kept me alive, if one could call it that. Weakened, chained, and dosed with extract of aspen enough to keep me only just conscious."

I felt the sharp flash of Ethan's magic. Peter Cadogan had died from the same substance—from his slow poisoning by a romantic rival.

Balthasar must have sensed the magic, and he nodded. "A small enough dose results in lethargy in the extreme. *Docilité*. It also impairs the ability to heal."

"I wasn't aware," Ethan said quietly.

"Nor was I," Balthasar said. "But I learned quickly. They held me in Spitalfields, in London. Questions were not asked about screams, about blood, about midnight activities. Not when need was great, and happiness was in short supply."

"You escaped?" Ethan asked.

Balthasar laughed, the sound like rough whiskey. "Nothing as romantic as that. The humans and their ancestors grew tired of caring for me, and they discarded me at an abbey in Walford. They either were gracious enough not to kill me, or believed I was nearly dead and the trouble would have been wasted.

"The abbey was a fortunate choice. The abbot was a kind man, and he'd sheltered supernaturals before. He helped me heal, to begin to function. And when it became clear I wasn't aging, he helped me find new lodging to avoid the obvious questions. I moved from one safe house to another. I was in northern Europe. In Aberdeen for many years. The custodians didn't know who I was, only that I needed refuge. And when anyone became suspicious, they moved me again. I ended up in Chalet Rouge. The safe house in Geneva."

"I know it," Ethan said with a nod.

"I improved slowly," Balthasar continued. "Recuperated as the extracts slowly—too slowly—left my system. It took decades before my memories began to return. And they came one at a time, like cards being dealt. A memory of you, of Paris, of Nicole. I eventually remembered who you were. And I discovered who you'd become."

Silence fell. Ethan watched Balthasar carefully. "And you've not contacted us in all that time? Or the GP?"

A lesser vampire might have squirmed under Ethan's stare, but Balthasar seemed mildly amused by it. "Our separation was less than pleasant. You had feelings toward me, as I did toward you. Strong feelings. You left without permission."

"You would not have granted it. You treated humans and vampires alike as if they were disposable. I grew tired of the depravity. Rémy took over the group when you were gone, and his behavior was no better. I did not go back."

Balthasar's eyebrows lifted. "It seems we are being frank. But it was a different time. I'll not apologize for what I was, nor will I request your apology."

Ethan's gaze darkened. "I owe you no apologies."

"Perhaps you do, perhaps you do not." Hands still linked between his knees, Balthasar leaned forward. "But do you owe me thanks? You owe your immortality, and all the benefits it has brought you, to me."

I felt the quick rise in Ethan's magic. "And why are you here now?"

"I'd say to make amends, but that sounds equally naive and pretentious. Let's say I became . . . unassailably curious."

"Because I have power?"

Balthasar dipped his chin a bit, managed a wicked smile that edged toward creepy and malevolent. "Because you've become so interesting. As have your . . . *accoutrements*."

"Careful," Ethan warned. "Or you will quickly wear out your welcome."

Balthasar made a vague sound of disagreement, then stood. He walked toward the bookshelf, long fingers lingering on the back of the chair. Before I could blink, he stood before the tall shelves, fingers now trailing across the mementos Ethan had collected over the centuries.

I'd barely seen him move.

God, but he was fast. Faster than any vampire I'd seen. He wasn't just a relic or an anachronism of an older age, but a powerful predator. And he was showing off.

In consideration of the threat, I straightened beside Ethan, felt his answering attentiveness.

Balthasar picked up a small crystal globe, let it glide across his fingers.

"I'll warn you again," Ethan said, "and for the last time. Use care."

"Care?" Balthasar asked. "The same care that you would show me?"

The world began to vibrate beneath my feet, as if the House had been suddenly perched on the edge of a machine large enough to spin the world on its tilting axis. It tilted around me—the entire room—while I stayed upright.

Me . . . and Balthasar.

CHAPTER THREE

✦ ❖ ✦

THE VAMPIRE'S GIFT

I gripped the back of the couch as the world shifted, saw Ethan's eyes go wide. Saw his mouth form my name—*"Merit?"*—but heard nothing but the pounding of blood in my ears.

I glanced up, vertigo racking me as perspective shifted, caught Balthasar's intense glance.

"What are you doing to me?" I demanded.

Balthasar smiled venomously as the sound grew louder and faster, as if hornets buzzed through my head. "I am demonstrating what it means to be one of my vampires."

I became a marionette, pulled toward him as if gravity's axis had shifted, sucking me sideways. I fought back—of course I fought back, tried to pinwheel my arms and legs to move. But the effort was useless. He dragged me stiffly forward, pulled me toward him by the sheer power of his will.

Balthasar had called me. Balthasar, who stood smiling through hooded lids, had managed to draw me in despite my obvious reluctance, my palpable fear.

This wasn't supposed to work on me.

When Mallory had brought Ethan back to life, her power over him had briefly lingered. She'd been able to funnel her magic through him, and he'd detested the violation, her presence inside the sanctity of his mind.

I understood that feeling now, because that's precisely what this was—a violation. By compelling me forward, he'd stripped me of my right and will, my ability to say no.

If this was glamour, the calling of a vampire to its Master, how did other vampires survive it? How did they live with the intrusion? The invasion? How was this different from what Mallory had done?

I glanced back, intending to scream for help, wondering why Ethan, Malik, and Luc hadn't risen to stop him, to help me.

But they looked frozen behind me. Not because Balthasar had stopped time, but because I was moving faster, at the same speed that Balthasar had demonstrated a moment before.

I fought for control of my own body, of my own mind. I'd long ago learned to keep blocks in place to keep my keen vampire senses from overwhelming me with sounds, smells, and tastes. I tried to pull them down, imagined their working like heavy metal shutters, creating a seawall between my mind and the buffering waves of his magic. But it was like trying to hold back a hurricane with an umbrella. The magic spilled around it, over it, under it, and through it like a leviathan.

And with the leviathan came a pulse of passion and arousal so keen it was nearly painful. My body felt suddenly electric, every nerve sensitive and attuned to Balthasar—the line of his neck, the nimble fingers that twirled the globe, the beckoning eyes.

All the while, Balthasar kept smiling. The psychic ropes he'd used to pull me forward tightened, each shuffling step bringing me closer to him.

I couldn't find breath to speak, and pled with my eyes for him to stop, to release me. But the fear only seemed to excite him, his arousal perfuming the air with old magic and the nearly overpowering scents of orange and cinnamon.

His eyes quicksilver with excitement, Balthasar bared his fangs with a hiss, needle-sharp tips gleaming as he prepared to bite, and extended a hand toward me.

"A kiss for a lovely woman," he said.

The closer I drew, the more the rest of the world faded, until he was the only thing I could see . . . and the only thing I cared to.

The silver in his eyes spun like sugar, and he looked like the hero from a Gothic poem, with sable hair and fresh-cream skin, his lips flushed crimson with desire . . . for me, for only me, because he and I were the only ones in the world.

He would bite me. He would pierce skin and vein, and he would take from me, and I would never want for anything else. I would never need anything else, because he would be everything . . .

His hand gripped my arm and drew me closer, my eyes drifting shut as his bared fangs promised simultaneous pleasure and pain, the vampire's gift. His lips found mine, made contact—

"*Arrêter!*"

Ethan's voice boomed through the room on a shock wave of fury. Suddenly, he was beside us, hauling me away. Balthasar dragged himself from my mind, the separation leaving me cold and empty. Without his bolstering magic, the floor rushed toward me like I'd been thrown against it. I landed on my knees with rattling force. Nausea welled as the world spun, and I squeezed my eyes closed until I felt the carousel slowing.

Malik was suddenly at my side. "I'm going to help you to your feet."

I nodded, unsure I'd be able to form words, and Malik put an arm around my waist, drew me to my feet. My knees wobbled but held.

"I won't let you go," he said quietly, and guided me toward the couch and away from the scuffle.

Even still, there was a terrifying part of me that didn't want to go, that didn't want distance from Balthasar, from the pleasure he promised.

Ethan grabbed him by the lapels, shoved him back against the bookshelves with enough force to snap wood and spill books and crystal to the floor.

Balthasar's laughter was cold as ice. "Perhaps you'll think twice the next time you lay hands on me, *mon ami*."

Ethan's voice was cold and sharp as Balthasar's, and he pushed him again into broken wood and glass to punctuate the words. "If you touch her again, come near her again, I will tear you apart with my own bare hands, Master or not."

Balthasar raised his hands between Ethan's arms, attempted to break Ethan's hold. But Ethan was driven by fear, love, and fury, and he had the upper hand.

Balthasar's voice was a cobra's hiss. "You would do well to release me."

"You'd do well to remember where you are. In my House, in my city, surrounded by my people."

"Your people?" Balthasar said. "I made you, *mon ami*, and a continent will not sever the bond between us. They are mine as much as yours."

"You misunderstand the nature of things." Holding Balthasar back with one arm, Ethan pulled a small dagger from his jacket with his free hand, held it in front of Balthasar's face.

"They are my people, every one of them, blood and bone,

mind and soul. I will warn you once, and only once, to stay away from them. I am not the child you once knew. My priorities have changed, as has my willingness to act."

This was Ethan at his fiercest. If there'd been any doubts that vampires were alpha predators, the swirling fury in his eyes, the gleaming fangs would have erased them.

"Do yourself a favor," Ethan said. "Leave Chicago tonight, and don't look back."

The office door burst open. Lindsey, Brody, and Kelley—another Cadogan guard—walked inside, swords in hand.

Ethan slammed the dagger into the wood beside Balthasar's temple, where it vibrated with force. And still Balthasar's expression didn't change. "Bored contempt" seemed the most accurate description.

Ethan stepped back, kept his malevolent glare on his maker. "Get him out of here. *Now*."

Balthasar stepped away from Ethan as the guards surrounded him.

"I will take my leave from your House tonight," he said. "But I'm only just getting acquainted with your fair city."

Luc gestured toward the door with his katana's curving blade, and Balthasar followed without comment. But he turned back in the doorway, found my gaze.

"Our reunion, so sweet, has only just begun. Until we meet again."

And then he disappeared.

"Have him followed," Ethan told Malik. "Find out where he's staying, who else knows he's here. I want someone on him—vampire and human—at all times."

Malik nodded, then rose and disappeared into the hallway to do a different kind of Master's bidding.

Ethan, still across the room—the distance heavy between us—looked at me. "You're all right?"

I swallowed, worked to collect my thoughts. "He glamoured me. He *called* me. That wasn't supposed to happen. I was supposed to be immune. I *was* immune."

A line of worry between his eyes, Ethan moved to the small refrigerator, grabbed a bottle of blood, uncapped it, and brought it back to me. "Drink."

"I'm not thirsty."

"The blood will help eliminate the remaining magic. Take it from someone who knows—you'll feel more yourself afterward."

"I don't want—"

"Just drink the damn blood, Merit." His tone was sharp, his words quick and angry.

"Why him? Why now, when I've been immune to everyone else?"

Ethan sighed, sat down beside me. "I'm not certain. He is powerful. A master manipulator. Perhaps his brush with death keened his abilities, or he practiced them in the intervening years. Or it could be the flavor of the magic." He paused. "Or it could be my fault."

I looked at him, saw the pinched fear and concern in his eyes. "What he did isn't your fault."

"Not Balthasar per se," Ethan said. "Your reaction." He pushed a lock of long, dark hair behind my ear, gaze tracking my face as if checking for injuries, evaluating my psyche. "The drugs. Your change."

My transition to vampire hadn't been easy or smooth. Ethan

had made me a vampire to save me from an attack. A noble deed, I could recognize now, but at the time I hadn't been able to consent. Feeling guilty about that, Ethan had given me drugs to help me through the cruelly painful transition. For most vampires, it was three days of bone-searing pain; for me, it was mostly a blur.

Unfortunately, in addition to protecting me from pain, it also kept me from fully transitioning to vampire, so my psyche was still split between human and vampire. They were slammed back together eventually, but maybe, as Ethan feared, there were other lingering effects, such as my immunity to glamour. And maybe Balthasar's magic had been the hammer that slammed that sensitivity back into place.

"We'd always thought you'd just been stubborn," Ethan said. "But perhaps the reasons were more fundamental than that."

I heard the guilt in his voice. "No. Balthasar did this because he wanted to prove a point."

"That he could get to you, and me," Ethan agreed. "Glamour is a trait intended to entice and manipulate prey. That he used it against you, against both of us, was cruel. Drink," he said again. "You'll feel better. And you don't want me to make you drink it."

I glanced at him. "You wouldn't dare."

His expression didn't change, so it seemed wise not to argue. I sat up and, with my eyes on him above the rim, drank.

He was right. It took the edge off, neutralized some of Balthasar's discomforting effect on me.

When I drained the bottle, I handed it back to Ethan, and he put it aside. "Good," he said. "Your color's already coming back."

"I didn't mean to kiss him." The words burst out in a bubble of sound, and even I could hear the strain of guilt in my voice. I hadn't meant to kiss Balthasar, but in that moment, I'd desired nothing less. "I didn't want to. Not really. I'd have done anything he asked. He had control over every part of me—mentally, emotionally, physically."

Ethan frowned at me. "Do you think I'd blame you for that? For what he did to you?" He shook his head ruefully. "I'm sorry I couldn't get to you sooner. That he got as far as he did. His magic . . . There's power in it."

He was angry at himself, believing he'd somehow failed to protect me. Since he'd been the one who intervened, who'd stopped Balthasar from drinking, he couldn't be further from the truth.

His arms moved around me, pulled me close. "Glamour is, and always will be, a weapon, no matter how prettily dressed."

A frighteningly powerful weapon.

"I'm not really sure how to feel. It felt like a violation. And it felt wonderful. And that makes me feel guilty."

He gently tilted my chin so our eyes met. "Glamour is intended to make you feel good, to make the idea of vampire feel wonderful. It wouldn't be very useful if it didn't. You are not to blame for your perfectly natural reaction."

I nodded, but that didn't relieve the sick feeling in the pit of my stomach. "I liked it better when I was immune."

"I wouldn't have had you discover it like this." He smiled a little. "Not that you had any more interest in glamour at your lively Commendation than you did tonight."

As he'd intended, a corner of my mouth lifted. "And I didn't like you very much then."

"No, you did not."

Luc appeared at the doorway, Malik beside him. He surveyed the room, looked at me. "You're all right?"

I nodded. "I'm fine."

Luc nodded. "Lindsey and one of the human guards are on

Balthasar. They'll keep tabs, and we'll cover him in shifts." He glanced at Ethan. "You believe his story?"

One arm across my shoulders, Ethan dropped his head back to stare at the coffered ceiling. "His explanation was internally consistent, and explains his absence rationally. You should still verify, confirm what we can." He lifted his head again, glanced at broken bookshelves, the shattered mementos, appropriately metaphorical. "But he's here now, so his explanation for his absence matters less than the reason for his presence."

"And what do you think that is?" Luc asked.

"To best me? To lay claim to whatever throne he believes he's entitled to?"

"So revenge and power," Luc said. "Those are perennial vampire favorites."

"Of his as well," Ethan said, rubbing his temples with his free hand.

"We could call Nicole," Malik said wryly, and Ethan barked a laugh.

"To thank her for sending him our way?"

"You think she knew?" I asked.

"I think he's canny enough to have visited her first, confirmed he had an ally, before coming here."

"She could have arranged to have the note left in our apartment while she was here for the Testing," I guessed.

Ethan nodded, and then his eyes narrowed. He glanced between me, Luc, and Malik. "If she knew he was alive, and if she knew it during the Testing . . ."

"Is he the reason she abolished the GP and created the AAM?" Malik finished, crossing his arms over his chest.

Luc sat on the arm of the chair across from us. "And how much of her maneuvering was just to give Balthasar a second chance?"

Ethan sighed. "We all knew she had ulterior motives—that she didn't propose the AAM because she's magnanimous."

"Did she say anything about it last week?" Malik asked.

"No," Ethan said. The country's Masters had met in Atlanta, Nicole's home, for the AAM's first meeting and to discuss the organization's building blocks: its location, its procedures, its decision-making apparatus, its finances, the possibility of holding a formal ceremony to celebrate the organization's creation. I'd missed that particular trip—Luc had accompanied Ethan as his body man. From the riveting discussions of parliamentary procedure I'd had with Ethan afterward, I hadn't missed much.

"The meeting was just as you'd expect a meeting of twelve egotistical and strategy-motivated vampires to be. If she's trying to maneuver us into some position to support Balthasar, she didn't show her hand."

"Next planning meeting is next week," Luc said. "Maybe this is step one."

"I don't know if I buy that theory," I said, looking between them. "To go through Testing, the election, the disbanding of the GP, setting up the AAM—all the work you've done in the last few weeks to get the organization up and running—there are easier ways to get power to Balthasar." I shrugged. "Hell, she could have just supported him as a candidate for Darius's position."

"That's a point," Luc agreed.

"Maybe you *should* call her," Malik said. "Acknowledge he is here. Find out what you can. Get it out in the open."

"That's what she said," I murmured, but loud enough for Luc to hear and grin approvingly.

"Nice, Sentinel."

Ethan rolled his eyes. "You two have clearly been spending too much time together."

"Two-a-days," we said simultaneously.

"You train more, you bond more," Luc said. "It's part of my trademarked regimen: 'Luc90X.'"

"That's not a thing," Malik said, "and it's not trademarked. It's probably a trademark violation."

"Details."

"Children," Ethan said, standing and glancing at his watch. "Dawn is coming soon, and I think we've had plenty of excitement for one night."

"Yes," Luc said, rising at the obvious signal. "Let that be a lesson to you about attempting to leave the House and have a private life."

"We'll keep our relationship purely professional in the future," I promised, which earned scoffs from all three of them.

"Tell that to the man who defended your honor with French and a blade earlier this evening," Malik said. He had a valid point.

Reminded of the blade, Ethan walked across the room, plucked it from the wall with a fist, slipped it into a nearby drawer. "Let's reconvene at dusk to discuss what we've learned about Balthasar, what we may need to prepare for."

"On it, hoss," Luc said, then glanced at me. "Assuming your 'purely professional' schedule allows, you've got small blade practice tomorrow."

Of course I did. Because God forbid I missed a night of Luc90X.

"She'll see you then," Ethan assured them. And the second they were gone, his arm was around my waist, and he'd snugged me against the hard line of his body.

Before I could react, his mouth was on mine, firm and possessive, passionate and insistent. He pushed me beyond thinking, into that sweet oblivion where there was only sensation, only the feel and smell and taste of him.

When he pulled back, nipping my lip in a final tease, both of us were breathing heavily.

"Always remember," he said. "Real lust beats old magic any day."

There was applause from the doorway. I turned around, found Catcher and Mallory offering a slow clap at the sight of us.

CHAPTER FOUR

✦❈✦

BOSOM BUDDIES

"What was I saying about lust beating magic?" Ethan asked quietly, and I patted his chest.

"Down, boy," I said, and waved them in.

"We heard you've had an evening," Catcher said. "Malik called Chuck, gave him a heads-up. We were closer to the House, so we stopped by to check in on things. Balthasar, eh?"

"So it seems."

"Magic?"

"As you'd expect," Ethan said, and slid his gaze to me. "And glamour that managed to penetrate Merit's defenses."

Or destroy them, I feared. And I didn't like the thought of Balthasar penetrating anything of mine, psychic or otherwise.

Catcher looked at me, head tilted and brow furrowed, as if I were a puzzle to decipher. "He changed her immunity?"

"Or slipped past it, yes," Ethan said.

I waved a hand. "Still in the room." But they were too involved in their analysis to care. Mallory walked over, rolled her eyes at their single-mindedness. She handed me a picnic basket.

"Thought we'd return this," she said. "Margot knocked it out of the park, as always."

I nodded, put the basket on Ethan's desk. "She tends to do that." I thought of the announcement they'd wanted to make. "Are you guys okay? Did you want to talk about something?"

She looked back at Catcher, opened her mouth as if to answer, but quickly closed it again. "We're good. We'll talk about it later. Really," she added. "It's no big deal. But this is." Concern crossed her face. "You okay about this Balthasar thing?"

"Yeah," I said quietly. "It was, I don't know, scary in a different kind of way. Not Catcher-throwing-fireballs scary, or even Ethan-facing-a-fiery-death scary."

"It was dark-spike-right-into-your-soul scary?"

"Yeah," I said. "Yeah. That's pretty much it exactly." Since she'd been assaulted by a serial killer, of course she'd have understood.

I lowered my voice. Ethan was upset enough that I didn't want to burden him with my lingering fear. "It was . . . personal."

She reached out, squeezed my hand. "I've been there. Feels good when you really don't want it to?"

I couldn't stop the flush that warmed my neck, but nodded. "I don't know how he's cooking up that glamour, but he's very, very good at it."

"Where's he been?" Catcher asked Ethan, who took a seat on the couch, gestured for them to join us. Mallory squeezed my hand again before releasing it, moving to sit in the chair beside Catcher's. I took my now-familiar seat on the couch next to Ethan.

"According to him, he was kidnapped by a cult, tortured, incapacitated by extract of aspen."

"You have doubts?"

"About his identity? I hardly could after tonight's display. For the period in between? Well, he's never been terribly well acquainted with the truth."

That was very diplomatic, I said silently to Ethan, and felt his answering warmth.

I am trying to remember, as a wise vampire once told me, that I am more than he tried to make me.

I'd been that vampire and appreciated the shout-out.

"So, what's the next step?" Mallory asked.

"I told him to leave the city," Ethan said. "I suspect he won't."

"And why's he here?" Catcher asked.

Ethan sighed, draped an arm along the back of the couch. "Hard to say at this early point, but add power, revenge, and possessiveness to the list. He said he wouldn't leave, but I'm not yet sure if that's because he wants to irritate me, finagle his way into our House and finances, or both."

"That's comforting," Mallory said, and Ethan nodded.

"He'll be well monitored, but to some extent we'll have to wait for him to make a move."

"You could," Catcher said. "Or you could provoke him into making one."

When Ethan's expression didn't change, I guessed he'd already considered that particular strategy.

I glanced at Ethan. "You've come up with a plan."

"I'm considering disavowal."

"Damn," Catcher said, shifting in his seat. "I haven't heard that word in a while."

I'd never heard it, but I had seen it in print in the *Canon,* the collection of vampire lore and laws. Every House Initiate got a desk reference, and the entire set of books—dozens of volumes— were stored in the House's second-floor library, one of its most spectacular rooms.

"What's disavowal?" Mallory asked.

"It's when a vampire publicly repudiates the one who made him," I said, earning Ethan's approving nod. "Being given immortality, whatever the circumstances, is considered a gift. It creates a bond—magically, biologically, politically—between the vampires. Disavowal severs the bond. It's considered an extreme action, an action of last resort, and ethically questionable."

"So, technically," Mallory said, "you could have disavowed Darth Sullivan?"

The question—and the nickname we used for him—was out before she'd realized what she'd said. She mouthed a curse, squeezed her eyes closed. "Crap."

Ethan sat up straight, slowly turned his gaze to me. "Darth Sullivan?"

I inwardly cringed, opted for defense. "You're so handsome."

"Merit."

"And really tall." I cocked my head at him. "Has anyone ever told you that you resemble David Beckham?"

"*Merit.*"

There was no avoiding it now. "We made up the name before we got to know you. In fairness, we only did it because we really, really didn't like you." I grinned. "But we really like you now."

"A lot," Mallory confirmed. But Ethan wasn't ready to let go of the bone.

Darth Sullivan?

You didn't like me, either, I reminded him. *I bet you had a crabby nickname for me, too.* When he didn't immediately answer, I looked at him sharply. *Ethan Sullivan. You had a nickname for me.*

In fairness, he said, mimicking me, *we really, really didn't like you.*

Are you going to tell me what it is?

No. Because I've no wish to sleep on the floor. His grin was wicked, but I was immortal. I'd get it out of him sooner or later.

"Do you ever get the feeling we're only getting fifty percent of the conversation in here?" Mallory asked.

"As long as they're keeping the sex talk to themselves, it's fine by me."

This isn't over, I told him, then turned back to Mallory. "It's not sex talk. And technically, yes, I could have disavowed Ethan. But I hadn't known about it then, and he'd have been really pissed, considering he saved my life."

"Hey, at least she concedes that now," Catcher said. "She was pretty pissed about it at first."

"Well aware," Ethan said. "So, to get back to the point, I could disavow Balthasar. In my so doing, he wouldn't be able to rely on his relationship with me for any material or political purposes."

"And risking the possibility of setting him off," Catcher said.

Ethan nodded. "That would be the concern. But it's an idea on the list."

Mallory yawned, and Catcher glanced at his watch. "It's getting late—or early. We should get home before they lock the place down. Don't want to be stuck with a bunch of bloodsuckers when the sun comes up."

Ethan regarded them thoughtfully. "Actually, that's another interesting idea."

"Getting stuck with bloodsuckers?"

"In a manner of speaking." He looked down, seemed to choose his words before lifting his gaze again. "Balthasar presents an unusual problem for us—a magical problem. And the two of you are obviously experts. How would you feel about staying at the House in the interim? You'd be an extra precaution, of a type."

The offer was met with stunned silence. The last time Mallory had spent an evening at Cadogan House, she had been so far in the depths of a black magic obsession that she'd stolen Ethan's ashes in order to make him her familiar. It hadn't worked that way, but it had brought him back to life, a result for which I'd be eternally grateful.

That had been months ago, and before she'd come through the other side of her addiction. But still, that he'd trust her enough to let her stay in the House was a very big step for both of them.

"I don't know," Catcher said, glancing at Mallory.

"You can discuss it," Ethan said.

"And I'll offer this—a basket of bedtime snacks, every night." I smiled at them. "That's a key for me."

"I know Chuck would appreciate it, given the circumstances," Catcher said. "And we actually would be closer to his office."

"That is true," Mallory said. "But—well, the other vampires may not like it."

"I am their Master," Ethan said simply. "Not the other way around. But I think you don't give them enough credit. You've helped this House considerably." He smiled. "And they're vampires. By their nature, they believe in second chances. For what it's worth, I'd consider it a personal favor."

He looked at me, and I suddenly understood. Ethan wasn't afraid Balthasar would attack the House . . . but that Balthasar would attack me, and Ethan wouldn't be able to get to me quickly enough.

Ethan held up his hands. "This is a big request, and it's completely up to you, and I understand if you'd like some time to think about it. And, of course, we'd prepare appropriate remuneration for your services." He smiled at Mallory. "Perhaps a donation to Sorcerers Without Borders?"

SWOB was a group Mallory had created to help fledgling sorcerers navigate their new magicks. It was a mission close to her heart, since she'd come out of the magical gate swinging some very bad mojo.

Mallory and Catcher looked at each other. She shrugged, and he nodded. "Fine by us," he said. "I could stand to be pampered at Hotel Cadogan a bit. Assuming Merit's right about the bedtime snack basket."

"If she's ever right about anything, it's food."

I gave him the arm punch that he deserved.

Ethan must have made his request psychically. Barely three seconds later, Helen, the House's den mother, appeared in the doorway in her typical ensemble—a tidy tweed skirt and jacket in her usual pale pink, her short bob of silver hair styled with Photoshop-worthy perfection. (It had only gotten more perfect since Ethan's transition to the AAM, as Helen was now his official social secretary.)

"Sire?" she crisply said.

"Prepare the guest suite, if you would. Mallory and Catcher will be staying with us for a few days."

Helen kept her gaze on Ethan, but she pressed her lips together in obvious disagreement with his choice. "They will."

"They will," Ethan said, in a tone that clarified the issue wasn't up for debate. Realizing that, she nodded, moved into the hallway again to make preparations.

"I don't want to cause trouble," Mallory said.

"Actually, I don't mind causing it," Catcher said. "Vampires have caused plenty of their own. What are the chances of getting an off-street parking space?"

Ethan just looked at him. Off-street parking in Chicago was a very serious matter. "That would require some maneuvering."

They looked at each other in heavy silence.

"How much?" Catcher asked.

Ethan smiled slyly. "A ward on the House to keep Balthasar out, constructed and managed by you."

"You're a sneaky bastard, Sullivan," Catcher said, and nodded. Not a bad deal for good parking.

While Helen prepared their rooms and Luc prepared their security access, Mallory and Catcher returned to their Wicker Park town house to grab clothing and essentials for Vampire Sleepover Camp. They'd return after the sun was up, but the human guards at the gate could get them inside. They'd set the wards, and we'd all enjoy a good night's sleep.

Vampires were unconscious during the daylight; theoretically, Balthasar would be, too. But he was conniving, and I wouldn't put a daylight attack past him. Catcher and Mallory being here— setting a ward, and being able to emerge in daylight if the need arose—made me feel a lot better.

I was often relieved at the end of a night to return to our apartments on the third floor, the Master's suite that Ethan and I shared. But nights like this made the respite even more important. We could be ourselves, for ourselves.

Just like the rest of Cadogan House, our rooms were as lushly appointed. Thick rugs, demure colors, French fabrics, gorgeous antiques. Tonight, it smelled of lilacs, and Margot, the House chef, had placed a horn and silver tray on a side table with cups of hot chocolate, fruit, and the tiniest sandwiches I'd ever seen.

As I'd mentioned to Catcher, Cadogan-style immortality had its benefits. And because silliness in the face of danger was one of them, I ate a small square of brown bread and what looked like smoked salmon while pretending I was a giant. Wearing Cubs pajamas.

"How many academic degrees do you have?" Ethan asked, walking out of the bathroom with a towel around his waist, scrubbing a second through his hair.

"Two and a half," I said. "But that doesn't mean I can't enjoy comically tiny foods." I held up a wee croissant. "Odds are good she assembled this tray for the comic appeal."

Ethan rolled his eyes good-humoredly before tossing the towel in his hand back into the bathroom, dropping the second onto the floor.

That left him naked—all hard planes and ridges of muscle, including a very impressive erection that left little doubt about his current line of thought. The seductive drowsiness in his eyes, part desire and part nearing sunrise, confirmed it . . . and enhanced the allure.

I dropped the pastry back on the tray, my appetite now shifted to something entirely different. "You are a gorgeous specimen of a man."

"Am I?" he asked, but when I crooked my finger in beckoning, he stalked toward me like a cat, muscles in his thighs and abdomen tightening, shifting as he moved. There was nothing about him that wasn't perfectly sculpted. Whether caused by the vampire mutation or his Swedish genetics, the result was undeniably tempting.

"You are," I said, and slid a hand down the flat of his abdomen, the muscle hard as steel beneath my hand. "And since you became Master of the universe, we haven't really had time to explore your various peaks and valleys."

"Colorado was a bit of a bust," Ethan agreed. He put a hand on my waist, leaned forward to nuzzle my neck, teeth just catching my earlobe. "Exploration sounds like a beautiful way to spend the last minutes before sunrise."

I closed my eyes, smiled, and tilted my head to improve his access . . . until my phone began to ring.

Since Ethan growled, I guessed I wasn't the only one frustrated. "I'll pay you not to answer that."

"It could be about Balthasar. I have to at least see who it is." I grabbed my phone from the side table, checked the screen, and found an equally unwelcome caller.

It was late for vampires, but early for humans, including my father, Joshua Merit, king of Chicago real estate.

I didn't especially want to talk to him, but seeing his name appear on my phone also didn't do much for my libido, so I gave Ethan an apologetic look, lifted it to my ear.

"Hello?" I said awkwardly as Ethan backed away, picked up his towel, and marched toward the bed. So much for the exploration.

My father skipped the introduction. "I'd like you and Ethan to join me tonight at an event."

The order, framed as a request, was so brusque it took a moment to catch up. "This isn't really the best time . . ."

"For me, either. I'm involved in the Towerline project, as I'm sure you'll remember."

That took a moment of memory searching. Towerline was a large real estate deal my father was trying to close. It would put four brand-new interconnected skyscrapers along the Chicago River.

"I helped you find those account numbers," he said, reminding me again—as if that was necessary—that to him, everything was a transaction.

Still, while his attitude was regrettable, he was right. He'd helped track down the owner of a Swiss bank account, which led us to a conspiracy to take out the GP's former head, Darius West.

"What's the event?" I asked, resigned.

"A party to raise money for some art-based charity or other. The charity isn't important." My father, the philanthropist. "The location is—it's at the home of Adrien Reed."

My father paused, as if his mere mention of the name would send me into excited apoplexy.

"I don't know who that is."

"Yes, you do. He owns Reed Logistics. I'm sure you've seen the facility near O'Hare."

Since I hadn't really been on the lookout for a logistics partner, or its warehouse, the explanation didn't do much for me. "Sorry, doesn't ring a bell."

I could practically hear the flat stare through the phone. "He sponsors free bat night at Wrigley," my father added, helpfully this time.

In my sunlight-tolerating days, I'd loved attending free *anything* night at Wrigley. And there was probably a box of mini Louisville Sluggers in the basement of my parents' home.

"Oh, Adrien Reed," I said. "I thought you said Adrien *Mead*." I knew it was lame, but I was committed.

Silence, then: "Given his new national reach, Reed's expressed interest in meeting Ethan."

And there was the pitch. Swing and a miss in my opinion, but that was ultimately for Ethan to decide.

"I'll mention the request and your offer, but I can't promise anything."

"Because of Balthasar?"

The question made me shudder with memory and concern. "How do you know about Balthasar?"

"The several ongoing live broadcasts." His voice was flat, radiating disapproval that we were making a spectacle of ourselves again.

"I have obligations," I said, in answer to his question. "So I can't make a commitment right now."

"Family obligations trump paramours," my father said. And with that, a four-word missive on loyalty—and apparent evaluation of my relationship with Ethan, and despite the fact that he wanted to use him for his connections—he hung up the phone.

I threw the phone into the bank of pillows on the bed, gave it a single-fingered salute for good measure. Not exactly classy, but sometimes even messy feelings needed expressing.

Ethan emerged from the bedroom in his favorite sleepwear, a pair of green silk pajama bottoms slung low on his hips. "Another quality conversation between father and daughter, I see. Did you know you pace when you talk to him?"

I looked down, realizing I'd traversed the apartment. "I guess I did. He wants us to attend a charity event at the house of the Wrigley ball night guy."

"Adrien Reed?"

I looked at him. "How do you know that?"

"Reed loves business, and you love baseball. I pay attention. Why does your father want us there?"

"Because you're 'national' now. That makes you a legit business lead—and a very big catch."

"I'm not sure if I should be flattered or not. I would like to meet Reed but don't especially like the thought of leaving the House vulnerable."

"Mallory and Catcher will be here, so that helps. But I'm going to need a dress."

Ethan smiled lazily. "I haven't proposed to you yet."

He firmly believed marriage was in our future, and enjoyed teasing me with hints of his proposal. He knew I wasn't yet ready to take that leap, but the teasing certainly kept me on my toes.

"Wrong kind of dress. I could wear one of the previous ones"—this wasn't the first fancy event Ethan and I had attended—"or you can work your sartorial magic and find something new."

"I'll do that," he said, grabbing his phone and sending a message. "Confirm with your father and get the details. We'll tell Luc at dusk."

I pulled my phone from the pillow array, muttering a few choice words about "obligation" and "loyalty" while I did it, but sent my father the message: WE'LL ATTEND. SEND DETAILS.

I put the phone on the nightstand, felt the sudden creep of the sun over the horizon as the room's automatic shutters closed over the windows. "That's it for me tonight," I said, and fell face-first into the pillows.

"Demure and elegant as always," Ethan said, and I felt the bed dip beside me. "Sleep well, my Sentinel. For tomorrow is another day."

"Inevitably," I murmured, and fell into sleep.

CHAPTER FIVE

— ❊ —

YOU MAKE ME FEEL LIKE
A NATURAL VAMPIRE

Many hours later, the sun crept below the horizon again, leaving the world dark, quiet, and cool. My eyes flashed open as the automatic shutters retracted, sending the orange glow of streetlights into the room.

I glanced beside me. Ethan's eyes were closed, his body resting atop a tangle of sheets—one leg bent, one arm thrown above the other, brow furrowed. A sheen of sweat covered his body, and there was a stale, lingering magic in the air.

It wasn't hard to guess the reason for his distress. I touched the back of my hand to his forehead. Clammy, but cool.

"I'm awake," he said, eyes still closed.

"You're usually up before me."

"I slept like the dead—no pun intended." He opened one eye, cast a glance down the length of his body. "And part of me *is* up."

"We haven't talked about Balthasar," I said, avoiding the direction of his gaze, lest I become glamoured by the promise of it.

"Not exactly how I'd prefer to get into the mood. Come here,

Sentinel," he said, and waited while I climbed atop his body, hard beneath me.

His eyes as green as glass, Ethan rocked his hips enticingly. "I can make you forget everything that worries you."

"I worry for you," I said, but let him slip my shirt over my head, let my head fall back when his hands found my breasts. Tension slipped from my shoulders as his hands worked cleverly to entice and arouse.

"We are immortal," he said huskily, eyes silver and focused on my breasts. "Let us live like it." He pulled me down toward him, tangled his hands in my hair as his mouth found mine, attacked with brutal force, willing to give no quarter. His tongue probed and tangled as his teeth nipped at my lips, his body growing impossibly harder beneath me as he deepened the kiss.

"I want you," he whispered, before trailing kisses along my neck. "Jesus, but I want you. Stand up."

"What?" I asked, brows lifted.

"Stand up."

It wasn't easy to stand on the mattress, but I managed it. I'd been standing only for a second when he bared the rest of me.

And then sat up, and his mouth was at my core, and my muscles went so lax I had to brace a hand against the wall in front of me to stay upright.

Hands on my hips, he pulled my body toward him as he devoured me. I fisted my hand in his hair, called out his name as pleasure hit me like a shock of lightning.

"*Ethan*."

Again, Sentinel. His mouth and hands continued to taunt and torture, until I wasn't sure I'd be able to keep standing. He didn't stop until I'd climaxed again.

"Knees," he ordered. And I gratefully complied, lowering quivering thighs as I situated my body atop his.

Ethan stripped himself of clothing, rocked his body upward, seating himself firmly inside me, then growled deep in his throat, a rumble strong enough to vibrate the bed beneath us.

He raked his gaze along my body, from strong shoulders to breasts, abdomen to thighs, to the junction where our bodies were joined. I loved watching his eyes, watching his silvered irises cloud with lust and arousal, watching his face go utterly blank when pleasure rocked him, hearing his possessive and primal groans. Ethan was undeniably gorgeous at any time of day, waking or sleeping. But when the veil of desire covered him, he was magnificent.

His lip curled with focus, his hands found my hips, long fingers squeezing my hips as I began to move, savoring the sensation of his body around mine, within mine, both of us becoming more than we'd been, because we were together. His hips lifted to meet mine, eyes narrowed, contorted with pleasure. Perhaps, I thought, I'd give him something to see.

I cupped my breasts, nipped my lip between my teeth coquettishly, watched his eyes widen in surprise, delight, arousal. His hips moved faster, pushed upward as I rocked above him, spinning my hips and watching as his eyes darkened. Sweat gleamed across his chest, his breathing harsher, faster, as his pace quickened further. I took his wrist, lifted it to my mouth, touched my tongue to the spot above his rocketing pulse.

"Merit," he said hoarsely, and, as his body rocked upward, I bit.

We lazed in bed, lying beside each other for a little while longer until Ethan glanced at the clock, sighed. "We need to get moving. The party starts in two hours."

It took me a moment to remember what he was talking about,

that we'd promised my father attendance at Reed's party, and that I was going to have to wear a dress and fancy heels. I'd need to figure out a way to carry my phone and, if not my katana, a dagger.

I'd also need to check in with Luc and, in case he hadn't already heard, update Jonah, the captain of the Grey House guards, about Balthasar's appearance.

Jonah was also my partner in the Red Guard, a secret corps of vampires who kept an eye on the Masters and the reigning council, now the AAM, to make sure they didn't infringe the rights of Novitiates. We hadn't spoken much since Nicole's GP revolution, as we'd both been busy helping our Masters with the transition. And, frankly, I'd been stung by RG comments that if Ethan had gained control of the GP, I was too enamored to keep an eye on him. I wasn't looking forward to rehashing the love-makes-girls-dumb argument.

"How long is the line?"

I picked up my phone, scanned for Luc's now-nightly announcement for the number of vampires who'd requested an audience with Ethan. Ethan was the only Chicago Master who'd agreed to provide an audience to Rogues, vampires who weren't affiliated with a particular House. That drew a lot of Midwestern vampires to Cadogan's gate.

"Only seven tonight," I reported back, and sent Luc the party details while I was thinking about it.

Ethan sighed. "I still won't be able to get to them all."

"If you don't, they'll come back. And there's a safe house if they need shelter in the meantime." We wouldn't house all the vampires who showed up at the door, so Ethan and Malik had established a boardinghouse down the block where traveling vampires could safely seek refuge while they waited for an audience with the Master.

I put aside the phone, glanced back at Ethan. "Balthasar."

"That isn't a question."

"It's a topic of discussion, which you're avoiding." I wrapped the sheet around myself, rose to sit on my knees so I could see his face, which was unreadable.

"Is the sheet really necessary at this point?"

"It will keep us from getting distracted."

"I can see you naked without getting distracted."

"That's not exactly a compliment, and quit changing the subject." I put a hand on his. "You haven't had a chance to talk about it—about him, about what happened—since it happened."

Ethan looked away. "Is there anything to say?"

"Well, he tried to seduce me in front of you, so we could start there."

As predicted, that got me a flaming glare. "It wasn't seduction. It was magic." But his tone belied his words.

"So it was. And a betrayal either way."

Ethan blew out a breath through puffed cheeks.

"You don't have to talk about it if you don't want to. But things get a little tense between us when we let things stew."

His look was flat. "Why do I have a sense you actually mean 'me' when you say 'we'?"

My responsive look was even flatter. "Blackmail."

"Irrelevant."

"Since Nicole attempted to blackmail you about Balthasar, I think that makes it pretty freaking relevant."

Ethan growled, pushed his hands through his hair, linked his fingers behind his head. "I'd like him to respect the fact that I intentionally separated myself from him, and perhaps take a graceful walk into the sun. But there is little chance of that."

He looked at me. "I don't worry about myself. I worry about you, and I worry about this House."

"Mallory and Catcher are here."

"For any *direct* trouble he might try to cause," Ethan agreed. He lowered his hands, linked his fingers across his abdomen. "But if he tries to re-create his little European kingdom here? If he treats humans in Chicago like he treated Persephone and the others?" He leaned forward, a line of worry between his eyes. "Consider, Merit, the storm that would rain down upon us, upon vampires."

He was right; I hadn't even considered the damage Balthasar might cause by leaving a trail of blood and bodies across Chicago. Our relative peace with the city was short-lived, and we'd only just managed to keep the torches-and-pitchforks types at bay.

"Damn," I said.

"Exactly." He sighed. "But we've done all that we can for now. Your grandfather is alerted, and he'll advise the mayor if necessary."

Mayor Diane Kowalcyzk wasn't keen on vampires, but we'd helped the city once too often for her to use us as the political lightning rods she preferred. And since Chicago had more vampire Houses than any other city in the country, we had the largest AAM contingent. That made Diane even more interested.

"And your plan? Are you thinking about disavowal?"

"I'm considering it. But I can't shake the fear he'd act out. I want to talk it through with Malik and Luc when we have time. Which isn't right now, since we have a real-estate mogul to entertain. Let's get moving."

"Do we have to go?"

"Yes. And there's probably breakfast waiting outside our door, if that's any incentive."

Of course it was. I slipped on a robe and opened the front door, found breakfast, newspapers, and Luc's daily security reports awaiting us.

I picked up the tray and closed the door. Ethan gestured me forward as if awaiting service. "Darth Sullivan desires breakfast."

I shook my head, placed the tray on the farthest corner of the bed. Someone had to keep his ego in check; might as well be me.

Ethan grumbled but reached for the paper and a mug of coffee. I grabbed a bottle of blood and headed for the closet to grab jeans and a T-shirt.

I wasn't getting into a dress until it was absolutely necessary.

When we were dressed, I followed Ethan downstairs to the House's foyer, where a small reception desk had been installed to handle the waiting vampires. It was currently staffed by Juliet, a red-haired House guard who looked delicate but was as fierce as they came. Supplicants sat on benches installed across from the table.

Juliet glanced up, nodded at Ethan. "Sire."

Ethan nodded at her, then glanced at the vampires—three women, four men—who waited for him.

They were a sociological sample: a variety of shapes, sizes, colors, nationalities, finances. Among them, a very tall, broad-shouldered woman with short hair and a square face. A man of average height with dark skin and darker hair, casual clothes, and a worried expression. A blond woman I'd have described as handsome in a sleek blouse and pencil skirt. Their reasons for waiting were probably also different, but they were unified in the hope that Ethan could solve their problems.

They began to rise when they realized Ethan was approaching, but he held up a hand. "No need. Please stay seated. Unfortunately, I have an engagement this evening, so my availability will be limited. But if I cannot see you tonight, Juliet will help you find shelter."

A few looked worried or perturbed by the delay; the rest seemed to be in awe of Ethan.

"Sire," they said in more or less unison, and Ethan smiled in acknowledgment before turning toward his office. That was where we'd have parted ways had we not seen Helen waiting in the doorway of Ethan's office, two garment bags in hand.

She was surveying Ethan's office when we reached her, her gaze stopping at the broken bookshelves. "I hadn't noticed these last night. It seems Malik did not exaggerate."

"Balthasar did not employ his best manners," Ethan said.

Helen placed the garment bags carefully across the couch, then stood ramrod straight again and looked at Ethan.

"You know that I normally do not speak out of turn. But with *him* in town, and sorcerers in the House, that seems a recipe for trouble."

"And if I told you the sorcerers were helping keep the House safe from Balthasar's tantrums?"

She paused. "Then I'll get the staff started on the repairs."

"I appreciate it." When she left the room, Ethan glanced at his watch. "I'm going to do what I can with the supplicants before getting dressed. You wanted to check in with Luc?"

I nodded. "I'll go downstairs, give him a few minutes to harass me about being overly fancy and missing tonight's training." That brought a smile to my face. "Oh, I forgot about that. No Luc90X tonight. Maybe dating a big shot does have its privileges."

"Since I am the big shot, and you're Sentinel, you could probably skip that training altogether."

I pointed a finger at him. "Don't tell Luc that. He likes to play boss, and you'd break his heart." I shrugged. "The training's good for me, and it does give me a chance to hang out with Lindsey."

It was much more fun to be part of the guard group, even if not quite one of them, than to stand alone as Sentinel.

"In that case, talk to him, and make it snappy. Our interlude this morning put us behind."

That interlude had been his idea, but considering how much I'd enjoyed it, I let it go. "I can read a clock. I'll meet you in the apartments."

Unless I came up with a really good reason to avoid the thing altogether.

Cadogan House had four floors—three aboveground, which held offices, gathering spaces, the library, and the vampires' individual rooms; and a basement, which held the training room, the arsenal, and the Operations Room. The latter was Luc's personal kingdom, a high-tech room with security monitors, computers, a giant conference table, and several vampires at his disposal.

Tonight, it also held a giant tin of popcorn with the seals of the three Chicago vampire Houses stamped in gold on an azure background.

"Nice," I said, reaching over the table and grabbing a handful. "I hope we're getting licensing fees for this."

"But of course," Luc said. While the guards sat at computer stations along the edges of the room, monitoring security, doing research, Luc sat at the end of the table in jeans and cowboy boots—like Helen, an exemption from Cadogan's black-suit policy—his ankles crossed on the table as he perused the day's *Tribune*.

The headline on the front page, which faced out, was jarring: MASTER MEETS MAKER above a photograph of Ethan and Balthasar facing each other. The opportunism was clear in Balthasar's eyes. The concern clear in Ethan's.

"Glad to see they aren't encouraging him."

Luc grunted, folded the paper lengthwise, then horizontally, and set it on the table. "Reporters love a good story." He tapped the folded paper. "That's a damned evocative one."

"Yeah," I agreed. Too evocative—too emotional—for my tastes. "Did every outlet pick it up?"

Luc gestured back to his desk, where a pile of folded papers had already been reviewed. "Across the world. We're the hot new dysfunctional family."

Lindsey rolled her office chair toward us, used red nails on the tabletop to pull herself to a stop. Her blond hair was pulled into a high bun, and she'd paired her suit with eyeglasses with trendy black frames that she didn't actually need. But she pulled off the "saucy librarian" look.

"Babe," she said to Luc, "you sound whiny."

"I'm entitled to be whiny," Luc said. "And don't call me 'babe' on duty."

Lindsey gave me a long-suffering look. "If I had a quarter, am I right?"

"Always." I pointed toward the glasses, the hairdo. "What's this?"

She smiled, shrugged. "Just trying something a little different. I'm going for intellectual femme fatale."

"And you're pulling it off," I said. "We'll be heading to Reed's within the hour, so I wanted to check in. Any word about Balthasar?"

"No," Luc said, "but the door's good and warded. He won't be able to get in or out."

"How'd they link it to him?" I wondered.

"Used a piece of wood from the office bookshelves. Residual magic, apparently. You know Mallory's into forensic magic?"

I nodded. "Yeah. How are the Novitiates taking her involvement?"

"There are grumbles, of course. Concerns about trustworthiness. But considering those are matched against concerns about Balthasar, most are chill."

"Where's he staying?"

"Condo on Michigan near Grant Park. We aren't sure which unit—we didn't follow him in past the lobby. We're looking through real-estate records to confirm the owner, and we'll keep eyes on him twenty-four-seven."

"What about his backstory?"

Luc leaned forward, tapped the touch screen built into the tabletop, and an image flashed onto the large wall screen behind us—a spreadsheet marked by black and green boxes.

"That's impressive," I said. "What is it?"

This time, Luc tapped a button on the conference phone.

"Yo," said a familiar voice after a moment.

Luc smiled. "Jeff, Merit likes your spreadsheet."

Jeff Christopher was a shape-shifting white tiger in the body of a lanky computer genius and, along with Catcher, one of my grandfather's employees.

"My spreadsheets bring all the girls to the yard. Hi, Merit."

"Hi, Jeff." I glanced at Luc with amusement. "You're giving orders to the Ombuddies now?"

"Requesting their assistance in our time of great need," Luc corrected, bringing his hands together prayerfully.

"Being bossy," Lindsey corrected with a grin, rolling back to her computer station at Luc's arch look.

It occurred to me that over the course of the last year, we'd become a strange and wonderful team. The Ombuddies, Cadogan House, the sorcerers, with occasional help from other supernaturals. Most of them friendly, all of them with unique strengths that contributed to a pretty weird, but wonderful, whole.

"I'm short on time tonight," I told the team members, "so tell me about whatever this is."

"So," Jeff began, and I could practically hear the smile in his voice, "we've begun the fact-checking process. Given the importance, we decided to be systematic about it, so we created this timeline."

"Green entries are verified," Luc said. "Black entries need to be. Red entries, if there were any, would be falsies. No falsies yet."

I nodded, gestured to the green entries. "What have you verified so far?"

Luc gestured to the beginning of the timeline. "We've started with Persephone's death, and Balthasar's not-quite death and capture by the Memento Mori. There was definitely cult activity in Spitalfields. In our particular case, men who wanted immortality and, ironically, didn't care who they killed to get it."

Luc switched the image on-screen to a small gold disc. ME-MENTO MORI was engraved around a center skull. "It's a signet ring," he said, spinning the picture so the band was visible. "Each member got one."

"Anything specifically about Balthasar being one of their captives?"

"Nothing we've been able to dig up so far," Jeff said. "But the Librarian thinks he's found some of the group's research materials. They're held by a private collector, but there's a library in London that has microfiche of the pages. Some of them are on-line."

The Librarian was Cadogan's aptly nicknamed research and book specialist. He worked in the House's extraordinary two-story library. I was green-eyed with envy for the job. Although ass-kicking definitely had its moments.

"The Librarian has reviewed some of them," Jeff said, "and we're working on getting copies of the entire archive. He's found some general mentions of vampires, but no names."

I glanced at Luc. "I'm surprised the GP didn't jump on that—a cult torturing vampires."

"I doubt this popped onto their radar," Luc said. "This wasn't a large-scale operation, but a cult in a very poor neighborhood."

"We looked at Walford Abbey next," Jeff continued. "Unfortu-nately, the building was destroyed in World War Two, and the monks have all died, so we're still searching for records there. That's as far as we've gotten tonight."

"And we'll let you get back to it," Luc said, and we offered our good-byes to Jeff.

I glanced back at the spreadsheet, surveyed the data. "It might all match up," I said. "He'd have known we'd check."

"I'd be surprised if it doesn't," Luc said. "He'd have pre-pared."

I looked back at Luc. "And for what, exactly? This isn't a cour-tesy call."

"No," Luc agreed. "He's got an agenda. And from his little display yesterday, you seem to be part of it."

"Oh, good," I said, smiling weakly.

"He'll use you if he can. Hell, he'll use any of us, I think, if he thinks it'll hurt Ethan."

"You think that's why he's here? To cause pain?"

"Why else? He couldn't have thought he'd get a warm reception from Ethan. Ethan suggested revenge and power, and I think he's probably right."

"What a mess," I said with a sigh. "Ethan hates to leave the House alone tonight, but my dad did help us. And Ethan's not going to pass up an opportunity to talk to Reed."

Luc grinned. "Nope. He's a savvy one. And we won't be alone. Me and Blondie"—that was Lindsey—"have done our fair share of supernatural butt-kicking. And we've got the sorcerers. You'll have Brody. You should take your katana, although you probably can't take it into the ball."

My eyes widened. "I'm sorry—did you say 'ball'?"

"Yeah. Reed's party. It's a ball. A full-on gala." He glanced up at me, amusement crinkling the corners of his eyes. "Did you not know that?"

"No," I said flatly. "No one mentioned that to me." Probably on purpose.

As the child of wealthy parents, I'd seen fancy parties through stairway balusters and cracked doors. I'd grown into a jeans-and-Pumas girl, evolved into a boots-and-leathers girl, and preferred both to crinoline and Spanx.

I lifted my gaze to the ceiling, considered the garment bag in Ethan's office, wondered what nightmare it held.

"If it's any consolation," Lindsey said, "all the cool kids will be there. The Schwartzes. The Lindenhursts. Michael Marlow and Todd Vanguard. They are very pretty. Tech billionaires or something, tall, dark, and handsome both, and very much in love."

"I take it you've been reading the society pages again," Luc said.

"It breaks up the bad news," she said, and I couldn't argue with that.

"Explain to me why people would spend money outfitting their houses and themselves for charity balls. Why don't they just give that money to the charity?"

"That is a question for the ages, Sentinel. In the interim, make sure your fancy ball gown has a spot for your phone. Or take one of those little purse things you ladies carry." He moved his fingers in the shape of a rectangle.

"A clutch?"

"That's it."

Lindsey chuckled. "Just call him Mr. de la Renta."

I blew out a resigned breath, rose, cast a baleful glance at Luc. "A ball? Seriously."

"Complete with theme."

I felt my lip curl. "Which is?"

Luc grinned. "That, Sentinel, is a mystery you'll have to solve on your own."

I left them to their work, reached the basement stairs when my phone began to ring. It was Jonah, who I still hadn't taken the time to call. I was glad he'd thought to do it.

"Hey," I said. "Sorry I haven't checked in."

"So Ethan's long-dead Master is alive."

"Hello to you, too," I said, bristling a little at his tone, which was snarky, but not in a good way. "And yes, that's what it seems. Have you seen him?"

"Only on television. You think he'll come here? What's his play?"

I gave him the overview and our analysis.

"I know you're probably busy with the AAM, but you'll want to keep an eye out for him. He's dangerous."

"So I sensed. This is going to make it even more crucial that we monitor Ethan."

I stopped on the stairs. "Wait. What?"

"I was going to talk to you tonight. We want you to install a camera, with audio, in Ethan's office."

Jonah was lucky he couldn't see my face. "Excuse me?"

"Ethan's part of the AAM. He's in a position of authority, and it's our job to monitor people in those positions. It's exactly what you signed up for."

In fact, I'd signed up for the RG when Ethan was gone. But that wasn't the point.

"I won't help you spy on him."

"Balthasar is alive, Merit, and apparently strong enough to call Ethan. He's dangerous."

"I don't disagree. But Ethan won't let Balthasar control him."

"You're assuming he'll have a choice."

"Balthasar isn't that powerful." I hoped. "Besides, there's an entire House of people who'd stop Ethan if we thought he was becoming someone's minion, including me. You sure know I wouldn't let him become a dictator."

"You have an obligation."

"So do you. Do you have a camera in Scott's office?"

"No."

"Are you going to?"

"No, but that's not relevant."

"How is it *not* relevant?" Realization dawned when he didn't answer. My anger rose, lifted like a hot cloud, and I dropped my voice to keep from screaming at him in the stairway.

"You cannot actually think I'd ignore Ethan becoming a dicta-

tor because I'm *sleeping* with him. I thought the RG was past that."
Another RG member, Horace, had raised the issue before, and I'd
believed we'd resolved it.

"Balthasar wasn't in the picture then."

"It's insulting either way."

"It's not meant to be an insult. It's meant to be a protection."

"Against what? My inability to logic through hormones?"

"You're taking this too personally." He sounded tired again,
like a parent talking to a petulant toddler.

I decided to give him the benefit of the doubt. "Look, I don't
know what's going on at Grey House. Maybe you're distracted;
maybe you're concerned about Scott and the AAM. I don't know. But
you know him better than this, and you certainly know me better
than this." And if he didn't, it wasn't flattering for either of us.

"You're saying you won't do it."

"Yeah, I am saying that. We all have lines, Jonah. This is one of
mine. I assume you trust me, or you wouldn't have made me your
partner. You think about that, and you let me know."

And for the first time that I could remember, I hung up on my
partner.

CHAPTER SIX

WHAT A DIFFERENCE A NIGHT MAKES

I was still stewing when I made it to the apartments. Ethan was gone, but the garment bag lay on the bed beside a glossy shoe box.

Hoping to direct my anger more productively, I unzipped the bag, half hoping I'd find a voluminous satin gown with mounds of rhinestones to rage against.

But I should have known better. Satin and rhinestones weren't Ethan's style.

"*Oh,*" I said as I unzipped the bag.

The dress was a slender column of black flared at the bottom. The sweetheart bodice was fitted but demure, and two panels of black tulle formed narrow sleeves that just covered the shoulders.

I turned to the box, uncapped it, found a pair of heeled sandals of crisscrossing satin straps that rose to the ankle and tied in a bow. They'd be tricky to walk in, but at least the straps would keep them in place if we needed to run.

I laid them out on the bed, climbed into the appropriate undergarments, and went to the bathroom to consider my hair options. My usual option, a high ponytail and bangs, wasn't going to do it tonight.

I dug through the bathroom drawers until I found a curling iron I'd probably used twice in the last five years. My bangs were long enough to sweep to the side and pin, and a few twirls of the iron left my hair in long, tousled curls. Mascara. Lip gloss. A hint of blush across pale cheeks.

And then it was time to don the dress.

I spent two minutes mostly naked in the bedroom, hair curling across my shoulders, staring at the dress.

Was I supposed to step into it? Drag it over my head? Surely the former, but it looked snug enough that I was a little afraid—even with a ballet dancer's build—that I'd get stuck halfway up.

Unfortunately, time was ticking, so I had to make a call. I let the dress drape to the floor, stepped carefully inside the middle, and began to pull it up the way a woman might don stockings. The dress was fitted, but the fabric had some give to it, so sliding it up wasn't as bad as I'd imagined.

The zipper was the tricky bit. It ran the length of the back, and even with my relatively long limbs I couldn't crook my arm enough to get the zipper up more than a few inches.

I was trying what I thought was a very creative approach—lowering the dress, zipping it up halfway, then sliding it carefully upward—when a knock sounded at the door.

"Merit?"

I snapped my hands over my chest as Lindsey's head popped into the room. The dress hit the floor, puddling at my feet.

"Um," she said with lifted eyebrows, walking inside and closing the door behind her. She put her hands on her hips, gave me an up-and-down appraisal. "Problem?"

"I'm getting ready!"

"I can see that."

I turned around, gave her my back. "Zipper?"

"Ah," she said with a nod, and strode forward, apparently non-plussed at the sight of the bare most of me.

"I like your hair like this," she said, pulling the sides of the dress together and raising the zipper with a satisfying *zwip*. "There's a hook at the top," she added, fastening it, then plucking at tulle and taffeta until she was satisfied.

"Very nice. Turn around."

I followed her directions, mostly relieved I wasn't hanging loose anymore, watched her nod.

"Very nice, indeed."

Apparently not content with playing at the dress, she fluffed parts of my hair, tucked in others. "This is fun. It's like you're my own vampire Barbie."

She stepped back, hands on her hips, nodding as she looked me over. "Shoes?"

"Box on the bed." Since there was little chance I was bending over to lace up the ribbons, I lifted the flare of the dress and let her tuck me into the shoes like Cinderella.

The heels were high, but the fit was good, snug. "I think I could run in these," I said, taking a few in-place steps.

"I doubt you'll need to sprint at Adrien Reed's house, but it's probably best to be prepared." She pointed to the closet, which held a floor-length mirror. "You want a look-see?"

"Yeah, I think I do."

She stepped aside while I carefully traversed the bedroom, trying not to snag the dress's flare on the heels or the spindly legs of Ethan's antiques.

The sound I made when I saw myself wasn't far off from the sound I'd made when I'd first seen the dress. I still looked like me, but sheathed in a gown that might have been worn by an actress on the red carpet, my hair softer than its usual knife-edge bangs and ponytail, I seemed softer. Not just a girl with immaculate comic timing and fine katana skills, but a woman who could hold her own with the city's elite.

That reminded me—I'd need something to hold my phone, so I grabbed a simple black clutch from the closet.

I'd just stepped into the bedroom again when the doors opened, and Ethan strode in like a man who owned the world.

He wore a superbly tailored black tuxedo—pants, two-button jacket, and bow tie—that accentuated his lean frame. He'd slicked back his thick golden hair, tying it at the nape of his neck, which enhanced his already striking features—cheekbones cut from marble, sculpted lips, piercing eyes.

He didn't catch our appreciative looks, because his gaze was on his watch. "I hope you're ready, because we're already behind."

"*Ahem,*" Lindsey said. "Sire?"

At the sound of her voice, he looked up, his gaze shifting from Lindsey to me, his eyes going enormous. "*Sentinel.*"

Lindsey lifted a finger, pointed it at the door. "And I'm just going to take that as my cue to leave. You know, before the panting and heavy petting."

Neither of us said a word as she slipped out.

Ethan took a step forward, then another. "I am . . . speechless. You look absolutely beautiful. Statuesque. Exotic. Poetic. Not that you aren't usually beautiful, but this is . . ."

"Different," I finished with a smile.

"Yes. Different." He touched a lock of hair, spun the curl around his finger. "Another side of you, of my dedicated Sentinel."

He lifted my hand, turned my palm, pressed his lips to the

pulse in my wrist. The kiss—the connection, the love, the magic—sent sensation up my arm, down my spine again.

"You look very handsome, too."

He arched an eyebrow with obviously wicked intent. "Do I?"

"You know you do, so don't pretend otherwise. You look like a prince."

He laughed heartily. "I am very much not—was not ever—a prince. I was, and remain, a soldier." He squeezed my hand. "Your soldier, as you are mine."

"Then we fit very well. We should probably go."

Ethan nodded, picked up our scabbarded katanas from the side table. "Just in case," he said. "We'll leave them in the car."

That reminded me—and I went back to the bureau, grabbed my dagger from the top drawer, and stuffed it into the handbag.

"You've got a weapon on you?" I asked, looking him over. I sensed the vague vibration of magic, but if he had a blade hidden anywhere, he'd done a very good job of it.

"Dagger and a small throwing knife I borrowed from the arsenal," he said as we headed toward the door.

"Ooh," I said, glancing up at him. "I've always wanted to try those. How's the weight?"

"Rather fantastic," Ethan said. "You should have Malik teach you how to use them. He's very skilled. And he knows it."

Both good facts to file away, I thought with a smile.

When we reached the stairs, I handed my clutch to Ethan.

He gave it the same look he might have given bad fish. "I'm not going to carry your purse."

"Then you'll have to carry me down the stairs." I took the handrail in my right hand, picked up the skirt's flare in my left. Took one careful step, then the next, sensed him descend with resignation behind me.

"Yes, a Master has to occasionally carry a purse," I said, anticipating his objection. "Just as a Sentinel must occasionally wear a very expensive dress."

"Did you make contact with Jonah?" he asked, catching up to walk beside me.

"He's going to keep an eye out for Balthasar." I opted not to tell him about Jonah's request. Both of us being angry at him wasn't likely to accomplish much.

Luc was alone in the foyer when we reached it, the supplicants already gone for the evening. He worked on his phone, tongue poked at the corner of his mouth, and looked up at the sound of our footsteps.

His eyes widened appreciatively as he took in my dress, heels, hair. "You look beautiful."

Ethan beat me to a response. "Thank you. But you should compliment Merit as well. She cleans up nicely."

Luc snorted, glanced at me. "And you don't look half-bad yourself, Sentinel."

"Thank you, Luc. He's just jealous. He prefers to be the arm candy."

"I think you'll both do," Luc assured.

"Anything?" Ethan asked, the question clear, even if unspoken.

Luc shook his head. "Quiet as a mouse, still as a rock."

I knew that line, had played the game in elementary school, a ploy to keep children still and quiet.

"I have an idea," Ethan said, "and I'd like your thoughts, your analysis."

Luc put his phone away, put his hands on his hips. "I'm listening."

"Disavowal."

"All right, all right, all right," Luc said with a grin. "I like an aggressive strategy."

I actually recognized that movie reference—an unusual win for Luc—but let the applause pass, since we were short on time.

"I'll talk to Malik, have the Librarian look into it."

Ethan nodded. "Brody's driving?"

"He's the best defensive driver we've got. He's waiting at the gate. I'm glad to see you've got weapons," he added, gesturing toward the katanas. "Although I do wonder about the purse."

"It's hers," Ethan said, handing it back to me. I supposed he expected I'd make the steps in front of Cadogan House single-handedly.

He must have guessed the line of my thoughts. *I'll hoist you over my shoulder if you can't make it down three steps.*

I'd make it just fine.

"Be careful," Luc said. "And, Sentinel? Try to have a good time."

I'd be at a fancy party in a fancy dress with my father and his fancy friends, while my boyfriend's narcissistic creator roamed Chicago. What could possibly go wrong?

The Reed house was a mansion of the old-school Chicago variety, located in the city's Prairie Avenue Historic District, a neighborhood south of downtown that housed some of the city's finest architecture. Reed's house, a monolith of stone with a sharply pointed red roof, had been built in 1885 for the owner of a successful mail-order company based in Chicago. The house formed a squared, elongated C, the open side closed with a long stone wall, creating a courtyard in the middle.

Tonight, limousines lined the neighborhood's streets. Brody plodded along in stop-and-go traffic, his frustration evidenced by occasional grunts.

"Eyes on the road," Ethan said when Brody checked the rear-view mirror again to catch a glimpse of me.

I bit back a smile, but gave myself a mental high five for being utterly fly.

"She just looks so . . . fancy," Brody said, which deflated my ego just a bit.

"Fancy," I decided, wasn't the equivalent of "astoundingly beautiful." And the dress had been too much work to get into for anything less complimentary than the latter.

"*She* can hear you," I reminded him. "And she outranks you. Eyes on the road."

"What did you say to me last night?" Ethan murmured with amusement. "Down, girl?"

I made a vague sound as Brody reached the front of Reed's house, where a human in a black shirt, vest, and pants opened the door.

"Stay close," I told Brody. "Find a spot, no more than two blocks, and keep your phone on."

"On that," he said, and merged back into the slow crawl of cars after Ethan and I had disembarked. I tucked hair behind my ear, adjusted the dress so it fell properly around my feet, noticed Ethan's soft smile.

"What?"

"You think you don't fit here, Sentinel," he said quietly, offering me his arm as we strolled the red carpet through lines of reporters who'd gathered to snap photos of the rich, famous, and infamous. "But you fit better than many of them, because you know exactly who you are."

The lucky photographer who snapped me after that compliment got a grand smile for her trouble.

After several slow minutes of walking, we reached the front door, where a petite girl with dark skin and hair piled in a voluminous topknot stood with a clipboard.

"Ethan and Merit," he said. "We're guests of Joshua Merit."

She scanned the list, nodded. "Welcome to the Reed house," she said, and gestured us inside.

The house opened immediately into an enormous two-story room, with marble dominating the first floor, including a large marble staircase bound in curvy marble balusters that marched to the second floor. The second floor formed a balcony around the first, surrounded by a railing of thick, dark wood.

The house's décor matched its large scale. Baroque furniture, paneled walls, heavy sconces, all of it oversized. There was something Old World about the tone, but the effect was jumbled, as if Reed had simply plucked items at random from an antiques store.

Adding to the heaviness, the furniture had been draped in jewel-toned silks and was speared with tall candelabras and dripping pillar candles. Reed had even hired performers. A couple in teal silk jumpsuits juggled painted clubs. Dancers in velvet ball gowns and harlequin ensembles, their identities concealed behind papier-mâché masks with large dark tears painted beneath diamond-shaped eyes, danced in pairs through the crowd. Most of the guests wore black, which offset the deep burgundy, gold, and crimson velvets of the performers' costumes.

"And the theme is," I murmured, glancing around, "Venetian masquerade."

"Very theatrical," Ethan said.

"It is." A man in a black jumpsuit spun past us, his face covered by a mask with round eyes and a beaklike nose.

And a little creepy, I added silently. *Very* Eyes Wide Shut.

And very Venetian. That's a medico della peste, he said. *It's based on a mask that was used by doctors to protect them from the plague.*

It's disturbing.

Some find that to be part of the appeal, Ethan said, but sidled closer as the masked man circled us, his eyes trained on us like a ballet dancer even as his body spun.

"That was creepy," I said as he finally moved away.

"It was," Ethan said, grabbing two flutes of champagne from a passing waiter's tray. He handed me one, then tapped his glass delicately against mine. "Sentinel, I'll say it again: You look ravishing."

Because I agreed with him, I shared his smile. "You have excellent taste. And I'm not just saying that because we're dating."

"But it doesn't hurt."

"It doesn't hurt," I agreed, and sipped. The champagne was smoky and peachy at the same time. An odd combination, but it worked. I hadn't yet seen a snack tray, but the drink gave me hope they'd also be good.

"Do you see him anywhere?"

I glanced back at Ethan. "Reed or my father?"

"Either. I'm surprised Reed isn't making the rounds—and your father isn't at his side."

"What do you know about this Towerline project?"

"Not a lot," Ethan said, shifting to avoid the swoop of a juggler snatching an errant baton. "I've read about it, seen the plans in the paper. It's reportedly the biggest deal your father has ever closed."

"And he wants Reed as an investor?"

"That would be my guess. A project that large will take a lot of financing." Ethan touched my arm, nodded toward the other side of the room. "And I believe we've just received our summoning."

I followed his gaze. A man on the other side of the room—also tall and lean, but with dark hair and pale blue eyes that matched mine—gestured with two fingers, beckoning me to him in the same fashion he called his servants.

I managed not to growl.

"Beware, Sentinel. Humans are the fiercest predators of all."

"Well aware," I said, using one of Ethan's favorite phrases.

With Ethan's hand at my back, we crossed the ballroom.

"Joshua," Ethan said when we reached him.

He offered Ethan a handshake. "Congratulations on your promotion."

"Thank you."

"Merit," he said to me, without pleasantries.

"Dad."

Always charming, Ethan said silently, then gestured to the room. "This is quite an affair."

"Adrien enjoys a good show. He'd like to meet you. I'll take you upstairs." He turned on his heel, headed toward the staircase. My father was undeniably absorbed by business, but for him to act as majordomo for anyone was utterly out of character. And oddly sycophantic.

The deal must not be done if he's doing Reed's business, Ethan said silently.

My thoughts exactly. But we'd come here for a purpose, so we followed him to the stairs, climbed treads of pink marble warped with age and the wear of thousands of footsteps. Thankfully, going up was a lot easier than going down, so Ethan didn't have to bear the burden of my purse.

Partygoers flowed around us with masks and champagne flutes in hand, the entire effect dizzying, like walking uphill through a waterfall of people.

The second floor opened into a long gallery flanked by marble columns, the walls marked by oil paintings in gilded frames: landscapes, still lifes, portraits. As with the first floor, his taste seemed to vary in everything except size. They were all enormous, which made their subjects seem that much larger.

Our Mr. Reed does not care for subtlety, Ethan said, our footsteps silent on the undoubtedly priceless runner that covered the marble floor as we traversed the gallery.

There were fewer guests in this room, which felt more like it belonged in a medieval castle than a businessman's home. The few men and women who'd sought refuge from the crush downstairs stood in intimate clusters, faces hidden by demi-masks.

The end of the gallery was marked by a set of wooden doors. They opened and a man strode out, closing them quietly behind him again. He was a big man—tall and wide—with a rounded crown of silver hair surrounding a shining bald dome. He walked toward us with heavy, steady steps, and looked very unhappy about whatever had gone down in the office.

"Sanford," my father said.

"Joshua," the man said with a nod, then carried on behind us, leaving the faint smell of cigar smoke behind him.

Sanford? I asked Ethan silently. His face rang a bell, but I couldn't place him.

Sanford King, Ethan said. *He was arrested last year for racketeering, bribery, extortion, and some manner of other financial ills. He was acquitted, as I recall.*

The arrest apparently hadn't hurt his reputation if he was getting private meets with Reed at the man's own gala.

We reached the doors, the apparent inner sanctum, and my father knocked. A moment later, the door opened, and a tall man in a black suit glanced at my father, then us. Bodyguard. He had the square jaw and broad shoulders for it, and the buzz of steel from the gun I guessed was holstered in a shoulder harness.

"Joshua Merit," my father said.

The door closed a bit while the guard did his checking, then opened again. The guard looked each of us over as we entered, then closed the door behind us and took his post again, shoulders back, hands clasped in front of him.

The room, an office with several walls of shelves, a large desk, and a sitting area, was spartan compared to the rest of the house. There were a few pieces of décor—a globe, potted palms, a blocky chandelier that might have been designed for a Frank Lloyd Wright house, but they were appropriately scaled and surprisingly tasteful.

A man stood across the room, leaning against the desk with one ankle crossed over the other, a phone in hand. He was trim but broad-shouldered, with dark, wavy hair and a goatee that had just begun to salt-and-pepper. I'd have put him in his early forties.

His charcoal tuxedo was immaculately cut, his square face well lived in but handsome, with a square jaw, a deep slash of mouth, eyes the same gray as his suit. He wasn't unhandsome, but it was the air of utter confidence, the sense of fundamental knowledge and control, that was interesting. He was absolutely certain of his world.

He hung up the phone, slipped it into his pocket, glanced at my father questioningly.

"Ethan Sullivan of Cadogan House," my father said. Apparently, the Master got top billing. "You'd wanted to meet him."

Reed shifted his gaze to Ethan, and I caught a moment of surprise, then irritation. My guess? His foundation of knowledge and control had been shaken because he hadn't known we were coming.

I glanced at my father, and the question on my face should have been obvious: Why was Adrien Reed surprised we were here? Wasn't his wanting to meet us the entire point? Or were we my father's hospitality gifts, to be handed over to the man like a bottle of good wine?

Regardless of his initial surprise, Reed was practiced. He moved forward, offered Ethan a hand. "Welcome to our home."

"It's a pleasure to meet you," Ethan said, then put a hand at my back. "My Sentinel and paramour, Merit."

It was childish that he'd used my father's word, but still satisfying to see my father's wince of impropriety.

Reed's nod was brisk, efficient.

"You have a beautiful home," I said. "The gallery is very impressive."

"I find, as I age, that I prefer intense to dull," Reed said. "More to less. There are only so many hours in the day, and much to be accomplished." He glanced at Ethan. "Immortality, of course, presents the opposite problem."

"There are more hours to fill, certainly, but more consequence," was Ethan's measured response. "One becomes eternally tied to one's choices."

Reed nodded in acknowledgment.

A door on the other side of the room opened, and a breeze from an outdoor terrace wafted in, along with the bright scent of fruity perfume.

"My wife," Reed said, gesturing to the statuesque woman who'd walked inside. She wore a long, sleeveless dress the color of new grass, a gleaming brass belt around her tiny waist. Her eyes were as luminously green as the fabric, her skin sun-kissed gold. Thick blond hair waved across her bare shoulders, one side pulled back by a barrette that matched the belt. She looked like she'd stepped from a 1970s fashion ad, or maybe the set of *Charlie's Angels*. Since she couldn't have been more than twenty-three or twenty-four, she probably wouldn't have gotten the reference.

"Sorcha," Reed said, holding out his hand.

She walked forward, offered him her free hand, the other holding a flute of champagne.

"Ethan and Merit, of Cadogan House. They're vampires."

"Oh?" she asked, her tone making it hard to tell whether she was surprised, confused, or disturbed.

"As I've finished my business, I suppose we should join the party again." He released his wife, gestured toward the door, and fell into step beside Ethan.

"I understand you're part of the AAM—the new national organization." They entered the gallery, the magnate and the Master, and chatted about the departure from the GP. My father and the bodyguard followed, and then Sorcha and me.

"This is quite a house," I said to her.

"Yes, it's very big. So, you're a vampire?"

"Yes. For almost a year now."

"Oh. How does that work, exactly?"

"Humans are turned when they're bitten by other vampires."

"Oh," she said again. Once again, I couldn't tell if she couldn't understand or didn't much care.

We reached the stairs and Reed stopped at the top, gestured Sorcha to his side. He signaled a waiter, who brought over a tray of champagne, stood at attention while Reed turned to his guests.

"Ladies and gentleman," Reed said, his resonant voice carrying across the space.

A hush fell over the room. Guests turned toward Reed, moved toward the stairs to watch him.

"I'd like to thank you all for coming to our small soiree tonight. I hope you'll enjoy the beverages, the food. You've all been generous, and I hope you'll consider being generous one more time. You'll see men and women with baskets in the crowd. Please consider making a donation."

The plague doctor danced through the crowd with two other masked friends, all of them carrying reed baskets, pausing occasionally as guests dropped money inside them.

The entire event had been theatrical, so when two men in harlequin masks jumped suddenly from the balcony and landed in the middle of the marble stairway, I thought it was part of the act.

But when they pulled gleaming katanas from black scabbards and the subtle vibration of vampire magic filled the air, it was obvious this wasn't part of the show.

It was an attack.

CHAPTER SEVEN

DRESSING DOWN

Ethan, I said silently, and he nodded, his body tense and ready to spring forward.

"We come for Sanford King," said the vampire on the right, katana pointed at the crowd. The humans talked and gestured nervously, looking around for the man who'd been called out. Unfortunately for him, Sanford wasn't difficult to spot, being nearly a head taller than everyone else.

"I believe you're at the wrong house," Reed said, voice booming and quieting the crowd again—except for the shuffle of cell phones as cameras snapped, messages were sent, and calls were placed.

This would need diplomacy, I thought, pulling my phone surreptitiously from my bag and sending Brody and my grandfather a message: VAMPS W/ SWORDS AT REED HOUSE TO HARM SANFORD KING. CPD DISPATCH PROBABLE.

"We're at precisely the right house," said the vampire on the left.

They moved down the stairs, one tread at a time, their swords extended and blades gleaming silver. With each step, the crowd moved backward, away from danger.

Sanford King might have been a criminal, but he wasn't a coward. He pushed through the humans and moved into the clearing, looked over the men. His face had gone crimson, sweat beading on his brow. "I'm Sanford King. The fuck do you want with me?"

"You're a killer," said the vampire on the left. "A criminal. A parasite on the city. You deserve to die. Tonight, we'll handle that."

They began to circle King, lions preparing for an attack, the gazelle cornered and nervous between them. Criminal, coward, or otherwise, Sanford was human, and didn't look like much of a match for the well-armed vampires.

Ethan and I simultaneously stepped forward to assist. But before we could take the stairs, Reed held up a hand, and his voice was low and threatening.

"Do not even think of drawing your weapons in my house. I will not have any more armed vampires here."

Ethan showed his teeth but stayed where he was.

His house, his rules, Ethan said silently. *Until we deem otherwise. Stay ready, Sentinel.*

Reed snapped his fingers, and his bodyguard pulled his gun from a shoulder holster, gripped it in a two-hand stance, and began moving carefully down the stairs, barrel pointed toward the vampires.

"On the ground!" he yelled when he hit the first floor.

The vampires ignored the order. As King disappeared into the crowd again, the vampire on the right launched forward, swinging his katana with a move the bodyguard barely evaded. But avoiding the strike left him off-balance, and the second vampire executed a perfect side kick that connected with the bodyguard's wrist, sending the gun into the air and then skidding across the floor.

The bodyguard didn't seem worried. "Fine. You want to play it that way, we'll play it." He lunged for one of the vampires, who neatly sidestepped the move, sliced upward with a strike that caught the bodyguard across the chest. He hit his knees, but it was a feint—when the vampire moved closer, thinking to finish him off, the bodyguard grabbed him by the calves, pulled him to the ground, attempted to muscle him into a hold.

The bodyguard was big and muscular and outweighed the vampires considerably. But they were faster, more efficient, more athletic. The vampire flipped, squirmed out of the bodyguard's hold, and jumped back to his feet, but he'd lost his katana. The bodyguard picked it up, grasped the handle with both hands, began to wield it like a foil, with pokes and thrusts that weren't well suited for the blade.

The vampires adapted, working together like the predators they were. While the vampire with the katana parried, the other moved around the bodyguard's back, peppering him with kicks to the legs and knees to keep him off-balance.

They were trained, which didn't bode well. Vampires trained in classic fighting styles meant someone with equal skills had done the training. And there weren't many vampires in Chicago with training like that.

The bodyguard stumbled, and the vampire with the sword jumped forward, blade disappearing into the bodyguard's gut. He screamed like a wounded animal, went down heavily. Someone reached out, helped him scoot across marble and back toward the crowd, applied pressure to the wound.

"Goddamn it," Reed muttered.

The vampires looked at each other, scanned the crowd. "Sanford King!"

Adrenaline became a dull itch beneath my skin. *Ethan*, I said again, this time the sound imploring, begging for action.

Ethan pulled out his dagger, light gleaming along the brilliant blade. "That's our cue," he said, not bothering to check Reed's response—or get his permission.

I shouldn't have been grinning, and my blood shouldn't have been *thrumming* like a Corvette engine at the thought of getting out there and mixing it up with these two idiots, and yet . . .

Without taking my eyes off the men, I pulled the dagger from my purse, shoved the purse back to Sorcha for safekeeping. *You want the right or left?*

The one on the right looks smaller.

I narrowed my gaze at the vampire, grinned. *Then I'll take the one on the left.*

You were beautiful before, Ethan said silently, *but with the fire in your eyes, you are a goddess.*

We'll see how divine I am, I said and, just as my grandfather had taught me decades ago, put two fingers in my mouth and whistled with earsplitting volume.

The vampires looked up at us, and fresh fear wafted up. They clearly weren't thrilled to see Ethan and me standing at the top of the stairs, blades in hand, and ready to rumble. And if they were Housed vampires, Chicagoland vampires, they'd have known who we were and what we could do . . . . and what the penalty would be for fighting Ethan.

Winner buys ice cream, I said as Ethan and I took the stairs one (careful) step at a time.

Done, Ethan agreed. *And gets to decide what to do with it.*

I barely suppressed the delicious shiver that rolled up my spine.

"Gentlemen," Ethan said, his gaze on the vampires. "You've made rather a mess here. I don't know you—yet—but I suspect you know who I am, and who stands beside me. And you know that what has happened here—your violation of this home, and what I suspect was a trespass without invitation—will not go unanswered. This is your one and only opportunity to lay down your weapons and peacefully surrender. There is no shame in knowing when to walk away."

The vampires looked at each other, made their decision, and turned to face us. They'd already brought war to Reed's house; they apparently weren't going to back down now.

"In that case," Ethan said, lifting his blade, "may the best vampire win."

The battle was on.

I moved slowly, methodically, kept my eyes on the vampire I'd selected. I hope it looked intentional, as if I were baiting him into impatience and an unwise move. I was, of course, trying not to trip on the stairs.

Since there seemed little doubt the voluminous garment was going to get nicked, I made a silent apology to the gods of fashion, flipped the dagger in my hand, and when I hit the first floor, dove in.

The vampire met me, blade for blade, steel against steel. A slice to my right, and I matched it with the dagger, used the force to spin him away. A slice to my left on his return spin, and I used the dagger to block, forcing the blade down and causing him to shift his center of balance. He bobbled backward but caught himself again.

I took the offensive. I sliced forward, using my blade as I might have used a paintbrush, with quick, fluid strokes designed to keep him moving at my speed, to keep him dancing and dodging instead of planning new attacks.

It was a good plan, but he was well trained. *Really* well trained. I wanted to smack the mask off his face. I wanted to know who he was, and who'd trained him to attack humans.

He was smart enough not to open his body completely, or give me access to delicate organs. There was something gentlemanly about his fighting style—and maybe that was something I could use against him.

I bobbled forward, pretending to trip on the hem of my dress—not entirely improbable. For a moment, he paused, instinct telling him to help me instead of hurting me. That put him off-balance, and I used a spinning sidekick against the back of his leg with enough momentum to send him lurching forward . . . but not enough to put him on the floor. It was the dress—it was too snug around the knees to give me kicking room. But crescent kicks, side kicks, front kicks were key pieces of my fighting repertoire. Which meant, unfortunately, that dress would have to die.

I'm sorry about this, I said silently to Ethan, before grabbing the hem and rending the dress up one side, giving me room to maneuver—and probably showing more thigh than I should have. The rip was audible, and I'm pretty sure I saw him flinch at the sound of thousands of dollars being shredded in the interest of victory.

But victory trumped fashion.

My legs freed of constraints, I spun the dagger in my hand, beckoned the vampire to strike again. He didn't waste time, moving forward with a jumping spin that sent the blade whistling. The human barrier shifted as we moved, morphing and changing shape around us like an amoeba to give us room to fight. I turned aside, outside his range, and punched forward with the dagger. I made contact, and the scent of vampire blood—the faint spice of it—blossomed in the air like a crimson flower—but he didn't react, and gave no ground.

Well trained, I said silently to Ethan, hoping he was faring well against his own opponent, but afraid to take his eyes off mine.

The vampire shook off the injury, regripped his katana, lifted it above his head in a perfectly telegraphed downward strike. I lifted my dagger to his, using our joined blades as a pivot point, and spun away. The katana struck only air.

"You missed," I said, and should have known better than to tempt fate. He struck again, and although I spun away, his aim was true enough that the tip of the blade caught my forearm, seared a trail of pain there.

I grunted as the scent of blood—mine, and not willingly shed—filled the air. *"Ow,"* I said, and when he stopped to look, cuffed him in the ear with an elbow.

"You cut me, you ass!" I said, and reached out for the mask. It was time for our mysterious vampire friend to reveal his identity.

He ducked the grab, but responded with one of his own, grabbing the tulle at my shoulder, but the fabric ripped and tore away in his hand, the bodice coming perilously close to dropping, but managing to stay in place. It was one of the rare times I was glad not to be especially buxom; had the girls been any larger, the gaping bodice would have put on quite a show.

A pulse of magic filled the air—and there was something familiar in it. The memory faded when I tried to grab on, like a faint star disappearing when you tried to look too closely. It was frustratingly out of reach, but close enough to bluff.

"I know you," I said.

He froze, just for a moment, and that was just enough time for me. I kicked his hand, breaking his grip and sending the sword through the air. I spun, grabbed it, and pivoted to aim the point at the pulse in his throat. His eyes moved from sword point to me and back again as he debated what he could do.

"Don't even *think* about it," I warned him.

With obvious concern, he lifted his hands into the air.

Chest heaving, I glanced at Ethan, a lock of hair across my face, tulle around one shoulder, my skirt slitted to the thigh, and my enemy's sword in my hands.

Ethan stood above his vampire, the vampire's katana in his hand, tilted down and just above the vampire's throat. His hair had come unloosed, gold spilling around his regal face, his tuxedo pristine but for a slice on his left arm. I relaxed incrementally; he was safe.

Ethan took in my near state of dishabille, and his eyes went hot . . . at least before he registered the dress's unfortunate state.

You've ruined another garment.

Technically, I corrected, *this asshat made me ruin the garment.*

I got a lifted eyebrow for my trouble, but since he hadn't lost his gleam of arousal, I decided he wasn't all that irritated. It was his fault for putting me in expensive dresses.

Men and women in their gowns and finery rushed toward King to offer aid.

He hadn't actually been part of the battle, but he certainly looked worse for wear. His face was red and puffy, his collar unbuttoned, chest pumping to pull in breath.

Sanford waved off some of the men and women around him,

loosened his tie. "Give me room. Let me breathe, for Christ's sake."

He looked up at Ethan, then me. "You saved my life."

"We did what anyone would have done," Ethan said, belied by the humans who'd taken the time to record the fight but hadn't offered to help, and probably so they could sell the video to the highest bidder.

Adrien Reed stalked down the stairs, fury radiating in his expression, his eyes on us, then the men on the floor.

Reed leaned down, ripped the mask off the vampire Ethan had bested. He was pale, with blond hair so light it was nearly white, and watery blue eyes. I didn't recognize him, and from Ethan's flat expression, he didn't, either.

Reed looked up at us. When we shook our heads, he moved to the second vampire, ripped the mask away, revealing familiar curly blond hair.

Oh shit, was my first thought.

Why? was my second.

As I'd suspected during the fight, I knew him. It was Will. The captain of the Navarre House guards.

I'd seen men angry before. Powerful men, supernatural men, whose anger seemed to rage like fire.

I'd never seen a man whose anger was as cold as Adrien Reed's.

The vampires sat on the floor of Reed's office beneath the point of our blades, and the barrels of handguns held by more of Reed's bodyguards.

We hadn't yet had a chance to talk to the vampires, so we were still in the dark about why, precisely, they'd come to Reed's house to attack Sanford King. I had found my purse and taken a moment to update Brody and my grandfather, asked him to ensure that an ambulance for the bodyguard was en route, and to pass word to Morgan, the Master of Navarre House. He'd have to deal with this one way or the other.

Reed hadn't spoken a word. Instead he watched with silent condemnation. His body was rigid, his eyes like frozen granite, hands in his pockets, lording his power over them.

"Mr. Reed," said a man in a dark suit over a dark shirt, his voice as prim and proper, his stance slightly subservient. A butler, I guessed. "The police have arrived."

Ethan and I exchanged a glance. It wasn't surprising the CPD had been called—God knew there'd been plenty of humans to make that call—but it promised the incident wasn't over.

Reed nodded, then crouched down in front of the intruders. "Who sent you?"

Both of them looked away, like schoolboys with secrets.

But Reed wasn't accustomed to anyone defying him. He took Will's chin roughly between two fingers. "I asked you a question. Who . . . sent . . . you . . . here?"

The tone, equally frigid and furious, lifted goose bumps on my arms.

Will was either brave or stupid. Or worse, and more likely, a deadly combination of both. He jerked his face away, Reed's grip leaving red marks across pale skin. "Sanford King is a monster."

So they're vigilantes? I wondered. *They believe they're on some sort of mission?*

If so, Ethan asked, *why fight us? We're not the enemies. And why here, putting so many humans at risk? That doesn't fit with the notion they're punishing King for transgressions against humans.*

He had a point. This was clearly a targeted attack—an attempt to get to Sanford King—and an oddly planned one.

The office doors opened, revealing my grandfather, in khaki pants and a button-up plaid shirt. He moved quickly with the help of a cane it didn't seem he'd need much longer.

In addition to several uniforms, my grandfather was followed by Arthur Jacobs, a CPD detective and good friend to supernaturals. Relief sang through me. Vampires attempting to kill an unarmed human was horrific, and having detectives unfamiliar with the city's vampires wouldn't have helped the aftermath.

Ethan pulled off his tuxedo jacket, draped it over my shoulders.

So as not to shock and awe your grandfather, he said as I pushed my arms into the sleeves and pulled the front panels together. I thought my bodice would hold, but I was essentially naked beneath, so there was no point in tempting fate.

My father, who'd only recently learned of my grandfather's position and hadn't been thrilled about it, certainly didn't look excited to see him now. He should have. My grandfather was the only thing currently standing between humans, vampires, and full-on panic.

"Mr. Reed," my grandfather said. "I'm sorry to meet you under these circumstances."

Reed's expression didn't change. "I'm interested in answers. Not excuses."

"And you'll get them," Jacobs said, stepping forward and introducing himself.

He and my grandfather looked at us, nodded. My grandfather's eyes widened at the sight of my dress beneath the jacket, and the gash on Ethan's arm.

"The EMTs are downstairs with your bodyguard," Jacobs said

to Reed. "Let's take the rest of this one step at a time. Your guests are excited and nervous, and we'll need to interview the vampires before we book them. Why don't you speak to your guests while we do that? Then Chuck can get your statement. That seems most efficient, and we won't want to make tonight any more diffi-cult than it's already been."

Arthur Jacobs was a good man and a good detective. He'd never been particularly argumentative, but I'd also never seen him quite as ingratiating as this. Reed, I guessed, had friends in very high places. I wondered how much that was going to cost us.

"Very well," Reed said. He walked toward the door but stopped when he reached my father, whispered something fierce that had my father putting a hand on Reed's arm, attempting to soothe.

When Reed disappeared, his butler behind him, my father looked at me and Ethan, and there was nothing pleasant in his accusatory gaze or his tone. "Is this your doing?"

Beside me, my grandfather sighed. "Joshua, really."

"It's all right, Chuck," Ethan said, smiling politely before slid-ing his gaze to my father. His smile narrowed to something much more predatory.

"If he believes even asking that question is appropriate con-sidering that his daughter and I just battled these men in front of several hundred witnesses, he's savvier than I've given him credit for."

My father's eyes flashed hot, and he pointed at Ethan with obvious fury. "Now, you wait—"

"No, I will not wait," Ethan said, voice as calm as my father's was angry. "We came here to repay a favor to you, and we resolved a problem on the verge of turning very, very ugly. That problem clearly had nothing to do with us, except that the perpetrators were vampires. And instead of offering thanks, you blame us? You have the nerve to ask if we planned it? You go too far."

I had never loved Ethan more than at that moment. My father's feeling, given the look on his face, was quite the opposite.

Jacobs sidestepped the heat and magic, walked toward the vampires. And any sense of graciousness or patience disappeared. "We know you're Will, Navarre's guard captain," he said, then glanced at the other vampire. "And your name?"

He didn't answer.

"Two hundred witnesses," Jacobs said slowly. "Your best option is to come clean and tell us the truth. Why you came to be here, and why you've done what you've done."

The vampire kept his lips pressed together.

Ethan rolled his eyes, peppering the air with irritated magic. "May I?"

Jacobs nodded. "Please."

"Name and House?" Ethan said.

When the vampire didn't answer, Ethan took a step closer. Where Reed's anger had been frosty, Ethan's was red-hot.

"I am speaking to you, Novitiate," Ethan said, bending toward the vampire, his tone low and dangerous, an inferno only temporarily banked. "For several reasons, including my rank and yours, you do not want to ignore me. Name and goddamned House!"

"*Zane,*" Will finally threw out, answering for him. "Of House Navarre."

"And do you, Will and Zane, have any excuse for what you've done here tonight? For attempted murder? For treachery? For acting precisely like the monsters humans believe us to be?"

"Humans attack each other all the time," Zane said, not realizing it was in his best interest to keep his damn mouth shut.

"We do not set our behavior by the lowest common denominator," Ethan said, magic flaring around him with a rush of searing heat. "We aspire to more, and we are held to a higher standard. We will be excoriated for this. I hope you and your Master are prepared for the punishments you have earned tonight. And where, dare I ask, is your Master?"

Ethan already had doubts about Morgan Greer's ability to hold Navarre House. This wasn't going to help.

"He doesn't know we're here," Will said quickly, with a warning look at Zane. "He doesn't know anything about this."

Ethan straightened, clearly dubious. "We'll see about that. Rest assured, Will and Zane. Regardless the punishments meted out by King, Reed, the CPD, and the people of this city, the AAM will have things to say about this trespass, this violence, this violation against all of us." Chest heaving with fury, Ethan stepped back, pushed a hand through his hair as he struggled to control his anger.

Jacobs took up the thread. "Why Sanford King?"

Neither answered.

"We'll find out. Whether you tell us tonight, or we find out from others." Ethan settled his gaze on Will. "You know Merit, and you know the Ombudsman. You know how skilled they are at resolving supernatural dramatics."

"We did the right thing," Zane said.

Ethan arched a responsive eyebrow. "How, precisely, was trespassing and attempting to kill a human who, I suspect, you've never met until tonight the 'right thing'?"

Will kept his lips pressed tightly together, but Zane clearly didn't mind talking. "Sanford King is a criminal."

"As are you," I pointed out. "And I seriously doubt Sanford King, whatever his transgressions, ever crashed a party at sword point and called someone out."

Neither one of them had an answer to that.

Ethan let the silence hang heavy in the air for a moment before looking at Jacobs. "Do with them what you will."

"Call Morgan," Will said as the uniforms pulled him to his feet, began to read them their rights.

"Morgan has been called," my grandfather assured him. "And we'll be having a very long talk."

CHAPTER EIGHT

SOMETHING IS ROTTEN IN THE
STATE OF ILLINOIS

Reed sent his guests home, and Jacobs and two uniformed officers accompanied the vampires to the station. My father, grandfather, Ethan, and I stayed in Reed's office, waiting for him to return.

My father stood across the room beside the globe, occasionally spinning it to watch its rotation. I sat beside my grandfather on a tufted leather couch of stiff burgundy leather, the type that had probably looked much more comfortable in the catalogue. Ethan stood beside me on his phone, updating the House.

Tensions, obviously, were high.

"It can't be a coincidence the attack was here," Ethan said to my grandfather, putting away his phone and breaking the silence. "I'm sure there would have been easier places to get to King, take him out."

"Undoubtedly," Chuck said. "We'll see what Reed has to say, supplement with our own background."

"You'll find nothing," my father said, putting a hand on the globe to stop its motion. "Reed holds himself to the highest ethical standards. That's why he refused King's business offer earlier this evening."

My grandfather didn't miss the implication. "He and King had words before the attack?"

My father rolled his eyes. "King made overtures, and Reed rejected them. He's a thug, and everyone knows he threatened the jury that acquitted him."

My grandfather just looked at him. "Our job is to consider all angles, tie off all loose ends, before reaching a firm conclusion. That's the nature of an investigation."

"You've talked to Morgan?" I asked, and my grandfather nodded.

"Catcher called him. I understand he was less surprised than he should have been."

You could practically hear Ethan's hackles rise. He wasn't a fan of Morgan or his leadership style, such as it was. Frankly, he was probably looking forward to berating him for his Novitiates' raging stupidity.

The door opened and Reed walked back in, Sorcha behind him. Without a word, she walked to Reed's desk, picked up a lighter and a cigarette case, disappeared onto the terrace again.

Reed walked to a bar of cut crystal decanters, poured a finger of Scotch, downed it. "They've been arrested?" he asked, without turning around.

"They're in custody," my grandfather explained. "They'll be booked and questioned, and the responding officers will consult with the prosecutor regarding the charges against them."

He took a small, spiral notebook from his shirt pocket, pulled an old-fashioned red and white ballpoint pen from the spiral, clicked the nib into place.

"Are you aware of anyone who would want to harm your reputation?" my grandfather asked, pen poised over paper.

Reed walked past us to his desk, took a seat in the leather chair behind it, rocked with an audible creak. "I'm a very wealthy man, Mr. Merit. Wealth attracts attention, and men who shape their own worlds are not infrequently the targets of crime."

"Any specific, credible threats against you lately?"

"Not that I'm aware of. If there'd been something credible, my staff would have told me."

My grandfather nodded. "What about Sanford King? Can you describe your relationship with him?"

"Perfunctory," Reed said, turning the chair to face the room and steepling his fingers over his chest. "We're acquainted, and that's nearly overstating it. He's a member of the charity's board of directors. His invitation was pro forma."

"So no business dealings?"

"None."

"I understand he presented you with a business opportunity earlier tonight."

Reed's expression flattened. "I don't hold with gossip. And I declined the offer. As I said, no business dealings."

"Thank you for clarifying," my grandfather summed, making a note in his book. "Sanford King likely has enemies."

"As I indicated, we all have enemies."

"And would there have been any reason for the perpetrators to believe you and Sanford had a closer relationship?"

"What are you asking?"

"I'm asking if you're aware of any particular reason they decided to attack him here and at this particular time."

"I assume they wanted to punish King as publicly as possible," Reed said impatiently. "Otherwise what's the point of attempting an execution at a gala? Why not just take him out on the street?"

"Was there anything unusual about his agreement to attend the party, or his interest in it?"

"I didn't organize the party or send the invitations. I have a staff. I allowed the charity the use of my house, made a substantial in-kind contribution with respect to food and alcohol."

My grandfather nodded. "There was considerable press coverage about the party, your involvement. You'll get even more publicity after tonight."

My father stiffened, apparently shocked by the insinuation. But my grandfather wasn't there to help my father kiss Reed's ass. He was there to probe, investigate, untangle.

"As I'm certain you're well aware, I don't need publicity. And I don't appreciate the tenor of the question."

My grandfather smiled his blandly polite cop smile. "I just want to make sure I understand the facts."

"The fact is, two vampires entered my house apparently with the purpose of killing Sanford King. If you want the cause, ask *them*."

"We have done so, and will continue to investigate their involvement," my grandfather assured him.

"I'm glad we're on the same page. I'll talk to my lawyers, decide how we'd like to move forward. I'll be in touch."

And just like that, Adrien Reed dismissed my grandfather.

We walked him back through the gallery and ballroom. The room was still decorated, but the guests were gone, adding a grim sense of abandonment.

No one spoke until we exited the house, stood together on the sidewalk.

"Jeff's in the van if you'd like to say hello," my grandfather said. "Or good-bye, since it looks like we're wrapping up here."

The van, clearly marked as Ombudsman property, sat just up the block. It was a mobile office and response center, fully equipped with computers and gadgets that only Jeff likely knew how to operate.

Brody had squeezed the Range Rover in front of it, and he and Jeff chatted quietly until we approached. Brody nodded at Ethan, who held up a hand, signaling him to wait.

Jeff had, as per usual, paired his floppy brown hair and smiling blue eyes with khakis and a blue button-down, the sleeves rolled up. His eyes widened as he looked me over.

"You took some damage."

I grimaced at the tatters of dress. "Actually, I did a lot of it myself. It's hard to kick in a sheath dress."

"I can't take you anywhere," Ethan said, but there was no mistaking the pride in his eyes.

"Sure you can. But next time, get me a gown with legroom."

"Or maybe just no random Navarre attacks," Jeff said grimly, glancing back at the House. "Sounds like a pretty bizarre situation."

"Very," Ethan agreed. "Have you heard anything about Navarre Novitiates being out of hand?"

"I don't hear much about Navarre at all," Jeff said. "What happens in Navarre House stays in Navarre House. Or so I assume." He tucked hair behind his ear. "I'm not sure if that's Morgan, or Celina's leftover crazy, or what. What about you?"

Celina Desaulniers was the former Navarre Master; she'd been forced out of the position after an attack on Ethan.

"Out of the blue," Ethan agreed, "even for Navarre House, which is saying something. But the severity here strikes me as something that must have festered or percolated for a while."

"What about supernatural vigilante groups?" I wondered.

"Nothing like that, either," Jeff said, sticking his hands into his pockets.

"What about Balthasar?" my grandfather asked. "Any further activity there?"

"He's in a condo on Michigan Avenue," Ethan said. "We've got eyes on him. It seems best for all involved to know what he's up to."

"No argument there," my grandfather said.

"Luc has the details about his location if you'd like it, or want to do any monitoring of your own."

My grandfather nodded. "We won't monitor per se, but I would like to stay apprised. Do you think he's looking for access?"

"If he is, he'll be sorely disappointed by what he finds."

"He can't think you owe him," Jeff said. "Not after what happened, all the time that's passed."

"A rational mind would expect not," Ethan said. "But he has rarely ever been rational. His needs are paramount, and damn anyone who stands in his way."

"I fear there is a lot of that going around," my grandfather said, and sighed heavily before trying a light smile. "I'd wax nostalgic about the good ol' days, but with age comes wisdom and sight, and the realization that every day is as good or as bad as the next. The difference is only in the margins."

Ethan nodded. "Very well said. And with that, we should probably get back to the House and begin planning our next play."

The cards would be dealt one way or the other.

"This is going to be a pain in the ass," Ethan said when we slid into the backseat of the Range Rover again.

The car shook a bit as Brody climbed into the passenger seat. "Home, Sire?"

"Please."

"And we thought this was going to be a networking event," I said.

Ethan laughed, a knot of mirthless sound. "The best-laid plans of vampires." He rubbed a finger across his forehead. "We must deal with this, but Balthasar will not wait long. I suspect this will be a long night."

"I suspect you're right." I glanced out the window at the lights of homes and businesses, wondered at the drama that unfolded there.

"Oh, Morgan," I said on a sigh.

Ethan slid me a glance. "Did you just say 'oh, Morgan'?"

"I did. In exhaustion, not desire. I'm not looking forward to dealing with him." Morgan and I had dated briefly, and he still harbored bitterness about the end of our relationship. Not, I think, because he'd truly loved me, but because he didn't like having been passed over for Ethan.

"I'm afraid we will not be able to avoid it. Not this time."

"I know. What did you think about Reed?"

"I didn't interact with him much, all things considered," Ethan said, skimming his fingers over my hand before entwining our fingers. "Likes material wealth, likes to show it off. Imagines himself very much the king of his castle."

"His gaudy castle."

"Just so. He has body men, which is relatively unusual for a businessman in Chicago. Is not used to people disobeying his orders. Certainly isn't used to those who dare breach the castle walls, interrupt his feast."

"I can't get a read on Sorcha. She's either really smart and very socially awkward, or really, really dumb."

"And she must be twenty years his junior," Ethan said, clearly not a compliment to either of them.

I just looked at him. "What?"

"Sorcha. She's at least twenty years younger than Reed."

It literally took me a minute to respond. "Of all the things we've seen tonight, *that's* what offends you? That he's in a May-December romance? Need I point out you're nearly *four hundred* years older than me?"

"That's different."

"How is it different?"

"Because I don't look a day over thirty."

The lack of logic was staggering. "That's got to be some kind of penis logic."

"Excuse me?" Ethan asked as Brody snickered in the front seat.

"One of your heads is significantly smarter than the other. She was pretty, though. I'll give you that."

Ethan sighed. "It has nothing to do with pretty."

"Not according to your brain," I agreed. "But once again—"

Ethan held up a hand. "No need to repeat the point."

"When I'm four hundred, do I get to date a twenty-five-year-old?"

Ethan narrowed his gaze. "If you date anyone other than me at any point in your hopefully long and fruitful life, there will be trouble for both of us."

"That's definitely penis logic," Brody said helpfully. I didn't disagree with him.

*　　*　　*

By the time we arrived at the paparazzi'd House, it was two o'clock. We were both tired and grouchy, and hadn't eaten in hours.

The jacket I'd returned draped over one arm, Ethan offered a hand to help me out of the car. When I joined him on the sidewalk, I put my hands on his face, stretched on tiptoes to reach him, and pressed my lips to his. "Thank you for standing up to my father."

Ethan wrapped an arm around my waist as shutters began to snap around us, capturing the moment, paparazzi yelling at us to look their way, make eye contact, increase the marketability of their particular photographs.

"Sentinel," he said quietly, the words only for me, "I will stand for you as long as I am able." And then he kissed me well and thoroughly. The words had been for me, but the kiss was for the audience.

"You two are making out every time I see you."

Ethan pulled away, glanced back at Catcher, who'd moved to stand beside us. "That speaks more to your interruptions than our affection."

Catcher made a vague sound, gestured toward the gate, where my grandfather stood waiting. Jeff must have dropped him off. "Shall we?"

I didn't especially want to, but big girl panties were made for times like this.

Morgan stood in the middle of the foyer, legs braced like a captain on a ship. His dark, wavy hair was short now, paired with a few nights' worth of dark stubble that set off his deeply blue eyes. He wore dark jeans over boots, a three-quarter-sleeve

Henley in a pale blue he favored, arms crossed defensively over his well-toned chest. Morgan was what I'd call broodingly handsome.

Unfortunately, he also had a disappointing tendency to brood.

He cast a glance at Ethan, then me, then the remains of the dress and scratches on my arms. His eyes flashed, and I wondered if he was bothered I'd been injured—or pissed that I'd fought with his people.

Luc and Lindsey waited nearby, moved forward when we walked into the foyer. I made a line for Lindsey.

"When you have a chance, can you talk to Margot, maybe arrange for drinks, blood, some snacks? It's been a long night."

Lindsey arched an eyebrow. "Babe, I know you better than you know yourself. Already put in the order."

I put a thankful hand on her arm, squeezed. "Thank you. I am starving."

"You pretty much destroyed that dress."

"But saved an apparently despicable human from a vampire ninja death, so that's something."

"It's something," she said quietly, her gaze on Ethan as he stalked toward Morgan. "They were really from Navarre?"

She wouldn't have doubted the truth of Luc's report, but she'd have marveled at the involvement of Navarre guards in a mess like this.

"They were," I confirmed.

"Morgan," Ethan said, glancing around at the suited Novitiates who lingered in the foyer and parlor to catch a glimpse of the trouble they expected would unfold. "Let's go to my office."

"Where are they?"

My grandfather stepped forward, voice quiet but firm. "Your

people are in custody. There's no way around that, considering what happened. Let's go to Ethan's office and discuss it."

Morgan glanced around the foyer as if gauging his move—whether to argue, storm out, or capitulate.

To everyone's relief, and my surprise, he turned on his heel and walked down the hallway.

"We'll go with him," my grandfather said, and he and Catcher fell in step behind Morgan.

"The House is secure?" Ethan asked, his gaze on the men moving into his office.

"It is," Luc said.

"Let's keep it that way," Ethan said. "Grab Malik and join me in the office."

"Roger that," Luc said, sending Lindsey back downstairs, then jogging toward Malik's office, which was just past Ethan's.

He glanced at me. "Would you like to get cleaned up first?"

"Please, yes. Give me five minutes? And don't start without me. I'd like to hear what he has to say."

He nodded. "If you'll be quick about it. And then we'll find out precisely what's rotten in Navarre House."

I cleaned up and pulled on jeans and a fitted, scoop-neck Cadogan T-shirt. I'd done my part for Cadogan couture already tonight; it was time for comfortable clothing. My hair had lost most of its wave, so I pulled it into a high bun. If they ever made vampire paper dolls, this would be the "Sentinel after a night of ass-kicking" ensemble.

The remains of the dress, in its tangled pile on the floor, looked nothing like the pristine gown Helen had delivered earlier.

"More's the pity," I said quietly, and had a terrifying mental image of Helen walking into the apartments, finding the dress, going utterly ballistic about its current condition.

So I stuffed it back into the bag, and stuffed the bag into the back of the closet—on Ethan's side. Because I was mature like that.

CHAPTER NINE

✦ — ≡✦≡ — ✦

WHAT THE WORLD NEEDS NOW . . . IS A
WINEGLASS OF UNUSUAL SIZE

There were a lot of people in the office, and a lot of tension. Ethan, Morgan, Malik, and Luc, along with Catcher and my grandfather, watched as Margot parked a food tray in the middle of the office, blazing a delicious trail of coffee scents.

Ethan, who'd ditched the tie and rolled up the sleeves of his battered shirt, moved to pour the coffee into a mug, offered it to my grandfather.

He walked over without his cane, which was parked beside the door, and took the mug with both hands.

"Thank you. Sugar, by chance?"

"Like granddaughter, like grandfather," Ethan said, moving aside so my grandfather could spoon sugar cubes into the mug.

Ethan took a bottle of blood, offered one to me. When I accepted it, but skipped delicately layered pastries for a protein-laced granola bar, he looked at me dubiously.

"Did you take a knock to the head?"

"Har-har," I said, and ripped the package open when I could feel hunger awakening with the ferocity of a starved panther. "This isn't a time for taste," I said, taking a bite. And thank God for that, since the bar tasted like a very unpleasant ménage à trois of malt, chalk, and dates. "It's a time for nutrition."

"Color me proud," Ethan said, and uncapped the bottle of blood, sipped. "If everyone's ready, we should probably begin."

We looked at Morgan, who stood across the room near the bookshelves, which had already been repaired, the displaced contents neatly rearranged.

"My people?" he asked.

"They're in the CPD's new full-dark facility," my grandfather said.

Morgan nodded.

"Let's sit," Ethan said, and we followed him to the sitting area, took seats. All except Morgan, who hadn't yet moved from his spot across the room. Not an unusual position for him—separate from the rest of us.

"What happened, Morgan?" Ethan asked.

Morgan walked to the cart, took a bottle of water, uncapped it. But as he walked to the seating area, he twisted the cap back on and set it beside the chair he lowered himself into.

"They weren't playing vigilante. They were trying to protect the House."

"From what?" Ethan asked.

Morgan closed his eyes, rubbed his hands over his face. He looked so young, and so tired. He was, I thought, the victim of time and circumstance, of having been given control of his House—the leadership of his House—before he was ready.

On the other hand, he'd had every opportunity to succeed,

and could have asked us for help. I suppose that meant the blame fell on him.

"It's better if I start at the beginning. Well, not better," Morgan said. "But you'll need the whole story."

For the second time in as many nights, Ethan nodded him on. "Then tell it."

"It's all about money," Morgan said. "Goddamn money." He cleared his throat nervously, like a man about to enter confession.

"Celina had very good taste. Her spending habits didn't match her assets, even the stipend she received from the GP. She borrowed extensively to fund her lifestyle, her tastes, her desire for the finer things. Clothes. Art. Food. Parties. Everything had to be big. Everything had to be perfect."

"Borrowed from whom?"

Morgan looked away, stared at the opposite wall. "The Circle."

Ethan and Malik shared a look, and my grandfather sighed heavily. I didn't recognize the name. It wasn't a supernatural group; if it had been, I'd have seen it in the *Canon*.

"What's the Circle?" I asked.

"A criminal enterprise," my grandfather said. "Based in Chicago, although they have roots internationally."

"You're talking about the mob?" I asked.

"Only in the mob's wildest dreams," Catcher said. "Bigger, more capital, more connections. And for all that, much more secretive."

Ethan looked at me. "Do you remember the murders in Lakeview a year or two ago? The alderman and her family?"

I searched my memory, recalled a black-and-white photograph, a tiny body on a square of grass that posed as a front yard. "They killed her, her husband, her children."

Malik nodded. "Because she wouldn't help the Circle push something through the Zoning Board. She'd apparently owed them a favor and hadn't delivered."

That didn't exactly lighten the mood in the room.

"That's how the Circle operates," Ethan said, then glanced at Morgan again. "What does tonight have to do with them?"

Morgan scratched nervously at the knee of his jeans. "Celina's notes are coming due because we've only been able to pay down the interest, which is high. Loan shark high."

"And they want repayment," my grandfather said.

Morgan nodded, adjusted in his seat, obviously uncomfortable. "The Circle came to me with a proposition—we take out King, the Circle wipes away some of the House's debt."

"And if you didn't agree?" Ethan asked.

"They start taking House assets. And taking out Navarre vampires."

Silence fell heavily in the room.

"Mother of God," Ethan murmured quietly, likely as aghast at the proposition as at the fact that Navarre was so far in the hole—and we were only just now hearing about it.

"Why didn't you come to us?" he asked, frustration barely veiled.

"My House, my problem. And I didn't say yes, so I assumed that was the end of it." The tightness around his eyes showed how wrong he'd been. "I get that your Houses operate differently. Mine doesn't. And for better or worse, I inherited the House I inherited."

I saw it in Ethan's eyes, the speech he wanted to give Morgan. Something about the Master making the House, and not vice versa, but he held his tongue. Morgan wasn't easily teachable, and he didn't take well to criticism, no matter how constructively intended.

"Keep going," Ethan said.

"I said no, obviously. But word got out."

"Word got out," Ethan said dryly, "of the Circle's attempted extortion and solicitation of murder?"

"Apparently," Morgan said, the word fierce not because of the House's apparent rumor mill, but because of Ethan's imperious tone. Having been on the receiving end of that tone, I understood the frustration. Not that I disagreed with Ethan here. "And I'm attempting to trace back that line."

"One way or the other," my grandfather said, "these guards found out, took it upon themselves to help."

"Yeah," Morgan said.

My grandfather nodded. "They probably imagined they were doing the city a favor, two birds with one stone. King's no Prince Charming."

"Why King?" Ethan asked. "Why did the Circle target him?"

"I don't know," Morgan said. "I mean, they tried to sell it like I was doing Chicago a favor. But it's not like they're interested in keeping the streets clean."

"King's got his own underworld connections," my grandfather said. "I hadn't heard he was involved in the Circle, and maybe it's because he said no. Perhaps this was an attempt to punish or take out King as a competitor."

"Why at Reed's party?" Ethan asked Morgan.

Morgan shrugged. "It was the designated location. They said they wanted to make an example of King."

"In front of Reed?" Malik asked.

"Reed's a very powerful man," my grandfather said. "His wealth, his access, would be very attractive to the Circle. Perhaps the Circle made overtures, and Reed didn't bite." He considered, nodded, pulled his earlobe methodically as he concentrated. "I don't know. I'll want to think about it."

"They might try again," I said, looking at my grandfather. "If they went to this much trouble to take King out, he's undoubtedly still on their agenda."

He nodded. "Jacobs is talking to King about protective custody. He might refuse—did refuse during his criminal trial when they wanted him to give up his colleagues."

"Did he?" Ethan asked. "Give them up, I mean?"

My grandfather released his ear, crossed his arms as if to avoid the habit. "As it turned out, there wasn't anyone to give up. He was prince of his particular syndicate. When you're at the top of the pyramid, there's nothing to be gained by giving over the muscle. "

My grandfather glanced at Morgan. "It's unlikely this is the last time you'll hear from them. They gave you a task, and they'll believe you failed to complete it."

"I refused it."

"But your people said yes," Ethan said. "And someone from the Circle will have seen the news reports by now, will know that an attempt was made, and it failed."

Morgan scrubbed his hands over his short hair. "This is going to destroy us. The media, the accusations, all of it."

"It was attempted murder," Ethan said, as if to remind him Navarre wasn't just having a spot of bad luck.

"I know that." This time, Morgan just sounded defeated. "You think I don't know that? They thought they were helping me, protecting their brothers and sisters, just as they're supposed to do."

"You cannot be blasé about this."

Morgan lifted irritated eyes to Ethan. "Do I seem blasé? Because I'm not. I'm aghast, sad, worried, completely at a loss. But I'm not at all blasé." He sighed, look at my grandfather. "Can I talk to them?"

"That's up to the CPD," my grandfather said, "but probably not until after they're processed."

"What do I do now?"

"How did the Circle contact you before?" my grandfather asked.

"They called my cell or my office phone, the same way they did with Celina. They used throwaway phones. A different number every time."

"Who called?"

"I don't know. They used a computer or a voice modulator or something."

"They'll know what did and did not happen tonight," my grandfather said, "and they'll make contact again. I can have the CPD trace the House phone, your phone. We can put security on the House. The organized crime division will be very interested in the possibility of getting closer to the Circle. They're very evasive, and this presents a unique opportunity."

"I don't want that," Morgan said. "I don't want to turn our House into a military state."

"Morgan," my grandfather said, "I'm going to be frank. We are well past the point of what Navarre House wants. Murder was proposed to you, and you didn't report it to the police. Two of your members attempted, at a very crowded event with hundreds of witnesses, to kill a human. Getting an indictment against them will be child's play.

"But we're also talking about very dangerous people, as you've seen. They are powerful, manipulative, and very, very resourceful. Considering the scope of the House's apparent debt, I'm frankly surprised they haven't caused more trouble for the House in the past."

Morgan just looked away.

I thought miserably of Shakespeare, of his advice not to be a debtor. Particularly when the debt was as dark as this.

Ethan leaned forward, elbows on knees. "Morgan, take Chuck up on his offer. Do what it takes to keep your people safe right now. In the meantime, have someone you trust—someone *outside* Navarre—look at your books and evaluate the House's connection to the Circle. Once you have that information, you can figure out a plan to move forward."

"And who can do that?"

"We can," Malik said, he of the numbers and figures and general math wizardry.

Ethan nodded in agreement. "We are not your enemies, and we've no incentive to lie to you. We have no ties to the old guard, and we aren't interested in disguising the depth of the problem or the sacrifice you'll likely need to make to fix it. If you don't want us involved, talk to Scott. Or another Master that you trust."

"I don't want this leaving Chicago."

Was he not familiar with the Internet? Two vampires in Venetian masks crashing a party at sword point? There were probably base stations in Antarctica that knew about this. The rest of the AAM wouldn't be far behind.

"It's undoubtedly too late for that," Ethan said crisply, obviously beginning to lose patience. "And I agree with Chuck: This isn't over. You did not do as they asked, nor were your guards successful. If you don't get to the root of this particular decay, they'll only want more. And it will be more than the murder of one man."

Morgan was silent again, gnawing the inside of his cheek as he considered.

If only he'd been older—less human and more vampire—when he took the House, or when Celina had forced our hands, and lit the fuse that ended with her own destruction. He was such a canny, witty, confident man. But he'd seemed to struggle with being a vampire, and certainly holding the reins.

How much of that, I wondered for the first time, was because of the Circle? Because of the mess he'd inherited from Celina? Sometimes a vampire was dealt a really shitty hand. Pity replaced the irritation I usually felt when thinking about Morgan's command failures.

Finally, Morgan looked up at Ethan, my grandfather. "We'd appreciate eyes on the House. I'm not comfortable having the House phones tapped, but I won't hide any future contacts. I'll come to you, directly." He looked at Malik, Ethan. "You can come by tomorrow night to look at the books."

Ethan looked at my grandfather, who nodded.

"Then that's what we'll do," Ethan said, rising. "You should get back to your House, your vampires. I'm sure they're worried."

"Since you're down two guards," Luc said, "we can lend you one, have Grey give you one. They'd be working for us, but living with you. It would give you some extra bodies, some different perspectives."

Morgan nodded, resigned.

"You're doing the right thing here for your people, for your House," my grandfather said, "getting Cadogan involved, letting them help you."

"Maybe," Morgan said. "But Celina is rolling in her grave."

"There is not enough alcohol in the world to fix this nightmare," Ethan said when Morgan and my grandfather were gone.

"It's not Navarre's finest moment," Malik agreed, rising to grab a bottle of Goose Island root beer, a personal favorite, from Margot's cart. He remembered that, held up another bottle for me, and at my nod, popped the caps. Margot had stored them in a silver bucket of ice, and a tempting little puff of frosty carbonation rose from the open bottle.

"Thanks," I said when he walked back and handed it to me.

"You've been quiet," Ethan said to Catcher.

Catcher crossed an ankle over the other knee, adjusted the hem of his jeans over the booted foot. "That woman has been the root of much misery. I hate to say that I'm not surprised she's screwed her House again, but if the shoe fits . . ."

"If Morgan's grasp of the situation is correct, she sounds like she was an addict," I said after a bubbling sip.

Ethan rubbed his temples. "She had no need of any of it. She was lovely. The House is beautiful. She was well connected, and very much a part of the GP's inner sanctum. I don't understand it."

"Respectfully," Malik said, taking a seat again. "We don't need to understand it. We just need to examine its depth and help them figure out a way to get them out of it."

"Best-case scenario?" Ethan asked.

"A manageable sum certain the AAM decides to pay off?" Malik suggested.

"I don't know," Catcher said. "I don't see the Circle being satisfied by any reasonable sum. You'll gauge the damage, of course," he said to Malik, "but what incentive do they have to turn off the faucet? I don't see them walking away from this. Not with a catch this large."

"Which means you don't see them backing off unless the entire organization is broken down," Ethan said.

Catcher nodded. "Morgan's got an opportunity to do that, which I suspect is why Chuck wanted to walk him out. It would be a coup for the CPD to bring down the Circle."

"If they're so big, so powerful, how are they still operating?" I wondered. "I mean, surely there are screwups, snitches, search warrants."

"I imagine what nearly happened to Sanford King is one of the reasons," Ethan said, glancing at Catcher for confirmation. "If you take out your enemies, perceived or otherwise, you tend to keep everyone else in line."

"And they are remarkably careful," Catcher said, "and remarkably well connected. And God knows I'm no fan of Seth Tate, but Diane Kowalcyzk doesn't have nearly the grip on the city that he did. As mayor, he wouldn't have objected to the Circle per se, but he would have demanded a cut."

"And Kowalcyzk?" Ethan asked.

"Not interesting enough to the Circle to bother with. Word is, they see her as a temp, and not worth the effort."

Ethan cocked his head. "You have contacts in the organization?"

"No," Catcher said. "That's the problem. With a lot of organized crime, there's an obvious family structure, a clear hierarchy. The hierarchy generally demands respect from the capos, the other players, so you know who they are.

"The Circle's not like that. They're not looking for glory; they're looking for long-term plays. Businesses, people, Houses they can sink their fangs into—sorry for the pun—and ensure an income stream over time. There's actually very little outright theft, not like the older-style gangs. A lot of this is cybercrime. Phishing schemes, transfer of international funds, hacking, extortion for cybercoin schemes. And the leadership is very decentralized, very big on anonymity, and very careful about giving any one individual too much information. That's why the CPD doesn't have them tagged in any significant way."

"How do you know so much about them?" Malik wondered.

"Accumulated knowledge. I was fascinated by the mob as a kid, even before I came to Chicago, and I'd read a lot about Al Capone, Bugs Moran, Johnny Torrio. I've kept up with the news, the stories, the talk, mostly as a hobby. Jeff knows hackers, and the Circle pops up in that community. And, of course, your grandpa hears things. Supernaturals trust him. And being supernaturals, they tend to stay on the sidelines, or get ignored by humans. Word filters down, and you put the pieces together a bit at a time."

Catcher frowned. "We figured they'd get involved with supernaturals at some point or other—I'd guessed magic, actually. Spell-selling, maybe trafficking in magical creatures, stuff that's actually within our jurisdiction. But we hadn't seen anything like that. Unfortunately, this tells us our thinking was accurate."

"And that they were very strategic," Ethan said. "If the interest was as high as Morgan suggested, they found—or perhaps 'cultivated' is a better word for it—what sounds like a very good source of revenue in Navarre House. But we'll see what the audit turns up."

Catcher sighed. "I've got no lost love for Morgan as a Master, although I thought he was a good enough guy before that. But I don't envy him this. This could be enough to break the House, certainly to cause a lot of pain, a lot of trouble, a lot of hardship for many, many years to come."

Ethan nodded. "Unfortunately, I tend to agree with you." He looked at Malik. "You'll make arrangements to review the books at dusk."

Malik nodded. "I do love math. Numbers are orderly."

"And real life rarely is," Ethan said.

Malik opened his mouth to respond, but before he could say anything else, Juliet rushed in, eyes wide, and skipping from Luc to Ethan.

"Sorry to interrupt, Sire. Kelley called. He's on the move. Kelley followed, has her lapel camera. We've got the feed live downstairs."

There seemed no point in asking who "he" was, or whether we'd make the journey to watch it.

CHAPTER TEN

━━ ✦ ━━

HE CAN DO MAGIC

We reconvened in the Ops Room, most of the guards' eyes already on the wall screen.

There, in the middle, stood Balthasar.

He wore black pants and the same high-collared coat he'd worn last night. He looked what I'd have called vampirically handsome—dark hair against pale skin, eyes gleaming with promise and excitement. His scars peeked from beneath the edge of the collar.

He stood in front of a tall, pale brick structure, a low stone railing behind him. A crowd of humans had gathered on the street in front of him, eyes wide as they watched him, waited for him to move.

I recognized the spot. "He's in front of the Wrigley Building. Those stairs go down to one of the boat docks along the river." It was a common spot for street buskers, performers who typically danced or played instruments for cash from passersby, mostly tourists who roamed the Magnificent Mile to browse, shop, or take in the energy of downtown Chicago.

Juliet brought Luc an earpiece, which he snapped into place. "Kelley, can you hear me?"

"Roger that," she said quietly, voice echoing through the room. "Tara's positioned at my three o'clock." She turned to the left, the camera panning until it focused on a lean woman with short brown hair at the edge of the crowd. She wore black cargo pants and a fitted black T-shirt. She stood at parade rest, but her eyes were cold and fixed on Balthasar. She was, I guessed, the human guard on this particular round of surveillance.

"Stand by for now," Luc said. "Keep your eyes and the camera on him. We're here and monitoring."

"Acknowledged."

Balthasar held up his hands as he addressed the crowd of humans below. "My name is Balthasar. I am a Master vampire, originally of France, but now home in your fair city."

It was an announcement uncomfortably close to the one Celina had made more than a year ago, the press conference that had changed the lives of supernaturals forever, and brought them— screaming, in some instances—into the light.

The humans murmured together, recognition dawning, since they'd probably seen his face in the articles and stories about his interaction with Ethan. Some looked intrigued.

"Do not be afraid of vampires. We are all creatures of the same God." He waved one hand over another, and when he turned both hands up, revealed a small white bird that fluttered into the sky. The crowd gasped with excitement.

"Magic tricks?" Luc asked. "Why is he doing magic tricks?"

"Illusions," Catcher gruffly corrected. "*Not* magic. He's fast, and he's got the coat to hold his props."

"And he's doing it for attention," Ethan said, "which he's clearly getting."

The knot of humans on the street grew as more gathered around to check out what the rest of them were gaping at.

"This looks like a setup," I said. "A play." Ethan, gaze on the screen, grunted in agreement.

"What's the play?" Malik asked. "Scaring humans? He's already told them he's a vampire."

"Kelley?" Luc asked.

"You see what I see. There's nothing else here—no obvious weapon, no partner."

Balthasar turned his wrist, fingers flicking, and a small silver ball appeared in his palm. He spun it around hypnotically, just as he'd done with the crystal globe in Ethan's office. "You may be aware that Chicago has three vampire Houses. Can anyone name them?"

"Grey!"

"Navarre!"

"Cadogan!"

I didn't like the context, but I was impressed by the humans' speed. They'd clearly been paying attention.

Balthasar smiled proudly, whisked the ball in the air, where it seemed to hover by its own magic. The crowd cooed appreciatively.

"*Très bon,*" he said, tucking the ball into his palm again. He moved his hands above each other, then opened his palms, and the ball was gone.

"As it turns out, I am not of those Houses. But I helped to make one of them."

"How?" one of the men in the crowd shouted back. Someone in his early twenties, I guessed from the voice, but his image was blocked by the crowd. "How did you make one of them?"

Balthasar didn't look impressed by the asker. "Who knows the answer?"

"Ethan Sullivan!" shouted a girl, mid-twenties, with waist-length blond hair pulled back in a low tail.

"Ethan Sullivan, indeed," Balthasar said. "I gave him immorality. Unfortunately, he doesn't seem to want my attention."

While the crowd waited, breath bated, for his explanation, Balthasar looked up, scanned the crowd, and when he found Kelley, smiled directly at her—and into the camera.

"Careful, Kelley," Luc said. "You've been made."

Ethan crossed his arms, his expression unfathomable as he stared at the screen. "I suspect he wouldn't be doing this if it wasn't for our benefit. And for theirs."

Balthasar moved two steps toward a woman, lifted her hand. Kelley adjusted her position so they were both in the frame.

The woman was petite, with coal black hair prettily tied into a topknot and held in place with a black patent headband. Deep-set eyes were poised above a Cupid's bow mouth, and she wore a short and stylish dress with flats. On her way back from a date, I guessed.

"What's your name, *mon amie*?"

"Park," she said with a smile.

"Make a fist, Park," he requested, and she did, eyes wide and bright with anticipation.

As the growing crowd twittered like excited birds, he lifted her hand to his lips, pressed a kiss there. "Perhaps," Balthasar crooned, "Ethan Sullivan simply doesn't want to share." He turned the woman's wrist so her fingers faced upward. "Open your hand," he said to the woman.

She did, and a small white bird, just like the first, flew from her hand and into the sky.

The woman laughed, put a hand on her chest in nervous excitement as the crowd erupted with applause.

"Thank you," Balthasar said, and looked at the camera again. "Sharing is how we show love and respect."

I know he hadn't meant me, not specifically, but the remembrance of his magic—as potent as it had been unwelcome—sent a cold trickle of unease down my spine. Ethan must have sensed my discomfort; he put a hand at my back, warm and gratifyingly possessive.

"May I impose on you one more time?" Balthasar asked. His voice was sweet as honey, his gaze warm and inviting.

Or maybe that was just his magic working overtime.

The girl nodded, extended a hand when he offered, and stepped forward beside him.

"We've never met before, yes?"

She nodded. "We've never met."

"And yet here, beside this beautiful building"—he gestured toward the Wrigley Building behind him—"in this beautiful metropolis, it is impossible but to be moved."

"What's he after?" Ethan murmured to himself, fingers rubbing his jaw as he watched.

"It's very beautiful," Park agreed.

Balthasar fanned and fisted the fingers of his right hand, then opened them to reveal a soft white flower in perfect blossom. The woman's eyes grew wide.

"For you," he said, and she took it, inhaled deeply.

Her gaze went slightly vacant, her lips parting in what looked like delicious agony. But I saw the truth in her eyes—the dilated pupils, the mask of arousal overlying fear, overlying lack of control.

A shiver ran down my spine in earnest sympathy. She wasn't pretending; she was *glamoured*.

"Ethan," I said, the word a bare whisper.

He moved closer to the screen, eyes wide in horror as he watched the scene unfold in front of us. "He's glamouring humans on Michigan Avenue." I caught the shock of fear in his voice, that Balthasar had done the very thing Ethan had feared.

"Right on the damn street," Lindsey muttered, eyes glued to the screen.

"Kelley," Luc said. "Is he doing what we think he's doing?"

"Glamour," she said. "I can feel it, but just the outer edge. It's pretty concentrated on her at the moment."

Luc glanced at Ethan. "Sire?"

Ethan didn't hesitate. "He cannot manipulate humans on Michigan Avenue. It's a violation against the humans, and they most certainly will crucify us for it. Send her in. Stop this."

Humans knew vampires existed, and over the course of the past year had learned about some of our strengths and weaknesses. But they weren't, at least as far as we knew, fully aware of vampire glamour—and its ability to influence and seemingly control.

"Roger that. Kelley, you are clear to intervene. Move forward and intercept. Get him off the damn street. Bribery, your own glamour if you have to. But no violence."

"Roger that," Kelley said quietly. "Moving forward."

The camera moved closer to Balthasar, to the woman in his arms. She put a hand on his chest, and as the crowd guffawed with amusement—as if she were only acting her coquettish part—leaned forward and pressed her lips to his.

Kelley pushed through to them, the camera jerking as she

tried to muscle through a crowd unwilling to part for her. The humans were too absorbed in the show to turn away or lose their seats.

Like prey scenting predator, Balthasar looked up and right into the camera, smiled broadly for all of us to see . . . and then pushed the hapless woman into Kelley's arms.

Kelley muttered a curse, grabbed the human, helped her to the ground, where the rest of the crowd surrounded them to offer aid.

"Shit," Luc said. "Kelley, get eyes on him! Get eyes on him!"

Kelley moved fast, and the camera panned up again . . . but he was gone.

"Move!" Luc barked out.

Kelley did, rising and tunneling through the arms, legs, and torsos of the humans who'd surrounded her and the woman, forcing her way back to the stone railing that marked the drop to the Chicago River below.

She looked down, left, right, scanned the stone dock where a water taxi sat empty, bobbing in dark water. There was no sign of Balthasar.

Luc spat out a curse.

"He can't have just disappeared," Ethan said, his voice low and dangerous.

"No," I said. "But he's fast. So fast that being in his spell makes it seem as if everyone around you has slowed."

The vampires in the room looked at me curiously.

"That's what it felt like," I said, forcing my voice to stay calm, "when he glamoured me. He is very, very powerful."

"He'll show up again," Ethan said ruefully, sounding suddenly tired. "He won't be able to resist. Tonight, he showed us what he can do, what he will do, to disrupt this city unless and until we give him what he wants."

"He can't get into the House," Catcher said. "Not with the wards."

"No," Ethan said. "But I suspect that won't stop him trying. Either here, or in the street, or wherever else he believes he can extort action from us. He hasn't made demands, not specifically, but he'll do that soon enough."

He muttered a curse. "I should have killed him when I had the chance."

After Luc turned off the screen and hurled his earpiece across the room in frustration, we reconvened in Ethan's office.

"Murder wouldn't have eased your conscience," I said quietly.

"No. But it would have rid the world of one more sociopath. He will not stop until he has achieved his goal, whatever that may be. Adoration? Power? Almost certainly. Perhaps to destroy everything that has been built here. Perhaps to destroy me and mine."

"We won't let him," I said, sliding my hand into his, squeezing our joined fingers.

He muttered something in Swedish. "What had I said about alcohol?"

"That there wasn't enough of it. But I bet some really old gasoline-style Scotch would take the edge off."

"Perhaps," he said, then leaned forward and kissed my forehead. "Perhaps."

My phone rang, and I pulled it out, found Jonah's number on the screen. I wasn't any happier to talk to him now than I had been before. If he had things to tell me—or an apology to issue—he could send me a text. Since he didn't, I put the phone away again.

Ethan looked at Luc. "How will we get rid of him?"

"Well, we haven't exactly had much time to research."

"What about the timeline?" I asked Luc.

"It's moving, but slowly. The Librarian's gotten some of the Memento Mori scans from London, and he's working with Jeff on an algorithm to search them for mentions of Balthasar or the other vampires."

I needed to get Jeff a gift basket. Did giant white tigers like catnip?

"What about the safe houses?" Ethan asked.

"Safe houses are safe houses for a reason; they aren't big on giving out information, especially now that we've given up our connection to the GP. But we've got a lead on the house in Aberdeen, and we're circling back to that."

"And the condo owner?" Ethan asked.

"I feel like I'm being interrogated," Luc said, yanking dramatically at the collar of his shirt. "Fortunately, the condo, being in Chicago, was much easier to find. Smallish real estate management company. Legit, and they've got several condos across the Loop. Tend to rent them out to executive types." He grinned at me. "I did check to see if it was one of your father's. No hit there, unfortunately."

"A small miracle," Ethan said.

"The Librarian did look into disavowal," Luc said, "at last, after a lecture about being overloaded. He said, 'It depends.'"

Ethan rolled his eyes. "If I wanted to hear that, I'd have called the damn lawyers."

"Actually, I told him the same thing. But he wasn't trying to sidestep—he had a good point. According to *Canon*, official disavowal takes place in front of a GP quorum."

"Ah," Ethan said, understanding. "And there is no GP."

"There is not, since Nicole abolished it. Does the AAM count for those purposes? Probably. But who's to say?"

"Does it really matter?" I asked. "He's not a member of Cado-gan House or the AAM, so it's not like they're going to be strip-ping him of any rights. If this is just an issue of a public denouncement, whether the AAM backs it doesn't seem rele-vant."

"It wouldn't be literally," Malik said. "But the move wouldn't have as much impact. It's a public denouncement, yes, but with-out the broader consequences—shunning by colleagues, the rela-tionship between the vampires being removed from the NAVR registry, et cetera."

I glanced back at Ethan. "Some of that stuff won't apply to Balthasar. Do you think he would care about the rest of it? You left him, disavowed him, once already. It didn't take."

"Being a narcissist, he is less interested in the opinions or de-sires of others. But your point is well taken. Even disavowal may not assuage him. Not if he's willing to go this far."

"If Scott and Morgan weren't already aware of Balthasar's antics, they'll need to know. They won't have known the depth of his egocentrism, but they'll begin to suspect it now."

"A good idea," Ethan agreed. "I'm not certain what to tell Scott about Morgan. It's better if he knows the truth, especially if the Circle decides the Houses can be used against each other. But Morgan, for various and sundry reasons, doesn't trust us."

Catcher, not being one to mince words, looked cockily at Ethan. "Does it kinda make you wish you hadn't set him up with Merit?"

I snorted.

Ethan gave both of us the imperious eyebrow. "I'm sure he was devastated when their relationship didn't progress, as I would have been, but I was thinking more about Celina."

"Also a problem," Catcher acknowledged. "And a trust barrier."

"A trust *Everest*," Luc said. "He's never going to trust us, not really. But that doesn't really matter. We're not in it for the glory, and we don't need the approval."

We all looked at him, waiting for him to credit the movie he'd likely stolen that line from, as he was a famous (or perhaps notorious) movie quoter. But his expression was defiant.

"What? I can't come up with something wise and clever on my own?"

"You can," Malik said, "but so rarely do."

As Luc made a juvenile face, Ethan's phone rang, and he pulled it out. We all stiffened a bit, awaiting more news. Ethan scanned the screen, put it away again.

"Morgan?" Catcher asked.

"Reporters," Ethan said. "Undoubtedly calling to discuss Balthasar's antics. We likely were not the only ones on the street with cameras, and I'm sure a dozen people have already spread it around the Internet."

"Sixteen," Luc said, scanning the screen on his phone. "As of right now."

"Just so," Ethan said, tapping fingers against the arm of the couch. "So a conversation with reporters is not likely to make me feel any better about our current situation."

"No," Malik agreed, "but that doesn't mean you should ignore them. We'll need to get ahead of this. If we don't, public opinion will begin the pendulum swing again. And where they go, Kowalcyzk will follow. Talk to Nick if you prefer, but talk to someone."

Nick was Nicholas Breckenridge, an award-winning reporter in a family of shape-shifters and members of the same pack as Jeff, the NAC. They were very wealthy and friends of my father's, and lived on an estate outside Chicago.

"What you need," Luc said, "is a plan to deal with this ass-hole."

"That is accurate," Ethan said, crossing one leg over the other. "And back to my earlier request: I'm entertaining options for get-ting rid of him." He checked his watch. "It's two hours until dawn. I want ideas at sunset tomorrow. Specific ideas from each of you about how, precisely, we should do that."

Catcher lifted a hand. "I'm not your employee."

"Much to my ever-present relief," Ethan said. "You're excused from the exercise."

Luc looked at me. "I'm guessing you're going to be busy with Navarre House tomorrow, but do remember us, withering away in the basement of Cadogan House."

I hitched a thumb at Ethan. "I go where he tells me to go."

"You need the training."

I'd known that was coming and had a response in the chamber. "I bested the captain of the Navarre House guards with a dagger, while wearing stilettos and a gown, in front of an audience. I have *all* the training."

"I'm taking credit for this one," Catcher said to the room, hand in the air. "Just FYI."

"I like to think it was a group effort," Ethan said. "All of us working together to shape our lump of girl into a Sentinel."

"I like to think I'm more than the sum of my training."

"You are," Luc said. "There's at least some hot beef or deep dish in there."

"I am also more than Chicago foodstuffs."

Ethan grinned at Luc. "Pumas? Diet Coke? Smart-assery?"

Luc snapped his fingers, pointed at Ethan. "Yes. And, like, three percent medieval literature."

"You're both hilarious. Really and truly. Comedy geniuses."

Mallory appeared in the doorway, stopped short when she saw the group of us. "Oh, sorry. I didn't mean to interrupt. I was just going to say hi."

"No problem here," Luc said. "I was just about to head downstairs." He looked back at me. "Tomorrow, before Navarre House."

I gave him a jaunty salute, and he disappeared.

"I'd like to go ahead and call Jeff," Malik said, "get some tips about digging online into the Circle. If they have a strong cyberpresence, it seems likely they've pulled Navarre House into some of that. Might give us a head start on the forensic accounting work."

"It's a good idea," Ethan said, and Malik waved, bowed out of the room, leaving the four of us.

"I hear you've had a night," Mallory said, moving toward us. "But you both look to be in one piece."

"We're fine," I said. "I assume Catcher filled you in?"

"He did, but not on the important thing—how did your father react to watching you fight? Was he utterly impressed?"

I hadn't actually noticed, but his reaction after the fact had been telling enough. "I wouldn't say impressed. At least for a moment, he thought we had set it up somehow." I glanced at Ethan. "He'll probably have things to say to both of us, separately, about how disappointed he is, about how the slate isn't clean."

"Ah, Joshua," Mallory said. "Such a charmer."

"That's one word for it."

"I actually wanted to see if you'd eaten, wanted to grab a bite."

Ethan gestured to the cart. "Margot brought in a tray, and I believe she included bread, meats for sandwiches."

"That actually sounds great," Mallory said. "I didn't go into the cafeteria; I wasn't really sure how everyone would handle me being there, and I'm starving."

"I told her to go anyway," Catcher said. "She didn't listen."

"I rarely do," Mallory said, moving toward the cart. "Can I help myself?"

"Please," Ethan said. Mallory walked over and removed a dome from a tray, revealing a spread of cheeses and meats.

Most were standard, with a few odd bits thrown in. One of the meats was pinkish purple and looked as though it had been jabbed through with olives; there was also a blue cheese so heavy on the blue that it leaned toward indigo.

"So I'll stick to cheddar," I said, nabbing a small square of yellow-white cheese, relieved to find, when I bit in, that I'd picked the correct one.

"Why don't we all grab a plate?" Ethan suggested. "I could use something substantial to eat."

I bit back a smile as I piled cheese and meat onto some sort of multigrain bread, smiled as Ethan held up a small bag of salt and vinegar potato chips. "I believe Margot left these for you."

"Offensively delicious," Mallory and I said simultaneously, remembering one of our long-ago-agreed-upon conclusions. We grinned at each other, and since our hands were full, we bumped hips in a kind of high five.

And frankly, it felt amazing to share that connection with her, that sense of history and solidarity. We were the living memories of our friendship, and being friends again seemed to make those memories more real, bring them into sharper focus. She smiled at me, nodded just a bit, and I knew she'd had the same thought.

CHAPTER ELEVEN

✦ ✦✦✦ ✦

SACRED AND PROFANE

We fixed plates, ended up at the end of the conference table, Ethan and me on one side, Mallory and Catcher on the other. Just like two couples on a double date, if a double date could be said to involve sandwiches around the conference table in the office of a Master vampire. But when times were troubled, as they so often were, you took your breaks when you could find them.

"How's SWOB?" I asked Mallory, thinking it would be nice to grab a bit of someone else's drama for a change.

"Good," she said, nodding, holding a hand in front of her mouth as she chewed. "We've got a Web site, T-shirts, business cards."

"Everything but sorcerers," Catcher said, crunching a chip.

"There aren't tons of them out there," Mallory said, elbowing him. "That's exactly why we need resources like this—so they don't feel any more alone than they already are. But I have touched base with a girl in Indiana and a guy in Iowa who were pretty freaked out when they accidentally did some magic. So we're hooking them up with the Order, making sure they get the support they need, not just handed off to a tutor with a fare-thee-well." Her tone darkened at the end, since that was precisely what had happened to her.

"I think that's awesome," I said. "Better to be overprepared than under-." The city had burned, after all, the last time we were underprepared.

"And speaking of underprepared, how's the mayor?" Ethan asked.

Catcher took a swig of beer. "I'm guessing she'll have some comments for Chuck given Balthasar's latest display. But he's communicating pretty regularly with her staff, and she's done a decent job the last few weeks of asking about supernatural situations instead of making accusations. Doesn't hurt that two human unions are on strike—gives her someone else to blame."

"She does like to play the blame game," Ethan said, a slice of tomato splurting out the side of his sandwich.

"You're not the sandwich architect I'd have figured you for," I said.

"I am, apparently, Darth Sullivan," he said, lifting a corner of bread to stuff the tomato back in. "I understand that building things, Death Stars or otherwise, isn't my particular strength."

My heart melted a little. "Did you just make a *Star Wars* reference? And a joke? At the same time?"

"Oh my God, that is so cute," Mallory said with a grin. "He makes jokes just like a human."

Ethan managed not to smite her for the comment, and we ate in companionable silence until the sandwiches were gone and Mallory and I had nearly finished the bag of chips, wincing with each successive bite.

Ethan tried one, but from the pursed expression, wasn't a fan. "My response," he said, "is 'why?'"

"Because delicious," Mallory said, reaching chip-greased fingers into the bag to dig for another one.

"Because delicious," I agreed, and spun the bag around so the open maw faced me.

"Finish them off," Mallory said, dusting salt and potato chip flakes from her hands and then wiping them on a napkin. "In the immortal words of Popeye, 'I've had all I can stands, and I can't stands no more.'"

While I grabbed another chip without argument, Mallory and Catcher looked at each other and shared a look that said we were about to return to the announcement they'd wanted to make.

"So, while we're all here," Mallory said, "we wanted to talk to you about something—again."

"Is everything all right?" Ethan asked.

"It's fine," Mallory said. "We're getting married."

Ethan's knife hit his plate with a jarring *clank*. "Sorry," he said, putting it aside. "Sorry. You surprised me. Congratulations! That's fantastic."

His recovery was fast. Mine was not, primarily because she didn't sound as though she thought it was fantastic. "You're getting married," I repeated.

"We are," she said, and tucked a lock of hair behind her ear. "So, Catcher is thinking about seeking reinstatement in the Order."

While I waited to hear the connection between her marriage and the Order, Ethan's eyebrows lifted. He met Catcher's gaze, something weighty passing between them. He and Catcher had a history I wasn't entirely sure about—it would take many years, I suspected, before I had a complete overview of Ethan's four centuries. Maybe it was Catcher having been kicked out of the Order that had brought them together in the first place.

"I didn't know you were reconsidering the Order," Ethan said.

Catcher nodded. "It's been on my mind. There are battles you fight from the outside, and battles you fight from within. I used to believe the Order was the former. Now I think it's the latter." He looked down at his linked hands. "Too much has happened in Chicago for the Order to still be so complacent. Mallory and I should be a force. Instead we're basically useless."

"Not to us," I said with a smile.

"No, not to you. But only because we work under the radar. I'm not saying we should go public, but we should at least be in the mix. And it would be nice to be official, for once."

"And how does this tie into marriage?" Ethan asked, glancing between them.

"The Order can ignore us as individuals." Mallory looked at Catcher. "We're powerful individually, but we're still just that—two separate units. The Order's got a lot of respect for the institution of marriage, for the idea of two souls becoming one."

"And if you're married," I said with a nod, seeing where this was going, "you become a unit."

"Worth more than the sum of our parts," Catcher agreed. "We figure they'll think it's better to deal with us than leave us on our own."

That didn't sound completely unreasonable. Maybe a little naive, but not unreasonable, especially considering what little I knew of the Order. But it was so unromantic. I had no objection to rational or logical, but I knew Mallory, and romance was important to her. Very important.

I glanced her way, caught her looking at me with cautious hope. She wanted me to approve. I could be happy for her, sure. I didn't need to agree with the circumstances, but I sure as hell wanted to understand them.

"And when are you thinking about doing it?" Ethan asked.

"As soon as possible," Mallory said, and Catcher nodded when she glanced at him. "Just at the courthouse, nothing big. But we'd really like you and Ethan to attend, to be our witnesses."

"To stand up for us," Catcher said.

Ethan blinked in surprise. "We'd be honored, of course. But I'm sure we could help with something a little more elaborate, if you'd like. You'd be welcome to use the House or the garden."

"Oh, I don't know," Mallory said, tucking hair behind her ears again. It was a nervous gesture, and reiterated that we were going to need to have a nice, long chat about whatever this was. "We're hoping to keep it really low-key. Efficient."

Ethan nodded, reached out, and touched her hands supportively. "We'll help however we can." He pushed back his chair and rose. "And I think this calls for something stronger than soda." He pulled a bottle of champagne from the refrigerator across the room, deftly picked up four champagne glasses in his other hand. I was grateful he was handling the situation with such aplomb, since I was clearly running behind.

"It's good to hear good news," Ethan said, bringing them back to the table, where I helped him disassemble the knot of them. "There hasn't been much of that tonight."

He removed the foil, then unscrewed the cage and pulled out the cork. Champagne frothed over the rim, which he tipped into the glasses. I passed them out, and Ethan raised his glass.

"To new beginnings and happiness. May you both have a lifetime of it."

"Hear, hear," I said, and we clinked our glasses together.

Mallory caught my gaze, hopefulness and trepidation in her eyes. I smiled and nodded, a promise of support.

Her relief was nearly palpable, and tears welled in her eyes.

We were definitely going to have to discuss this. But that was a discussion for another time, preferably with two fewer men in the audience.

Mallory and Catcher were tired, so they begged off Ethan's offer of a special dessert or more champagne by the backyard fountain—and what might have been an opportunity to chat with Mallory about the sudden interest in marriage.

We were an hour before dawn, and despite said drama—or probably because of Mallory's—I was utterly wired. Sleep wasn't going to come quickly, so I decided to force its hand.

I'd skipped a night of training (for a perfectly legitimate reason), but recognized that I still needed to work out, to hone my skills. So when Catcher and Mallory returned to their room and Ethan turned back to House business, I climbed into workout gear and headed outside.

I didn't think about anything as I ran down the path that followed the interior perimeter of the Cadogan grounds. My mind was primarily focused on putting one foot in front of the other, keeping my form correct, keeping my speed consistent.

I pushed myself until my breath was quick and rhythmic, my body sheened with sweat, and my legs felt like iron. And by the time I'd slowed in front of the House, my limbs were warm and loose and my brain was relatively calm. Exhaustion tended to do that, and the faint lightening at the edge of the horizon probably wasn't helping.

The foyers were empty when I walked through, the House's

vampires tucked in and prepared for daylight. Probably a good thing, since I was hot, sweaty, and still panting.

The stairs, however, did not feel so good. My body felt leaden, and I nearly sighed with relief when I finally reached the third-floor landing.

The apartments were empty, so I ditched sweaty clothes and headed directly for the shower, washing off the sweat, the fear, the anxiety.

I emerged wrapped in a towel, a second wrapped turban-style around my wet hair, and found Ethan standing in front of a small table, flipping a stack of what looked like mail. "The House is locked down."

I nodded, gestured. "Is that mail? Do vampires get mail?"

He looked back at me, grinned. "Why wouldn't they?"

"I don't get mail."

"You aren't Master of the House."

I padded toward him, glanced at the envelopes he'd already discarded. Credit card applications, catalogues, charity updates, bills.

"Would you like a Cadogan House platinum card?"

"Can I have one?"

"No. You have a full library, all the clothes you could ever need, provided you don't destroy them, and a cafeteria at your disposal. For what purpose, precisely, would you need a platinum card?"

I dodged the question. "Spoilsport," I said, but spied the magazine peeking from the bottom of the stack. Its glossy cover featured three men and women in sharp suits, arms crossed in businesslike efficiency. TONIGHT'S HOUSE was written in a tidy font across the top of it.

"My God," I said, picking it up and holding it against my toweled chest. "Is this a magazine for Masters?"

"It's for House staff," Ethan said with a chuckle, unfolding a letter. "Why?"

Why? Because it featured headlines such as "The Best Bang for your Blood Buck," "Weeding Out Problematic Initiates," and "Décor 101: Sprucing Up Your House."

"I'm going to need to flip through this for both edutainment and infotational purposes."

"He who reads *Today's House* also pays today's House's bills."

"Don't push your luck."

"I already did," he said, refolding the letter and putting it back in the pile. "I called Nicole."

It took me a moment to adjust to the segue; he'd clearly been eager to get that off his chest. "And how is her royal highness?"

"Acting very royal, which doesn't really do credit to her democratic leanings."

I put the magazine back on the pile. "Did she know about Balthasar?"

"He visited Atlanta," Ethan said. "I don't have the sense he was there very long, but long enough at least to meet her, to reconnect, to convince her of his identity."

"When?"

Ethan's eyes fairly glowed at the question. "You don't miss the details, Sentinel. Two months ago. Before the Testing. Before she came to Chicago."

"And she never mentioned it. You think they're working together on something? That that's why he's here?"

He put his hands on his hips, frowned. "Our conversation was brief, but I didn't have that sense. She sounded, I suppose, starstruck. In my experience, Balthasar enjoys more of a challenge than that."

"So the next few weeks should be really quiet around here."

Ethan chuckled, kissed my forehead. "As before, after. Let's worry about that tomorrow, Sentinel, and get this night behind us."

I had no objection to that.

I pulled on pajamas, dried my hair, and brushed my fangs like a good little vampire. I checked my phone, found Jonah had left a voice mail I didn't especially want to listen to.

And being a good little vampire, I sat down on the bed, lifted the phone to my ear.

"Merit," the message said, "it's Jonah. We need to talk. You can't just ignore me. We're partners. Call me, and we'll talk about the monitoring. I'm sorry if you took it personally, but it's not personal. It isn't. It's just caution. We all want to believe the best in those who lead us. But every empire has fallen, Merit. Every empire will fall."

The message cut off.

I liked Jonah. Respected him, and what he stood for. He was my partner, after all. A partner I'd agreed to serve with, and a man who'd helped me and the House countless times.

Frankly, I didn't disagree that every empire would fall eventually. Hadn't we just seen that happen to the GP? And I could admit my sensitivity to Balthasar's glamour was concerning. Hell, it concerned me. But I'd adjusted. Jonah's insistence that I'd be blind to what might happen, that I'd miss the signs of Ethan's becoming utterly dictatorial—or that I'd purposely ignore them—that I'd let all vampires suffer because I loved a man, was just wrong. And coming from someone I thought I'd known, and certainly had respected, it hurt. A lot.

I tossed the phone onto the nightstand, but it spilled over the end and landed on the floor at Ethan's feet.

He'd emerged from the bathroom in dark boxer briefs that

hugged his thighs. He picked up the phone, placed it on the nightstand. "Everything all right?"

"Just an irritating message."

"From Jonah?"

I looked up at him suspiciously.

"I saw your phone when he called you. And when you didn't answer." He cocked his head. "You aren't speaking to him?"

"Not at the moment."

"Would you like to tell me why?"

I fluffed my pillows with cathartic thumps. "Nope."

This time, his brow lifted. "Is this something I should also be irritated about?"

I caught the thread of possessiveness in his voice, almost wished it was that simple. I didn't think Jonah was interested in me anymore, but even if he had been, handling that would have been comparatively easy.

"No," I said on a sigh. "He's just being unreasonable about something RG-related."

Ethan didn't answer. He just looked at me, waiting, with his face drawn into Masterly features.

"I can't talk about it," I insisted. "It's nothing dangerous to the House. Just—something between us."

"Ah," he said, and walked around the bed, sat down, and turned off the light. "I see."

"Do you?"

He stretched out beside me, then snaked an arm around my waist and pulled me tight against his body. "I do. You're in the RG, and you're dating—very seriously—a member of the AAM. It's not unforeseeable he'd have concerns. The RG is an organization, Merit, which is built on a certain fundamental sense of fear. That those in power will erode the very rights they've promised to protect, and that if we are not careful and vigilant, it will happen sooner rather than later."

"So you're saying he's being reasonable?" I asked.

"No. But I am suggesting he's being rational. For some—and the RG is among them—vigilance isn't paranoia; it's inevitability. Consider this: If he was dating Lakshmi, would you have the same concerns?"

Lakshmi was a member of the now-defunct GP, and a woman who'd had a definite romantic interest in Jonah. She'd helped during the GP's reign, but she was undeniably manipulative.

"I wouldn't trust her," I said. "But I'd trust Jonah's judgment. I'm not getting the same trust. That's what's frustrating."

"Ah," was all he said. "Would you like me to talk to him?"

"No. I can fight my own battles." And would. I just wasn't looking forward to it.

"I've no doubt of it," he said. "In other news, it appears Mallory and Catcher are to be married."

"So they say."

"You don't sound enthused."

"They sounded like they were discussing getting a small business loan, not making a lifetime commitment of love and fidelity."

"You have doubts about their love and fidelity?"

"Well, no, not in the abstract. I know he loves her, and vice versa. But that's not what I heard from her tonight." I shifted, suddenly restless, and stretched out beside him. He gave me the room but linked our fingers together.

"I heard business. And I heard nerves. Once upon a time, she'd wanted this big wedding in New Orleans, for God's sake, on Bourbon Street. With fire-eaters, a jazz band, a second line, the entire shebang. And, okay, we've grown since the last time we talked about it, so maybe her tastes have changed. But she didn't even sound excited. That's what bothers me, I guess. It's her wedding. She should sound excited."

"You will be."

"When I get married, yes, I probably will be excited. I'll let you know if anyone proposes."

Ethan humphed.

I sighed, turned in to him again. "It's been a long night. Let's go to sleep."

Ethan wrapped his arms around me, and I instantly relaxed, my lids growing heavier, drifting closed.

I woke alone in an empty room, with wooden floors and walls of robin's-egg blue. The bed was tall, with four posters of thick, spiraling wood that rose at least five feet into the air. The bed was down, with its juxtaposing softness and lumpiness, the sheets ivory and soft. Light from a candelabra on a small wooden desk flicked shadows across the wall.

This isn't my room, some part of me realized, but it was a dim and quiet voice. I sat up, touched the white shift that covered me from neck to ankles, rubbed against bare skin.

"You're awake."

The words were spoken aloud, but they also reverberated in my head just as a silent conversation with Ethan might have, and my heart began to pound in response.

I looked up, found him standing in a corner. He wore fawn leather breeches, knee-high boots, a white linen shirt that draped open at the neck. A small book was open in one palm, one knee lifted and a booted foot flat on the wall, as if he'd been lazily reading.

Balthasar.

"Merit," he said, his smile slow and seductive. "I am so glad we have this opportunity to get acquainted."

"Where are we?"

Balthasar gestured at the room. "A little place I created. It allows you a sense of how Ethan and I used to live."

It wasn't real. Couldn't have been real. But the scents of beeswax and bay rum belied that belief. Mallory had warded the House. So how was he here? And how was I with him?

Too many questions, not enough answers. But I'd seen enough of Balthasar to know that he'd take advantage of any indication of weakness, so I kept my voice smooth.

"He told me how you used to live."

Balthasar moved closer. "Did he?"

"I know that you used humans. That you used women. How you discarded them. And he told me about Persephone. How you used her. How you killed her, used her to punish Ethan."

His expression went momentarily blank. She'd meant so little to him that he hadn't bothered to remember her name.

"If Ethan was punished, it was for good reason. He was my child, after all."

"He hasn't been anyone's child in a very long time. Where is he?"

A flash of anger. "Not here. This place is for me and you, so that we can become better acquainted. Don't you want to become better acquainted with me, Caroline?"

"That's not my name," I said as Balthasar took a step forward. I scanned the room for an exit, but there was no doorway, only the window across the room, which was covered by slatted shutters that locked in place with metal braces.

If there wasn't an exit, I'd have to find a weapon. I slid across the bed to the other side, hopped onto the floor, putting the bed between me and him. I walked across rough floorboards toward the desk, hoping to find a letter opener, a dagger. Or if I was really lucky, a sharpened aspen stake.

"I'm not going to hurt you, *chérie*," Balthasar said, closing the book and kicking off from the wall. He walked toward me, putting the book on a side table as he passed.

"Then let me go."

His smile was slow. "You are not here because you are trapped, Merit. You are here because you want to be. Because you are intrigued by me. Because you understand *le désir*."

"I'm not intrigued by you."

He shook his head, smiling softly as if talking to a child. "You were so wonderfully sensitive to me yesterday. I was surprised by the depth of your . . . *passion*."

"It wasn't passion. It was magic."

"Are you certain of that?" And yet the tendrils of his magic stretched across the room, reached for me.

"I love Ethan." I said the words with force, like they were a talisman, a charm against Balthasar's appetite.

"You can love more than one thing, *chérie*. I am sure Ethan shared his past with you, told you of the women in which we took pleasure. There was always room for more."

Focus, I told myself. *Find a way out. There is always a way out.*

I reached the small desk, trailed my fingers across it as if I were just exploring the room. The candelabra was stuck to the surface, and the drawer pulls were decorative. The desktop held only an open notebook, slanted writing across its yellowing surface.

"I don't want to love more," I said.

"That is unfortunate, poppet. Because I am owed much by your Master."

I moved closer to the window, glanced at the shutters. I might be able to pry off one of the braces, but I'd need time for that. "Why would he owe you anything?"

"Because I made him what he is." The words were heavy, and they fell in the room like thunderclaps.

I glanced back at Balthasar, and the silver in his eyes made my heart hammer against my ribs.

"I made him *everything*."

I swallowed, forced my voice to steadiness. "You made him a monster. He made himself a Master."

Balthasar hissed, teeth gleaming and bared, glistening with hunger for whatever he thought he could get from me. He walked closer, maneuvering his body between me and the bed.

I needed a weapon. My heart sped, and I put my back to the window, using the oversized shift to shield my hands as I tried to work one of the braces loose. To keep him occupied, I kept talking.

Balthasar chuckled, and that was nearly as disturbing as his anger. "Are you seeking escape, Merit? For that is not to be. Our business is not done."

Damn it, the brace wouldn't budge. Fear began to tighten my chest, send flutters through my stomach. I had no weapon, and no exit, and an enemy who was eager to hurt Ethan. It was a bad combination.

"What do you want from Ethan? From us?"

"*Je veux tout.* Everything I might have had. Everything that was taken from me."

"Ethan took nothing from you. Your captors did."

Balthasar moved so fast I didn't even see it. He grabbed my arm, the mere touch enough to send desire rushing through my body like liquid fire, and began to drag me across the room.

I pulled back, tried to free my arm, kicked at his calves, but his grip was steel-solid. "What do you want from me?"

"Ah, *chérie*, let us not be coy. Not now."

As he pulled me toward the bed, a new kind of panic set in. Not fear for my life, but for my body, and the sanctity of it. For what he meant to do, and who he meant to hurt by it.

"You can't use me to get to him."

Balthasar's smile was wide and feline. "We would both disagree with you."

"I won't let you. I'll leave him first."

Balthasar clucked his tongue. "No, that is not the truth. I have seen how you look at each other."

Magic moved in a whirlwind around him, a cyclone that transmuted body, hair, clothes. Light flashed, and when the light and magic dissipated, Ethan stood before me.

My body bucked with shock.

No, I told myself. *No. This is* not *Ethan.*

But he looked so much like Ethan. Tall, rangy, his body honed and sculpted, his eyes sharply green. If they'd stood side by side, I'm not sure I could have told them apart.

Balthasar pulled me tighter against the line of his body. Of Ethan's body. He looked like Ethan, smelled like Ethan, and the touch of his hand carried the same strength and warmth. Thought and need warred, made enemies by love and magic.

It's an illusion, I reminded myself, digging my fingers into my palms until bright pain radiated, hoping the sensation would wake me up, send me home, or break whatever spell Balthasar had worked on me. *So break it.*

I used mental blocks to keep my keen vampire instincts—and the sights, smells, and sounds they revealed—from overwhelming me. *Maybe that's what I need,* I thought, and closed my eyes, blocking out the sight of him, then the sensation of his arms around me, then the magic that flowed around the room as easily as water.

The pain was nearly immediate—a searing pressure that

threatened to burst my head from the inside, a vise pressing against my skull. And the more I tried to fight it, the taller I tried to raise the walls against him, the worse the pain became. My hands curled into shaking and sinewy fists, my body shaking from the exertion, the inside of my skull booming like the percussion of a thousand flash grenades.

The force in my head kept building, the blood roaring in my ears, until I was certain I'd pass out.

And then what would he do to me? Exactly, I feared, what he wanted.

Instantly knowing I'd rather be conscious and fighting as best I could, I gave up, let the blocks fall away . . . and as my body went limp, felt the warm rush of heat as his magic spilled over me like wine.

Suddenly, his mouth was on mine, the taste of wine and blood on his lips, his teeth and tongue demanding.

I turned my head away. "Get away from me!"

He kissed me again, his teeth nipping tender flesh and drawing blood. I slapped him, whipping his head to the side and leaving a scarlet mark across his face.

Balthasar hissed and led me toward the bed again, which left little mystery about exactly what he planned to do—and how he planned to use me to hurt Ethan.

"I *made* him," he spat as I dug my feet into the floor, splinters biting into the soles, in a last effort to avoid the horror he'd inflict on both of us.

But he used his weight, his strength, to slingshot me onto the bed.

I sank into the feather bed, rolled toward the other edge, trying to think, to keep the panic from overwhelming me.

Balthasar grabbed my ankle, and I kicked out with the other.

The strike was good; I nailed him in the shoulder and sent him tumbling backward, but he righted himself and with that blurring quick speed was suddenly on top of me, hands pinning down my arms with bruising strength, one knee between my thighs, and Ethan's green eyes staring back at me.

The expression on his face, the gleam of success in his eyes, was nothing like Ethan's. He smiled, all teeth and fangs, weapons meant to penetrate, rip, *kill*.

He lowered his face to my neck, and I struggled beneath him, trying for any advantage in strategy, in physics, that would reverse our positions. But in the soft pile of sheets, I couldn't get purchase. I was trapped, and my heart began to pound like a timpani drum, faster and faster, fear tightening my belly, sweat peppering my arms.

He'd hurt me without remorse to punish Ethan, to hurt him, or to distract him. Or best yet, all three.

"You will never know him like I know him," Balthasar said, his face only inches from mine, fangs gleaming. "As long as you may live, as strong as you believe your love to be, you were not there with us. You did not see what made him."

His gaze dropped to my lips, and his tongue snuck out to moisten his lips. "But, perhaps, we can share what you have now, and we will all be closer for it."

"You'll never know what *we* have," I countered, trying to force air through my lungs. "No matter what you do to me now, you'll never have Ethan again. Because he grew up, and you never did."

He slapped me hard enough to put stars in front of my eyes.

It was the best thing he could have done.

My eyes silvered as fear transmuted into fury, filling me with a gorgeous and righteous warmth. I used that burgeoning fire, stoked it with thoughts of the pain he'd caused others, the terror, the deaths. I thought of the humans he'd violated, the misery and tragedy made by his hand.

Balthasar's eyes widened with pleasure. "Oh, *le chaton* has claws."

Anger lowered my voice to a growl. "Don't call me kitten."

With a scream more animal than human, I raked nails across Balthasar's face, clawed at him like a penned animal.

He cursed in French, low, guttural sounds of indignation that I'd dared refuse him.

"You little bitch," he said, trying to grab my arms. "When I am in control of your House, when I am your Master, we will see how you use those claws."

"I am not Persephone," I said, raking nails across his face again. "I'm already a vampire, and you can't hurt me!"

"Merit!"

"Stop using his voice!" I screamed it at the top of my lungs, slapped him hard, would have done it again except that I felt a different viselike grip around my wrists, and the sound of another voice, raining down like freezing water.

"Merit! Stop!"

The world rushed suddenly back, covering and choking me as I tried to rise through the tumult and break the surface.

As suddenly as it had begun, I was back in our bedroom. I sat atop Ethan's chest, his hands around my wrists, his face striped where I'd raked my fingernails across his skin.

And his eyes were wide with fear.

CHAPTER TWELVE

TRUTH AND CONSEQUENCES

I made an animal sound, tried to pull my wrists away from his grip. "I hurt you. Oh God, I hurt you. *Let go*," I cried, and his hands flashed open.

I scrambled off the bed, backed toward the corner of the room. I didn't stop until the wall was cold against my back.

I slid to the floor, hands in my lap, fingers bloodied from scratching him, the stain clear even in the dim light of the lamplit room. I stared at the blood on my hands until my body began to shake with an emotion I couldn't name. Fear? Violation? Mortification that I'd hurt the man who'd given his life for me?

"Merit, what's happened?"

My gaze flashed to Ethan. The scrapes had already begun to fade, but they were still there. Taunting me. Reminding me. "I hurt you."

"I'm fine," he said, throwing away the covers and standing up. "What's happened?"

My hands began to shake, and I crossed my arms, tucked them against my sides. "Balthasar. He was here. I was with him."

Ethan's gaze darted around the room. "No one was here. He wouldn't have been able to get past the ward."

I shook my head. "He took me somewhere. Together. In a room, an old room, a French room. It was old-fashioned. And then he looked like you." My voice shook, sounded far away. "He looked like himself, and then he looked like you."

Ethan looked as though he wanted to touch me, wanted to move forward, but I shook my head.

"Stop. Stay where you are."

I could feel the panic building again, filling my chest with iron, squeezing my lungs as if I'd never get a lungful of air again.

"Breathe, Sentinel."

But I shook my head. Not to disobey, but to protest. My head began to swim, my vision fading at the corners as panic swamped me.

"*Sentinel.*" Ethan's voice, his tone, was like a slap to my mind. "I gave you a direct order, and I expect you to follow it. Take a breath!"

I sucked in air through painfully tight lungs.

He took a step closer, visibly flinched when I pulled back farther.

"Stop."

"I won't come any closer," he promised. "But I'm going to hold out my hand. You can take it when you're ready. Each time you inhale, you squeeze. Each time you exhale, you squeeze. All right?"

I nodded. Ethan reached out his hand. It took effort, but I slowly lifted my shaking fingers to meet his.

"Inhale slowly," he said, and I squeezed his hand as I sucked in air.

Ethan watched me, nodding. "And exhale, slowly."

I nodded, blew out air through pursed lips.

"Again," he said softly.

It took time. I don't know how long. Seconds. Minutes. He stood there the entire time, his arm outstretched, but otherwise making no move to invade the boundaries I was trying to rebuild. For a man as commanding as Ethan Sullivan, that must have killed him.

When my breathing was finally steady, I drew my hand away, wiped dampness on my pajama bottoms.

Ethan's scratches had already disappeared, but the fear from his eyes hadn't.

"You're all right?" I asked.

"I am scared to my bones."

I nodded, tried to swallow past the lump in my throat. "I'm going to just . . . take a minute." With a hand against the wall for support, I rose slowly, making sure my quaking knees would support my weight, then walked toward the bathroom and turned on the light.

I was always pale, but in the mirror I seemed preternaturally so, with blue shadows beneath my eyes. And across the left side of my face was the faint red flush from Balthasar's hand, from where he'd slapped me.

No, not just that—from where he'd *marked* me.

Wherever we'd been, whatever we'd done, he'd been able to touch me. To hurt me. And if I hadn't found my way out of that place when I had . . .

I shook my head. I was here now. I was here now, and he wasn't. I'd made it out of wherever I'd been, and now I had to deal with it.

I had to find a way to deal with it.

First things first: I'd be damned if he'd mark me. I turned on the faucet, confirmed the temperature with my fingers, and splashed cold water onto my face over and over again until the memory and color had faded again.

I turned off the water, pressed a towel to my face, and when I put it down again, found Ethan standing in the doorway.

The expression on his face was ferociously possessive, and intensely uneasy. "Tell me what happened."

I nodded but walked past him into the bedroom, felt a pulse of guilt that I'd avoided touching him. But he didn't mention it.

I sat down on the edge of the bed, gathered my hands in my lap. Ethan stayed in the doorway but pivoted to face me, an uneasy distance between us.

My head was a jumble of words and thoughts, but I tried to order the pieces chronologically. "I was in a bed in an old-fashioned room. I think it was supposed to be like a room you'd been in before. With him. An inn, maybe? He was dressed in old-fashioned clothes, and I was, too. He wanted to talk about me, about you, about himself. He tried to be clever, to romance me." I paused. "And when that didn't work, he was suddenly you."

Ethan grew very, very still, and even the buzz of magic around him seemed to freeze solid.

"He looked like you. Smelled like you." Tears blossomed again. "I tried to get away, but there weren't any doors, and the window was barred, and I couldn't get the brace off." Panic rose quickly, a shot of cold from stomach to head, and I squeezed my eyes closed, trying to erase the memory of violence at Ethan's hands. *Get it out*, I told myself. *Get it out, and it's done, and you won't have to say it again.*

"And he tried to kiss me." The words flew out and away like startled doves. "He touched me. He tried to . . ." I shook my head, tears dawning again. "Well, he tried."

Cold magic flashed again. "Did he hurt you, Merit?" Every

word was like the snap of a twig in the dark—a sharp, surprising bite of sound. And his eyes left no doubt about his intentions: Had Balthasar been in the room with us right now, he wouldn't have made it out alive.

"No. *No*," I repeated, when Ethan looked as though he might lunge for the door. "He touched me, but he didn't . . ." Instinctively, I crossed my arms over my breasts, swallowed past the lump in my throat. "He didn't hurt me that way. I don't even know if he could have, really."

Ethan struggled to understand. "You mean to say it was a dream?"

"It *wasn't* a dream." His voice had been kind, the question well intentioned. But it hit me wrong, and my voice was shaking with defensiveness.

I shook my head, collected myself, found my voice. "It wasn't a dream," I said again. "It was real. I don't know how it was real, but it was."

He frowned. "How are you so sure?"

I lifted fingers to my cheek. I didn't want to tell him what Balthasar had done, incite him just as I suspected Balthasar wanted me to do, but he deserved the truth. And, more important, we needed to figure out what had happened.

"He slapped me. I could see the mark in the bathroom mirror."

That flash of cold magic again, but Ethan stayed absolutely silent, clearly holding his temper in check.

I glanced around the bedroom, at the seemingly solid walls, at the fact that I was still in a tank and pajama bottoms, not the white linen shift Balthasar had put me in. But it had felt real. Impossibly real.

"It doesn't matter," I said.

"It doesn't matter?" His tone was icy now, that fury only barely banked, his eyes like cold green glass, nearly translucent and undeniably deadly. "It doesn't matter that he hurt you? That he assaulted you?"

"To Balthasar," I clarified. "It doesn't matter to Balthasar, because I don't matter to Balthasar. He doesn't care about me." I looked up at him. "He's using me to get to you. To show that he's powerful. To prove that he can still hurt you. To prove that he could get to me just as he did Persephone. That he could ruin something else of yours, force your hand against him."

"Hurting you doesn't gain him anything."

"But it does," I said. "He doesn't think you'll run away this time, but that you'll stay and fight, because you love me more than you loved Persephone. He believes he'll win, Ethan. That he'll kill you and stake a claim on the House. He's decided he wants it, that he's owed it, and he'll take it however he can."

There was a knock at the door. Ethan moved to answer it. Mallory rushed in, Catcher behind her, both of them in Cadogan T-shirts. She wore pajama bottoms; he wore jeans. Ethan must have called them while I was in the bathroom.

"What happened?" she asked. I could tell she debated whether to touch me, to embrace me, and held herself back.

"Balthasar attacked her. He got to her in this room, in this House, and I want to know how that happened."

"Attacked her?" She looked me over, eyes wide with concern. "Jesus, Merit. What happened?"

"He got to her," Ethan repeated, "while she slept in our bed."

Mallory looked at me, then the room's exterior wall. Her expression transmuted from horror to utter confusion. "I'm sorry, but I don't understand what you mean. There's no breach in the ward. He couldn't have gotten in."

"That's impossible," Ethan said. "She said it wasn't a dream."

Wordlessly, Mallory rose, turned to the wall, held out her hand. In the space of a heartbeat, with no obvious effort, a glowing yellow orb appeared in her hand. That was something new. Before, it would have taken closed eyes and concentration for her to achieve. She'd gotten better at harnessing her powers, or at least in making them look effortless.

Mal flicked her fingers, and the orb flew toward the wall like a fastball in a no-hitter. It made contact with an electric sizzle, vibrantly green light shimmering across the wall, across the ward, like dappled sunlight across the bottom of a swimming pool.

When the light faded, she glanced back at us. "The ward is in place."

That didn't seem debatable, but Ethan wasn't satisfied, and his words were biting and bitter. "If the ward is in place, how did he get past it?"

Catcher took a step forward. "You're going to want to watch your tone, Sullivan."

"And you'll want to make sure your magic functions the way it's supposed to."

"For fuck's sake," Catcher said. "You can see the ward as well as she can, and it's not been breached. Can you not tell that she's exhausted?"

I looked at Mallory, for the first time saw the dark shadows beneath her eyes.

"A ward for a structure this large doesn't operate automatically," Catcher said, quieter now. "It takes energy to maintain it."

But Ethan couldn't see past his fear. "If the wards are in place, how did he get to her? How the fuck did he get to her?"

"Ethan," I said softly, "he didn't get past the wards."

"Maybe it was just a bad dream," Catcher said. Now Catcher's protectiveness was making him stupid.

"Do you honestly think I can't tell the difference between a bad dream and someone in my mind? Someone attacking? Because I have to say, there's a pretty big difference."

"All right," Mallory said, and when Catcher muttered a curse, slugged him in the arm. "I said all right! Everybody take a step back. Something awful has happened here tonight, and you know Merit wouldn't cry wolf. If she says it happened, then it happened. So instead of griping about it, we figure out what the hell it was. All right?"

When no one answered, she poked Catcher in the arm with a finger. "All right?"

"All right, all right. Damn, woman." He took a step backward, ran a hand over his shorn scalp.

Mallory nodded, exhaled heavily. "The wards are in place. And yet Balthasar attacked Merit. So if he didn't attack her physically . . ."

"The attack had to be primarily psychic," I said. I hadn't been in a room in France, and Balthasar certainly hadn't been in here with us. Some sort of psychic connection—strong enough to leave a physical mark—was the only other possibility.

"Vampires can't—" Catcher began to argue, but Mallory cut him off with a look.

"We'll assume," she said, "that nobody has heard about that kind of thing happening before. Regardless, it happened tonight, so let's discuss how." She looked at Ethan. "I assume you aren't aware of him trying this when you two were buddies?"

"We weren't buddies," Ethan snapped, but after a glance at me, the anger drained from his face. "And no, I've never heard of it happening before, either with him or anyone else."

"So what's the range of vampire psychic power?" Mallory said, looking at us.

"Glamour, and the ability to call, to reduce inhibitions," Ethan said. "Those are relatively common psychic skills. Lindsey's skill is somewhat more unusual. She's empathic. She can read emotions. Translate them, as it were."

Mallory looked at me. "Was he trying to compel you to do something? To kill Ethan or hand over the House keys, or whatever?"

I thought back. "No. He wanted sex. He didn't get it, obviously, because I started hitting him, and Ethan called my name, and that's when I woke up. He made himself look like Ethan, tried to use that to get under my skin. He wanted to hurt Ethan through me."

"Sex. Nightmares. Glamour. He sounds like an incubus," Mallory pronounced.

An incubus was another night-dwelling supernatural, a sensual creature that sought sex with women while they slept. Or forced them into it. And being a student of the occult even before her magical coming-out, she'd have known.

I wasn't sure incubi existed, but she had a point. The sensuality. The seductive power. Those were marks of the incubus myth, and I'd seen weirder in my year as a vampire.

I glanced at Ethan. "Is that possible?"

"Incubi do not exist," Ethan said flatly. He sat on a corner of the console table. "But vampire strengths—psych, strat, phys—can have their own flavor. Like Lindsey's being empathic."

Ethan glanced over, arranged three of the objects on the console table—a rune stone, a small stone figure of a bear, and the autographed baseball he'd once given me, now home among the knickknacks—in a straight line, the objects spaced equally apart.

"Most vampires have moderate strength." He pushed the rune above the others and out of alignment. "Occasionally, a vampire will be moderately strong in two categories, extra strong in one." Now he pushed the bear together with the rune. "And sometimes the vampire will have two strong attributes—strength and psych—and sometimes the flavor of those attributes runs toward the sexual."

"And that's really the origin of the incubus idea," Catcher said.

"Precisely," Ethan said with a nod. "Balthasar enjoys all things carnal, sexual or otherwise. His ability to glamour has always been strong, as we saw in my office, but I wouldn't have considered him a Very Strong Psych."

"Why not?" I asked.

Ethan frowned, as if trying to explain his hunch. "I suppose I've always considered him more of a *physical* actor, not a metaphysical one. He prefers seducing a woman with his charms—and the ego boost that comes from success."

"Maybe it wasn't just the force of his personality," Mallory said. "Maybe there was some magic or glamour in there, too."

"Or maybe I just never wanted to see it," Ethan said, then glanced at me. "I was still learning to be a vampire at his hand. Especially during the earlier years, vampires didn't think overmuch about strength or categorization."

I nodded. "So, if he's got this skill, or developed it while he recuperated, what do we do to keep him out?" I looked at Mallory. "Can you adjust the wards somehow?"

They looked at each other, brows furrowed as if they were engaged in silent deliberation.

"I don't know why that wouldn't be possible," Catcher said. "If we can create a physical barrier, why not a psychic one?"

Mallory twirled a lock of blue hair. "Yeah, I'll need to think about it, poke around the library for a bit, if that's all right?"

"Fine by me," Ethan said. "Do you think you could prepare something tonight? By dawn?"

"I won't know until I know," Mallory said. "But I'll get started and keep you updated."

Ethan nodded. "We have to go to Navarre to discuss the Circle."

"That'll be a good time," Catcher said.

"If by good time, you mean something akin to a fang root canal, then yes, it will be."

I looked at Ethan. "That's not a thing—fang root canals."

He smiled. "It's not, no. But it makes a very good metaphor. And it made you smile."

"Aw," Mallory said. "That's so cute. Work on boosting each other's moods, because you probably shouldn't kill Morgan in frustration. Navarre has enough problems at the moment without adding vampiricide."

She reached out, hugged me before I could stop her. "I'm really, really sorry about what happened."

"It wasn't your fault," I assured her, but the hug—the breach of my personal bubble, even if it would normally have been fine—still lifted a clammy sweat at the back of my neck.

Another score for Balthasar.

They left us alone, but the apartments were still crowded with emotion, with memories, with the repercussions of what Balthasar had done.

Ethan's fury had faded, replaced by grief. "I am so sorry this happened. I wouldn't have had you know him, Merit. Not like this, not ever like this, or any other way."

"I know."

"There is such childishness in his narcissism."

I nodded. "If you don't play the way he wants," I suggested, following the logic, "he'll destroy your toys."

"That is, and was, Balthasar to a tee."

"The attack really sucked," I said. "But I think there was one benefit."

Ethan's brow furrowed. "What's that?"

"He's told us what he wants—drama. He thrives on it. Feeds from it. And he wants more of it. He wants the House, Ethan, and he wants revenge. He'll expect you to confront him about this—about me. To find him, give him your time and attention, fight him. You shouldn't do that. Not yet."

Ethan's eyes narrowed savagely. "And why, precisely, shouldn't I? Why shouldn't I find him and rip every limb from his body? Why shouldn't I leave him for the sun to find, scatter his ashes, and salt the earth behind him?"

"Because that's what he wants."

"I doubt that."

"Well, not the earth-salting or limb-ripping, but the theater. He wants you to come after him. He wants to, I don't know, feast on your outrage. So don't feed him. Don't give him the satisfaction—at least, not on his terms." I paused, considered. "Like you said before, we'll draw him out. We'll give him an audience, but in a setting we control and manage."

Ethan tilted his head. "What setting? We've essentially ruled out disavowal."

"I don't know," I admitted. "I'll have to think about that. But if we do something big, I promise you he'll show up and cause trouble."

"And force our hand."

I nodded fiercely. "Exactly that. We'll write the story," I said. "And he'll write the end."

He let me shower, get dressed in my traditional black Cadogan suit. I paired my suit with a tank that matched the blue-gray of my eyes. Ethan had paired a perfectly fitted jacket and trousers with a white button-down, the top button open and revealing his glinting Cadogan medal. We'd both donned our professional best, a good thing since we were due at Navarre House—and the twilight drama had already made us late.

"You don't have to go," Ethan said as I checked the blade of my katana, slid it home again.

"Not after what you've been through. I've already sent Malik over to get started on the books—and I sent Juliet with him as a precaution. He'll be better with the numbers than either of us."

As much as I appreciated having an excuse to avoid bookending a visit from Balthasar with a visit to Morgan, locking myself in the House wasn't going to do either of us any good. For one, I couldn't just chill out there. I'd be pacing the halls, worrying about Ethan because Balthasar was out there. And avoiding Morgan would only make me feel more cowardly.

"Thank you, but I should go. I'll feel better if I have something to do. Something else to think about." Someone else's drama to focus on.

"I called Luc," Ethan said. "I didn't give Luc all the details about the attack, but told him enough so that he'll be prepared. Guards were posted at the condo all night; he didn't return."

"He'll have to find somewhere to bed down and stay out of the sun," I pointed out.

Ethan nodded. "Luc's going to contact the rental company, see what he can find out. Or have Kelley do it." He paused. "I don't want you alone. Not when he could get to you."

"Okay."

He clearly expected a fight, looked shocked and suspicious that I wasn't arguing.

"I don't have any desire to be alone with him. But I can't ask Jonah right now."

"Then I'll be with you."

"You have a House to manage. And a vampire congress to build. You're a fanged founding father. You don't have time to babysit me."

His eyes flashed hot. "You're my future wife and the mother of my future child. I will well protect you against any threat, living, dead, or undead, just as I promised in my oath to this House."

The reminder of marriage and children set an entirely different set of nerves on edge. Gabriel Keene, the leader of Jeff's Pack, had prophesied a vampire child was in our future. And since no vampire child had ever been carried to term, that was a Very Big Deal for vampires, and for Ethan.

"I don't want to play into his hand," I said. "Or give him an opportunity to get to you because you're sticking too closely to me."

"Do I seem like the type of man who forces others to take my hits, handle my battles for me?"

"Of course not. But things are what they are."

"Things are what they are," he agreed. "But Balthasar will not stand between us." Silence fell. "We could be married."

My heart galloped. "What?"

"Like Catcher and Mallory. We could be married. Now. Quickly. For the practicality."

My heart sank at the phrase. "For the practicality."

Oblivious to my tone, Ethan nodded. "He is an old vampire with old values, however fresh his memories. As it stands, he'll see you as a Consort." He frowned, as if choosing his words carefully. "You declined the position quickly enough that we didn't discuss it, but it is—was—not entirely dishonorable. A Consort has power, prestige, the ear of his or her Master. She can choose those with whom she consorts; the power is hers. If he believes you stand as Consort now, he may believe you can be swayed."

"Even while I sleep," I suggested, and Ethan nodded.

"Giving you my name, securing our relationship, would give you security. Safety. Day or night."

I knew Ethan had planned to propose; he'd made that clear enough. That proposal would have been for love, for companionship, for me. But tonight, he looked so earnest. So practical. And that was too much a reminder of Mallory's situation.

I appreciated the sentiment, and his obvious concern for my welfare. But his offering a marriage of convenience wasn't my ideal proposal. I'd been imagining him on his knees in a tux with a book of Byron's poetry and a ring box, reciting the first stanza of "She Walks in Beauty" while his green eyes glinted in the moonlight.

It might have been fantasy, but it was *my* fantasy, and I preferred it to cold practicalities.

I shook my head, glanced up at Ethan. "As flattered as I am that you'd offer me your name to protect me, I don't want our lifetime together to start like this."

A corner of his mouth lifted. "At least you appear to acknowledge we will have a lifetime together."

"One step at a time," I said in a warning tone.

"All right, Sentinel. I'm not going anywhere. Nor, I believe, are you. And if you need a proposal with candlelight and poetry, probably one of the Romantics, so be it."

When my eyes widened at the reference, he smiled.

"I told you that I pay attention, Merit. I always have."

---------•→ ⇥⬧⬧⇤ ←•---------

CHAPTER THIRTEEN

SUIVRE L'ARGENT

W e'd reached a personal accord, but Ethan was still silent as Brody drove us north to Gold Coast and Navarre House, where another round of drama awaited us.

The silence wasn't all because of me, or Balthasar. Ethan had left a cadre of unhappy supplicants in the Cadogan lobby, men and women whose problems he once again wouldn't have time to address because we had other vampires to protect. Most of those waiting had accepted his apologies with grim resignation. A few had grumbled under their breath about his obligations, how he'd forgotten the vampires who got him where he was. (Since he hadn't been elected, and he didn't actually know these non-Cadogan vampires, I questioned the logic.) One had made a move toward him, tried to step toe-to-toe and blame Ethan for making things worse, for bringing new CPD attention to vampires, and causing them to constantly harass him.

He hadn't looked stable, and he certainly hadn't appreciated my stepping between him and Ethan. But we'd had to leave, so we'd dispatched Luc to make sure he was escorted off Cadogan property.

Nicole had warned me that dissolving the GP wouldn't solve our problems, but create new ones. Put a new and different kind of target on Ethan's back. As much as I hated to admit it, she'd been right. But we still had to try, and that meant handling one problem at a time.

Sometimes triage wasn't just the best you could do—it was the *only* thing you could do.

As if Ethan could sense my worrying, he reached out to touch me, to put his hand on my knee, and I hated that I flinched. It was instinct, a reaction to my attack, to the personal barriers that Balthasar had so obviously violated.

Ethan froze.

I'm sorry, I said silently. *I just . . . I need time.*

I could feel the wall rising between us. It was a wall Balthasar had prompted, and it was wholly unfair to both of us. But there it was. I needed time to regain my control, to feel that I was the one in charge of me, and not that someone else was running rampant inside my head.

He nodded sharply, seemed to battle between fury and hurt. *I'll give you time, as I always have. But he will not stand between us.*

I hoped he was right.

Despite the drama, we found Navarre House unchanged. It was still a beautiful dame of a building with a turret on the corner, pale stone on the exterior, and a view of Lake Michigan that even my father would have admired. Perfectly manicured boxwoods in terra-cotta pots were placed at intervals in the small strip of (also perfectly manicured) grass in front of the building, while hydrangeas that hadn't yet bloomed marked each corner of the building. Celina had undeniably good taste. But then, that was part of the problem.

"Katanas?" I asked, with a hand on the door.

Ethan looked at my scabbard, then his. "You've got your dagger?"

"In my boot."

He likely compared politics to risk. "I've got mine as well. Let's leave them in the car for now. Brody, stay close."

"I'm not going anywhere," he assured him.

We walked up the stairs and opened the front doors, found the interior also the same, with a pale, museumlike chill. Marble floors, spare furnishings, and the occasional bench or piece of artwork arranged and lit as if part of an exhibit. I couldn't help wondering how much the Circle had paid for Celina's carefully curated home. And how much her vampires would have to pay for that now.

The House's demilune reception desk, previously staffed by three brown-haired beauties, was manned tonight by three brawny men I pegged instantly as off-duty cops. They had the broad shoulders and flat eyes of men used to seeing all manner of inappropriate behavior. So Morgan had upgraded his security, but that might have been due to the last round of Navarre House dramatics: A killer had gained access to Navarre House a few months ago and killed two Navarre vampires.

The man in the middle looked up as we approached, scanned us. "Name and business?"

Ethan looked mildly irritated by the question, but answered, "Ethan Sullivan and Merit, Cadogan House. We're joining Malik, also of Cadogan House. We're here at the behest of Morgan Greer."

They looked duly unimpressed by the explanation and that the Master of Cadogan House was visiting. But that was the point of having cops at the security desk. No fangirling, and no famous vampires sneaking into Navarre House without permission.

"One moment," the middle guy said, then confabbed with his

colleagues, checked clipboards, surveyed lists. After a moment, he rolled his chair back to the middle position, pulled two Navarre House lanyards and security badges from a drawer, and pushed them and a clipboard across the counter. "Sign in."

Ethan looked up at him, opened his mouth to give what I guessed would be a dressing-down. I knew what he thought, because my thoughts were the same—that this was a power play by a Master who wanted to remind us he was in charge within his halls.

If Navarre's situation was as bad as we suspected, that hardly seemed to matter.

"I'll sign us in," I said, and scribbled our names on the clipboard, plucked up the lanyards, and handed one to Ethan.

"Someone will be out in a moment," the guard said, then picked up a handset and dialed up a number, whispered into the receiver.

By the time he put the phone down again, footsteps were clipping on marble toward us. Nadia, Navarre's Second and Morgan's paramour, emerged from a hallway.

She was gorgeous in an exotically European way, with generous features and golden brown hair. She wore slim-cut black pants, a flowy black top, and laser-cut high-heeled booties. And tonight she looked thinner, her cheekbones sharper, dark circles beneath her eyes, and a deep sadness still set there. Her sister, Katya, had been one of the murdered Navarre vampires. It appeared she was still in mourning.

"Nadia," Ethan said. "It's lovely to see you again, although I'm sorry the circumstances are what they are."

Nadia nodded but didn't say a word. She gestured us to follow her up the staircase that flowed to the first floor. The stairs were also marble, the handrails gleaming brass. And as beautiful as the House was, she was the only Navarre vampire we'd seen enjoying it. Maybe the others were locked in their rooms, lest the Circle should come calling.

We rounded a corner and walked down a hallway with marble floors and white walls covered in black strokes and slashes. Not graffiti, but woodcut prints blown up and reproduced on the wall. They were images of Navarre House through history, I realized, from an elaborate French chateau to the Gold Coast graystone. Had the Circle funded the artwork?

"In here," Nadia said, pausing by an open door. Ethan nodded at her, and I followed him inside. It was a large room dominated by a glass conference table with leather and chrome chairs. There were separate seating areas on both sides of the enormous room, and a wall of mirrors along one end.

I wasn't an expert on home décor, but living with Joshua Merit had taught me enough to know the furniture in this single room was probably worth tens of thousands of dollars.

I can no longer walk into a room in Navarre without assessing its cost, Ethan confessed.

Me, too. I suppose Morgan could always hold a tag sale if things got too bad.

Why would he sell tags?

I just shook my head.

Juliet stood in a corner near the door in full Cadogan black, a yellow katana scabbard belted at her waist. She nodded when we walked in, and Ethan did the same.

Morgan, Malik, and a woman I didn't recognize sat at the opposite end of the conference table, a laptop in front of each of them. Malik wore Cadogan black; Morgan wore a fitted blue-gray T-shirt and jeans.

The woman had a thick bob of wavy blond hair that hit two

inches above her shoulders and framed vividly blue eyes. Her skin was pale, her generous lips perfectly shaded with crimson. She'd paired a pale blue sweater with a capelet together with an ochre pencil skirt and deadly looking stilettos. She was effortlessly beautiful, the type of woman others seemed to hate, or at least envy. And she didn't look as though she'd much care either way.

I didn't know her, but Ethan seemed to, and he stiffened at the sight of her.

She and Malik stood; Morgan kept his seat at the head of the table.

"Ethan Sullivan and Merit," Morgan said. "This is my new Second, Irina. I don't know if you heard Nadia requested a different position after Katya's death."

"We hadn't heard," Ethan said. That was an important fact not to have made its way to Cadogan House, but Navarre was insular. Considering that it had also hidden its evidently thorough connection to the Circle, I shouldn't have been surprised.

From the tightness around Morgan's eyes, I wondered what else we hadn't heard about Nadia. Were she and Morgan on the outs, too? There certainly hadn't been any noticeable heat between them—or even acknowledgment—when she'd dropped us off. She hadn't even entered the room.

"Nice to see you again, Irina," Ethan said. "I'm sure you'll flourish in your new role."

Irina nodded regally, clearly certain she'd flourish.

"We've reviewed most of the basic debt and asset information," Morgan said. "Tried to give Malik a sense of the big picture."

Ethan nodded. "Are Will and Zane still in custody?"

"They are. The lawyers think a deal would be in their best

interest, and in the House's. I don't know how much leniency they'll get, circumstances being what they are."

Ethan nodded. "Has the Circle made a new demand?"

Morgan shook his head. "I'm not naive enough to think they'll let us off the hook when the attempt went south, so I assume they're formulating their next step."

Or it's already in play, I said, frustrated that Morgan didn't seem to have considered it. That was the most frustrating thing about him—he was wickedly intelligent, had a great sense of humor, and clearly was dedicated to his vampires. But something—perhaps all those years under Celina's tutelage—had blinded him to the ever-present dangers of life as a vampire. Perhaps Navarre vampires really had lived a charmed life until Celina's death. And maybe it was our experience with adversity—and the fear and paranoia it spawned—that kept us prepared.

"I don't think we need either of you right now," Morgan said. "I believe we have this under control."

It couldn't be called lack of cooperation, since Malik had a literal seat at the table. But it wasn't exactly collegial. It probably was, like the request that Ethan sign in at the front desk, a stretching of masterly muscle—especially in front of his new Second.

Not that animosity by Navarre vampires toward Cadogan was new. They'd typically imagined themselves better and more genteel than the rest of us. That prejudice, ironically, was due in part because Cadogan historically allowed drinking from humans or vampires. Like in many other Houses, Navarre's vampires only drank bagged or bottled blood. That was one of the reasons they felt superior to us, classier certainly, even if they were denying part of their biological heritage.

Whatever the reason, those prejudices, which should have been long past, seemed to be in full effect tonight. But Ethan was no wilting lily, and hardly the type to wither under Morgan's stare. Instead he kept his gaze on Morgan, let the silence build. I could only imagine the silent conversation he and Malik were having. Likely not suitable for children.

Morgan blinked first. "You can stay if you think it'd be helpful, but I'm sure Malik's skilled enough."

It was, apparently, enough of a retreat for Ethan. He smiled, slid that slow gaze to Malik.

"I believe I've got it covered," Malik said with an admirably straight face and smooth tone. "But I wouldn't mind taking a break before getting to the next round. Grabbing a bite to eat."

Ethan glanced at me, questioning eyebrow arched. *Have you infected him?*

You're hilarious, I said.

"Perhaps we could arrange for food?" Ethan offered. "We'd be happy to do so. Especially if you don't need us."

Morgan didn't miss the snark, and his voice was bland. "Fine by me."

"Any preferences?"

"None." Morgan didn't bother to ask Irina. Maybe they were also communicating silently.

"In that case, we'll get out of your hair."

Malik rose and pushed back his chair. "I'm going to step outside with my colleagues for a few minutes."

Irina didn't bother to respond but looked away in reprobation, as if it was bad form for him to leave, and despite the fact that he was doing a favor by being there at all.

I'd always liked Malik, but felt a new and fierce protectiveness. *I don't think she likes Malik,* I said silently. *How could anyone not like Malik?*

She doesn't like the rest of us, either, if that gives you comfort.

Then I look forward to that story.

We followed Malik toward the door. Juliet made no move to follow us but kept her eyes on Morgan and Irina. That, I suspected, was the result of a bit of silent direction from Ethan, in the hope of gathering casual intel from the Navarre vampires while we were away.

"Let's go outside," Malik said. "I could use some fresh air."

We stayed silent for the trip back down the stairs and, instead of walking toward the front of the House, snaked around behind them to a set of glass double doors that led to the House's garden.

The rectangle of neatly clipped grass was divided by a long and narrow granite stream that trickled as it stepped down across the courtyard. There was a row of boxwoods cut into perfect spheres along one long wall, the sticks and orbs of white allium growing between them. A row of bright green hostas, only just beginning to unfurl, lined the other. Rectangular benches of polished marble were placed at intervals through the neatly clipped grass, and a large, low deck of dark wood planks rose slightly over the grass on the garden's opposite end. The garden's design was careful and precise, but didn't look especially cozy. It wasn't a place for barbecues or romantic walks. But it did seem weirdly appropriate for a frank accounting discussion.

We walked to the middle of the courtyard, away from as many prying ears as possible. Unable to resist, I reached down and skimmed fingers over soft, thick grass, comforted by the confirmation that spring was on its way.

When I rose again, Malik's eyes were on me, concern tightening the corners of his eyes. "You're all right?"

Luc must have called him. I nodded, but the mere fact of his asking was nearly enough to move me to tears again. "I'm okay."

"The attack was psychic?"

Ethan nodded.

Malik's eyebrows lifted with interest. "Does that match your memories of him?" he asked Ethan.

"I knew him as 'strong,' sometimes frighteningly so. And always with a sensual bent."

Malik nodded.

"Tell me about Navarre," Ethan said.

"I've only reviewed the first layer, but it's bad enough. Celina did no favors for the House; Navarre and the Circle are entwined as intimately as lovers."

"So not just debts?"

"Not just," Malik said. "The House certainly owes money, including several large promissory notes. As Morgan suggested, Celina was not well accustomed to thrift. She had excellent taste, and liked to dabble in the finer things. She got some return on her investment—she purchased some art and antiques that have retained their value—but much was spent on consumables. Clothing. Shoes. A very well-stocked wine cellar. We're still determining the full scope. Celina and Carlos are both dead, and she apparently didn't confide in anyone else about her arrangements."

"The Circle just kept giving her the money?" I asked.

"Considering the interest rates we've seen so far," Malik said darkly, "it was a good strategy for them."

I couldn't argue with that.

"And beyond the debt?" Ethan asked.

"She gave limited powers of attorney over several of the House's investments and bank accounts to a variety of questionable corporate entities, and put some House properties in trust for the benefit of others. I'd bet all of them are connected to the Circle."

"Can you get the list of companies to Mr. Merit? Perhaps the CPD can use them to ID the Circle's members."

"Of course. But I expect linking them will be difficult." Malik rubbed the back of his head. It wasn't even his House, but his concern was obvious. "They look like anonymous LLCs—limited liability companies—and the names are all random three-letter acronyms. FAH, GLR, OMQ, that kind of thing. You take that much care to set up bogus LLCs, you're probably pretty good at laundering the money that comes out of them. It would take time to unravel."

Ethan nodded. "We'll leave that to the CPD."

"How long has this been going on?" I asked.

"She began incurring the debts approximately seven years ago—or that's the earliest we've seen so far."

"Before she outed vampires," I realized, and Malik nodded.

"She was fairly social, as you know. Morgan has suggested she might have made a connection to the Circle that way, through some social engagement or other. The Circle would have known much about the House's operation—and probably about the existence of vampires well before she announced it to the rest of the city."

We considered that silently. "Is that why she outed us?" I wondered. "Because the Circle forced her hand? Blackmail, maybe?"

Ethan whistled. "This keeps getting better. Riddle me this," he said. "If the Circle's so worried about King, why haven't they made contact again with Navarre?"

"And why haven't they skipped asking altogether and just taken the properties and investments they apparently have an interest in?" I asked.

"Both are excellent questions," Ethan said, then glanced back at Malik. "And another one: Since when is Irina Second?"

"Since Nadia resigned two weeks ago. That's all I know."

"You were going to tell me about Irina," I reminded him.

"She was one of Celina's very close friends," Malik said. "Many thought she'd be appointed Celina's Second after Carlos. When Morgan got the job instead, there was dissention in the ranks. Those who supported Irina were vocal about their belief Morgan got the position because he and Celina were sleeping together."

I'd suspected Celina's and Morgan's relationship had been intimate, but I hadn't known his promotion to Second had been controversial.

"So that group was probably especially pissed when he got the House," I guessed.

"They were," Malik said. "The faction only strengthened—because now they had something specific to be pissed about, particularly when he appointed Nadia as his Second."

"She didn't have a position in the House before that," Ethan explained. "She was Russian, had protected her sister during the revolution. She was fearless. She was not a bad pick for Second, but nor was she the most connected to the pro-Celina contingent."

"So now he's appointed Irina to keep that contingent happy," I suggested, and paused to consider Morgan's difficult history as Master. He'd had the Circle to contend with, and now I realized he had also been trying to prevent Celina's supporters from revolting.

"What a mess," I said.

"It is," Malik agreed. "And given the faction's love of Celina, I'd strongly suspect no one has any idea how bad things truly are. And we're only through the surface layers."

My stomach picked that moment to grumble, and I squinted with mild embarrassment.

"Let's not delay the inevitable," Ethan said. "We'll get some food. Keep at it," he said to Malik. "Don't hesitate to call if any problems arise."

"Let us hope it doesn't," Malik said.

For vampires, hope literally sprang eternal.

———— ❦ ————

CHAPTER FOURTEEN

SHE BECKONS

We trekked back to the first floor, handed back our guest passes, and signed out again. The guards were no more enthused by our exit than they had been by our entrance.

"Glum dudes," I said quietly as we pushed open the heavy door and walked outside.

"Would you want that job?"

"Excellent point, and no."

The mood between us was lighter now, perhaps buoyed by the reminder that ours wasn't the only House with troubles. I knew denial wasn't going to improve my comfort level, not really, but for the moment—and with Ethan at my side—I was happy to pretend Balthasar was merely a memory from Ethan's past.

"Did you have a place in mind for food?" I asked when we reached the sidewalk that ran in front of the House.

Ethan glanced left, right, at me. "Actually, I thought I'd let you follow your nose."

"That's very nearly insulting."

"You don't think you can sniff out the best restaurant in Gold Coast?"

I probably could, but that didn't make the question any less insulting. "I'm not a bloodhound. But pizza sounds good."

A corner of his mouth lifted. "And in this neighborhood?"

"Lou Malnati's, Gino's East, Birbiglia's." Three more possibilities sprang to mind, but I stopped offering them when I realized I was only helping his argument. "Those are from memory. Not scent."

Ethan chuckled. "Which way, Sherlock?"

"I'd suggest you go to hell, but if you mean pizza, we should go left. You think it's safe?"

"Rarely," he said grimly. "But I think it's unlikely Balthasar would have followed us here, plans to attack us as we walk down the street for pizza."

"Not enough ceremony," I said, following the train of thought, and he nodded.

"Precisely."

So we set off down the quiet street in the warm spring air. He'd normally have taken my hand, or put his long fingers at the small of my back to remind me he was there, or to remind others I was taken. I didn't mind the machismo, but either he could tell I still needed space, or he was still stinging from my last physical rebuke.

I couldn't think about that, I told myself. Had to worry about my own needs, had to take care of myself. And hopefully, when all was said and done—and all *would* be said and done—we could find each other again.

Six blocks later, we stood in front of Two Brothers' Pizza, a new-to-me shop squeezed in a small commercial chunk of the neighborhood between a coffee shop and luxe real estate agency.

Two gold pots stood beside the door, each holding tropical flowers that looked decidedly genital—a white-cupped petal with blushes of pink in the center, and a large protruding stamen right in the middle.

I snickered like a fourteen-year-old boy.

"Interesting décor," Ethan said, glancing through the window.

The restaurant was entirely white—white tile floor and walls, white stone bar, white leather bar stools on spindly brass legs. Even the liquor had been poured into white bottles. A giant chalkboard hung behind the bar, a list of apparent possible pizza toppings written in pretty chalk script.

"Intriguing," Ethan said, scanning the list.

"I don't know. I just don't really see carrots on pizza. Or radishes." I had an unpleasant memory of Catcher eating "shepherd's pie" pizza covered in mashed potatoes, peas, and meat. I wasn't exaggerating to say it was a felony against pizza, and the mere idea of it put me off vegetable toppings completely. If it wasn't meat or cheese, it had no business atop a pie.

"The vitamins are good for you."

"I'm immortal."

"Strong fangs," Ethan said, walking inside and stepping up to the counter.

Fortunately, he was willing to compromise. He'd try the triple meat I selected, and I'd try his beet, carrot, and mortadella concoction. Being the gentleman that he was, Ethan offered to carry the boxes back to Navarre House.

The night was beautiful—a light breeze, white clouds moving across the darkened sky, humans walking dogs or chatting with neighbors in the small, gated entryways that characterized the houses in the Gold Coast. It was a neighborhood of wealth, of luxury and relative safety. No turf wars, no abandoned lots, very little crime. Those who lived there were lucky, at least materially.

We were two blocks from Navarre when Ethan's phone beeped. He pulled it out and stopped short, his magic filling the air. Even the flavor of Ethan's fear and hatred for his maker was becoming recognizable.

"Where is he?" I asked, my stomach knotting with nerves.

He handed me the phone. Luc had messaged him a photograph—a grainy black-and-white of Balthasar standing on the sidewalk across the street from Cadogan, his coat billowing around his ankles as he stared at the House.

I handed Ethan the phone again, my buoyant mood suddenly deflated. "He's showing us that he can get to us. That he's here and he isn't leaving."

"And, as you mentioned, that he's waiting for my response." Ethan looked at the phone, which beeped as more messages arrived. "He left an obvious trail, and Kelley and Tara are on him again."

"He wants to be found. Wants you to know where he is. Wants you to be able to find him." Dread settled low in my belly. "He'll try to find me again, Ethan. Try to get to me again while I sleep."

"Mallory and Catcher will figure something out. They won't let him get to you. I won't let him get to you."

I looked up at him, let him see the fear in my eyes. There wasn't much these nights that scared me, other than losing him or Grandpa or Mallory, or someone else I loved, but Balthasar had scared me, and badly.

There was nothing equivocal in his gaze, in the steadiness of his green eyes. "He was my nightmare, Merit. You are my miracle. He will not touch you again. Yes?"

When I nodded, he smiled.

"We have pizza, each other, and a very good accountant. Let's go back to Navarre House and get this job done."

Just another fun evening for the vampires of Cadogan House.

We turned the corner on Navarre's street, the hulking white building glowing beneath streetlights and spotlights in the careful landscape.

Nadia stood on the lawn talking to a tall and well-built man with ruddy skin and reddish hair that fell in tousled curls around his square face. He wore jeans and a bright yellow T-shirt beneath a bulky leather jacket.

I thought, at first, they were embracing. That Nadia had a new lover, and they were sharing a quiet moment on a spring night in Chicago outside the confines of her House. And when they hit the ground, I first thought they'd fallen into a sordid coupling there on the narrow strip of grass, and nearly at the feet of her former lover.

It took me precious seconds to realize they were fighting—grappling like MMA fighters in the final round of battle. Her legs were twined around his waist, and he'd pulled her arm at an awkward angle as she spat out phrases in quick, staccato Russian. I didn't recognize the words, but it didn't take a genius to figure them out—or that she needed help.

"Get away from her!" I yelled, and took off toward them. At the sound of my voice, the man looked up, spotted us, and stood. Then he pulled something from his jacket, which he pointed at Nadia.

"Stop!" Ethan called out, at the same time the man hit the trigger. And then the Taser's darts were in the air and Nadia's body was convulsing, jerking stiffly on the ground as she screamed in pain.

He'd Tased her, shot her with bolts of electric current and smiled like a psychopath as she writhed on the ground. His quarry addressed, he looked up at us, dropped the weapon, and bolted.

Take care of Nadia, I told Ethan silently, and hauled ass after her attacker.

I was fast, but shorter; his strides were longer, and he seemed to gain ground with each step.

He ran toward the lake, took a sharp right toward downtown when he reached inner Lake Shore Drive. For a moment, he disappeared from view, and my heart stuttered with fear that I'd lost him. I pushed for more speed, forcing my feet to move faster, lengthening my stride, trying to make up the distance between us.

I took the turn sharply, nearly barreled into a group of teenagers on skateboards, ignored their complaints as I scanned the street ahead of me for a sign of him, finally glimpsed his yellow T-shirt and red hair ahead of me.

Faster, I demanded. *Just a little faster.* I reached down deep for any bit of energy I could find, promised myself Mallocakes and deep dish for the effort. Exhaustion was irrelevant. The pounding of my feet in high-heeled boots—and that had been a mistake—was irrelevant. The only relevant thing was the man in front of me, the human who'd Tased a vampire in front of her House.

I didn't generally wish harm to humans. But if there was ever a time I could use the opportunity to beat someone senseless, this was it. After the beating, sure, I'd probably spend some time considering the ethics of my choices. But for now, there was only the anticipation of battle.

And the anticipation grew sharper, because he was human, and he was getting tired.

As North Lake Shore turned into Michigan, and condos became retail space, as shaded residential windows became plate glass designed to show off luxury handbags and watches, I gained ground. He glanced back once to check the distance between us, and I let my eyes silver and fangs descend.

The little bastard had the nerve to smile at me.

That was the first time I thought to really wonder who he was—and why he'd assaulted Navarre's former Second on Morgan's front porch.

Because he'd been sent by the Circle, I realized belatedly, ignoring the blare of a taxi as he dashed across Michigan and I followed. He was muscle, come to enforce the Circle's will, come to punish Navarre House for failing to take out King when they'd had the chance. Morgan said they'd threatened to take the House's assets; they'd clearly meant it, and intended to enforce that threat one vampire at a time. On the other hand, his timing had been appalling. He'd made the strike in front of two vampires, both of whom were trained fighters.

Regardless, if I could catch him, we'd have an actual, human link to the Circle.

Push, I demanded, and pumped my arms harder.

He reached the Hancock Building, its sharp gray glass ribboned in black, and turned toward the river again. I guessed his strategy—if he couldn't beat me in a straight-line race, he'd head into the buildings and alleys of Streeterville, try to lose me there.

He was twenty yards ahead of me. He passed a trash can, paused just long enough to push it over into my path. I vaulted it, landed smoothly again, and kept running.

"Try that again, asshole!" I yelled, ignoring the shouts of humans who jumped out of the way of our chase. Someone would inevitably call nine-one-one, probably while filming the damn thing. That was fine by me, as long as I got to him first.

Unfortunately, he turned and pulled a handgun. He'd been smart enough not to waste bullets on Nadia, probably thinking the Taser would be more effective. A single shot was highly unlikely to kill a vampire, but it sure wouldn't feel good.

He kept moving, slinging his arm behind him to get off shots. He fired twice, the bullets flying to my right and above my head. His aim wasn't great, but it was good enough to send me to the ground for cover while he dodged into an alley.

"Shit," I muttered, and climbed to my feet again, pulling the dagger from my boot and running toward the gap between buildings.

I crouched at the edge, trying to remember Luc's handgun training, which had been a pretty slim lesson compared to the blade work, and how many shots would have been in the magazine. Maybe seven, maybe ten, maybe fifteen, depending on the gun and whether he had extras.

Long story short, I'd be dodging bullets for a while.

I peeked around the corner, just long enough to see Ginger heading through the brick-lined alley toward the next street, and ducked back again as two bullets whizzed past me.

That was four, I thought. Not that counting them would give me any real indication of how much firepower he had left, but the act helped settle my nerves, at least enough to get me moving again.

I dove into the alley, let the first Dumpster take the brunt of three more bullets.

"You keep shooting at me," I yelled out, "and we won't be able to have a nice conversation about why you attacked that vampire."

"Why don't you bite me, bitch?"

"Sticks and stones!" I yelled back, and waited for sound. There were footsteps this time, but no bullets, so I glanced around, saw the coast was clear, and hauled ass to the end of the alley so I didn't lose him on the next street.

Squinting, I darted into sudden lights and people, as a stream of humans dumped out of the open doors of a ten-screen movie theater. I pushed between them, spied the red-haired perp dodging cars to cross the street, and took off after him.

A taxi honked as I dashed across in front of it, the driver swearing at me with a fist out the window.

"I'm chasing a murderer!" I yelled back, exaggerating a little, but hitting the truth close enough.

I made it across the street in one miraculous piece, raced across a concrete courtyard in front of a skyscraper that gleamed with blue and red lights. They cast a colorful glow across the ground, highlighted the runner as he dodged tourists and late-night workers, shoving them into one another to create obstacles for me.

He darted into a long, narrow park bound on both ends by circle drives. The southern circle dropped down to the river; the northern one dropped to lower Illinois Street.

He ran to the southern end of the park, turned back to me, grabbed his crotch. "Why don't you come and get this?"

What a class act.

"Because I've seen bigger," I said dryly, stepping onto grass still soft from the winter snowmelt and walking toward him. I spun the dagger in my hand, watched his eyes widen as it caught the light. "But I know how to get dirty if that's what you want."

"Oh, I bet you do."

"Who do you work for?"

"Fuck you." His tone was as mean as his gaze. He didn't know me or anything about me, but I was his enemy, and he didn't care if I lived or died.

"Not in a million years. Do you work for the Circle?"

"You think it'll be that easy?"

I shrugged casually. "I'm pretty sure I just chased you across Streeterville and managed to keep up."

I flipped the dagger rhythmically through my fingers as casually as I might have scratched an itch, watching him, waiting for a lean or movement that would signal his next move.

"Not bad for a girl."

"That's what the last guy said—right before I kicked his ass." I beckoned him forward, dipped my chin, smiled thinly. "If you're so manly, come and get me."

Sirens began to wail nearby. Someone had called the cops; I could only hope Ethan had managed to contact my grandfather, ask him to intercept. It wouldn't do to have vampires arrested tonight, too.

Ginger didn't want any part of cops. He feinted left, then barreled forward. But I'd been distracted by the sirens, caught the fake too late, shifted my weight too slowly. I jumped for him, extending my body, managed to grab his legs and bring him down. He kicked out, boot connecting with my cheekbone and sending a bolt of bright pain across my face. He jumped up and took off again.

I blinked back tears, but without pausing to think, relied on muscle memory and flipped my dagger toward him.

It connected, lodging in the back of his thigh. He cursed feverishly and hit the concrete on his knees, then yanked the blade out and tossed it away. Gaze narrowed, spittle at the corners of his mouth, he rose again, limping as he vaulted down the stairs to the road below.

"Damn it," I muttered. A jackhammer pounding in my skull, I

jumped to my feet and started for him, pain jolting through my head each time I made contact with the ground, and ran toward the small wall that overlooked the street below.

He was taking the stairs at a gallop, nearly to the ground.

There was no time to hesitate. I put a hand on the rail and vaulted over it.

The ground disappeared beneath me; for a moment, I was airborne. For whatever chemical or physical reason, gravity was more forgiving for vampires, so the jump from the upper street to the lower felt more like one big step than a twenty-foot leap.

I hit the middle of the street in a crouch, horns blaring deafeningly as an eastbound CTA bus roared toward me. I rolled out of the way, hair whipping around as the bus barreled past, four inches from my face, forcing the breath right out of me.

"Crap on toast," I said, sucking in air before kicking up my legs and vaulting to my feet again.

I dodged the next car for the sidewalk, scanned the street both directions.

He was gone.

I cursed but set off at a jog, peering into the windows of a bodega, a fast food restaurant, and the fancy lobby of a fancier skyscraper, hoping he'd ducked inside to wait for me to give up, and I'd catch a glimpse of red hair in a corner behind a pop machine or a potted plant. But there was nothing.

This apparently being the CTA hub of Streeterville, a second bus sped past me, this one heading north. I glanced up. There, in the back left window, was Ginger, middle finger raised.

The bus turned and disappeared, taking him with it.

I stared, openmouthed, at the empty street for a full minute before pulling out my phone, sending Ethan and Catcher the information, hoping they'd be able to intercept the vehicle and give us back our lead. Because I was going to feel pretty crappy if I'd managed to let him, our only connection to the Circle, get away from me.

I cursed again, circled back to grab my dagger off the ground. I opted not to wipe off the blood, thinking the CPD might be able to process it for DNA, and tried to carefully conceal it inside my jacket. Uniforms would be circling soon, if they weren't already, to track down the source of the gunfire—uniforms who probably didn't know me or my grandfather. No point in exacerbating the situation with a visible and bloody blade.

There were still cabs to be had, but I decided to walk back to Navarre and steam off some of my irritation.

"Halfway across downtown Chicago and he hops a motherloving bus," I muttered to the horror of a human couple who walked past as I turned back onto Michigan. At least they'd head back to Eau Claire with a good story.

Foot and car traffic lightened as I moved north, the streets quieting as I hit the Gold Coast again. Humans done with the day's work enjoyed walks in the warm spring night, heading to a late dinner, to the river for a boat ride, or to the lake for a boat tour of the skyline.

What if I had that kind of life now? What if life became peaceful for Cadogan, and Ethan and I could settle down and become domesticated vampires, with a library full of books, a House of Novitiates, and possibly a child? After all the battles, the terror, the injuries, the grief, would we enjoy that life without drama? Hell, Balthasar was even older than Ethan, and he still wasn't ready to settle down.

Since there was no end in sight to the current drama, the questions were purely rhetorical. But someday they might be. Could I go back to that quiet life—what Ethan had once called my small life—and be happy again?

As I turned toward Navarre House, I saw the city's three Masters—Ethan, Morgan, and Scott—in front of Navarre House with Jonah, and my grandfather the Ombudsman's van parked in front.

Yeah, I thought, and walked back into angst, political and otherwise. I could probably deal with a quieter life. As long as I got to keep my katana.

CHAPTER FIFTEEN

━━━━◆◇◆━━━━

A VAN DOWN BY THE RIVER

G rey House had an amenity for sports of all kinds and varieties, and its heavily male population, including Scott Grey, looked the part. He was tall and broad-shouldered, with short dark hair and a matching soul patch beneath his bottom lip. Jonah, tall and auburn-haired, with generous lips and knife-edge cheekbones, stood beside him. They both wore jeans and Cubs T-shirts in lieu of the Grey House jerseys Scott had favored over medals.

Jonah glanced at me, nodded a silent greeting. There was a hint of sadness in his blue eyes, disappointment, probably, that we were still on the outs. Or maybe that I hadn't yet given in to the RG's demands.

I was sad, too. He was my partner, and he'd become an important part of my life—and dealing with the drama vampires in Chicago seemed to frequently face. But what could I do? I was certain I could help the RG without sacrificing my relationship with Ethan. Love hadn't taken my honor. But since I wouldn't concede that love could make me blind or stupid, I supposed we were at a standstill.

"You appear to have injured yourself, Sentinel," Ethan said, his gaze on the tender spot beneath my eye.

"He kicked me in the face, so I stabbed him. Is it bruised?"

He angled me for better lighting, frowned at my face. "It's swollen and purpling but doesn't look broken. You should heal. You're all right otherwise?"

"I'm fine. How's Nadia? And Malik and Juliet?"

"Nadia's resting," Morgan said.

"And Malik and Juliet are in the House with Irina," Ethan said. "We thought it best for them to keep untangling the knot, such as it is."

I nodded.

"The perp ran?" Scott prompted.

I nodded. "Down Michigan, into Streeterville. He pulled a gun and used it," I said, glancing at my grandfather. "I can give you the details of the route if you want the bullets for forensics. And there's this," I added, sliding the dagger from my sleeve, and extended it with two fingers to my grandfather.

"Blood?" he asked, scanning me for injuries.

"His, if you've got an evidence bag."

He nodded, pulled a plastic baggie from the pocket of his jacket. "Just in case," he said with a light smile, and opened it so I could slip the knife inside. Then he closed it, sealed it, wrote the information on the outside with a felt-tip pen he'd pulled from the other pocket.

"Any word on the bus?" I asked.

"Uniforms stopped it," my grandfather said. "He wasn't on it."

I dropped my head back, squeezed my eyes shut. He'd

been my responsibility—a responsibility I'd taken on—and I'd blown it.

Sentinel, Ethan said silently, in a tone meant to comfort. But it didn't help. Not this time, when I'd been so close to such a good lead. *No one is questioning your efforts.*

I am. I'm questioning the hell out of them.

"I'm sorry," I said to Morgan, lifting my head again. "I was so close, and then he moved onto one of the lower streets. I followed him down, but I didn't realize he'd hopped the bus until it was moving."

Morgan just nodded.

"He wouldn't have gotten far," my grandfather said. "The uniforms are canvassing in case there's any sight of him."

"There won't be," I said. "He didn't want anything to do with the sirens. And he wouldn't confirm he was with the Circle, but I presume that's what we're thinking?"

"That's the logical conclusion," my grandfather said.

"Why would they hurt Nadia?" Morgan said. "She had nothing to do with this. Nothing at all. They should have come after me."

"Because it isn't money they're after," my grandfather said.

Which meant Morgan was going to have to figure out a way to satisfy them, or hope the CPD could bring down an enormous criminal enterprise before they got to anyone else. Neither of those options sounded especially easy.

"When we have all the information," Ethan said, "we'll chart a course."

Morgan nodded but didn't look at all convinced.

"I'm going to get this to Jeff," my grandfather said into the intervening silence, lifting the evidence bag, then glancing at me. "Walk with me?"

I nodded, fell into step beside him as we walked slowly across the grass, at his pace, toward the van.

"Did I ever tell you about the Moody case?"

"I don't think so."

"Darryl Lee Moody had a very bad habit of stealing cars. Twenty-three before anyone identified him. Twenty-seven before anyone found him. I was twenty-eight years old, had just gotten my detective's shield. I wanted to prove myself, did some investigating, found a man who knew a man, and was able to locate his shop. I scoped it out, realized he was the only one in there—and with two cars. If I waited for backup, he'd have disappeared. I knew that in my gut. So I went in, gun blazing, all by my lonesome. It did not, let's say, go well."

"What happened?"

"General Tso's chicken," he said, each word heavy as it dropped from his lips. "Moody had just ordered dinner, and the delivery arrived five seconds after I'd walked in. Kid was nineteen years old, walked in to find his customer being held at gunpoint by a cop."

"Yikes."

My grandfather nodded. "Moody grabbed the kid, used him as a shield to get out of the room. He didn't hurt him, thankfully, but Moody was gone by the time I made it outside, made sure the kid was safe."

"Did you find him again?"

"I didn't—not in so many words, anyway. Four months went by without a single sign of him. And then, one night, I pulled over a car for running a red light. Darryl was behind the wheel."

"I doubt I'll get that lucky."

My grandfather chuckled, turned to me, and smiled. "Maybe, maybe not. The point of the story, Merit, is that not every op is successful, even if you tried your best. Sometimes there's General Tso's chicken."

"And it is infuriating. Delicious, but infuriating."

"So it is. You're a perfectionist, just like your father."

I humphed.

"I know you don't care for the comparison, but it's the truth, baby girl. You've both worked very hard to craft your particular worlds. You, with school, ballet, now Cadogan House. Your father with, well, every other house. You won't succeed every time. But if you're lucky, and you work hard enough, you'll come out on top more often than not."

We reached the van, and he stepped carefully down from the curb to the road, knocked on the back door twice. After a moment it swung open, revealing Jeff and Catcher in matching red Ombudsman T-shirts and khaki shorts. Jeff had opened the door with a grin; Catcher sat at one of the very swank van's computer stations, eyes tracking across the black-and-white image currently on the monitor.

"You ran a good race," Catcher said, without looking at me.

"Did I?"

He clicked something, typed, clicked again. "Security cams say you did. You kept up with him, handled some shots and obstacles."

That actually brightened my evening quite a bit. Compliments from Catcher were few and far between, because he was at least as much a perfectionist as my father and I. Their rarity made them more meaningful.

"The jump was a nice touch, too," Jeff said, sitting down on his swiveling stool again. "But you might want to put a little more space between you and the bus next time."

"The bus?" Ethan asked, stepping behind me.

"I had plenty of room," I promised him, which was entirely true, if four inches counted as "plenty."

"I'm mapping the route," Catcher said to my grandfather, "so we can backtrack, pull any casings."

"Excellent," he said, then handed over the plastic bag to Jeff, who looked it over.

"You've also got some pretty good throwing skills," he said. "We caught that shot at the perp on camera."

Ethan's eyebrows lifted again. "Throwing skills."

"The dagger," I explained. "It was a lucky shot, and that's not false modesty. But it was kind of fun." I really was going to have to talk to Malik about knife throwing.

Jeff nodded, unlocked a small metal cabinet, and placed the knife inside. "Were you able to get a shot of his face from the cameras?"

"Eh," Catcher said. "I get motion, but not a lot of detail. You want to give me a summary, I'll add it to the APB."

"Six foot two or three, medium build. Muscular but lean. Red hair with some curl to it. Blue eyes. Pale skin. Human, and in good shape. Possibly not very experienced with supernaturals."

"Why do you say that?" my grandfather asked.

"He had a gun and a Taser, used the latter on Nadia, the gun on me. He was smart enough not to use the gun first—knew it wouldn't be entirely effective—but not experienced enough to use a blade or stake, which would have taken me out altogether."

My grandfather nodded. "Good observation. There's a task force on the Circle—they come together when new information arises—and we'll get the description to them, see if it rings any bells in the organization."

"Malik also has a list of organizations he's gleaned from his financial review," Ethan said. "He'll get them to you. He's confirmed the Circle's close financial ties to Navarre, but I think we can agree this has moved well beyond finances."

"He's already sent them," Catcher said, tapping another screen.

Curious, I hopped into the van and leaned behind Catcher to check the list. As Malik had said, the companies were strings of three seemingly random letters. None consisted of names or words, at least not in English.

"Yeah, those aren't exactly helpful," I said. "'The Circle, LLC' would have been better."

Catcher glanced at my grandfather. "What's the end game here?"

"King being a Circle rival is the most likely motivation for the Circle's hit on him. I suspect they wouldn't get a financial return on taking out Nadia, which makes this punishment, pure and simple. A direct hit on Navarre House, showing what they're able to do if Navarre doesn't pay up, or successfully carry out their next assignment."

"So they've got another project lined up," Catcher said.

"That would be my take. It might be another hit on King, might be something else entirely."

Ethan nodded. "They have to suspect Navarre can't simply write a check."

"Suggesting we'll have to wrap up the Circle first," Catcher said, "or someone's going to lose people."

"This is going to get worse before it gets better," I said.

My grandfather nodded. "That's quite possible." Concern tightened his expression when he looked at me. "Catcher filled me in on Balthasar. You're all right?"

The thought of it—the reminder of Balthasar—made my stomach twist. I didn't want any more reminders. And I didn't want him in my head.

"I'm fine. Frankly, it felt good to get out there just now, mix it up a little."

My grandfather nodded, looked back at Ethan. "You've had no sign of him tonight?"

Ethan pulled out his phone, checked it. "Not as of yet, although he made an appearance outside the House, apparently to remind us he could."

Everyone leaned forward as Ethan handed his phone around, showed them the grainy black-and-white of Balthasar.

"Tenacious, or crazy?" my grandfather asked, his tone somber.

"I'd suspect both," Ethan said, tucking the phone away again after it made the round. "He essentially admitted to Merit that he wants the House, believes it's his due."

"Because he made you?" my grandfather asked.

"And I left him."

My grandfather nodded, considered. "There any room there to draw him out? To force his hand?"

Ethan gave a smile, but there was nothing happy about it. It was pure predator, pure warrior, and very much vampire. "Your granddaughter has suggested there is. We'll speak with you—with all of you," he added, glancing at Catcher and Jeff, "when we're ready to move."

They all nodded, knights prepared to come to their lady's honor, and I felt my cheeks pinken with pride and a little bit of exhilaration. I was a capable warrior but didn't mind having a Master, a cop, a shifter, and a sorcerer in my corner.

Ethan looked at Catcher. "How's the ward coming along?"

"She's working on it," Catcher said flatly. "I obviously was called away."

"We're juggling resources," my grandfather said calmly, as if to avoid any argument between them. "And all doing the best we can under very unusual circumstances."

"I understand," Ethan said, his gaze on Catcher. "And your time is appreciated." It was as close to an apology between them as I expected they'd get. "For now, we'll get the Navarre vampires out of harm's way."

"You've got ideas?" my grandfather asked.

"I do. But I'll need to talk to Scott, Morgan."

My grandfather nodded. "Do that. We'll deal with the evidence, touch base with the CPD about the forensics." He smiled. "Nice that we can blame random violence and gunshots on someone other than a vampire for a change."

"Sad, but true," Ethan said. "Let's follow up with the Masters, Sentinel."

I nodded, and we said our good-byes and turned to walk back to the House.

"And how are you?" he asked. He moved to lift his hand to my back, but dropped it again, as if remembering my flinch. That sent a new wave of guilt through me, but I pushed it down. This wasn't the time for Balthasar.

"At the moment, frustrated. My grandfather gave me a pep talk, but I don't know that it helped. The perp could have given us a good lead about the Circle."

"He might have," Ethan agreed. "But more likely, he'd simply have refused to talk. The Circle does not continue to exist because its members snitch, and I'd surmise there are serious punishments for those who break the rules. Likely rewards for those who stay quiet. The CPD will have blood from the dagger, fingerprints from the Taser. That will likely give them as much as they might have gotten out of the man."

I nodded. "That helps. Thanks."

"Anytime, Sentinel."

I caught a glint of something in the grass, stopped, and glanced across the grass until I saw it again.

"What is it?" Ethan asked.

"Give me a second." I nudged it with the toe of my boot, then bent down. There in the grass, near the spot where Nadia and the man had fought, was a gold coin about the size of a nickel. Inscribed in the top was a circular symbol, a kind of ouroboros—a snake coiled in a circle, the tail in its mouth. In this case, there were three snakes composing the circle.

"It's a coin," I said, and handed it to Ethan.

"Chuck," he called out, after he'd looked it over, and my grandfather walked toward us.

"What've you got?"

Ethan handed him the coin, and my grandfather nodded. "The Circle's calling card," he said. "Your perp must have dropped it. And I believe that confirms the reason for this particular visit."

He pulled another evidence bag from his jacket pocket, dropped the coin inside. "Navarre's debt has come due, and it appears the Circle intends to collect."

We joined the vampires again, headed inside Navarre House to discuss the specifics of the response. This time, the House's lobby was stuffed with vampires in trendy clothing and obvious nerves, their magic peppering the air. Morgan waved us past the guards, who still watched us grimly as we passed, as if certain we were the cause of the trouble outside, instead of the ones who'd handled it.

Morgan passed them in silence as we followed him to the staircase, his Novitiates' gazes on the group of us as we moved, the city's Masters together. It was odd, I thought, that he didn't address his vampires. But if he wasn't going to talk to them, it certainly wasn't our job. I wasn't even sure how much they knew about the Circle, although Will's and Zane's absences and Nadia's attack should have at least tipped them off that something big was happening.

"What's going on out there?" a vampire called out. "We need some answers, Sire."

Morgan stopped on the staircase, hand on the banister, and turned back to look at them. We moved out of the way to give his vampires a look at him.

"Something happened here today," he said, his eyes dark and somber. "Something that was set in motion years ago. It is the result of many years of selfishness and superficiality and, yes, malfeasance. Of greed and short-term thinking. We are investigating the problem, and looking for a solution. That solution may not come today, but when it comes, it will undoubtedly require a change to the way in which we do things here." He looked around at the marble floors, careful lighting, expensive furnishings. "We may have to examine who we are and what we wish to be." His voice was soft, wistful, with a heady dose of regret in it.

After a moment, Morgan looked down at them again. "Stay in the House tonight. Don't leave, even with an escort."

There was an outpouring of argument, a volley of questions, a few arrows of accusation. Morgan stood there, took the brunt of it, and I caught Ethan's mild but curious glance.

What are you thinking? I asked him.

I'm wondering if he intends to sacrifice himself for her, and despite all that she's done to him, and to them.

I hoped it wouldn't come to that, that he wouldn't fall on his sword for a person so unworthy. But Celina's cult of personality was powerful, and if he thought Navarre needed to believe in her,

I wouldn't put it past him to sacrifice the king in order to save the queen. Vampire politics: chess with more fangs.

Morgan lifted his hands to get their attention, and even then it took several seconds for the noise to quiet. "I've issued my order, and I'll update you when I can. Until then, I expect you to behave like Navarre vampires."

With that, he turned and walked up the stairs.

Yet again, I didn't envy Morgan Greer.

Irina and Malik were still in the conference room when we arrived, laptops still open, although the pile of papers around them had grown since my last visit. Juliet still stood at parade rest in the corner, her gaze on the Seconds at their work.

As the Masters arranged themselves around the table, I glanced around the room, scoping out a drink cart or refrigerator. I was parched, and hadn't had a thing to drink since my running tour of Streeterville. I walked toward Irina, who looked as perfect as she had two hours ago, from her golden hair to her ruby lipstick. I could easily imagine her and Celina as friends or, since it was difficult to imagine Celina having true friends, as confidantes. She was light to Celina's dark, both of them fashion-forward and gorgeous.

Irina slid her gaze toward me as I approached, clearly unhappy about the interruption.

"Sorry to bother you, but could I get something to drink?" I asked her.

Irina gave me a full up-and-down appraisal before gesturing to the door. "The kitchen's down the hall."

I was apparently neither highly ranking enough nor Navarre enough to merit her going to any trouble.

"I'll take you," Juliet said quietly, moving near me and gesturing toward the door.

I didn't want to leave the room without Ethan's okay, so I waited until he made eye contact, nodded, then followed Juliet out the door again.

"She's a piece of work, isn't she?" I whispered as we walked down the hallway. It was empty, but magic and sound from the drama below still filled the air. Navarre's vampires were very, very unhappy.

"She's a hateful shrew." She gestured me to a room on the left with a swinging door. We walked inside, found a crew of white-clad chefs in an immaculate kitchen, every one of them wearing toques, preparing delicate dishes of food over long white counters. They stopped as we entered, watched us carefully as Juliet walked to a large, glass-doored refrigerator, grabbed two bottles of water.

"One for Ethan," she said, wholly ignoring the stares around her. She handed me one of the bottles and walked back through the gauntlet as if the room were empty, then out the swinging door again.

When it closed again behind us, she shook out her entire body. "Seriously, this place gives me the willies. They're just so *pretentious*."

"Yeah," I said, uncapping the water. "I get that." I stopped, took a hearty drink. "Can you imagine living here? Learning to be a vampire in this place?"

"It was her House," Juliet said, not saying Celina's name, just as we'd done with Balthasar. "Everything here, every one of them, has been touched by her. And not in a good way."

"Yeah," I agreed as we passed a framed line drawing of what

looked like a particularly unpleasant erotic coupling. "Not in a good way."

When we returned to the room, Ethan, Morgan, and Scott sat in the middle of the table. Jonah had joined Malik and Irina at the end. I gave the bottle to Ethan and took the seat beside him, across the table from Jonah. He looked at me, nodded, and I did the same.

"The Circle will come back again," Ethan said, beginning the grim conversation. "King is still alive, as is Nadia, and the debts are outstanding. Tonight is not the climax of the Circle's aggression toward Navarre. It is the beginning."

Scott nodded. "We believe it's best if the Navarre vampires go to safe houses."

Irina's response, at least, was quick and angry. "Navarre vampires will not be forced out of this House."

"Irina," Morgan warned, but she paid him no heed and lifted her chin defiantly.

"We won't go into hiding like cowards."

Morgan's eyes fired dangerously. "Navarre vampires will do as they're directed, as I deem best. In case you've forgotten, I stand Master of this House."

"If it weren't for your failure—"

He held up a hand. "I'm going to cut you off there. It's been a difficult night, and there are guests in our midst. Because of that, I'm going to ignore your tone."

"You should have protected this House."

"You know how this started, and why. Celina did this. She indebted us—and severely—to the mob. Do you understand that?" He gestured at the room around him, filled with expensive furniture and décor. "This, all of this, was bought with Navarre blood. And those debts, my dear, as Malik has undoubtedly informed you by now, have come due. That's why Nadia was injured. That's why they're here. Because of her mess."

Irina looked away. "The result could have been avoided with care."

"It couldn't have been avoided. She has destroyed us, Irina. She rammed the ship into the iceberg, and we're left to rearrange the chairs." He ran a hand through his hair. "Look around you. Look at what's happened, at what she has reduced us to. Be angry if you must, but don't be oblivious. Don't play coy when lives are at risk.

"And for right now, apologize to our guests. I also suggest you leave the room until you've regained your senses. Otherwise I can have you escorted out."

Magic burst into the room from both directions, filling the air. This was as awkward to watch as a couple fighting at a dinner party. And just as secretly entertaining. If the situation hadn't been so dire, and Irina's obnoxiousness so deplorable considering the circumstances, I'd have asked for popcorn.

Irina rose. "You should never have been her Second."

Morgan's smile was thin but grim. "It wasn't up to you to decide, but her. And since you're so eager to beatify her, I'd think you'd respect her decision. Regardless, she is not here, and we are. Your apology?"

"Your guests are responsible for her death."

That raised my hackles.

"You bring them here, flaunt them in our faces, as if they'll help us. Do you know what that does to us? To those of us whom she made?" She gestured at me, her hand flung wildly. "It feels like a betrayal."

"She made me, too. But that does not negate her bad acts. And that wasn't an apology."

Irina's eyes silvered and her fangs descended. She put a hand on the handle of her katana. She was ready to fight. And if the look in her eyes was any indication, she was aching for it. "I will not apologize to them, or to you."

The Masters stayed seated, but their bodies went on sudden alert. Sharper gazes, squarer shoulders, just in case action was necessary.

"You do not want to start a fight with me, Novitiate," Morgan said. And he didn't just use words to convince her. Glamour flowed through his words, through the room, streaming like water across a dry creek bed.

It overwhelmed me.

The sensation of fluid magic, of intrusive magic, raised a cold sweat on my arms, down my spine. I put my hands flat on the tabletop, trying to focus on the cold of the glass to distract me from the memory of Balthasar. I tried to breathe through pursed lips, slowly in and out, just as Ethan had shown me.

The magic wasn't even directed at me, but it affected me as if I'd been targeted by a maelstrom. Was this what my life would be like from now on? No longer immune to glamour, but unable to be in the same room with it, even if it wasn't directed at me? I'd be a magical creature that couldn't stand magic.

Just keep breathing, Sentinel. I'm right here.

I glanced up at Ethan, and his expression was utterly calm.

It's his magic. It moves—it feels like it's going right through me.

Your body is new to glamour, so you're sensitive to it. Be still and breathe, he said, his voice soothing even psychically. *You're feeling anxious, and it's normal. The distress will pass. I promise you that.*

I had to keep it together. Had to stay calm, had to hide this reaction. There were too many enemies around us, too many threats toward Ethan.

The others—, I began.

Can't tell you're fighting it, Ethan said. *You're doing fine. Keep breathing. And when we get back to the House, talk to Lindsey. She'll help you with techniques.*

I nodded infinitesimally, kept breathing. Watched as two vampires rushed into the room in black shirts and cargo pants, swords unsheathed.

"Sire," the guards said, hurrying to Irina with swords pointed, so it seemed we weren't about to witness a coup d'etat on top of the dissolution of the House's senior staff.

"She's threatened mutiny, insulted our guests, and refused to obey orders." He gestured vaguely at us. "They can verify if need be."

It occurred to me that Morgan had wanted us there—in the House, in the room—because he suspected, or hoped, Irina would cause a scene and he'd have to act. We were his witnesses. We could verify that she'd been disruptive, and that whatever punishment he doled out to her—and to Celina's faction—would be justified.

Maybe he was cannier than I'd given him credit for.

"Take her to her room. Stand guard until I get there."

Their hands on her arms, Irina nailed Morgan with a glare. "We'll take the House back, one way or the other."

"In that case," he said, "I look forward to the challenge."

I thought that was true. But I still wasn't certain he wanted to win it.

---◆◆◆---

CHAPTER SIXTEEN

BECAUSE THE NIGHT

I t was a full ten minutes before the room was clear and calm, before the magic dissipated like clouds after a deluge.

"I'm sorry you had to see that," Morgan said, at a bar tucked into a cabinet, where he'd poured himself two fingers of amber liquid, drained it in an equal number of drinks. That Irina had sent me out of the room for a bottle of water made me dislike her a little more.

"Are you?" Ethan asked. "Or are you glad you had witnesses?" He'd also apparently guessed it wasn't a coincidence Morgan picked that moment to bait Irina.

"Let's say both." Morgan came back to the table. "She wanted to air her grievances, and I wanted evidence of her insubordination. Two birds, one stone. And a House that's falling apart."

He sighed heavily. "I'm pretty well convinced she's the one who told Will about King, about what the Circle wanted us to do. He'd have seen King as an enemy to Chicago, and it probably wouldn't have taken much for her to convince him to act."

"You haven't questioned him yet?" Ethan asked.

"Oh, I questioned him," Morgan said, crossing an ankle over the opposite knee. "He wouldn't give her up. Played the dutiful soldier."

"You think he supports Irina's faction?"

"I don't know," Morgan said. "And I haven't yet decided how or whether to play that particular card with her. I'm not political," he added, throwing the word out as if it left a bad taste in his mouth.

Ethan let that pass. "We were discussing rehousing the Navarre vampires? We need to reduce the risk they'll be targeted, used by the Circle to punish the House, or you."

"We propose to divide them among the safe houses by blind lottery," Scott said. "They're the only ones who'll know where they're going. That reduces the likelihood they'll be found, targeted."

Morgan shook his head ruefully, tapped fingers on the table. "It will take time to get that arranged. We've got nearly one hundred and twenty in residence."

"We've got our Novitiate liaisons working together on it," Scott said. "Our hope is to arrange the housing and transportation tonight, possibly move a first group of vampires. The rest would go at dusk. We're now unfortunately skilled in the mass transport of vampires." Grey House had been targeted by vampire-hating firebombers, forcing the vampires to move. They'd sheltered temporarily at Cadogan before taking up residence in a high-rise.

He looked at Ethan. "We propose to handle the transportation. While Cadogan handles the Circle."

I wasn't sure how much "handling" we could do of the Circle, but Ethan nodded his agreement. "Acceptable terms."

"I don't see any way around it," Morgan said, looking briefly around the room, perhaps realizing that he had no Navarre vampires to commune with. His Second had mutinied, his captain and one of his guards were in custody, and there was apparently a faction of vampires eager to see him dethroned.

"And Morgan will come to Cadogan House," Ethan said.

Morgan looked torn between argument and praise. "Because?"

"Because you'll need to be involved in the negotiations."

"For what?"

"The Circle wants something from Navarre House," Ethan said. "They've decided they have a right to it. We determine what they want, and we figure out how to get it to them."

"And you don't think it will be money?" Morgan asked.

"We don't," Ethan said, then gestured at me, apparently willing to let me share my previous realization.

"Navarre has money," I said. "Even if not liquid, there are antiques, art, property. And the Circle has legal and accounting connections to the House."

Scott didn't react to that announcement, so Ethan must have filled him in. But Morgan scowled, probably irritated the House's dirty laundry was becoming ever-more public.

"If the Circle had wanted money," I continued, "they could have simply taken it. They'll want something else. Power or blood, or possibly both, like with Sanford King."

Ethan let heavy silence descend, then leaned forward in his chair. "Let's get your vampires safe. And then we'll deal with the Circle."

It was nearly two by the time we made it back to the House, but paparazzi still waited outside the door, supplicants in the foyer. A few of the faces looked familiar—vampires from the night before Ethan hadn't had a chance to get to.

One of the temp vampires manned the desk, and he smiled apologetically at Ethan. There was a silent pause while, I guessed, they communicated telepathically.

They've been waiting since we left, Ethan reported silently, and even his silent voice sounded tired. *I need to give them time. They have earned it.*

That gave me an idea, so I nodded. "Let me walk you to your office first."

I waited while he gave the temp instructions, held up a hand to his subjects. "Your patience is appreciated. I'm going to get organized, and you'll be escorted in."

Thank-yous sounded as we moved down the hallway.

The lights were on in Ethan's office. A cold bottle of water, condensation patterned along the sides, sat on a coaster on his desk, waiting for him.

"Bless you, Helen," he said, sitting down, uncapping the water, and taking a heady drink. When he was done, he held it out to me, but I shook my head.

"I'll grab something in a minute and go downstairs. But before I do that, I think I have an idea about Balthasar. About how to call him out."

"I'm listening, Sentinel."

"He wants an opportunity to show himself, show off his power. And I don't think he's the only one—the vampires outside, they come to you for help, for reassurance, for advocacy. They trust you as much as the vampires of your own House. But they haven't seen you formally Invested." I smiled cannily. "I think we need to fix that."

But Ethan frowned. "The AAM hasn't decided if there will be an Investiture."

"You're an AAM member, and you're all equal, according to Nicole. Tell Nicole it's important in Chicago to acknowledge the Master's new roles. Call it an Investiture, a coronation, a GP Independence Day celebration. Whatever the name, make it a very big deal—something the media outlets will pick up on. And don't tell Balthasar. But let him find out."

He raised his eyebrows. "Nicole might tell him directly."

"She probably will. And that will only tempt him further."

"You think he wouldn't be able to resist."

"You said earlier he'd want the ceremony, and I think you're right about that. The ceremony, the excitement, the media coverage. And this would be on our turf, with our players and our rules."

Ethan considered, then began to smile slowly.

I didn't care for that smile. "What?"

"You, Sentinel, are also the House's Social Chair."

My gaze flattened. "You gave me that position as a punishment."

"And it's still in place. I won't make you plan it," he assured me, and I relaxed incrementally. "But it's a good thought. I'll talk to Malik, Scott. If we can figure out the play, it might be worth the risk."

When my stomach growled again, I remembered our interrupted errand. "What happened to the pizza?"

"I tossed the boxes down when I went to help Nadia. They didn't survive the trip."

I didn't mourn the beets, but I nodded. "I'm going to grab something to eat, then head to the Ops Room."

"There are many irons in our fires," Ethan said, then glanced up at me. "Take care, Sentinel."

I promised I would, and left him to his supplicants.

The dining room was empty, but light seeped beneath the kitchen door, as it usually did. I peeked inside, found Margot in front of the stove, bouncing to Beyoncé. Definitely not the same atmosphere as the Navarre kitchen.

Margot was gorgeous, with a curvy figure and beautiful face, her seductive eyes accented by her bob of dark hair and bangs that fell to a point in the middle of her forehead. She wore a black chef's jacket over leopard leggings and the heavy rubber clogs chefs seemed to favor.

She looked up but kept swirling a small saucepan with the other. "Hey, Mer," she said, then frowned. "Looks like you got nailed pretty well."

I touched fingers gingerly to my cheekbone, which had dulled to an ache. "Is it still bruised?"

"It's a little purple, yeah. How's Navarre?"

It always surprised me when word of our off-campus shenanigans traveled, and I had no idea why. Vampires loved to gossip at least as much as humans, and since this particular gossip involved a vampire attack, Luc would have advised the House just as a precaution.

"At the moment, not great. Internal conflict, external conflict. It's kind of a mess."

"I ever tell you I applied there?"

I drew my gaze away from neat square tins of chopped vegetables at the station next to her stove to her face. "No. Before Cadogan?"

"Same time as. I wasn't sure which House I liked better—Cadogan was in my gut, but I had a friend in Navarre."

"And why'd you pick Cadogan?"

"I trusted Ethan more than I trusted Celina."

"Good instincts."

"No kidding, right? Ethan was—still is—very practical about vampirism, about being a Novitiate. Our responsibilities to the House, his responsibilities to us. Celina was more . . . I don't know. Particular. I mean, Ethan's particular in his own way, sure. But he's particular about things that matter. She was particular about our being vampires with a capital "V." Seeming, at all times, the best vampires in town. It was exhausting."

"Yeah. That's the vibe I got tonight. Lot of expectations about how to 'be' a vampire."

She nodded. "That hits it pretty well. What brings you by?"

"I know it's between meals, but could I grab something to eat?"

"Sure. Just a second while I get this where it needs to be." She swirled the pan for another moment or two, and when she decided it was done, she poured the contents—caramel-colored liquid—into a nearby glass dish.

"I'm browning butter," she said, then put the pan in the sink, walked to the fridge, and pulled out a small take-out container. "Ham and a very nice white cheese on baguette. Sides of Dijon and mayo, pickle, chips."

I took it from her, smiled. "You made me a to-go box?"

She closed the refrigerator again. "Ah. You must not know about Executive Order Two Hundred Eleven."

"What's that?"

"Basically, we're required to keep sack lunches ready for you. Ethan thinks you get hangry."

I was torn between irritation and admiration, as the order was both incredibly apt and utterly insulting. "That's ridiculous. I do not get hangry."

"Are you hangry now?"

I paused. "Maybe," I said with resignation.

She flicked a hand toward the box. "And there you go. Eat your regulatory sandwich and be happy about it. I threw in two chocolate chip cookies."

That was something anyway.

I was hungry/hangry enough that I didn't think company was a good idea. It also wasn't often I found myself with a few moments to sit quietly, so I sat in the dark cafeteria for a few quiet minutes, eating my take-out dinner with bottles of blood and water I'd grabbed from the cooler.

One wall of the cafeteria was composed of windows that looked out over the Cadogan grounds. The landscape lights were on, highlighting a group of trees just beginning to bud, tulips just beginning to blossom. I could see the yard's French fountain from there and, if I was quiet enough, could hear the gurgling water. While I ate, I kept my gaze on the sculpted yard, my mind on trickling water, on gently blowing limbs, on the fresh possibilities that spring would bring to Chicago.

By the time I'd finished my meal, my mind was quiet again, and my sense of perspective was restored. I cleaned up, walked toward the bright hallway, and prepared to enter chaos again.

The Ops Room was buzzing with activity and alert magic, as per usual. Temps sat at the computer stations and Luc sat at his desk, pulling a handful of popcorn from the tin as he stared at his laptop and tapped one key at a time with an index finger. Kelley and Juliet were at the conference table, working busily on laptops and tablets. Lindsey was gone, probably patrolling the grounds.

He glanced up when I walked in. "Ah, the prodigal Sentinel returns. Ethan upstairs?"

"Meeting with supplicants. They'd been waiting for him."

Luc nodded. "We hooked two up with your grandfather yesterday. Intersup conflict stuff that's out of our jurisdiction." He fixed his gaze on my cheek. "It looks like you had a very interesting evening. Internet confirms that."

I stopped. "What is that supposed to mean?"

"Kelley," he prompted with a grin, and Kelley, mouth pursed into a smile, filled the wall screen with videos of me chasing down our suspect.

"Son of a bitch," I murmured, although I did look pretty kick-ass running down the street in leathers, ponytail streaming behind me. My "Serious Vampire Warrior" face was fairly convincing.

On the other hand, "Did any of the assholes who had time to take these videos consider stopping the guy who'd just assaulted a vampire?"

"Evidently not," Luc said. "But they had ample time to contact the news channels and sell the footage."

I walked over and grabbed a handful of Luc's popcorn, leaning a hip on the edge of his desk while I munched. "Any word from the Ombuddies?"

"Yes. Jeff was able to run a photo search. On-screen," Luc ordered in his best Picard, pointing a finger at Kelley.

It wasn't an especially good Picard, so I gave Kelley a sympathetic look. "Has he been like this all night?"

"Unfortunately," she said, eyes on her tablet. "'Make it so' has made several appearances."

"Make it so!" Luc said again with verve and a very bad British accent. No matter how dire the world outside, we could count on Luc for a bit of levity.

The image popped up on-screen, a mug shot of the redhead, although his hair was shorter in the image and one eye bore an impressive shiner.

"Looks like an upstanding citizen. Who is he?"

"Name's Jude Maguire. Got a helluva sheet. B and E, assault, larceny. Mostly relatively petty stuff, but plenty of it. You stabbed a felon."

"What about his connection to the Circle?"

"The CPD's actually aware of it," Luc said. He grabbed another handful of popcorn, rose, and walked to stand by me. "He's muscle, enforcement. Not high enough to control the money. He's done four short raps already because he won't give up his compatriots. Won't snitch, and won't even take a deal. He does the time quietly, apparently earns a lot of respect because of it."

I nodded. "Muscle makes sense given the position he was in. It was right on the street, Luc. Dark, yeah, but there are plenty of streetlights in that part of Gold Coast, and he was right outside the House."

"Ballsy, which is the way you send a message to Navarre."

I nodded.

"CPD checked his usual haunts, but there's no sign of him. He'd been living with a girlfriend, hard-bitten woman according to Catcher, but she says she hasn't seen him in a couple of weeks."

"Bolted," Kelley said, and Luc nodded.

"Hiding out with the rest of the crew somewhere, but the CPD doesn't know where that spot is. Jeff's trolling the Net for any clues, information. The Circle hasn't contacted Navarre yet, but I can't imagine that's not coming soon based on what we've seen so far."

"How's the evac going?"

"Slow and steady. Grey's gotten surprisingly good at handling the logistics. Upside of someone firebombing your House, I guess. Last count, twenty-three percent of the House was out. They're pretty well spread out—the safe houses within city limits can't hold them all—but they'll have better security, at least."

"The Circle hasn't interrupted?"

"Not so far. Doesn't mean they won't, but they also probably didn't expect a response this quick or head-on. I don't give Morgan credit very often, but he's been overseeing the evac himself, making sure the vampires get out, and get out safely."

"It isn't over," I said. "Even if the Circle doesn't hit the vampires, or the safe houses now, they'll wait. They have no incentive to just let it go."

"Agreed," Luc said. "And we don't want to draw this out. The vampires will talk, and the safe houses won't be secure forever. We've got a limited amount of time while the Circle's playing catch-up to get ahead of them. When Morgan gets here, I expect we'll try to get him to ping the Circle. Get a demand, negotiate, something."

I nodded.

"And then there's Balthasar."

The mere sound of his name curdled my stomach, and the chocolate chip cookies currently residing there. "Has he shown up again?"

Luc shook his head. "No. Juliet's arranged for one of the human guards to call the real-estate office during business hours tomorrow. Like the Circle, he's spiraling around us, getting closer with each turn. He seems to enjoy the gamesmanship."

"That matches my experience."

Luc turned to me. "Anything in that experience you think would help us find him? You've had the most intimate discussion with him so far. And I'm sorry about that, by the way."

I shrugged awkwardly at the concern, nodded. "I'm not sure what I can tell you. When I 'woke up,' or whatever, we were in an old-fashioned room. No electricity, roughly built. Eighteenth century, maybe nineteenth." I closed my eyes and thought of the surroundings, the objects in the room. "Four-poster bed. Window. Candle. Small desk. There was an open notebook on it. Another small table."

"What kind of notebook? Any writing?"

I opened my eyes, gauged the size with my hands. "Maybe eight inches by fourteen? It looked old. The paper was yellow. There was handwriting in it, but the ink was faded."

Luc nodded. "Do some research on the room as you remember it. Maybe he picked that room for a reason, those objects. Maybe that notebook means something, and maybe we can use it to find him."

"Sure. I talked to Ethan about an idea to draw him out," I said, and told Luc about the possible Investiture ceremony.

"As ideas go, I don't hate it. Our people, our location, our terms. But there's no guarantee he'd show up."

I nodded. "We'd have to get someone friendly in the media—Nick, maybe—to do a story, build it up into something Balthasar and his ego won't want to miss. That's the core of him, Luc—his ego. Everything he does is to satisfy it."

"A narcissist and a psychopath."

"Yeah," I said.

Lindsey walked in, threw her leather jacket on the back of a chair. "The paparazzi can bite me, one at a time. You're on, babe," she said to Kelley, who grabbed an earpiece and headed for the door for her own round on patrol.

Luc's eyes lit at the sight of his significant other. "Trouble in paradise?"

"All news is bad news," she said. "Balthasar this, Navarre House that."

"Are you irritated they're being nosy," Luc asked with a grin, "or just irritated they aren't asking about you?"

Lindsey had once been featured as a vampire cover girl on a weekly gossip magazine, and she'd enjoyed the attention. "I don't have to respond to that. But possibly both." She looked at me, irritation morphing to concern. "You're all right?"

I nodded. "Cheek's sore, but I'll be fine. It's getting better already."

"Good." She patted my hand, and I didn't flinch, which sent a fresh wave of Ethan-related guilt through me. "What's new in here?" she asked.

"As it turns out," Luc said, "Balthasar this, Navarre that. Merit's going to consider the setting of Balthasar's attack, see if that gives us any clues. Why don't you coordinate with Jeff, see if there's any help you can provide about the Circle?"

Lindsey nodded.

"Actually," I said, "before you get started, could I talk to you for a minute?"

Brows lifted in curiosity, she nodded. "Sure."

She followed me into the hallway. I opened the training room's door enough to see that it was empty, then pushed it open and stepped inside, beckoning for her to follow. The ceiling was high, ringed by a balcony where vampires could watch sparring matches or training sessions. On the walls hung ancient weapons of war, and on the floor was a layer of tatami mats, ready for battle or practice.

"What's up, chica?" Lindsey asked, making sure the door was closed behind us again.

"It's about Balthasar. About last night. About glamour. I'm wondering if there's something you can teach me about fighting it off. If he does it again, I want to be ready. I don't want . . ."

I cut off the sentence when tears threatened and looked away, focusing on one of the ancient pikes hanging on the wall, the painted bands of color, the swag of leather strips and feathers at one end. When I thought my control was back again, I looked at Lindsey, found her expression soft and supportive.

"I don't want to get that close again," I said. "If it's happening in my head, I can stop him from coming in, right? Stop it from happening?"

"I can try," she said, then lowered herself to the floor and patted the mat across from her. "Tell me how it felt," she said as I sat down cross-legged in front of her. "Physically, I mean."

"Well, I was asleep, and then I was awake in this room." I gave her the same brief description I'd given Luc.

"I don't remember feeling any magic, not going in. I did feel magic coming out of it, like I was being pushed through a tunnel. I felt that same sensation when Balthasar glamoured me in Ethan's office. That tripped something, triggered some vampire sensibility. We think my immunity was actually a malfunction, that glamour is now affecting me the way it's supposed to."

Lindsey nodded. "Like when Celina kicked your ass and your senses fell into place."

It wasn't my finest moment as a fighter, but it was an important moment for me as a vampire. "Yeah, like that. I'm becoming a vampire in bits and damned pieces. And now, either because of what happened then or what happened in his room, or both, I'm extra sensitive to it. Morgan used glamour tonight, and I nearly lost it."

"I would really like to have a few choice words with Balthasar."

"You'd have to get in line. Ethan's first."

She nodded. "So, back to this particular instance, it's not that Balthasar was literally in your head, right? And you weren't actually in some other room. It's more like there's a"—she paused, clearly thinking of the right phrase—"joint psychic space. A psychic spot he's pulled you into."

I nodded. "I tried to put up walls—mental blocks. They didn't help much."

She nodded. "Unless you're an amazingly strong psych—top one percent—mental blocks aren't going to work against that kind of glamour."

"What if he tries to pull me into a joint psychic space again?"

"Well, first, you remember it's a metaphysical construct, not a real thing."

"But he hurt me. Slapped me and left a mark." The reminder made my cheek sing sympathetically.

"Psychic wounds have physical manifestations," she said. "Just because he connects with you psychically doesn't mean there's no physical effect. But remember—it's still glamour. He can't really force you into that psychic space—not physically anyway. But he'll try to convince you he can. That's what glamour's all about, after all. And second, if he gets you in there, you let it ride."

"I let it ride?"

She nodded. "Have you ever ridden a bus, and there's no seats left, so you have to try to stand up in the middle, hold on to one of those 'oh shit' straps?"

"Uh, sure," I said, just deciding to go along for the metaphorical ride.

"Well, to stay upright, you have to be fluid. If you lock your knees, you'll tip right over. But if you keep your legs loose"—she hopped to her feet, waved her arms snakishly—"you'll stay upright. You can't just ride the bus. You have to *ride* the bus."

"Okay."

"Glamour's like that. Your instinct will be to fight—to put up mental blocks. For most vampires, that won't work. You have to keep your knees loose and ride it out."

"Ride it out," I murmured, thinking suddenly of a late night last April, when I'd first met Celina. She'd tried to intimidate me, but I was still naive to her power, and I let her magic flow right around me. That had managed to piss her off, which made the effect doubly fun.

"I've kind of done that before," I said, and told her the story.

"But even then, casual magic didn't affect me this way. This is overwhelming, even the light stuff. Even the stuff not directed at me."

She nodded. "I think the strategy would still be the same. You're standing on the bus, or floating through waves, or whatever analogy you prefer. But you let it ride over you, flow past you. Let the magic move in and out, across you, without actually touching you."

"Lot of metaphors," I pointed out.

She grinned, chucked me on the shoulder. "You're the lit student."

"And you're a Yankees fan and the daughter of the pork king of Dubuque."

"All that and a bag of chips," she agreed, then jumped to her feet, and held out a hand to help me up, too.

"Thanks for the help."

"No worries. Least I can do since you held back my hair during my last psychic barfathon."

"I did do that," I agreed. "Listen," I said, toying the zipper on my jacket absently, "while we're here, can I ask you a personal question?"

"Is it about my sex life?"

"I will never ask you a question about your sex life."

"Fair enough. Carry on."

"It's about being called…" I paused, gathering my thoughts. "It really sucked, Lindsey. Balthasar was in my head, and there was nothing good or comforting about it. It was manipulation, pure and simple, and in the most fundamental way." I frowned. "I guess my question is this: If there are ways to fight it, why do any Novitiates let their Masters do it?"

She looked saddened by the question, which made me feel like a freak for having asked.

"Because immortality is a long time, Merit. Humans and empires will come and go in that time. Sorcerers and shifters will come and go," she added quietly, and I refused to think about the implications of that statement. I refused to consider the possibility my beloved humans, shifters, and sorcerers wouldn't be around forever.

"That's the crappy part of our reality," she continued. "But your connection with your Master? It's there as long as you're alive. A wisp of flame in the darkness. You're never alone. Not really." She tilted her head at me. "Didn't you notice when Ethan was gone? I mean, in your head?"

How could I separate that? I'd felt his loss utterly and in so many ways—emotionally, physically, psychically. Yes, I knew he wasn't there any longer, but his sudden absence had been devastating, the mental silence only one small sliver of it.

"I was grieving," I said. "I don't know that I could separate it out."

She nodded. "I get that. Actually, now that I think about it, I wonder why Ethan didn't sense Balthasar out there somewhere."

"Maybe he did," I said. "He's never said that he didn't."

But we still looked at each other, added that fact to the growing list of concerns about this man we'd called Balthasar, a man who was powerful enough to call our Master and invade my brain, and brave enough to glamour humans in the middle of downtown Chicago.

We weren't sure who he was, but the "what" was clear enough.

He was a threat.

CHAPTER SEVENTEEN

(MALLO)CAKE OR DEATH

After the session, I went back to the Ops Room, searched (unsuccessfully) for anything I could find about Balthasar's room until Luc accused me of looking tired, which I was, and sent me upstairs.

There were two hours until dawn, and I wasn't exactly looking forward to sitting in our apartments and obsessing about Balthasar or the Circle, or my strategic failure today. I hated screwing up. My grandfather's and Ethan's support notwithstanding, I still felt that that was exactly what I'd done.

I was too tired to exercise, and didn't look forward to my cheek aching from more running, so I'd decided to lose myself in a book that had nothing to do with vampires, mobsters, or magic. I was rounding the banister to head from first floor to third when I spied Mallory heading toward me.

"Hey," she said, "do you have your apotrope?"

It took me a moment to catch up with the question. "My who what?"

"Your apotrope. Your good luck charm. The raven bracelet I gave you," she finally said, with obvious exasperation.

"Oh, sure." She'd given it to me to help ward off bad juju when Ethan and I provided security at a shifter Pack convocation. "Why?"

She gestured from her head to toes with a finger. "Because I am mother-loving exhausted—the ward is killing me. It's all day, all night. Catcher gave me a boost"—she winged up her eyebrows suggestively—"which helped, but I'm still pretty pooped. The long and short of it is, we can't keep him physically and psychically out of the House at the same time. That's more power than we've got. But if I use the bracelet, as a focus, I can at least keep him out of *your* head."

"Okay," I said, realizing she was offering me precisely what I'd needed—a distraction. Or some distracting magic to watch, anyway. And besides, she and I still had chits to chat about. "It's in the apartments. Wanna come upstairs?"

"Is it okay if I make magic there?" She held up a hand. "And ignore that I just set you up for a comment about Ethan's sexual prowess."

"You tell me about Catcher's sexual prowess all the time," I said as we began to climb the stairs.

"That's different."

"Because?"

She grinned. "Because I like talking about it."

We reached the apartments and walked inside.

"Damn," she said. "I really didn't get a good look at this place earlier."

"You hadn't been in here before?"

"I had not." She walked to the bathroom, peeked in, sat on the edge of the mattress, bobbed to check the weight, poked into the closet. "Holy balls. Darth Sullivan has a lot of suits."

"Yeah," I said, moving into the bedroom. "He does."

"You got pretty nice digs here, Mer. Much better than that closet he called a dorm room."

"Sleep with the Master, get the best digs."

"I guess. Good for you. For both of you." She yawned, covering her mouth with the back of her hand. "Sorry. I'm nearly gone. Bracelet?"

I walked to the cabinet in the closet, pulled out the bracelet. It was antique gold link, with a small raven-shaped charm.

Mallory moved to the desk, pulled the Louis XVI chair into the middle of the room. She put the bracelet on the padded seat, arranged it just so.

"You think he'll care if the fabric gets singed?"

I just looked at her.

"You're right. It's Darth Sullivan. Better bring me a towel."

Because she was tired and doing me a favor—protecting me from a crazy person—I did, handing over a fluffy bath towel Ethan probably also wouldn't want singed. But scorch marks could be hidden with careful folding.

Mallory arranged the towel, put the bracelet on top of it. "Come stand behind me," she said, and I did, well back and out of the way. I'd already seen one of her fireballs today. I didn't need a repeat performance—or my own singeing.

She stood between me and the chair, eyes closed, wringing her hands as if to warm up. And then it began—the warm, slow spin of Mallory's winding magic.

This was magic, clean and astringent, but not the kind Balthasar or Morgan had used. Glamour was viscous and syrupy compared to the energy Mallory pulled into the room. Catcher had once explained that sorcerers didn't *make* magic, but pulled it from the universe using the force of their own will, moved and manipulated it. In that case, she was pulling the best of it tonight.

I peeked around her shoulder, watched as the bracelet began to glow with a faint amber light and shiver on the seat cushion. It jumped once, then twice, before lifting into the air and beginning to rotate, its speed increasing until it spun like a Frisbee.

Mallory smiled, flicked a finger to the side as if to direct it, but its spin suddenly wobbled.

"Ah, crap," she said, turning and yanking me to the floor as the bracelet whirled through the air like a blade and launched across the room. It buzzed over our heads and hit the opposite wall with a resounding *crack*.

Mallory looked up, climbed to her feet, grimaced. "You think he'll notice that?"

I glanced up at the ruler-sized burn mark on the wall.

"He might," I said, the bracelet clanking to the floor as I climbed to my feet. A painting hung a couple of feet away from the mark, mounted by wires from a hook over the crown molding. I scooted it over to cover the hole, then moved back to stand beside Mallory and survey my handiwork. The picture was in an awkward place, but it was a landscape I didn't especially like; no British pastoral scene was complete without a linen-shirt-clad man emerging from a pond.

"You know, we're both adults. We could just tell him what happened."

She chuckled. "Yeah, but toying with Darth Sullivan is so much fun."

I could hardly disagree with that. "What do you do with the bracelet now?"

"Maybe I'll just finish this the old-fashioned way," she said, and touched a finger to the bracelet. It lifted slightly, gave one delicious shiver, and then fell back to the floor looking entirely ordinary.

"Done," she said, but wobbled a little on her feet.

"You all right?"

"Just tired." She pushed hair behind her ears, moved her head side to side, neck popping with the movement. "Nothing a monthlong vacation in Bimini couldn't fix."

"I got you," I said, reaching out a hand to help steady her. "I think your magic's getting cleaner. Is that a thing?"

She brightened. "Really? That's definitely a thing. Kind of like"—she paused as she thought of a metaphor—"a diamond with better clarity. Or a beer with less filler."

"Cool. Is that a practice thing?"

"It's a no-longer-delving-in-the-dark-arts thing. And yeah, practice. When you first learn how to do this, to harness the magic, you pull in a lot of crud. Emotions, magical castoff, atmospheric energy. The relative magical dirt."

"The stuff in the joined psychic space?" I asked, thinking of Lindsey.

"Yeah. Like that. And as you get better, you know what you're looking for, can see it a little clearer, can pull in the good stuff." She walked to the bracelet, blew on it before gingerly picking it up.

"Hot," she said with a smile, switching it from hand to hand. "Metal does that sometimes. Something about magic and atoms and quantum mechanical jargon I don't understand." The bracelet's apparently having cooled enough, she extended it to me. "Put it on right before you go to bed; take it off when you get up. It might make you tired."

"Because?"

"Because to keep Balthasar out of your head, it has to stay 'on.' And since I'll be holding the House ward in place, it will be using you to operate. I'm the maker; you're the battery."

I held it out with two fingers. "I'm not sure I'm comfortable with that."

"Sure you are. I'll be doing the same thing, except while you're protecting your own ass, I'll be protecting the collective asses of all your fanged brethren."

When she put it like that, my objection seemed pretty weak. "All righty, then," I said, and put the bracelet on the nightstand so I wouldn't forget it.

"You know what?" I said, glancing up at her after checking the clock. "We've got a little time until dawn. Why don't we just hang out in here?"

She cocked her head at me. "What did you have in mind?"

"Mallocakes and low-budget sci-fi movies."

"How low budget?"

"*Orca Attack: The Rekindling.*"

Her eyes lit like the sun at dawn. "You had me at 'orca.'"

That was what they all said.

She paused to update Catcher while I gave Ethan a rundown on the ward and asked him to give us a little time to rest. And, since we had unfinished business, some time for me and Mallory to discuss some things . . .

When I'd changed into comfy pants and a Cubs T-shirt, I switched on the television and found the correct channel. Mallory kicked off her shoes, and we fell across the bed and on a box of Mallocakes I'd been keeping in a drawer for just such emergencies like hyenas at a kill. If hyenas had been magically stressed supernaturals with an addiction to chocolate.

"How's the chocolate drawer?" I asked, tearing the cellophane on a Mallocake, taking a heady bite of chocolate sponge cake and cream, and closing my eyes to savor it.

"It misses you," she said, pausing midbite to watch an orca devour the torso of a swimmer in one bite. "But I keep it company." The chocolate drawer was, as the name suggested, a drawer in Mallory's kitchen that, when we'd lived together, had held my chocolate stash. I should have asked her to send me a care package. Not that Margot or Ethan spared any expense where treats were concerned.

Mallory adjusted pillows behind her, snapped into a Mallocake wrapper.

"You ready to tell me about the wedding?"

She chewed, eyes on the screen. "There's nothing to tell."

"Mallory Delancey Carmichael. I know you better than anyone else in this world, except possibly Catcher, and that's only because he knows you carnally."

"I don't like the sound of that word. Carnally."

"I didn't like saying it. Spill."

She rolled her shoulders, groaned. "It's not a big deal. We just think it would be better to go ahead and do something simple."

I put down the Mallocake and stared at her. "Please tell me his proposal was more romantic than that—than he wants to just 'go ahead.'"

"We're just not at that white-lace-and-big-veils kind of stage right now."

"Then what stage are you at?"

"I don't know." She made a sound of frustration, then stuffed an empty wrapper in the box, grabbed another. "I don't know. But not everything has to be a big dramatic production."

"Said the girl with the blue hair who dresses up for Halloween, has a room dedicated to sorcery and spells, and is currently watching the second movie in the Orca Attack trilogy."

"I still can't believe you let me skip the first one. What if I missed a crucial plot point?"

"Big sea mammal eats people with extreme prejudice. Humans kill it. Respawn. Repeat. Now you're caught up. The point is, much like the Orca tales, you *like* dramatic productions."

"I *liked* them," she clarified. "When I was younger and love was about romance and flowers." She looked at me. "Love, as you well know, is about a lot more than that. It's about effort and patience and commitment. I love Catcher. And I want to marry him. And I want you to be happy for us."

I scooted to sit sideways, facing her. "Look, I guess I just figured, when the time came, you'd announce your wedding with a town crier and full-on party. If that's not what you're into right now, so be it. I get that the wedding isn't the important part. The marriage is. And if you're happy about this, then I'll be happy. But that's the part I can't really tell. Are you happy? Is this what you want?"

She looked away, moistened her lips. "I just . . . I know he loves me, and I know he wants to be with me. But I'm having a hard time telling if he wants to get married because he wants me, or because he wants back in the Order."

That was a tough one, and I wasn't entirely sure how to answer it. "That puts you in a tough position."

"Yeah," she said. She hadn't opened the Mallocake, but played with the ribbed edges of the plastic wrapper. "I understand that I made the world we live in now. I understand that I didn't exactly help his relationship with the Order. And he accepts that, just like I accept him. I'm very content. I mean, circumstances being what they are."

That was the phrase I didn't like. The blame she was putting on herself for a problem she didn't really create.

"Circumstances being that you're a brilliant sorceress and a good person who pulled herself back from a total shit storm. I'm not excusing what you did—but you took responsibility for it, and you've tried to make amends. That's all you can do. As for Catcher and the Order, that's history. That's between him and the Order, which, as far as I can see, is completely worthless anyway."

She laughed through welling tears. "Yeah, I kind of feel the same. But as much as we'd like to, we can't ignore them any more than you could ignore the GP. I just—I don't know. I don't need him to prove that he loves me. But I sure wish he'd focus on us a little more."

She brushed away tears. "I'm just being silly."

I reached out, wrapped my arms around her. "You aren't being silly at all. You've got needs, and you're entitled to them. And you need to talk to him."

She nodded, laughed a little. "Who'd have thought you'd be giving me relationship advice?"

"Who'd have thought you'd be marrying the world's grumpiest sorcerer? I love you, Mallory. If this is what you want, then this is what I want for you. You just tell me when and where, and we'll be there."

Because that's what friends would do.

Once upon a time, I'd have said it was impossible to eat too many Mallocakes. That my vampire metabolism made up for my enormous appetite, and I could feast to my little heart's content and never pay the price for it.

That was, shall we say, a mistakenly optimistic approach.

Four Mallocakes later, I begrudgingly admitted defeat. Which was why Ethan returned to the apartments to find Mallory and me lying on the bed, television on, pooched stomachs taking a much-needed breather.

"Oh, this is quite a sight," Ethan said with obvious amusement, then spied the empty box of Mallocakes. "A vampire and sorceress done in by chocolate snack cakes."

"Mallocake 'splosion," Mallory said weakly. *"Pew, pew, pew."*

"I think there's one left." I moved just enough to skim fingers against the box, tip it up. "Yep. One. You can have it."

"Wait," Mallory said, and put a hand on my arm while she deliberated, as if there was a chance she might be able to squeeze in one more. "No." She waved me off. "I can't. Go ahead."

"This scenario isn't really selling the Mallocake concept to me," Ethan said.

"We're having girl time."

"Not the girl time I prefer to imagine, but so be it."

"Perv," Mallory said with a grin, rolling off the bed and trundling toward the door. "I'm going to roll myself downstairs."

"Take care," Ethan said. "And thank you for the ward."

She burped indelicately.

"And that's our powerful sorceress," Ethan said, locking the door behind her.

"That is," I agreed, and stuffed wrappers into the Mallocake box, then slid off the bed to throw it away and shake any remaining crumbs out of the duvet. "What's new in Cadogan House?"

"We're trying to assure Diane Kowalcyzk that vampires don't intend to destroy Chicago. Oh, and a ghost from my past is on the loose, and we've moved a few dozen vampires into temporary housing. But, as you might say, no bigs."

I readjusted the blankets again. "I'm not sure I've ever said that."

"I'm sure you have."

I glanced up at him. "I have nearly a Ph.D. in literature."

"And you just ate what I'm guessing is a significant number of processed snack cakes. Having a degree doesn't guarantee good choices. But you can probably analyze Chaucer like a champ."

"Damn straight. How were the supplicants?"

"Remarkably straightforward," he said, taking off his jacket and hanging it on the back of the desk chair we'd resituated at the desk. "How is Mallory?"

"Good. I'm not sold on this elopement situation, but she seems to have accepted it, so I'm not sure there's anything for me to do."

He nodded, hands on his hips. "She's an adult, as is he."

"I know. But it's marriage, and I'd like him to pull that stick out of his ass. Maybe you could talk to him."

"No."

"Ethan—"

"No," he said again, this time more firmly, and walked into the closet. "His relationship is between him and Mallory," he called out. "Let her vent, if that's your friendship. But they have to make those decisions for themselves."

"Stubborn ass," I murmured.

He emerged in emerald green silk pajama bottoms and an arched eyebrow. "I heard that. And I suspect Catcher's the stubborn ass here, not me."

I couldn't argue with that. "Is Morgan here?"

"He's coming tomorrow night. Wanted to stay at the House

tonight, make sure the remaining vampires at Navarre were safe. Grey's already got guards on the House, and we've contracted for a few humans as well. That should keep the Circle at bay during the day, at least."

"What about the Investiture?"

"We've discussed it, but only generally. Scott's and Morgan's minds are on something else."

I nodded, but Ethan's furrowed brow didn't relax.

"What's wrong?"

"Nothing," he said. "Everything. I worry for you."

I pointed to my trusty bracelet. "I'm covered."

One corner of his mouth lifted, and he walked to the bed. "I'm worried about more than just tonight. He's already tried to get to you twice."

"He won't get to me."

"I know he won't, Sentinel, because I won't let him."

Ethan lay down beside me, my eyes wide-open even as I felt the slow tug of sleep as the sun breached the horizon.

I was nervous, I admitted. I didn't want to sleep, even with Mallory's apotrope. Didn't want to fend off pulling fingers and dripping fangs or feel as if my body was a pawn in their game. I didn't want to fight.

"You are mine," Ethan said, opening his arms to me, embracing me when I curled toward him. This time, I hadn't hesitated, exhaustion at least tempering that fear.

"Let me hold you in the darkness," he whispered, lips against my ear. "Let me fight him for you. Let me keep you safe."

The depth of the love in his voice, the feel of his body against mine, made my pulse pound with want. But while my body was responsive, my brain was not. It was fully in protective mode. Not just that I'd think of Balthasar, but that every new intimacy with Ethan would give Balthasar another bullet to use against us.

"Soon," Ethan promised, reading me even in the darkness of the room. "Soon, and inevitably. For you are mine, Sentinel," he said, words slower and softer as sleep overtook him.

"*Mine.*"

CHAPTER EIGHTEEN

DIASPORA

I woke with a sudden start, legs sprawled across the bed, arms crossed beneath my head so that the bracelet pressed into my face.

"Sentinel," Ethan said quietly.

"I'm all right. I'm fine." I sat up, pushed damp hair from my face. My body was dotted with sweat, my pajamas damp with it. I'd slept like a rock—deeply, heavily, and with no memory of Balthasar.

"Did he . . . ?"

I shook my head. But I had dreamed about a bevy of white-toqued Navarre chefs, carving me up with very large knives. No more late-night Mallocakes.

"You look a bit peaky." He cocked his head. "You also have the imprint of a raven in your face."

I rubbed groggily at the sleep wrinkles. "I feel like I ran a marathon."

"You did a lot of running yesterday, which was long enough, and you've slept in the embrace of magic. Blood, I think, would help."

"Shower first. Blood later."

He paused. "I'd like to join you. But I don't want to push you if you aren't ready."

I must not have been ready, since my first reaction was to tell him no.

"He hurt you," Ethan said, pushing a lock of hair behind my ear. "It's all right to take time to heal, to feel yourself again." He smiled softly. "As I said at dawn, Sentinel, I'm not going anywhere."

I knew what he was doing—little touches, small caresses, intended to comfort and help me adjust to him again, help me build comfort in intimacy.

"I'll be fine," I promised him. "I'm sorry that I'm letting him use me to hurt you."

"You're doing no such thing. You're taking care of yourself. As I love you, I prefer that you do just that." He ran his hands down my arms. "Let me do what I can, Sentinel. Let me take care of you."

Ethan Sullivan had many fine qualities. He was honorable. Intelligent. Funny. Sexy as hell. Sarcastic at all the appropriate times. And when the need arose, the very alpha Master of Cadogan House cared for his Sentinel very, very well.

"Stay there," Ethan said, pulling on jeans that slung low on his hips. While I lay among pillows and quilts, he opened the apartment's door, brought in the tray Margot had left outside. I watched with amusement as he arranged and simplified the contents, then carried it to me. Blood, bacon, a still-warm croissant.

I looked up at him. "Are you wooing me?"

"I've been wooing you since the moment our eyes locked on the first floor of this House."

I gave him a flat look. "No, that's when you accused me of being spoiled."

"Details," he said lightly, mouth drawn into a crooked grin. "Helen is helping move the Navarre vampires, and Morgan won't be here until that process is done. We're allowed to take a few minutes to ourselves before we rush out the door to solve others' problems. Let me tend you, Sentinel."

I could hardly have argued with that, so I nodded, watched him rise and disappear into the bathroom. A moment later, the water in the bath began to run.

I ate the croissant slowly, tried to put aside lingering nerves, the fact that the House—or vampires, anyway—currently faced trouble from two directions—the Circle's issues with Navarre, and Balthasar's reemergence into Chicago, into Ethan's life, our lives together. It would have been glorious if we could have locked the door, kept the world on the other side, and simply lived there in peace and quiet for just a little while.

With Margot occasionally leaving trays outside, of course.

When I looked up, Ethan was in the doorway, hand outstretched, green eyes fairly glowing. "Your bath awaits."

I smiled, thinking of a movie scene. "Are you going to paint my nails, too?"

His eyebrow popped up. "No. Should I?"

"No," I said on a laugh, then put aside the tray and walked to him, looked up at him. He was beautiful enough to still take my breath away, and I knew I hadn't been the first—and wouldn't be the last—vampire to think so.

Understanding dawned.

Once upon a time, Ethan had used women. He and Balthasar had both done so, seeing women as merely a different kind of pleasure that, like blood, was theirs for the taking. Persephone, in particular, had died from Balthasar's mistreatment. Ethan hadn't been able to comfort or soothe her. But he could comfort and soothe me now.

"I don't see you in him, you know."

He looked up at me, green eyes fire bright and very startled. "What?"

"When you look at me. When he looked at me, even when he looked at me through your eyes—or what he imagined were your eyes—it was different. You have a depth that he doesn't. And you don't look at me like I'm a thing to be acquired."

When Ethan arched an eyebrow, I couldn't help laughing.

"All right, you do have an unusually strong interest in acquiring me."

"You're mine," he said simply, again.

Ethan dressed first and headed downstairs to check on Morgan and Navarre. I was dressed in my leathers and nearly out the door when my phone rang.

I frowned when I read the screen, but lifted it to my ear. "This is Merit."

"I'm calling on behalf of Adrien Reed," my father said. "He'd like an update regarding the investigation, the vampires' punishment."

"He should talk to the Ombuds' office about that."

"Don't be difficult."

"I'm not being difficult, I'm directing you to the appropriate parties. If you want to know what the CPD is doing, you'll have to talk to the CPD. The vampires weren't from Cadogan, so I don't know what their punishment was."

"So you could find out as easily as me, but you won't." He

didn't seem to grasp the fact that I didn't want the particular answers he was looking for.

"That's not the issue at all, but all right." There seemed little point in arguing with him.

"You should watch yourself. You've already put yourself into the middle of the vampires' battle."

Said the man who'd offered to pay Ethan to make me a vampire. He said he'd done it for the immortality, to ensure that I'd live longer than the daughter my parents had lost before I was born. Unfortunately, he hadn't asked my opinion before making the move.

"I am a vampire."

"You know what I mean. Reed is a powerful man, with a lot of friends. It would behoove you to tread carefully where his interests are concerned."

Having offered his advice, he hung up the phone.

Ten minutes later, I was at the table in the Ops Room, fuming at my father as I sipped a bottle of water and flipped through an image search of antique notebooks, four-poster beds, candelabras, simple desks, still looking for something that would lead us to Balthasar.

I had absolutely nothing to show for it.

There were pictures of all those things. But nothing that connected to Balthasar, at least as far as I could tell, and nothing that connected that particular room—the layout or the furnishings—to anything else. It seemed to be just a random room he'd picked or invented in order to attempt his seduction. Because that, I thought, was what he'd believed it would be. He'd worn a romance novel rake's clothing, put me in a lush bed dotted with candlelight, and had been holding a book when I woke up. When he'd failed to woo me on his own, he'd determined to look like Ethan, hoped that would work. It didn't. Wouldn't have. But he'd seemed to believe it would . . . He'd thought he'd be able to seduce me with his charm and his glamour and the scene he'd believed he could set.

"I've got something about Balthasar, where he's staying now." We all looked up as Juliet pulled off her headset.

Luc rose from his spot at the head of the table. "Talk to me, Jules."

"Our guard did a very good job. She went to the real-estate company, flirted with one of the account managers, bought him drinks. He loosened up, told her about Balthasar." She looked down at the notepad in her hand. "He gave the manager some malarkey about how he wasn't satisfied with the amenities in the old place. Requested another condo specifically."

"Oh, really?" Luc said. "Where'd he go?"

"The penthouse in the Palisade Building." That was one of the glass high-rises along the Chicago River, its sleek, stacked columns frequently a highlight of river architecture tours.

Luc whistled. "That's quite an upgrade."

"Ya. Condo's owned by Ram, LLC, but the account manager didn't know anything about that company. But—get this—both units have been comped. Balthasar's not paying a thing."

Luc's eyes went flat. "Go. Get visual confirmation he's at the location, follow if he goes anywhere. Keep your distance, and do not approach. Report back if you get a visual, and update on every hour. Take a temp with you, and no heroics."

"On that," Juliet said, and Brody followed her out the door.

Ram, LLC, I thought. I'd heard of a lot of LLCs lately, and a lot of three-letter LLCs. Was that really a three-letter word . . . or three-letter acronym?

I pulled out my phone.

"You got something, Sentinel?"

I held up a finger to hold Luc's inquiry while Jeff answered my call.

"Merit!" Jeff said. "What's the good word?"

"That's my question for you. That list of entities Malik gave you—the ones from Navarre House. Can you send that to me?"

"The corporations? Sure. I'll send it."

"Thanks. I'll call you back." I'd barely hung up the phone when the list came through, eighteen three-letter acronyms that looked more like stock abbreviations than names . . . including RAM, LLC.

My heart began to gallop. "It's not Ram, LLC, Luc. It's R-A-M, LLC. It's one of the companies that Celina gave a limited power of attorney over the House's investment accounts." I scanned the list, the accompanying Navarre connection. "In this case, Navarre's *largest* investment account."

The room went silent.

"The Circle owns Balthasar's condo?" Luc asked quietly. "That's quite a coincidence."

"Yeah. It is. Who owned the first one? The one he moved from?"

"Uh," Luc said, tapping the screen to pull up old data. "Company called Element, LLC."

One of the temps, a square-shouldered kid with thick, dark hair, equally dark eyes, and a wide smile, spun around in his computer chair. "I'm not sure it's Element, sir."

"Merit, this is Keiji the Temp. Keiji the Temp, Merit." We

waved at each other. "Why don't you think it's Element?" Luc asked him.

"I don't think Kelley was saying a word. I think she was saying letters."

"Letters?"

"L-M-N."

"L-M-N," Luc said, playing with the sound. "L-M-N. Damn. How did I miss that? Good call, Keiji the Temp."

Keiji nodded, smiled knowingly. "You can leave off the Temp part."

Luc lifted a shoulder. "I like using titles. It adds to the atmosphere. I'm gonna do it again: Sentinel?"

I nodded, having already checked the list while they enjoyed their pas de deux. "LMN, LLC is on the list. It's got an interest in one of the House's real estate trusts."

Luc frowned, rose from his chair, walked from one end of the Ops Room to the other. "So Balthasar's stayed in two condos. The first one isn't good enough, or he's pissed he gets made by us, so he asks for the second one. Both of them are owned by companies that have, over the course of time, managed to get their hands in Celina's kitty."

I grimaced, and Luc stopped short, shook his head, considered what he'd just said. "No, undo that. Delete it. Just pretend I didn't say it." He glanced back at me. "That's quite a link, Sentinel."

"Yeah, but to what, really? The LLCs were created by the Circle. Balthasar has apparently stayed in two condos owned by those LLCs, and therefore by the Circle. It's a coincidence, I'll grant you, but what does it tell us?"

Luc took a seat at the table, lowered his voice. "They could have sent him here. They could have found him, dug him up from his safe house, sent him here."

"Why?" I asked.

Luc shrugged. "The Circle's mostly got Navarre. Maybe they want Cadogan, too. This would be a helluva way to get there."

Helen appeared in the doorway. "Morgan is here."

Luc nodded. "We'll be up in a moment." When she disappeared, he glanced back at me. "This could get really, really ugly."

That seemed inevitable.

Morgan, in his usual jeans and T-shirt, sat in one of the leather chairs in Ethan's office. Ethan and Malik chatted quietly in the corner, and they looked up when we entered.

"A moment, Sire?" Luc asked, gesturing them into the hallway.

"Excuse us," Ethan said to the room, not waiting for a response before we stepped outside and closed the door.

"Something new?" he asked, scanning our faces.

"We think we've found Balthasar's new home, and I've got Juliet and Brody on the location. They won't move unless we say. But your Sentinel, who has a pretty good memory, made a connection between the Circle and the condos."

Ethan looked at me. "Oh?"

"Both condos are owned by companies Malik found in the Navarre House records."

"The Circle's LLCs?" Malik asked.

"Yep. And the LLCs have comped both stays."

Ethan looked at Luc. "Coincidence?"

"You know my position on those."

Ethan crossed his arms. "So we think the Circle is funding Balthasar's stay in Chicago. Why? Because they want him here? Because he's part of their efforts to rule the city's vampires?"

Luc nodded. "That's what we were thinking."

Silence, then, "I don't know why that would surprise me. He loves power, but never sought to attain it through traditional channels . . . and yet . . ."

"They're humans," I said, voicing something that bothered me about the entire thing. Ethan glanced at me, nodded briskly.

"That's it precisely. Balthasar thinks humans are weaker, less, than us. They are mice to his cat, things to be toyed with and discarded. I find it hard to believe he'd willingly partner with them."

"Maybe he doesn't think it's a partnership," Malik suggested.

"We're missing part of the story," Ethan said. "But it makes tonight's negotiations that much more important. Let's get to it."

We all turned at the sound of footsteps in the hallway, found Jeff, Catcher, my grandfather, and Detective Jacobs walking toward us.

"The cavalry has arrived," Ethan said, extending a hand to my grandfather and Detective Jacobs. "Gentlemen."

"We understand the Navarre evacuation is complete," Jacobs said.

"It is," he said, "and Morgan's in my office, ready to begin. And we've gleaned one additional bit of information. The Circle is apparently paying for Balthasar's condo while he's in town. The entities that own the two condos are on the Navarre list."

My grandfather's eyes widened appreciatively. "Isn't that interesting?"

"We thought so," Ethan agreed. "We don't yet know how much they're in bed together, but there's certainly some connection." He gestured toward the door. "Shall we?"

Morgan stood when we walked in. I gave him credit for not objecting to the CPD's involvement, although the flash of irritation in his eyes was impossible to ignore.

But Ethan did a pretty good job of it. "Morgan, I believe you know Arthur Jacobs."

Morgan nodded. "Sure. What's the plan? Am I going to call him? Set up a meet?"

"That depends, in part, on the Circle," Jacobs said.

"And the electronics," Jeff added, who pointed to Luc.

"If you'll follow me," Luc said, "we'll get to it."

We convened in the Ops Room, vampires, humans, sorcerers, and shifters at the conference table, our collective gazes on Jeff.

"So, the Circle previously called Morgan's cell or the Navarre office phone to make contact, yes?"

Morgan nodded. "Yeah. I've got a number, but I've never used it. I'm supposed to call it, wait for the return call."

"Probably a throwaway phone," Jacobs said. "But if you haven't used it, the number should still be good."

My grandfather clasped his hands on the table. "We know the Circle wants something. Hopefully, you've interrupted any immediate plans to take that payment in violence by getting your vampires safe. That was a very smart move, and a very impressive effort by the Houses."

Morgan nodded.

"Now you'll reach out to the Circle, find out what they want. As we've discussed, it seems unlikely that's money at this point. It may be another job. It may be more House access. Considering the time that has passed since the unsuccessful attempt on King, I suspect they'll be ready to tell you."

"Okay," Morgan said.

"Can I see your phone?" Jeff asked, removing a small black box from his pocket.

Morgan pulled out his phone, handed it over.

Jeff nodded, pried a tiny card from the side of the phone, then slid the card into a slot in the black box. The box's glossy exterior began to glow.

"New toy?" I asked.

"A little multifunctional device I've been working on. Does a little of this, a little of that. A little telephony, among other things."

After a moment, the box turned black again, and the tray popped open. At the same time, the Ops Room's wall screen filled with graphs and charts.

"And there we go." Jeff popped the card out, put it back in Morgan's phone, returned the phone to him.

"I've borrowed your telemetry data," Jeff said, spinning his chair around to look at the screen, bringing one chart to the center.

"All right," he murmured. "I'm going to eliminate any calls that came from the same number more than once, and any that match your contact list." That left a handful of plotted points on the screen. "You recognize any of those?"

Morgan eliminated a few numbers, leaving four on-screen.

"Those are burn phones' prefixes," Jeff said, gaze scanning the screen. "All different numbers. No apparent connection between them, and the calls all pinged different towers."

"They're very careful," Jacobs said.

My grandfather nodded. "That's how they've stayed in business so long. They are a remarkably careful group."

"So the number you have will probably be another burner phone," Jeff said. "When they've called you, how long does each call last?"

"They're short. A minute, maybe?"

Jeff nodded. "Probably too short to trace, but we can at least determine which tower they're using. So, when everybody's ready, you'll place a call to the number you've got, and I'll do what I can to nail it down."

"How do I play this?" Morgan asked, looking around the table.

"We've got two goals," Jacobs said. "Addressing the situation with your House and, if possible, acquiring enough information to identify the Circle's key players and shut them down."

"The latter being the only real way to ensure that the former happens."

"Frankly, yes."

"When they call back, you'll be matter-of-fact, but polite. In their minds, Navarre owes them a substantial debt, and they want to collect. They'll have a demand, and you want to know what it is. You don't have to negotiate with them, argue with them. You just need to know what they want. There's a chance they won't want to make that demand on the phone. That's fine, and we can cross that bridge when we come to it. The key is to engage them in communication so we can move forward."

Jeff looked at Luc. "Can we use your earbuds? I can dial them in so we can all hear the call."

Luc nodded, pulled the box of earbuds from a locked desk drawer, lest his vampires should steal the tiny plastic nubbins.

Juliet beat me to the teasing. "You afraid we're going to borrow those without asking, Dad?"

"You take my car, you stay out after curfew, you don't call your mother regular," Luc said in his best Chicago accent. "Bet your ass I'm locking up the silver."

Luc passed the box around the room, and we took earbuds, slipped them in.

"We work long hours," Luc said to Morgan. "Many of them are

hard. We try to keep the tone light—but that's no reflection on the work quality."

Morgan nodded, but there was weariness in his gaze. Too many nights spent worrying, instead of commiserating with his vampires, his Novitiates and staff. And now those vampires were spread across the city like cottonwood seeds in the wind.

"We're ready if you are, Morgan."

He nodded, pulled a slip of paper from his pocket, tapped in the numbers, lifted the phone to his ear.

The room went silent.

"Gold star," Morgan said after a moment, and then hung up the phone again.

"Gold star?" Ethan asked.

"That's the code for our account."

"How long will it take them to respond?" Ethan asked.

"I don't know," Morgan said, and we all prepared to wait.

It took less than five minutes.

Morgan's phone rang, the ring tone a soft, alternative song I recognized, the vocalist mourning the end of a relationship. My chest squeezed sympathetically, but I kept my thoughts to myself. Morgan wouldn't have appreciated the sympathy, especially not from me.

"Give me three . . . two . . . and one," Jeff said, then pointed at Morgan. "You're a go."

Morgan blew out a breath, lifted the phone to his ear. "Navarre."

The answering voice—deep and slowly and clearly affected by a voice modulator—echoed in my ear. "You were not instructed to call."

"And you were instructed in the beginning not to touch my people. You did it anyway."

"You first refused your assignment, and then botched it."

"You came to my House, assaulted one of my vampires. They are not on the table."

Merit, Ethan said silently, and I nodded my understanding, did my part.

Morgan, I said silently, activating the unusual telepathic link between us. *Calm down. Remember what this call is about.*

He still looked furious, but rolled his shoulders in an apparent effort to calm himself.

"We're not especially concerned about your preferences," said the voice. "Your loan is in default." There was a moment of silence. "We will afford you the opportunity to negotiate."

Morgan pursed his lips, blew out a relieved breath. "That's acceptable."

"One hour. Michigan Avenue helipad. The copter will be waiting."

"Helicopter?" Morgan said. "Why do we need a helicopter?"

"We select the location, Navarre."

Morgan looked around the table, settled on me. "You want to deal, I want a guest. Merit, of Cadogan House."

Ethan's magic bloomed hot and bright beside me, and I covered a hand with his. His wasn't the only irritation. My grandfather, Jeff, and Luc looked pissed on my behalf.

But their reactions, while appreciated, were irrelevant. We couldn't let Morgan go alone, and I was as reasonable a choice as any. Certainly more reasonable than having another Master go with him, handing them both over to the Circle.

"One hour," the voice said, and the line went dead.

Morgan put the phone down, then was brave enough to meet Ethan's furious gaze.

"That you would dare to volunteer Merit without her, or my, consent absolutely astounds me."

"I had to take someone. Who else at this table would you send?"

"So you'll throw her to your wolves without even asking her permission?"

"Did you ask her permission to make her a vampire?"

Ethan's body went rigid, and he moved to stand, but I squeezed the hand on his arm.

"Morgan," I said, "quit being an asshole. Ethan, he's right. I'm the best person to go. I've dealt with Jude Maguire, I've got skills, and I can talk to Morgan telepathically. That's a big advantage."

"He might have asked you."

"He should have," I agreed, leveling an unflattering gaze at Morgan. "But he didn't, and it's done."

Ethan's gaze didn't waver. "How long will it take to get to the helipad?"

Jeff scanned the map he'd already pulled up on the screen. "Current estimate is twenty-three minutes."

"We get there early, scope it out. That gives us twenty minutes to get this operation ready to go." He glanced at Morgan. "And when it's done, you and I have business."

Morgan nodded, and the preparations began.

I let them deal with the logistics, ran upstairs to change clothes. This wouldn't be a social call. I'd need as much protection as possible, so I pulled on leather pants, a red tank, my leather jacket, black boots. I wanted to tuck a dagger into my boot, but the CPD still had it. Not that it mattered; the Circle would undoubtedly search me and take it, and since it had been a gift from Ethan, I didn't want to lose it.

The possibility that Balthasar would be there, would be involved, occurred to me, and turned my stomach. I was looking forward to a good down-and-dirty fight, but not one that took place in my mind. I considered, grabbed the bracelet from the nightstand, fastened it. Better to be safe than sorry where he was concerned.

I splashed water on my face, brushed my hair so I could tie it up. When I emerged from the bathroom, pulling my hair into a ponytail, Ethan stood in the doorway, hands in his pockets, still vibrating with irritation.

"He's put you in a damn fine position."

"It was an asshole move," I agreed, snapping the elastic into place and ensuring that the ponytail was snug. "But he's right—he didn't have a better choice."

"They now know you're coming," he said as I walked toward him. "They'll be prepared for you, and might consider taking you as an asset."

I nodded, offered up the realization that had made my heart thump beneath my chest like a nervous rabbit.

"If they really wanted to negotiate, to give him a new assignment, they'd have done it over the phone. Bringing us to their HQ is risky. Which means they don't really want to negotiate."

Ethan's brow furrowed, and he nodded. "We think you're right."

"So they want to kill us, or use us as bait to get something else. Like Sanford King, who is currently inaccessible to them, since he's in protective custody. And they'll assume my grandfather knows where he is."

"And they'll assume they can use you to get to your grandfather."

I nodded. That was a lot of weight on my shoulders, and I really didn't want to get kidnapped again. I'd already been held by a demon and a group of jingoistic elves, and didn't want to make it an even three.

"Morgan's aware of all this?"

"He is. Your grandfather spoke with him about it."

I nodded, considered. "I think we go in with the assumption this will be a hostage exchange, that they'll come out swinging. From our perspective, we're trying to nail a location, identify players, so we can turn the mess over to the CPD."

"I am so proud of what you've become," Ethan said quietly. "And it terrifies me."

I grinned at him. "It terrifies me, too. But it's also surprisingly fun. In between the bouts of terror and anxiety." I put a hand on his chest, felt his own heart pound beneath my pulse, and was relieved when it didn't add to my anxiety. "I know you've already planned an escape route. What is it?"

He smiled, just a little. "Brody will have the car ready, your grandfather will have two CPD units and the van ready to go, and I've arranged for a helicopter, just in case."

"Any sense of where they'll be taking us?"

"Either someplace they don't want to be followed on the ground, or a place offshore."

"An island in the lake?"

"That was Arthur's thought."

I nodded. "That could work. It would also explain why the CPD hadn't been able to find their lair. Depending on its location, they may not even have jurisdiction over it."

"Your grandfather thought of that as well," Ethan said with a smile. "He's contacting authorities in Wisconsin and Michigan, just in case. Those seemed the most likely possibilities."

I put a hand on his chest. "I'll take care of myself."

"Oh, I know you will," he said, and pressed his lips to my forehead. "Because if you don't, you and Morgan will both have to answer to me."

We met in the lobby, each group standing together in its own cluster, Morgan standing alone.

"Brody's outside with the SUV," Luc said. "Ethan, Morgan, Merit, and I will ride together. Detective Jacobs and the Ombuds' folks will follow in the van." He glanced at me. "You've got the earbud, and we'll communicate that way. We'll also want to track your location."

"They'll take any electronics," Jeff said. "So we can't track her with GPS."

"What about my raven bracelet?" I asked, lifting my wrist and glancing at Catcher. "If I wear it, could Mallory use that to find me?"

He considered. "Actually, yeah. She could."

"Get her," Ethan said. "And get her on it."

Catcher nodded, ran for the stairs.

I glanced at Luc. "Has Juliet found Balthasar yet?"

"No visual confirmation. We'll let you know if we find him."

Morgan looked alarmed. "Balthasar? What's he got to do with this?"

"We don't know," Luc said. "Possibly nothing. But keep your guard up." He looked us over, the jeans-clad man, the leather-clad woman, going into battle without so much as a dagger.

"Your instincts are going to be your best defense here. We've got the chopper on call to get you out, but if there's any delay in finding you, you'll have to keep yourselves alive."

"That's on me," Morgan said, looking at me. "She's my responsibility, and I accept and acknowledge it."

"And when you return?" Ethan prompted.

"Then we'll settle our accounts."

┈━≡◈≡━┈

CHAPTER NINETEEN

FLIGHT OF FANCY

Ethan and Luc escorted us into the building, past the empty security desk, and toward the elevators, where Luc selected the top floor.

"Any questions?" Luc asked.

"Not from me." I looked at Morgan. "Anything else you'd like to say before we do this?"

Morgan shook his head.

"In that case," Luc said, "be careful." He looked at me. "Remember your training, keep your stance strong, and don't be afraid to kick 'em in the balls."

Luc obviously favored a sentimental motivational speech.

The elevators opened to a tile-floored foyer and glass doors that led to the helipad outside. The helicopter was waiting for us, a sleek white oval with orange stripes, its blades already thushing, the door open, a big man in black fatigues standing outside, waiting for us to enter.

My heart began to thud with nerves, excitement, the likelihood of battle, the possibility of loss.

Ethan slipped a hand around my neck, pulled me forward, pressed a hard and possessive kiss to my lips that nearly left me breathless in a completely different way. *Be careful,* he said silently.

I will. Keep that helicopter ready.

He drew back, and I put a hand on his face, took a long look at him, committed his features, his mouth, his eyes, to memory.

I followed Morgan to the helicopter, and the man directed us into our seats, strapped us in. And then we were lifting into the air, the sensation so much as if I'd suddenly been able to sprout wings it brought inexplicable tears to my eyes. I glanced down, watched Ethan grow smaller in the distance, and hoped to God I'd see him again.

The city disappeared behind us in a matter of minutes, and we floated above the darkness of Lake Michigan.

An island, I said to Morgan, an eye on the shoreline so I could keep my bearings, and explain, if it provided necessary, where we were.

Yeah. There aren't that many close to Chicago. They'll be able to find us. If we have to play sacrifice the pawn, don't volunteer.

You, either. You're a Master, and I'm a Sentinel. We can handle this.

Some minutes later, a light began to glow in the darkness, a pale hulk growing larger in front of us.

I tapped Morgan's hand, pointed to the shape.

He leaned over to peer out the window. *What is that?*

I'm not sure, I said. But when the helicopter began to descend, I decided we were about to find out.

Unfortunately, landing didn't really improve my understanding. We'd approached a large island and landed on a concrete helipad, the lights bright enough to obscure anything else around it.

We hopped out of the helicopter, duck-walked away from the rotors, looked back in dismay as it lifted off again into the night.

Shit, Morgan said, squinting from the light.

Yeah, I agreed.

As the helicopter receded, the sound of waves crashing on the shore some distance below us filled the air.

"Let's go," said the man in fatigues. We followed him to the edge of the helipad where two more figures, also in black and carrying automatic weapons, gestured us toward a well-trimmed and mulch-covered path through dense woods not yet greened by spring. After a moment, we emerged onto the small, flat lawn of what looked very much like a traditional Midwestern ranch-style house, except this one was much, much larger.

"What is this?" Morgan asked.

"Torrance Hall," the guard said, apparently not seeing the need to be circumspect when it wasn't expected we'd be leaving the island again. That was concerning.

"It's where some of the old-school Chicago mobsters kept their booze and money. Ferried it back and forth to the city when supplies ran low." He shrugged. "Boss likes the ambience."

He walked to the front door, opened it. We stepped into a tidy home with 1970s décor, heavy on the oranges and ochres, with tweed furniture and shag carpeting.

The house smelled slightly musty, like a vacation home just opened for the season. Since winter had only just begun to break its hold on Chicago, that might not have been far from the truth.

"It's dark out," I whispered now that we were inside, using the agreed-upon code to activate the earbud, but heard only static in response. We must have been too far away for a signal, which meant not only did we not have weapons, but we didn't have any way of communicating with the House.

Technology, I thought with a curse, really, really hoping Mallory was having better luck with magic.

"This way," the guard said, and we followed him into a living room. "Stop."

The guards with guns stood at our backs. The first guard gestured us to spread out our arms. He patted me down, then Morgan, and when he was satisfied, began moving again.

We walked past a kitchen with avocado-toned appliances, into a den with a sunken floor dotted with throw pillows. The house had been updated by someone since the mobsters had used it, but not in the last forty years.

The guard took a passageway to an outbuilding, and when the guards with guns looked at us menacingly, we opted to follow him inside . . . into a very recently updated game room. Bar on one end with a few high-top tables, a pool table in the middle, arcade-style video games along the wall.

Jude Maguire, shirtless and bearing a placket of bandages below his ribs, leaned over the pool table.

I cursed silently. And since I hadn't injured his ribs, I guessed the Circle had been pissed about our little Streeterville outing.

"Mr. Maguire," the guard said. "They're here."

Jude looked up, glanced at us, then looked down at the table again. He aimed, released, and the balls sailed across the table with a *crack* of sound.

There were three other men in the room, in addition to the three guards who'd accompanied us. All of them were thick-necked and broad-shouldered, and the air vibrated from the volume of weapons they carried.

One of the other men stepped forward for his turn, and Jude stepped back, held his cue like a pike, crossed one ankle over the other.

"They cause any trouble?" Maguire asked.

"No, sir."

Sir? Since when was Jude Maguire a "sir"? He was muscle, not leadership. Leadership didn't put itself in the line of fire, in clear view of the public. And it certainly didn't get broken ribs after a failed operation. But that hardly mattered now. Nobody in the room argued, and we weren't exactly in a position to do so.

The second player made his selection, sent a couple of balls spinning ineffectually before giving up the board to Maguire again. He walked around the table, checking angles.

"We're ready for your demands," Morgan said into the tense silence.

"Our demands," Maguire repeated, then pulled back the cue, snapped it forward. The ball ricocheted across the table, hit the bumper, then sailed into the diagonal pocket. He rose, looked us over. "Your former Master borrowed a lot of money from us, asked for a lot of favors. And you don't want to pay us back."

"I'm not here to argue about the debt. I'm here to resolve it."

Maguire handed the cue to the man closest to him, walked toward us. "Are you? Are you in charge? Because what I see here is a man begging for relief. Begging so hard he brought a girl with him." Maguire stopped a few feet away, crossed his arms, gave me a slow and salacious look. "A girl I didn't finish the first time around."

I barely managed not to growl, but didn't bother to hide the fangs and silvered eyes. "Just for the record, you won't be finishing me now, either."

"Just get on with it," Morgan spat out. "What do you want?"

Slowly, Maguire shifted his gaze back to Morgan. "We've already told you what we want, and you apparently sent children to do a man's job. We wanted King, and we wanted him dead."

"Why?" Morgan asked.

"Because—that's all you needed to know to perform your task, which you failed. That means he's in the wind."

"I won't kill for you," Morgan said.

"That's pretty obvious." This time, Maguire slid his gaze to me. "What would you do for her?"

Maguire's gaze snapped to something beside me, and I pivoted, lifted a hand instinctively to duck the pool stick one of Maguire's goons was yielding like a club. I wrenched it away from him, shoved the blunt end into his gut, pushed him backward until he bobbled and hit the ground on his ass.

Stick in my hand, wielded like a weapon, I looked back at Maguire. "I don't need anyone to kill for me."

He put a hand on his chest in mock apology. "I guess I misspoke. We don't want him to kill someone for you. He's already fucked that up. But you, we can use. There are plenty in Chicago who want you alive, and who'd pay a pretty penny to keep you that way."

"Using me to get King isn't a very good idea." Given Maguire's sudden sneer, we'd guessed his plan accurately.

"Even assuming my grandfather knows where he is, he won't give him up. He won't negotiate, even for me." I wasn't one hundred percent confident my grandfather would make that choice, but I was pretty certain. He was an honorable man, and believed in duty.

"I'm willing to take that chance," Maguire said. He gestured, and the man I'd pushed back barreled forward again. I gripped the pool cue, angled, and struck, intending to box his ears. But this time, he knew the blow was coming. He ducked to dodge it and aimed for my lower body, trying to grab me. I jumped backward to avoid him, my arms wide to keep my balance . . . and just within reach of two more humans.

One grabbed the pool cue. The other grabbed my arm, twisting it backward and nearly doubling me over. I kicked backward with the opposite leg, caught his knee. He bobbled, but retorqued my arm, sending shocks of bright pain from fingers to shoulder. I hit my knees hard, my arm high and awkward behind me.

"A little help here," I said, trying to wiggle myself free without dislocating my shoulder.

"Little busy," Morgan said quietly, and I glanced his way. Maguire had an enormous handgun, nothing you'd want to meet in a dark alley, aimed point-blank at Morgan's head. That, I guessed, would be the kind of shot that even a vampire wouldn't survive.

"Let her go," Morgan said, hands in the air. "You don't have any argument with her."

"You're wrong there, but then you weren't part of our escapade yesterday. You were in your House, nice and comfortable, while your vampire was assaulted on the street. Just like Celina would have been." Maguire's smile was mocking. "Point being, you aren't really in a position to make demands."

Maguire had done his research, knew just where to push Morgan's buttons.

"Neither are you, if you think her family will give you anything. Her father's an asshole, and her grandfather's a cop. She's right; he won't give up King, even to save her life."

Maguire lifted a shoulder. "Once again, that's a risk I'm willing to take."

"You'd be bringing the wrath of the entire CPD down on the Circle, on you."

He laughed haughtily. "You think the CPD can touch us?

There is nothing that's happened in this city for ten years that we haven't approved. That includes your father's little pet project."

I might not have liked my father overmuch, but that didn't mean I wanted him involved with the Circle. "Stay away from my family."

"That's quite impossible, since your family keeps jumping into my business. You may be immortal, doll, but we're connected."

"We?" I asked, and Maguire's expression darkened. "You mean you aren't running this little shit show yourself? Color me surprised."

His eyes flashed with fury, and the man behind me offered the punishment, twisting my arm harder. I winced, but kept my eyes on Maguire.

"I don't respect a man who doesn't fight his own battles. And speaking of which, if you're truly a 'Circle,' where's the rest of your gang? Is it these guys? Because . . ." I glanced around, tried to look patently unimpressed.

The man behind me wrenched my arm again, this time maneuvering it up, forcing my head down, my cheek to the sticky wooden floor, littered with dirt, crumbs, and probably worse.

"You like to run your mouth," Maguire said. "A pity, since I bet it could be used for so many other more interesting things."

"Tell me about Balthasar."

"I don't know what you're talking about."

"We know the Circle's paying for his condo. Why?"

"You think I have anything to do with that freak? No. He's not my idea. He's fucking nuts, is what he is."

Stay down, Morgan said, his gaze still steady on Maguire.

It took me a moment to adjust to his voice in my head, but it's not like I could have moved anyway. *What?*

Stay down. I'm moving in three . . . two . . . one.

With blurring speed, Morgan dropped his arms, crossed them, pulled something small and flat from his jeans pockets, wrenched them out again. I dropped my head as something whizzed millimeters above it. There was a cry, and my arm was free.

Pain shot through it from shoulder to wrist as circulation returned and nerves pulsed. I ignored it, pushed past it, jumped to my feet while looking to see what damage Morgan had done.

Maguire and the man who'd grabbed me had small discs—plastic throwing stars—extruding from their chests. They must have missed them on the pat-down.

They were screaming with pain, gripping with slick and bloody fingers at the barbed coins, trying to pull them out.

"Get them, damn it!" Maguire yelled, even as he stumbled backward into a chair, still groping at the missile. "And don't kill them. We need them alive."

The rest of the muscle rushed forward.

I didn't waste time. I jumped onto the pool table, darted across green felt, and jumped down again to the case of pool cues on the opposite wall. I grabbed two.

"Morgan!" I yelled out, and jumped onto the table again, just missing the outflung arms of one of the men who'd sat quietly during the rest of Maguire's little show. They must not have been the first string.

"Clear!" Morgan said, and I tossed a cue to him. The man tried to grab my boot; I kicked him in the face, bone and cartilage crunching. He yelped, covered his face with a hand, and stumbled back, making room for the next one. He'd thought to bring a cue, swung it at my shins. I jumped to avoid the first swipe, hopped onto the table's wooden edging, flipped onto the floor again, and brought the broad end of the cue around, nailing him in the shoulder.

The thrill of the fight—the flood of adrenaline—rushed through me, dampening doubt and sharpening my movements, my focus.

I knocked one man to the floor, but another followed him, as if emerging from the house's crevices like a scuttling insect. He'd grabbed his own pool cue, and swung it at me like a hitter who'd pointed to left field.

I brought up my cue to strike, and he shattered it with enough force that it reverberated down my spine. With a thunderous *crack*, my cue splintered in half, and I instinctively turned from the sound and shards of flying wood that I really, really hoped weren't aspen—the only wood that could reduce me to ash if well aimed.

The man cursed with victory, reset for another swing, this one higher—and aimed at my head.

I didn't wait for it to land. I dropped the broken cue, pivoted into a kick that nailed him in the side, and jerked the cue from his hands.

"Bitch," he said, and I flipped the cue into the air, caught it backward, and nailed him between the eyes with the blunt end.

He teetered backward, fell atop a table, and both of them crashed to the floor. We hadn't killed any that I could see, but we'd incapacitated some of them, at least for a little while. Maguire was still maniacally clawing at the disc. For all his ferocity, he didn't handle his own injuries very well.

"Damn," Morgan said, chest heaving beside me. "You've gotten better."

"Yeah, I have." I tossed the cue to the floor, gestured toward the stairs. "Let's get the hell out of here."

We went out the way we'd come in, running back down the passageway and into the house, then out the front door again.

"Ethan," I said into the earbud, "if you can hear me, we need an evac, like, yesterday."

Between bouts of static, I caught the intermittent words "mechanical" and "delay."

"I didn't catch that. Repeat: We need an evac right now."

I caught "helicopter" and "broken." The rest of the response was only garbled static.

"You are fucking kidding me," Morgan said.

I didn't think so.

"We're gonna have to find another way off the island," I said as gunshots echoed behind us. I looked right, left, found a path that led away from the concrete pad down toward the shore.

"There," I said as voices began to sound behind us. I ran toward the path, began to half jog, half hop down the dirt- and rock-covered path, Morgan's footsteps behind me.

The trail, narrow and rutted, ran up and down through a forested area, with switchbacks as tight as bobby pins. The forest was silent around us, whatever animals might have scampered in the dark smart enough to stay still while the predators roamed around them.

The path opened up almost instantaneously, shooting us onto a rocky, sandy shoreline where water lapped in the dark. There was an ancient picnic table, the remains of a circular fire pit surrounded by rocks. Maguire and his cronies—or Capone and his—had enjoyed a picnic or two on the Lake Michigan shoreline. Unfortunately, there was absolutely no sign of a boat.

"Shit," Morgan said, propelling out of the trees behind me, grabbing my body for balance as he nearly ran straight into me. We fumbled, separated, looked around, saw nothing but trees and water.

"There has to be a way off this godforsaken island," I said, scanning left and right, but the shoreline was dark.

We couldn't outrun these guys forever. They knew the island better than we did, and the sun would be up soon enough.

The darkness seemed to suddenly contract, to close in around me, as if I'd been shoved into a room without doors, a room with a barred window. Like a man with a key to unlock my head were standing beside me, and his words were in my ears again. *Our business is not done.*

No, I thought, trying to stem the rising panic, the memory of Balthasar that seemed right on the edge of swamping me. There was always a solution. I just had to think, had to slow down and think.

Crap, I thought as my vision began to spark around the edges. *Panic attack.*

I grabbed Morgan's arm as my heart began to thud. The air was chilly, but a cold sweat broke out, peppering my skin with clamminess.

"What the hell are—oh, shit, are you okay?"

My throat felt snug as a straw, my head beginning to spin from lack of oxygen.

"Hey, breathe. Breathe, Merit. In, out. In, out." He mimed the motion, then walked me to the picnic table. "Sit," he said, but cast a nervous glance around him, waiting to hear humans running through the trees.

But why should they be in a hurry? This was their island. We were the interlopers here, and apparently with no exit.

"This isn't a big deal," Morgan said, squeezing my hand. "No need to panic. This is just a minor setback. There's another way out of here, and we'll find it."

I followed his breathing, caught the rhythm of it, forced myself to breathe on counts. In, one, two. Out, one, two. Over and over again, until my heart began to slow its frantic pace.

"You can't be afraid of the dark, you know. That's not a thing a vampire can even have."

He was trying to make me laugh, and I chuckled in spite of myself and my racing heartbeat. "Not afraid. Just—a memory. A bad one."

"Then you need to replace it with a new one," Morgan said, looking down, up, around as if he might find a replacement on a nearby shelf.

"Ah," he said, his gaze on the sky. "Look up."

"What?"

"Look up," he said, and tilted my chin upward.

It was as if the moon had exploded and spilled its light across the sky—stars sprinkled the dark canvas like diamonds, the cloudy Milky Way gleaming among them.

I'd seen a similar sight in our few nights in Colorado, when the universe had flung open its arms to us. It was majestic, and it made me feel small in the best possible way.

"There is always light," Morgan said quietly. "The stars are always shining, even if we can't see them."

He was the last person I'd have expected to hear something that philosophical from. And it helped.

A dog barked nearby. "We've got to go," he said.

"Wait," I said. "I have an idea. Just give me a minute. Keep an eye out."

I closed my eyes, tried to slow my beating heart, tried to listen to the darkness for an idea, a suggestion, the hint of an escape plan.

My heartbeat thudded in my ears, and I focused past it, strained for sound. It took precious seconds, but I finally heard the soft scampers of animals in the woods, the hoot of an owl, the rhythmic slap of water against the shoreline.

And there, in the back of the sounds, in the darkness, the squeak and groan of metal, just as rhythmic.

I opened my eyes again, stood up, looked in the direction of the sound.

"There," I said, and as he followed behind, I jogged down the shore until I saw it: a metal dock, about twenty yards away. It floated on booms that squeaked with each soft wave.

Beside it, bobbing lightly in the water, was a boat. It wasn't large, and it wasn't new, but it was floating. And that was something.

Voices echoed through the darkness behind us, and they were getting louder.

"Dock," I said, and we took off running. I pushed open the small gate—thankfully unlocked—intended to keep interlopers off the equally small pier, hurried to the boat docked at the end of it.

It was a powerboat, something a family might use for skiing on a day at the lake. A seat for the captain behind a control panel and short windshield, a seat beside for a passenger, a line of cushions across the back. Nothing fancy, but the outboard engine looked serviceable enough.

I hopped down onto plastic carpeting, the boat swaying beneath me. I hadn't been on a boat in a very long time. Hell of a time for a reunion.

I sat down in the captain's chair, checked the relatively simple dashboard—ignition, speed, fuel gauge, throttle. The key was in the ignition, and it looked as though the tank was full. There were other bits and pieces of high-tech equipment, which could have been whale-tracking machines for all I knew.

When I realized I hadn't felt the boat bobble with Morgan's weight, I glanced back, found him standing on the dock, staring down at me.

"Get in the boat!" I told him.

"You know how to drive a boat?"

"I *remember* how to drive a boat," I clarified. "My grandparents had one on the lake for a few years, and my grandfather taught me how to drive. Get in," I said, and when he hopped down, I pointed him back toward the dock. "Untie the ropes and pull in the buoys. Push us off from the dock."

"We're clear," Morgan said, and I popped the ignition, felt the engines roar to life behind me. I nudged the wheel enough to point her away from the dock, just as voices rang out behind us, and gunshots began to *ping* through the air.

"Get down!" Morgan screamed, covering his body with mine as bullets rained around us. An old soda can, sitting forgotten in a cup holder, was hit, spraying soda into the air like a fountain. Morgan tossed it overboard.

"Go," he said, and I pushed down the throttle. The boat's nose lifted, the hull skipping over waves as we roared into darkness.

————◆✦◆————

CHAPTER TWENTY

THE PICTURE OF DORIAN GRAY

The lake was dark and quiet, the hum of the engine and the slap of water against the sides of the boat the only sounds. If the circumstances had been different—if it had been Ethan beside me instead of Morgan on the rear bench, silently mulling over his fate, and if we hadn't been running from gangsters—it might have been a romantic trip.

As if he'd known I'd been thinking of him—and maybe he had—Morgan moved up to the front of the boat, took a seat in the opposite chair.

"It always seems to come so easy for you," he said.

"What comes easy for me?"

"Being a vampire."

The sentiment was so utterly absurd I laughed. "Did you miss the panic attack?"

"All right, present circumstances excluded. And do you want to tell me what happened back there? Because I don't think it was really about getting off the island."

I pushed windblown hair behind my ears. "Just something

that happened to me a few nights ago. It made me a little panicky."

"A little?"

I nodded, kept my eyes on the dark water in front of me, squinting to see the lights of Chicago, praying I'd recognize them before we ran out of gas . . . and that dark panic circled me again.

"Anyway, other than that, being a vampire seems to come easy for you."

"There is no part of my being a vampire that has been easy, from the first attack to tonight's little pool party. I was kicked out of school. I watched Ethan die. My best friend unleashed a demon onto the city. None of it has been easy. Some of it has been pretty great. Most of it has been awkward."

"You have a House," he said. "Solid from the ground up."

He was right about that. And ironic, I thought, since my father's first words to me after I told him I'd been made a vampire were to denigrate Cadogan House. "They're old, but not as old as Navarre House," he'd said. Perhaps not. Perhaps not as chic, or as historic, and God knew Cadogan had had its share of bumps. But ultimately, when you dug down to it, we were solid. The foundation was solid, because Ethan was solid.

"Yeah," I said. "I got really lucky. And you got the really short straw in that respect."

He looked surprised by the admission, as if he'd expected me to rail against him, blame him for the House's issues. But that wouldn't have been fair.

I paused, not sure we'd reached total candor. On the other hand, what did I have to lose from honesty?

"Navarre has always been standoffish, at least in my experience. And it's been harsh when dealing with Cadogan. The city's faced a lot of crap the last few months, and you haven't exactly been helpful. How much of that is due to the Circle?"

He didn't answer at first, as though he couldn't decide whether to be pissed.

"I'm asking if you want me to give you the benefit of the doubt. You're only responsible for your actions," I said. "Not hers. And I know you loved her—that you all loved her. That she was very, very important to you. But it sounds like she gave you a crumbling castle."

Morgan sighed, sat back in the chair, glanced at me. "Yeah. She did. And yeah, I avoided most of your shenanigans because I had shenanigans of my own to deal with. We've been walking a very thin line since I came on board. That line keeps getting thinner, but the other vampires don't seem to appreciate that. They'll try to take the House for this. Because of what's happened."

"Irina's faction?"

He nodded. "I have tried to do right by Celina's vision, but how can I, when it was built on sand? I mean, look at this." He laughed, but the sound was entirely humorless. "We're on a boat, trying to escape an island of mobsters who'd kill me in a heartbeat if it gave them a chance to get a return on their investment."

I glanced back. There was only darkness behind us, the gurgling sound of the engine the only thing I could hear.

"We've escaped," I said. "Now we find our way back to shore. And that's the same thing you have to do. It's your House, Morgan. For better or worse, and whether Celina chose you for the right reasons or not, you're its Master. Own it."

The sky was overcast, the city lights gleaming orange beneath it. The dashboard held a small compass, so we used both to guide our way back to the city.

Chicago looked so peaceful in the darkness, a strip of light at the edge of the world, shapes emerging as we drew nearer. The height of the Willis and Hancock buildings, the sprawl of lights along the lakeshore, of cities stretching from Indiana to Wisconsin, the lights of Navy Pier.

"Where exactly are we going?" he asked.

That was an excellent question. Driving a boat was one thing; parking it was something entirely different. There were several marinas around Chicago, but I didn't really know how they were arranged.

There was one obvious place in Chicago to park a boat. Lots of boats, as it turned out, were already parked there, if much bigger than this one. I'd have to negotiate around the breakwater, lines of riprap that protected Navy Pier and the Chicago Harbor from the worst of Lake Michigan, but that, I thought, would be relatively easy. The entry point was beside the Chicago Lighthouse, which also served as headquarters for the RG. Hell, I could even wave at Jonah on the way in. Not that I'd do that right now.

I directed the boat toward the lights. "We're going there."

Morgan glanced at the horizon, then back at me. "You're not seriously going to park this thing at Navy Pier."

"It's a pier, isn't it? And a *navy* pier at that. It's in the damn name. If they didn't want boats parking there, they should have called it something else."

"You're getting loopy."

"My adrenaline has run its course," I admitted. "I'm going to crash really, really hard later."

I pulled the boat up to the end of the pier where a ladder dropped down into the water, grimaced as fiberglass groaned against concrete.

"Grab the ladder!" I told him, then switched off the engine

and ran around the chair, flipping the buoys over the side of the boat to provide some protection against the waves that already lifted it. Morgan tied off the boat, climbed up the ladder, and gave me a boost. When I'd followed him up, we stood on solid concrete, but I could still feel the phantom movements of the water beneath my feet.

"They're going to be pissed," Morgan said, eyes on the water.

I looked down at the boat, which looked ridiculously small bobbing in the waves against the dock, its significantly larger brothers and sisters—a yacht for dinner cruises, a three-masted schooner for the historical experience, a bevy of tour boats— parked along the dock in front of it.

"Probably so. But all things considered, this is just a drop in the bucket."

Morgan sighed, ran his hands through his hair. "Yeah, I suppose you're right. And that little guy got us halfway across Lake Michigan, so we should be grateful for that." He looked at me, and for a moment I saw Morgan in there, not just the Master he was trying to be. "You did good."

"So did you. Nice job with those throwing stars. You got any more of those?"

"Maybe one or two. I'll set you up."

"Cool."

We looked up at the sound of footsteps, caught the silhouettes of people running toward us. Ethan, Luc, Mallory, and Catcher emerged from darkness, my grandfather and Detective Jacobs behind them.

Sentinel? Ethan asked silently.

I'm fine, I said, glanced at Mallory, and held up my bracelet. "You tracked me?"

She nodded. "Glad it worked, since the earbuds crapped out. And I'm glad you're okay."

"The helicopter was just about to lift off when you started across the lake. Mallory guessed you'd taken a boat."

Luc stared down at the water, then back at me with amazement. "And the Circle's boat, at that."

"Only after they tried to take their payment out in our hides." A series of large waves rolled in, nudging the boat against the pier with a grinding sound that didn't really speak well of its future seaworthiness. Or lakeworthiness.

"They're on Torrance Island," I said when Jacobs reached us. "Former mobster hangout. There were at least six men there. I don't think they've really opened the house for spring yet. There's a helipad, but no longer a boat." I gestured toward the water.

"Negotiations?" my grandfather asked.

"They want King, decided they'd take me as a hostage to get his location."

"He's important to them."

"Apparently, but we didn't get a reason out of them. Either Maguire knew and wasn't telling—which seems unlikely, because he was pretty talkative—or he just didn't know. He played like he was leading the organization, but eventually threw out a 'we.' And besides, he's muscle. Maybe well-connected muscle, but just muscle. No one else looked familiar, and there was no sign of Balthasar. But Maguire basically acknowledged they knew who he was, and that he's crazy."

"Well done, Sentinel," Luc said approvingly, and my grandfather nodded.

"We've gotten the location of their hole, or one of them, anyway, and the boat. We'll investigate the jurisdictional issue, send boats and a chopper to bring them in if we can, and keep you posted."

"This boat may not make it through the night," Morgan said, eyes on the water as another wave surged toward it, even the water in the harbor rough tonight.

"Can we go home?" I asked. "It's been a long night."

"One moment," Ethan said pleasantly, then gave Morgan a right cross to the face.

Morgan staggered back, eyes wide. When he found his footing again, he put a hand to his jaw, wiggled it. "What the fuck, Sullivan?"

"That was our unfinished business. Now we're even." Ethan's eyes slitted. "Think carefully before you decide to use my people as ballast again." With that, he put his hand at my back, turned me toward the gate.

Morgan cursed. "Anybody ever tell you you're an asshole, Sullivan?"

Beside me, Ethan grinned, but kept his gaze on the boardwalk in front of us. "It wouldn't be the first time."

My grandfather and Detective Jacobs stayed behind to oversee the boat's forensic processing, with Jeff and Catcher promising to assist with research.

Morgan, Luc, Ethan, and I drove back to Cadogan House. Ethan sprang for hot beefs on the way home, and I finished mine in the car before we'd left downtown. The fight, the anticipation, my acting as a battery for Mallory's ward, put my hunger on overdrive.

Morgan excused himself to check on his vampires, ensure that they were still safe. We found Kelley and Malik waiting in Ethan's office, their expressions grim.

"What's happened?"

"It's Balthasar, or at least it seems like Balthasar. Downstairs," she said, and we followed her down to the Ops Room.

Once again, the screen was on, tuned to a news broadcast, the ticker at the bottom of the screen chilling: HOSPITALIZED WOMAN CLAIMS ASSAULT BY VAMPIRE IN DREAM.

"Jesus," Ethan said. "Can we have ten minutes without a crisis?"

"What about Juliet?" I asked Luc. "I thought they had him. I thought they found his condo."

"They sat on the building for two hours, didn't see him, so they checked with security. Turns out, security heard him contact the account manager in the lobby about something or other, and the account manager spilled that we'd checked in on him."

I had choice words for humans that I decided not to verbalize. "So he's gone again?"

"Unfortunately, yes." He gestured toward the screen. "I'd presume he's pissed we're keeping him away from his penthouse. So this attack could be punishment for that. But if the Circle and Balthasar are connected, and the Circle's pissed at us, it could be punishment from their direction, too. I doubt the Circle would have condoned it—it doesn't seem like their kind of play—but it wouldn't the first time Balthasar did something violent."

"Why not just come for us?" Luc asked, glancing at Ethan. "For you? What is he waiting for?"

Ethan's eyes darkened. "Consider the man. He's waiting for me to beg, and I'll be damned if I'll do that. We must put a stop to this. We cannot allow him to hurt anyone else, to destroy the goodwill we've tried to build."

"The Investiture," I said. "Navarre's vampires are stable, and it's time to take care of our own. We have to draw him out."

Ethan perked up an eyebrow.

"We have to draw him out, *Sire*," I added politely. "As you think best and such."

"Nice cover," Luc muttered.

"Her Grateful Condescension leaves something to be desired," Ethan said. "But she's right. I'll talk to Scott and Morgan. We'll say two nights hence. I'll also talk to Nick," he added, eyeing Malik. "I was thinking, if we'd decided to finalize it, that I'd suggest it's been in the works for several weeks, and we only just decided to announce it to humans."

"That adds weight and interest," Malik agreed with a nod.

"Location?" Luc asked.

"I'd prefer here. If there's to be an engagement with Balthasar, I'd prefer it happen on our territory and our terms. But perhaps in a tent on the grounds, weather permitting, in order to keep him out of the House proper?"

I nodded, looked at Luc. "In the meantime, we'll go back through Balthasar's timeline again, back to the beginning. We didn't know about the Circle the first time we looked. Maybe, with fresh eyes, something will pop."

I hoped it would. Because no one else deserved the trauma he seemed hell-bent to put people through.

When Ethan and Malik had gone, Luc skimmed fingers over the controls in the tabletop, and the timeline appeared on-screen. Most of the events were now green, meaning they'd been verified. A couple were still black, meaning they needed corroborating. None were red.

"So he told the truth about his past," I said.

Luc nodded. "The facts line up, except for the couple we haven't yet verified."

"Which are?"

Luc used a handheld tablet to zoom in on the chart. "Jeff's algorithm didn't pop any mention of Balthasar's name in the Memento Mori ledgers, but Jeff's not confident in the results. Thinks it could be due to the program, the inconsistency of the handwriting. The error rate's too high. He's going to keep looking."

I nodded. "What else?"

He pointed to another black box. "The safe house in Switzerland. Chalet Rouge. It's still operating, but I haven't been able to reach anyone yet. That's a phone tag issue."

I considered, but shook my head. That wasn't anything, either. "Go back to the beginning."

"What?"

"The beginning of the timeline. Go back to the beginning."

Luc zoomed out, resituated the timeline at the beginning. It began with Persephone's death, Ethan's departure, the attack on Balthasar by, as he'd put it, the "relative of some girl or other."

I suddenly remembered the look on Balthasar's face when he'd attacked me, the blankness when I'd mentioned her name. The utter lack of recognition.

The memory swamped me, raised a cold sweat down my back, a bubble of nausea in my throat. I closed my eyes, pursed my lips, forced myself to breathe in and out until the weight on my chest subsided.

"Sentinel?" Luc asked quietly.

I held up a hand, let my breaths come and go quietly until the panic passed. And felt dread settle low in my abdomen again, that I'd be living with terrifying and humiliating bouts of panic for the rest of my immortal life.

"Okay," I said a moment later. "I'm okay." I shook my head,

accepted without argument the bottle of water Lindsey handed me, took a long drink.

"He didn't know her name," I said when I was done.

Luc looked confused. "Who?"

"Persephone. When he attacked me, I mentioned her name. Balthasar looked completely blank, like he had no idea who she was."

Luc looked at the chart, contemplated. "He'd been tortured. Could have forgotten it."

"Yeah, but that seems to be the only thing he *doesn't* remember. He was attacked by a band of 'some girl's' relatives, held by them for magical purposes for years, can tell us every place he's been since then, but he doesn't mention the girl's name?" I looked at Luc. "If they show up at his house to punish him, to kill him, damn straight they're going to mention her name, tell him they're avenging her death, or his attack on her, or whatever. I'd sure remember it."

"He didn't say he didn't know it," Lindsey pointed out. "He just didn't mention it. And we're talking about Balthasar. He's not gonna win Feminist of the Year."

"And even if you're right," Luc said, "and he didn't remember her name, why does it matter?"

Because her name mattered. To Balthasar, to Ethan, to the story. And maybe, I thought, dread beginning to rise thick in my chest, to all of us.

"A vampire comes back into Ethan's life," I began, "centuries after his supposed death, and tells a story about where he'd been the entire time. But he doesn't know one of the most important parts of that story. We also find out he's being funded by an organization that's out to control all the vampire Houses in Chicago."

My heart thudded, but I asked the question anyway. "What if the story he told wasn't actually about him?" I looked at Luc, then Lindsey. "What if he isn't the real Balthasar?"

The Ops Room went deathly silent.

I wasn't sure which possibility was worse—that the vampire who made Ethan was psychopathic and misogynistic enough to forget the name of his most important victim, or that he was a magical imposter who'd gone to a hell of a lot of trouble to play that psychopath.

"Even if you're right," Luc said quietly, as if speaking the words more softly would minimize their power, "even if there's some way he could have gotten the information, made himself look like Balthasar, there would be easier ways to get to Ethan."

"Easier, but not with more legitimacy. Not with a tie to Ethan. Not like this. He's got the Circle behind him, Luc. They are strong, and they are wily. They've already got Navarre under their thumb. What's the best way to stake a claim on Cadogan?"

"Jesus Christ," Luc murmured, staring at the timeline.

I nodded, walked toward the door.

"Where are you going?" Luc asked.

"I want to talk to Ethan about Persephone, about that night."

And if this vampire, this man who'd thrown our lives into chaos was nothing more than a very powerful grifter running a long con, he was going to answer to me.

My palms began to sweat on the trip upstairs to Ethan's office. I wasn't looking forward to making him focus on Balthasar again, and certainly not to suggest that Ethan had been wrong from the beginning.

His office door was open a few inches. I put a hand on the

door, nearly pushed it open, until I recognized Jonah's voice in the room.

I froze, shifted so I could see them through the crack in the door. They stood in the middle of Ethan's office. Ethan had a glass in hand. Jonah had his hands in his pockets, and he looked profoundly uncomfortable.

"She is sad, Jonah," Ethan was saying. "She feels you're underestimating her. As you are."

My eyes widened in surprise, just as Jonah's did.

"She told you?"

"Not the details. She didn't have to." Ethan turned back, looked at him. "Her relationship with me, my involvement in the AAM. Of course you'd see that as a potential asset." He paused. "I know you have feelings for her."

"*Had.*"

"That's debatable. If your emotions weren't coloring your analysis of this situation, you'd see it differently. That's what makes it disappointing."

"And how, exactly, would I see it differently?"

"If I were you, instead of seeing her relationship with us as a liability, I'd see it as a bonus." He put a hand on his chest. "I'd consider the information she'll be privy to, the access she'll have. I'd wager her situation is unique in the United States, and I'd be grateful for that situation. I wouldn't hold it against her. And I wouldn't use it as an excuse to question her loyalty. And if you have any doubt that she would put power and gain above the welfare of her friends, her colleagues, her family, then she's the one who needs a new partner."

"She made an oath."

"To the RG, and to me, and to her House. And she made an

oath to you, of a kind, and you to her. She isn't the one breaking that oath now."

"Balthasar could—"

"Balthasar is irrelevant, as you well know. He is trouble, yes, and we are dealing with him. But he has no bearing on my rule of this House, or her.

"Look," Ethan continued. "Either you earnestly, and wrongly, believe that she'll be suddenly blind to my incompetence, or my succumbing to Balthasar—or someone else in the RG believes it, and you won't stand up for her. Neither option is particularly flattering for you."

He finished his drink, set it aside. "You should get back to your House, keep an eye on your Master, just as you suggest Merit keep an eye on hers. Although Balthasar has no bearing on my leadership, he's still dangerous. Until we get him squared away, I recommend you stay close to Scott."

Jonah nodded. "Thanks."

"Anytime."

Jonah turned toward the door, and I nearly ran down the hallway to duck out of sight. But since I wasn't a child, I cleared my throat and pushed open the door as if I'd only just come by.

"Oh, sorry," I said, with what I hoped was admirable acting. "I didn't see you had anyone in here."

Ethan looked amused. "No trouble, Sentinel. Jonah was here to discuss the Investiture and look over the grounds. He's just heading back to Grey House."

Jonah nodded. "You were at Torrance Island?"

"Yeah. It would have been a cool tour but for the murderous criminals."

"I bet. I should go," he said, and slipped out without another word.

"Did you enjoy our conversation?"

I looked back at Ethan. "What conversation?"

He smiled. "I saw you outside, Sentinel. Although I don't think he did."

"Thanks for taking up for me."

"I'd say I was taking up for your partnership. Whether I like it or not, it's a valuable asset to the House. You two work well together and could continue to do so if he wasn't being so stubborn."

"Yeah." I walked to him, slipped my arms around him, relieved that I hadn't questioned the gesture before doing it. "What do I do?"

"I don't know, Merit." Ethan paused, clearly surprised by the embrace, before wrapping his arms around me, his relief nearly palpable. "I'm afraid he's not giving you many choices. He certainly doesn't believe he has many. You came up for something, and I presume it wasn't Jonah."

My stomach twisted again, and I pulled back. "I have a question about Balthasar, actually."

"Ah."

"You said you believed it was Persephone's family who assaulted Balthasar. Held him."

"That's correct."

"How do you know?"

His jaw worked for a moment, his expression still unusually cautious. "I told them."

I blinked. "You told them?"

"What he'd done and where to find him." One hand on his hips, he ran the other through his hair. "I couldn't save her, couldn't kill my maker to avenge her. But I could let them know the truth and give them an opportunity to avenge her death, and prevent any others."

Ethan walked a few steps away, giving himself space, looked back at me. "It is not something I'm proud of. It was cowardly to ask a human to do work I should have done. But there had been so much death . . ." He looked away.

So Balthasar had killed Persephone, and Ethan had told her family about it. They'd hunted him down and planned to kill him, and one of them decided he'd be more useful scientifically. But still, through all that, Balthasar didn't remember her name? Had he not thought about the timing? About the fact that he'd been attacked just after Ethan left? Surely he could have put that together. And if he had, why hadn't he mentioned it?

"What's on your mind, Sentinel?"

"Puzzle pieces that don't fit well," I said. "He didn't know about Persephone."

"What do you mean?"

"He didn't mention her when he was here. And when he attacked me, he didn't recognize her name."

"He could have forgotten, repressed it," Ethan said, but he didn't look convinced by that. "He called me. Knows all the history."

"True. But his appearance, right now, was oddly coincidental. And he's here, at least in some part, because the Circle is paying for it. Just at the moment when the Circle is making a concerted bid for control of the city's vamps."

"You're suggesting he's an imposter." Ethan's tone went hot. "I'd know if he wasn't who he says he is. It wouldn't be possible for someone to pretend that well."

But we lived in a world of fairies, gnomes, harpies, shifters;

that's what bothered me. Since when was anything impossible, magically or otherwise?

Before he could say anything else, my phone rang. I pulled back, found Catcher's number, answered it. "Merit."

"We've got something new on Jude Maguire, starting with the fact that Jude Maguire isn't his real name. Jeff did an image-surf—"

"Hey, Mer," said Jeff's voice in the background.

"Hey, Jeff. Image-surf?" I prompted.

"And we found a photograph, think we found Maguire's previous identity. His name was Thomas O'Malley."

"Does that matter?"

"Yeah," Catcher said. "I think it does. Judge for yourself."

"Send it to Ethan's mail," I said, and walked to Ethan's desk, sat down behind his computer.

"Oh, do help yourself," Ethan murmured, watching.

I pulled up the program, waited for the photograph to come through, and when the alert rang, clicked it.

I nearly dropped the phone. "Crap on toast," I said, borrowing Mallory's curse, and gestured Ethan to come look.

It was a photograph from a college yearbook, two guys standing side by side, an arm over each other's shoulder, bottles of beer in their free hands. Their hair was fashionably long, just brushing their popped shirt collars. They looked casually wealthy, confident, and very content with their lot.

They, according to the caption below the photograph, were Thomas O'Malley and Adrien Reed.

"I'm going to put you on speaker," I said to Catcher, and put down the phone so Ethan could hear.

"They went to college together," Catcher said. "O'Malley got popped for larceny, changed his name, if not legally. Jeff says there's no record of it."

"When you're friends with Adrien Reed, who needs a judge?" Ethan muttered.

"Yeah," Catcher agreed. "There was barely a record of the photograph—Jeff found it buried in an online alumni forum. Wouldn't surprise me if Reed tried to scrub the records. In order to hide the connection."

"Let's not get carried away," I said. "I'm sure Reed took a lot of pictures with a lot of people."

"This wasn't just a throwaway," Catcher said. "They were buddies, frat brothers. O'Malley was in Reed's first wedding. Pre-Sorcha. First wife's name was Frederica. No pictures that we could find—also likely scrubbed—but there's a line item in the society pages. Reed and Maguire are friends," Catcher concluded. "Which makes me wonder if Reed is also part of the Circle."

"Jesus," Ethan said. "All the money. All the connections. Why would he risk that?"

"Maybe that's the wrong order of things," I said. "Maybe he got the money, the connections, *because* of it. But if we're right, why the attempt on King at Reed's house?"

"Maybe Reed wanted a bird's-eye view of King's downfall," Catcher said. "Wanted to watch a competitor suffer."

"Or wanted to confirm the hit had gone down," Ethan said. "There was, after all, some question whether that would take place. And to let it happen in his own home, he was incredibly confident King's death wouldn't be traced back to him."

"That could be," Catcher said. "For now, this is just speculation. We don't have any hard evidence linking Reed to Maguire, as he's now known, the Circle, or anything else. But it's a first step. I have to go. We're going to look into the King-Reed angle more. I'll keep you posted."

By the time I said thanks and hung up the phone, Ethan had grabbed his suit jacket and was headed for the door.

"Where are you going?"

"I'm going to pay a little visit to Adrien Reed. And this time, I'm driving."

◄═══►

CHAPTER TWENTY-ONE

FRANKLY, SENTINEL

He didn't give me time to argue, tattle, or grab Brody. In order to keep Ethan from going alone, I had to settle for sending Luc a message as I climbed into Ethan's Ferrari and he squealed out of the basement parking garage and onto the street, just missing the gate by a hair.

"What, exactly, is the plan here?" I asked as the engine hummed through Hyde Park.

"I want to talk to him. I want to talk to him about Balthasar. I want to talk to him about Navarre. I want to talk to him about the hell he's put us and our friends through for the last week. I want to talk to him about attacking my Sentinel and attempting to use her as a hostage."

"All good questions," I said, nodding my agreement. "But keep in mind that we don't actually have any evidence he's done any of that."

"Frankly, Sentinel, I don't give a damn about evidence right now. I care about this unmitigated asshole having the stones to admit what he's done so I can begin planning how to destroy him."

"So this is just going to be a light social call to a millionaire in the middle of the night, then."

When Ethan growled, I decided this wasn't the time to mitigate tension with sarcasm. Seeing as how I didn't have much else to contribute, I settled back and began to answer Luc's panicked messages.

The front door was locked, no welcome party tonight, no cadre of limousines in line to drop off visitors. Ethan pressed the security panel beside the door.

"May I help you?"

"Ethan Sullivan for Adrien Reed."

"One moment please."

There was a pause, then a beep, and a woman in a dour black dress opened the door, gestured for us to come inside. The moment we did, two guards stepped forward, scanned us with hand-held wands.

Metal detectors?

Looking for weapons and, more likely, recording devices, Ethan said.

When they decided we were clear, they gestured us forward. "Mr. Reed will see you in his study. I understand you know the way."

"We do," Ethan said through clenched teeth. "Thank you."

The house had been stripped of its Venetian party decorations, but hadn't diminished the excessiveness. Every nook and cranny was still stuffed with objects, art, furniture.

"Is he a hoarder?" I asked quietly.

"One wonders," Ethan said. "That would certainly explain his criminal interest in accumulating more of it." His voice was dry as toast.

We traveled the ballroom, the stairs, the gallery, made our way to his office. A new guard stood by the door, hands clasped in front of him, gaze suspicious. After a look-over, he nodded us in.

Despite the hour, Reed sat behind his desk, pen in one hand as he scanned a sheath of papers. "I'm a busy man, Mr. Sullivan," he said, without looking up.

Ethan walked into the office, his gaze on everything in the room except Reed, his stride dangerously blasé. He walked to the bar cart, poured a finger of liquid into a glass, finished it.

So our Master vampire intended to toy with his prey a bit. If I wasn't supposed to focus on his safety, I'd have pulled up a chair to enjoy the show.

Reed's eyes widened at the move, but the facade snapped quickly back into place. "Help yourself."

"Done," Ethan said, putting the glass on the cart, bottom up, with a heavy thud.

Reed put down his pen, the move slow and deliberate. "Your manners leave something to be desired."

"My manners?" Ethan said, turning back to him. "Do you know, Adrien—may I call you Adrien?—what isn't mannerly? Being a loan shark. Facilitating a vampire's addiction. Extorting murder. Assault. Oh, and leading a criminal enterprise."

Reed's eyes widened, this time with amusement. "Have I done all that? That's quite a list of accomplishments."

"Games are beneath you."

He clucked his tongue. "I'm sad to say that's wrong. All the world's not a stage, but a game. Most are pawns. Some are kingmakers. Only a chosen few are kings."

Ethan tilted his head. "Are you a king? Is this your castle?" He paused. "Is the Circle your kingdom?"

Reed went very quiet and very still. "I understand you fancy yourself a leader of vampires and think highly of your connections and your power. But I'm not sure you have as much of either as you believe, Mr. Sullivan. That could be dangerous for a man in your position."

As if Reed had paid him the highest compliment—or been baited right according to plan—Ethan grinned wildly, took a step forward.

"And I'm not sure you understand real danger, Adrien. Celina made a bad business deal? That's not my business. But you threaten vampires? You attempt to hurt my people? That makes it personal. And when it's personal, it will be your house and mine. It will be you and me, and there will be no one to stand in front of you. No one else to fight your battles. *That* is the dangerous situation."

But Reed knew how to play the game, just as Ethan did. His gaze shifted to me, and the chill in it lifted the hair on the back of my neck. There was nothing soft, nothing compassionate, barely anything human, about Adrien Reed.

"The personal matters to you, does it?" he asked, the implication obvious. If Ethan wished to battle Reed, Reed would simply target me.

Ethan's magic seeped forward, a cold and sinking fog. "You'd be wise to keep your eyes on me and your men away from my people."

"My 'men'? Unless you're interested in mergers and acquisitions, which I highly doubt, I can't say I know what you're talking about."

"We've had several unpleasant run-ins with Jude Maguire. He's one of yours."

Reed frowned, pursed his lips, feigned confusion. "I'm not sure I know anyone named Maguire."

"You might remember him as Thomas O'Malley," I suggested pleasantly.

His smile widened. "Oh, I haven't heard from Tom in years. I hope he's doing well."

This time, I let my smile bloom vampiric. "Actually, he's nursing some fairly serious injuries at the moment. Accident with a throwing star."

Ethan glanced at me, grimaced. "Oh, that sounds unfortunate."

I nodded. "It was. And bloody. I'd like to get some of those stars."

"I'll see what I can do."

Reed's lip curled at the comment and the byplay, but only for an instant. However dangerous he might have been, he was very well schooled at masking his emotions, playing the businessman. It was an attribute a vampire could appreciate. "I don't know what you're talking about."

"In that case," Ethan said, "how about Balthasar? Are you aware your companies are paying his way?"

"Don't confuse me and my companies, Ethan. I don't oversee every decision made in my expansive, shall we say, kingdom."

"You may have money," Ethan said, "and you may have friends in very high places. But you forget one thing: You are human, and we are not. We are strong, and we are immortal."

Reed snapped out a laugh. There was no mirth in it, only insult. "You are two-bit celebrities with short memories and whose popularity shifts like the tide."

Footsteps echoed down the hallway, drawing nearer.

This time, the smile was all Reed's and a bit maniacal. "Ah," he said, lifting his cell phone, wiggling it a bit. "It looks like help has arrived. And lest you think I've called them because I fear you—let me clarify things for you." He put the phone on his desk and leaned forward. "I've called them to remind you that you don't hold the upper hand. You never have, and you never will. This city is beholden to me, and its debt has come due."

I'd thought Balthasar narcissistic, psychopathic. But the crazed desire in Balthasar's eyes had nothing on the utter malevolence in Reed's.

With that statement freezing the air, Detective Jacobs walked in, two uniformed cops behind him. Reed pasted on a relieved smile with shocking speed. "Thank you for getting here so quickly."

"Of course, Mr. Reed," Jacobs said, glancing at us. "I understand your visitors are unwelcome."

"What they are," Reed said, "is harassing me. And I understand the CPD takes vampire harassment very seriously these days."

"Of course they do." Jacobs looked at us with disappointment in his eyes. "And my apologies for the delay. A transformer burst, so traffic and streetlights are out. It's very dark out, and they've had to reroute traffic."

Adrien made some vague sound, didn't seem to care much about the CPD's logistical concerns. But we understood it. That was our code phrase, the signal we'd worked out before visiting the Circle on Torrance Island. Jacobs wanted us to play along.

Jacobs took Ethan by the arm, and Ethan made a good show of shaking him off. "Get your damn hand off me!"

"You know I can't do that, Mr. Sullivan. Not when you've come into someone's home, threatened them."

Ethan's expression was perfectly superior. "I did no such thing. The housekeeper let us in!"

"Mmm-hmm. Your lawyers can discuss that with you at the

station." He smiled back at Mr. Reed. "Once again, sir, I'm very sorry for the interruption. Chuck Merit doesn't appreciate his reputation being tarnished, and I'm sure he'll have some choice words for his granddaughter."

"I hope he does," Reed said, not bothering to hide the gleam in his eyes as an officer led me to the door with a heavy grip on my arm. "They should learn to respect those who've earned their success."

"My thoughts exactly," Jacobs said. He glanced at the clock on the wall behind Reed's desk. "I hate to inconvenience you further considering the hour. Perhaps I could call you tomorrow for your statement?"

"That would be acceptable," Reed said, clearly pleased by Jacobs's apparent deference.

Jacobs nodded. "In that case, we'll clear out and leave you to your evening. Do take care to lock up afterward. You never know who you'll find on the doorstep."

This might be the worst date I've ever been on, I mused as the officers escorted us silently down the gallery and out of the house.

Oh, I doubt that, Ethan said behind me.

That's not flattering, Sullivan.

It wasn't meant to insult you, but the boys you dated. Had any of them the guile to win you, they'd have done so. But seeing as you're here with me . . .

Just stop there, I advised him, *before you dig that hole any deeper.*

"Put them in my car," Detective Jacobs said to the uniforms. "I'll take them back to the station."

The cops looked at each other. "You don't, uh, want us to go with you?" asked the one who held me, free hand on his club as if there was a possibility I'd take a swing at a cop.

"Unnecessary," Jacobs said with a smile. "I've handled these two before." He patted his coat as if he held a secret weapon there. "And I know just how to do it. I'll even take care of the paperwork."

"That'd actually be great," said my cop, looking very relieved. "I've got a pile on my desk. I mean"—he glanced at his partner—"it's not exactly protocol . . ."

"But, then," Jacobs said, "neither is coming to the home of a millionaire to arrest vampires he's apparently invited through the door."

"He does have a point," said Ethan's cop. Ethan watched the discussion with amusement, apparently nonplussed about the fact that his arrest was the topic of conversation.

"If you could just get them into my car," Jacobs prompted, and they nodded, opened the back door of a sedate gray sedan, gestured us inside. I squeezed in after Ethan, and they closed the door with a heavy *thud*.

"Twenty-eight years without so much as a speeding ticket," I said, glancing at him, "and you get me arrested for trespassing."

Ethan snorted. Jonah usually accompanied me during investigations, so Ethan didn't often get the chance to do the fieldwork. He seemed to be enjoying it—both the highs and lows. Maybe he saw it as a break from administration and paperwork. Or maybe he just appreciated being my partner in the other sense of the word.

Jacobs gave parting instructions to the cops, climbed into the front seat. He watched as the uniforms drove away, then glanced at us in the rearview mirror. "You have anything to say for yourselves?"

Ethan smiled. "Can we throw ourselves on the mercy of the CPD?"

Jacobs humphed. "Now that we're alone, would you like to

tell me why you're here in the middle of the night worrying Chuck Merit?"

I winced, but Ethan didn't mince words. "There's evidence Reed's involved in the Circle. And considering his money, finances, connections, I'm guessing he's at the helm."

Jacobs, being a cop to the bone, didn't so much as flinch. "What led you to that conclusion?"

My grandfather must not have filled him in on what the Ombuddies had found.

"Jeff and Catcher dug into Jude Maguire's past," Ethan said. "He's actually Thomas O'Malley. O'Malley went off the radar several years ago, and Maguire took his place. Reed and Maguire went to college together. They're friends; close ones. O'Malley was in Reed's first wedding."

Jacobs considered quietly. "That doesn't link Reed to the Circle."

"Not definitively," Ethan agreed. "But he as much as admitted it in his office."

"Admitted it, or as much as?" Jacobs asked.

Ethan nodded, taking his point. Reed hadn't expressly said anything about being in the Circle.

Jacobs turned on the car. "We'll look into it," he said. "In the meantime, I recommend you stay away from Mr. Reed. Whether he's part of the Circle or isn't, he's a very powerful man, as I'm sure he informed you. Your transportation?"

"Black Ferrari, one block north."

Jacobs nodded. He eased the car onto the street, and after doing a figure eight around the block in case Reed was watching, pulled up in front of the Ferrari.

He glanced at Ethan in the rearview. "Perhaps, next time you decide to play junior detective, you'll let one of us in on the investigation."

I elbowed Ethan in the ribs.

Jacobs put the car in park, got out, and opened our doors, making a grand gesture as we climbed back to freedom.

"Don't worry your grandfather," he said to me. "I'll talk to him. And do try to have a nice evening."

We climbed into the Ferrari, and I, for one, was relieved to be leaving the neighborhood. At least until I pulled out my phone, found the waiting message from my father.

Reed had apparently gotten to him, too, and he was pissed.

"I cannot believe you. Your disrespect for yourself, for your family, for your grandfather, for me. To barge into a man's home, to accuse him of wrongdoing, of all people. A trusted friend and business partner. To be escorted out by the *police*. What if there'd been reporters? Or a tourist with a camera? Do you have any idea the damage you've done to this family, to the Towerline project? We're going to talk about this. We're going to talk about this *tonight*."

I guessed Reed hadn't just called the CPD.

"Trouble, Sentinel?"

"Reed tattled. That was a very unhappy message from my father."

I watched Ethan's gaze dart from windshield to rearview mirror to side mirror, then back again. Magic began to lift, slowly but steadily, raising goose bumps on my arms.

"What's wrong?"

Ethan's gaze tracked the sequence again. "Someone is following us. White sedan, dark windows, three cars back."

I glanced at the side mirror, and when the car immediately behind us turned onto a side street, I caught a sliver of white.

"One of Reed's men?"

"Unless your father's hired a hit man. Send Luc a message. Tell him Reed may be pissed, and to lock down the House. Same message to Scott and Morgan."

I typed the messages as Ethan turned a sharp corner, tried to lose the car behind us. The movement wasn't good for accuracy.

"I might have just told Helen to lock down the House."

"Close enough," Ethan said, his gaze darting between the windshield and rearview mirror. We were flying down a residential street. The Ferrari had no problem with that, but Chicago traffic was hairy on the best of nights.

The street opened, became two lanes in each direction. The white car used the opportunity to go around the remaining car and slipped back in behind us. It was an Audi, and I caught a glimpse of red hair when he drove beneath a streetlight.

"It's Maguire," I said. "And he's moving faster."

Ethan nodded. "He knows he's been spotted and doesn't want to lose us."

"He doesn't have to worry about that. He knows where we live."

"That's only true if he wants us to arrive safely. I don't believe that's the case, Sentinel."

There was a flash, a bang, as gunshots ricocheted around the car. There was a *thwack* behind me as a bullet made contact with a back panel.

Ethan jerked the Ferrari to the left, the right, avoiding another spray of bullets. Maguire had upgraded his arsenal.

"Either Reed was particularly distressed by our meeting, or Maguire is acting out. Either should know better than to waste a Ferrari on vengeance."

Ethan wrenched the car to the left across blaring traffic and onto a side street. The white car followed, leaving the crash of metal and tinkle of glass in its wake as cars hit one another to avoid smashing into it. He zoomed down a narrow street, dodging around parked cars like a skier on a slalom course.

The Audi maneuvered behind us, mirroring every swerve. Maguire was an asshole, but a capable driver. Ethan turned right, tires squealing with the motion, had room to speed up. But the Audi was right behind us, and inched closer.

"Hold on," Ethan said, and we jerked forward as the Audi slammed us from behind.

"He is fucking insane!" I said, gripping the armrest to keep my seat.

"I fear you're right." Ethan sped up, but the Audi kept pace, knocked us again.

"All right," Ethan said, "I am done with this asshole. Hold on." He grabbed the parking brake, yanking it up as he wrenched the wheel so we spun around to the left, drifted down the street as the tires screamed in protest.

Ethan hit the gas and we darted down the street in the opposite direction. But Maguire knew the same trick, or close enough, and spun the car around to follow us.

No—not just to follow us, but to reach us. As we zoomed down the empty residential street, blowing past houses and cars and sleeping humans, the Audi darted forward so we were even.

Maguire flipped us off through the window, then slammed his car into ours.

"Shit," Ethan said, and held the wheel, tried to keep us stable, but wind caught the car like a sail, and suddenly we were airborne. For a moment, time slowed, and Ethan gripped my hand, squeezed it with bone-crushing strength.

Take care, Sentinel, he said silently.

We rotated, flipped, soaring through the air like a luxury projectile. The world spun, dark sky now our floor, the pavement our sky . . . and then we landed with a jolt I felt in every bone, muscle, and tendon. We bounced once, then again, before skidding to a stop.

Sound and pain and smell returned with a roar like an ocean wave cresting over our heads. I tasted blood, felt a stabbing pain in my side.

I'd knocked my head against the seat back, and I blinked until the world stopped spinning. When the carousel slowed, I glanced over, the movement wrenching something in my neck.

Ethan sat beside me, utterly still, eyes closed, head bleeding from a visibly nasty gash in his forehead. Smoke began to fill the car from the crumpled hood.

I cursed, unhooked my seat belt, kicked the car door until it opened, and climbed out. I staggered on my feet and grabbed the side of the car because the world had started to spin again.

"Do not pass out," I ordered myself, my knuckles white as I fought to stay upright while darkness circled around my vision. I clung to consciousness, taking one step at a time, my ribs screaming, both hands on the car for balance, moving around it to Ethan's side of the car.

His door was dented, but I wrenched it open.

"Ethan!" I slapped him, got no response, tried our psychic connection. *Ethan.*

The silence was deafening. I put a hand to his throat, felt a low and steady pulse. The car was filling with smoke; I was going to have to move him.

I unbuckled the seat belt, leaned him forward, reached around his chest, pulled him out of the car. It wasn't easy hauling one hundred and eighty pounds of undead weight with what I'd diagnosed as a broken rib and probably a concussion, but I managed it, and got him to the curb when sirens began to scream in the distance. I laid him on the sidewalk, tore a strip from my T-shirt, pressed it to the unpleasant-looking wound in his forehead.

I didn't stop to consider the possibility he might have been killed, that both of us might have been killed. That, I knew, would have set off an entirely new wave of panic, and I didn't have time for that.

When Ethan's eyes fluttered open, my hiccupping breaths sounded suspiciously like sobs.

"Ferrari?" was all he said.

I laughed between sobs. "Totaled. You're going to need *another* new car. And Luc is never going to let you drive again." Hell, Ethan would be lucky if Luc ever let him out of the House again.

"You drive," he said, and closed his eyes again, a smile flitting around his mouth. "Headache."

"You took a good knock. Amazingly, your head is not actually filled with rocks."

Ambulances, fire trucks, CPD vehicles streamed down the street. EMTs climbed out of the ambulance with gear in hand, rushed toward us.

"I'm fine," I said to them, ignoring the pain in my side. "He's a vampire, so he'll heal, but he's got a pretty bad cut."

"We'll clean it up," one of them said, and I moved aside, climbed to my feet as they began to work.

I looked across the street, found Maguire's car wrapped around a light pole. Either contact with us had sent the car on a collision course, or he'd been too busy watching us to see the obstacle.

Techs had already pulled him from the car, were attaching a cervical collar and stabilizing him for transport.

"I'm fine. I'm fine." I glanced back at the sound of Ethan's voice. He was sitting up, if slowly, and waving the techs away.

They'd managed to get gauze and padding on his forehead, which was apparently the most he was willing to let them do.

The Ombudsman's van squealed to a stop at the curb, and my grandfather climbed out of the passenger seat, searched for us. I held up a hand, waited until he made eye contact, saw the relief in his eyes.

Maguire was loaded into an ambulance, and the techs jumped into the vehicle, closed the doors. The sirens came on and the bus zoomed down the street.

I'd have sworn I saw my father in the streetlight where the ambulance had been, staring at the scene in front of him. But when I blinked, looked again, he was gone.

Two bottles of blood later, we'd told the story to my grandfather three times. It didn't change in any of its repetitions, but he wanted to ensure that he'd gotten all the facts straight.

By the time we returned to the House—once again in the back of a CPD cruiser, since the Ferrari was toast—dawn was flicking rosy fingers at us.

I was so exhausted that I didn't even argue when Ethan lifted me into his arms, carried me into the House. It had been a really, really long night, and the raven bracelet I still wore probably wasn't helping.

Luc met us at the front door. "Sire?"

I heard the words, but I was already drifting to sleep, and they sounded so far away.

"She's fine," he said. "Just tired. The House?"

"Fine." Luc closed and locked the door. "And I hear Maguire's out of surgery, stable. We'll plan to debrief about all of it at sunset."

Ethan nodded, kept walking toward the stairs. When we

reached the apartments, he unlocked the door, carried me into the room, kicked it closed once again.

"You can put me down," I said groggily.

"Mmm-hmm."

He waited until he reached the bed, stood me carefully beside it. "Get undressed. I'll get some pajamas."

"Pervert," I said, but pulled off everything except the raven bracelet I still wore. I hit the bed naked and fell asleep immediately.

⫸⫷⫸

CHAPTER TWENTY-TWO

THE PRESTIGE

We woke at dusk, both of us naked, to a knock on the door.

"That's never a good sign."

Ethan grunted, pulled on a robe, walked toward the sound. I heard mumbling, and then footsteps approaching again.

"Your father is in the foyer," Ethan said, when he rounded the corner again. "Helen reports that he seems upset. He wants to talk to you."

"I'll bet he does. Tell him I've moved to Botswana."

"Why Botswana?" was his only inquiry.

"First place that came to mind. Which is weird, because I bet I've never said 'Botswana' before." But I was procrastinating, so I pushed off the covers and climbed out of bed. "I'll get dressed."

Ethan nodded. "As will I, and we'll tackle this particular obstacle together."

That was fine by me.

* * *

We didn't dawdle, but we didn't hurry, either. I wasn't in any rush to listen to my father explain to me—especially after last night— how wrong I was about Reed. On the other hand, I was more than willing to give him a lecture of his own.

We walked downstairs wearing black clothing and grim expressions.

"Front parlor," Lindsey said quietly when we reached the foyer.

We walked inside at the same time, two vampires in the threshold, a united front against all enemies. My father stood in the middle of the room in an immaculate suit, hands in his pockets. He glanced back, moved quickly toward the door when he saw me.

"Merit."

"Joshua," Ethan said, moving just enough to put his body between ours.

My father kept his gaze on me. "I need to talk to Merit."

Once upon a time, I might have shied away from conflict with my father. I'd have avoided it by running to New York or California for college or my first round of graduate school, or I'd have simply locked myself in my room. I was no longer that girl.

I also had a champion.

My father took a step closer to me, but Ethan held out a hand.

"Stop," he said, quietly, but firmly. "She needs no more berating from you. If you cannot speak to her civilly, respectfully, I won't allow you to speak to her at all."

My father's jaw twitched. Most of the men and women in his acquaintance kowtowed to him; it wasn't often he was challenged.

He looked at me, as if to confirm that I agreed, and found my position no softer.

"He's right," I said. "You've had your say, and there's no need

to repeat it. It's pretty clear what you think of me. Of all of us."
The irony being that he'd been the impetus for my being there,
for being a vampire at all.

"I didn't know he was a criminal. Reed," he clarified. "I didn't
know what he was involved in."

The words, spoken with a flavor I'd never heard from my
father—uncertainty—hung in the air for a moment.

"Let's go to my office," Ethan said. "Joshua, I believe you
know the way?"

My father nodded and walked past Ethan into the hallway.

When he disappeared, Ethan glanced at me, held out a hand.
"Come, Sentinel. Let's go hear what your father has to say."

Malik and Morgan already waited in Ethan's office. They rose to
leave when we walked in, but Ethan motioned them down again,
closed the door behind us. The three of us joined them in the
sitting area.

"This pertains to Reed," Ethan had said. "So it pertains to all
of us. You should stay."

My father looked at me. "I didn't know Reed was a criminal,"
he said again, then swallowed heavily. "I was on my way to Reed's
home. We'd been on the phone, and he said you'd just barged in.
I told him I'd call your grandfather, and I did."

Reed must have called him as soon as we hit the front door.
That explained why Jacobs had shown up with the officers and
how'd they'd gotten there so quickly.

"That's when you left the message for me?" I asked.

He nodded. "I didn't know everything then."

Ethan frowned. "And what do you know now?"

"I saw the police escort you out. And when the police were
gone, he went into the house."

"He?" Ethan asked.

"The redhead." My father paused. "Maguire. I'd seen him on the news. Knew my father was looking for him. Knew he'd accosted Merit."

"Wait," I said, holding up a hand. "You saw Jude Maguire walk into Adrien Reed's house?"

"Only for a moment. He walked inside, couldn't have been in there for more than a couple of seconds. Then he walked out again, slammed the door, got into his car. The white sedan." He shook his head. "I thought Maguire was the perpetrator, the one who'd hired the vampires. I thought my father was wrong about Adrien. He's a business partner, a friend. He wouldn't hurt my family. He wouldn't hurt my daughter."

"You followed Maguire," Ethan prompted.

My father nodded. "When I realized he was shadowing you, I called your grandfather, told them where you were, where to find you. And then I saw the Ferrari flip, and my heart stopped." Eyes on me, his gaze darkened. "I thought I'd lost you."

"I'm all right," I said quietly. My father and I didn't get along, and weren't especially close, but that didn't mean I couldn't sympathize with his fear for his child. My sister, the first Caroline, had died in a car accident that left my parents nearly unscathed. I'd been, or I'd always felt that I'd been, her replacement. It must have wrecked him to have witnessed the crash, to fear history would repeat itself and he'd lose another daughter—and his connection to that beautiful child he'd lost.

"You saw us," Ethan said, "but you didn't help?" There was a note of disapproval in his voice.

"By the time I got to the vehicles, Merit's grandfather had arrived, and the ambulances." My father looked down, clearly embarrassed, a rare condition for him.

"You were in good hands," he continued after a moment, when his eyes had hardened again like chalcedony. "And I had other business. I went back to Reed's house."

I didn't scare easily. Not anymore. But that scared me. "You went back? After what had happened? Why?"

"I told him I'd seen Maguire, that I knew who he was, that I'd seen what he tried to do to you and Ethan. Reed was cagey, but said you'd gone to his house to harass him, had probably led Maguire to his doorstep, and that security hadn't let Maguire in."

Convenient, and likely scripted by Reed just in case someone was watching, Ethan observed silently. *He is very, very clever.*

"This is our fault."

We all looked at Morgan, saw the guilt etched in his face.

"If it wasn't for her, for Navarre, you wouldn't be in this position. None of you. Not if Celina had been satisfied with what she'd had. Not if she'd had any self-control." He ran a hand through his hair. "Maybe I can sell the building. It must be worth something. Maybe that would take care of part of the debt. I could sell the art, the furnishings."

"You don't have to do that," my father said. "It's unnecessary."

Ethan went very still. "What do you mean, Joshua?"

"I gave him Towerline."

For a moment, I didn't understand what my father had said, the implication of it. "What do you mean?"

"I gave Adrien Reed my interest in Towerline. In the investment, in the building."

I was staggered. Baffled. Utterly bewildered by the act, the apparent sacrifice. I stood in silence for several long seconds—just trying to catch up with my raging emotions—before looking at my father again. "I'm sorry, but I don't understand. You paid off Adrien Reed?"

"He didn't call it that." His tone was dry. "Said it was a good-faith proffer against our future business."

"I can't say I'd recommend any future business with Adrien Reed," Ethan said.

"I can't say I disagree with you. The suggestion was his, but carefully couched, of course." Talking about business seemed to return my father's color, his poise. "But he said it settled the debt of the Navarre vampires, and he'd draw up the paperwork accordingly."

"Thank you," Morgan said. "My God, those two words are staggeringly insufficient, but they're all I can think to say. Thank you."

My father nodded.

"How much of a hit will Merit Properties take?" Ethan asked.

"Towerline was a . . . substantial investment. It's a hit. We can recover, but not this year."

I was still flummoxed, still trying to come to terms with the sacrifice my father had made, the fact that he'd simply handed over his pet project in order to keep me, *us*, safe. And that wasn't all.

"I can't believe Reed gave up so easily," I said. "Not because the project isn't worth a lot"—it was skyscrapers in Chicago, after all—"but because he'd be giving up Navarre House. Reed seems like the type who'd want to draw out the punishment as long as possible. Or, in this case, the extortion and loan-sharking."

"He is tenacious," my father said, and looked at Ethan. "He said something about the game not being done. He may be done with Navarre. But I suspect he isn't done with vampires. And I would be very, very careful where Adrien Reed is concerned."

Ethan looked at me. *The Investiture.*

His connection with Balthasar, I agreed. *He isn't giving up Navarre House out of some sudden sense of magnanimity. He's finishing the first*

*round of his game—Navarre—in order to focus on the second. Which
would be Cadogan House.*

But one thing bothered me, and I looked back at my father.
"The party at Reed's house. He was surprised to see us—didn't
expect to see us there. He didn't invite us?"

"He'd said a day or two before he wanted to meet you, although he hadn't mentioned the party specifically." His expression dimmed with obvious irritation. "He took care to remind me
of that."

Ethan nodded. "He knew the Navarre vampires would attempt to take out King. He wanted a front row seat, but he hadn't
wanted us there to interfere. Which is precisely what we did."

My father nodded, and I belatedly realized how tired he
looked. His cheeks were drawn, and there were shadows beneath
his eyes. "Do you want us to call Grandpa? He can pick you up.
Take you home."

"No. You should tell him what you know now, and that Navarre's debt has been settled. But leave me and Towerline out of it."

My eyes widened. "Leave you—you're a witness. You saw Maguire go into the house. We can't leave you out of it."

"But I didn't," my father said. "Not really. Just as Reed said, I
saw him refused entry at Reed's house. And I want no one to
know about Towerline. Our business will recover, but publicity
about the reason for the transfer won't help that. I promised him I
wouldn't. That was part of our transaction."

"And you trust him to keep his word?" Ethan asked.

"He is a keen and brilliant businessman. Looking back, I cannot say how much of that is hard work, skill, luck, grift. But we
have a truce, and I won't be the one to break it." My father rose.
"My car's outside. I want to go home and see my wife."

I nodded, rose as well. "I should say thank you, but I feel like that wouldn't be enough. You did a very generous thing. It's not the kind of thing I'll ever be able to repay."

My father looked down at me from his few extra inches of height. "I am a decision maker. For my company, for my family. I make decisions using the best available information, the best data. That data does not include liability. It does not factor popularity. My family, my company, are not democracies. When everything falls down, I fix it, because that is my job. That is my responsibility. That is my weight to carry."

He looked at Ethan, stared at him for a good, long while. "You'll protect her?"

The question, the moment, hung in the air like smoke. It was a changing of the guard, not because I needed protecting from either of them (I didn't), but because the obligation to protect me was passing from one to the other.

"I have since the beginning," Ethan said, his words holding a keen edge, a reminder that he'd saved my life when my father had inadvertently set my death in motion.

"Then I suppose we're done for tonight." With that curt phrase, my father walked to the door, disappeared into the hallway.

I sat down again, stared at the empty doorway, the room silent around me.

"I'm not certain what to say," Ethan said when the front door's opening and closing echoed down the hallway, "although I believe chocolate would be appropriate?"

I shook my head. "I need a drink. A stiff drink."

Ethan walked to the bar, poured something into a glass that was probably older and more expensive than I'd appreciate, and brought it to me without comment.

I downed it, squeezed my eyes shut against the burn. "Thank you," I said hoarsely.

"Mmm-hmm," he said, and took the glass back, placed it on the coffee table. "Gasoline?"

"Pretty much." But the warmth was comforting.

Ethan smiled, glanced at Morgan. "You can probably begin moving your vampires back to Navarre."

Morgan rose, nodded. "I'm going to make some phone calls."

"Consider having your lawyers adjust whatever documents are necessary to get the House back in control of its affairs," Ethan said, and Morgan nodded again.

After a final long look at me and a look of acknowledgment, Morgan left the room. Maybe he finally felt that the scales had been balanced.

"Can it be that simple?" Malik asked when Morgan was gone. "That Reed would simply hand back Navarre with no strings?"

"I think it was the simplicity that bothered Reed," Ethan said. "He is a player. He wants a challenge, and Celina made Navarre easy prey. He'd have enjoyed conquering Navarre, but it would have been over too quickly, the round too easily won."

I looked at him for a long, quiet moment. "He wants Cadogan."

"Possibly," Ethan agreed. "We beat Maguire in the chase that I presume Reed arranged, survived the accident. I suspect he's decided we're now legitimate competition. Or it could be more than that. All vampires? All supernaturals? All we know is that he has tired of this game and is ready for the next one."

"And in the meantime?" I asked. "What do we do?"

"We eliminate the threat we can eliminate. We focus on Balthasar. Let's go talk to Jude Maguire. But before we go— Malik, could you give us a moment, please?"

"Of course," he said with a knowing smile, rising and leaving the office, leaving Ethan and me alone, my father's generosity still buzzing in the air.

My smile was cautiously hopeful. "Did that just happen?"

"So it seems," Ethan said. "How are you?"

"I'm fine. Just stunned." He sat down beside me, and I looked at him. "Have I been misjudging him all these years? Has he been this generous, and I never saw it? Or was I right, and this is just an anomaly and he's going to demand repayment down the road?"

He brushed a lock of hair behind my ear. "I am sorry that you're forced to ask questions like that about your father. About someone who should always protect you, and without condition. It may be that he's remembering your sister, and wanted to make amends in the only way he knows how. That is, I think, why he tried to make you a vampire in the first place."

I sat back, closed my eyes. "Families are complicated."

"Living creatures are complicated," Ethan amended. "And since Jude Maguire still numbers among them, let's go hear what he has to say."

Chicago Central was a hospital complex of disparate buildings and architecture, at least a third of the buildings under construction at any given time. But then again, most hospitals seemed constantly in the process of morphing from one style into another, wings sprouting here and there like mutant insects.

My grandfather, Catcher, and Jeff waited for us in the hospital's bright and spacious lobby, which I guessed from the spotless floors and immaculate seating had been recently rehabbed.

"For you," Catcher said, handing back my dagger.

My relief at having it in hand again was almost palpable. I tucked it into my boot as discreetly as possible, felt better for that simple act.

"What's this I hear about Navarre?" my grandfather asked.

"We aren't privy to the details," Ethan said smoothly. "But a benefactor made an anonymous donation to address Navarre's outstanding debt. We understand Reed considers the debt satisfied."

My grandfather turned his cop's eyes on me. "A benefactor?"

I kept my gaze straight, unwavering, and I bluffed like there was no tomorrow. "That's what we hear."

He stared at me, unblinking for another long moment before turning his gaze onto Ethan. "That's all I'm going to get."

"That's it," Ethan agreed.

"So Navarre's debt is paid," Catcher said. "But what about the vendetta against King?"

"Still not settled, any more than Reed's interest in us, at any rate. But I suspect Reed is a patient man, and he'll be willing to wait for King."

"King will have to stay in witness protection until Reed's under wraps," my grandfather muttered almost to himself.

"Reed is rich, connected, and apparently has supernatural benefactors at his disposal," Catcher pointed out. "He won't be under wraps anytime soon. But for now, we've got Maguire. We bring down Reed one step at a time."

"One minion at a time," Jeff agreed.

"How is he?" Ethan asked.

"Conscious, under guard," my grandfather said. "He'll be arrested formally once he's clear. Let's go up and hear what he has to say."

As a vampire, I didn't have much use for hospitals, much need for them. But there was still something about the pale green walls, the antiseptic scent that made me nervous.

We followed a complicated trail from elevator to passageway to elevator, and finally through a gauntlet of nurses and cops before we reached Maguire's room at the end of a hallway. Two uniforms stood by the door, and they nodded when my grandfather approached.

"Mr. Merit," said the one on the left. "He's awake. Watching *COPS*."

"Ironic," my grandfather said.

"I'd have to agree with that, sir. Three of you can go in at a time."

"Me, Merit, Ethan," my grandfather said, then gestured for Catcher and Jeff to wait.

"Let me talk to him first," I said. "I think we have a rapport." Mostly of the ass-kicking variety, but I think that still counted.

"Lead on," my grandfather said, and we walked inside.

The room was small, as most hospital rooms were. A couple of counters, small bathroom, bed.

Maguire lay in the middle of it, looking weirdly small. Some of his hair had been shaved and his face was swollen, a thick pad of gauze around his head. He wore a blue hospital gown, his body covered by a thin white blanket with a waffle texture.

Maguire looked up when we entered, smiled at the sight of me, then winced at the pain the motion had apparently caused. "What do you want?"

"Answers, preferably," I said. "And thanks for destroying the Ferrari. Are you going to write us a check for that, or . . . ?"

"Fuck you," he said.

"Not interested. Tell us about Reed, Tommy."

His eyes flashed. "My name's Jude Maguire." He lifted his wrist, the plastic bracelet snapped there. "Says so right here."

"We've seen your picture with him, O'Malley. Reed didn't destroy them all. He missed one."

"Bullshit."

I smiled. "Absolute truth. It was a college photo—both of you with popped collars and keg cups. Very charming. And since we've got that photo, this would be a perfect opportunity for you to cover your own ass by explaining Mr. Reed's involvement in the Circle."

"I don't know anything about the Circle. Everything I know about Reed, I learned by watching television."

"You'll go to prison," my grandfather said.

"It won't be the first time, won't be the last." Maguire turned toward the window.

I thought of what Maguire had said about Balthasar on the island, his apparent distaste, decided to use it. "Balthasar attacked a woman last night."

"What's new?" he mumbled.

"She says he attacked her in her mind."

Maguire's eyes darkened. "You think I'm bad? I'm nothing compared to him. He's the one you should be afraid of."

"How so?" I asked.

"He hunts women. With no regret and no remorse. You ask me, he's just an asshole."

So there was dissention in Reed's ranks. "I wouldn't disagree with you." I took a chance, offered my unsubstantiated theory. "We know he's not the real Balthasar." Behind me, my grandfather and Ethan stiffened. "Who is he? What's his real name?"

Maguire smiled crookedly. "And spoil all the fun? No."

Ethan's magic flared behind me at the realization, the implicit confirmation, that the man who'd wreaked havoc in our House hadn't just been a monster—he'd also been a fraud.

But we'd have to deal with that later. First, we had to find out who he was.

I walked closer to the bed. "Then tell me how he got the details right."

Maguire coughed, winced again with pain. "Do your own work."

"Why? I know you don't respect him, Jude. And I'm guessing he's not making things easy for you—doing magic tricks on Michigan Avenue, for God's sake. That's not exactly helping the Circle stay underground. We bring him in because he's being an idiot, and I'd bet Reed reduces whatever percentage of the profits he's getting."

His jaw worked as he considered, but there was anger in his eyes, and I didn't think it was directed as us. "He was there."

Ethan pressed forward. "He was where?"

"With Balthasar. He was a prisoner of the Memento Mori."

CHAPTER TWENTY-THREE

WALK LIKE A (WO)MAN

Ethan needed time to breathe, to process, to cool off. Jeff, Catcher, my grandfather, and I gathered in the hospital lobby—Catcher standing, me on the floor in front of the bench Jeff and my grandfather shared—looking at the small tablet Jeff operated. Through the window, Ethan paced the sidewalk, phone pressed to his ear, probably talking to Luc or Malik.

Jeff continued to tweak his ledger-searching algorithms, still looking for mentions of Balthasar, but without success. "I got bubkes," he said, obviously frustrated. "The algorithm isn't working. It's not even catching words I can verify are actually in there. I can go through the microfiche by hand, but I'll want my own comp and scanner for that."

"We can provide staff to assist you with that. I'd bet the Librarian would be happy to help."

I looked up to realize Ethan was behind us, arms crossed over his chest.

You're all right? I asked.

No. But I will be as soon as I wrench his head from his body.

Jeff nodded. "That would be good. It'll go faster the more eyes we have."

"For the moment, let's think more broadly," my grandfather suggested. "Reed knew about this vampire. How?"

I looked at Jeff. "You said the ledgers were at a library in London?"

"Not the ledgers themselves," Jeff said. "Just the microfiche. A private collector owned the ledgers."

"A private collector?" Ethan asked.

"On that," Jeff said, diving into his tablet again. His response was nearly immediate. "Well, Odin's balls."

We all blinked, not sure whether to respond to the very creative curse, or the fact that he'd been excited enough to issue it.

He looked up, obviously exhilarated. "The Memento Mori's ledgers were purchased at auction by a private investor. The collector was represented at the auction by LMN, LLC."

"Odin's balls, indeed," I said, and glanced at Ethan. "That's one of the Circle's companies that paid for Balthasar's condo. When were they purchased?"

He scrolled. "Looks like four years ago. Oh, this is something. I've got the text from the auction catalogue. The ledgers were described as an 'intriguing exploration of the inner workings of a London cult, including references to monsters and vampires.'"

I glanced at Ethan. "Celina's relationship with the Circle started seven years ago, and we guessed the Circle learned she was a vampire at some point. Maybe that point was four years ago."

Ethan nodded. "He learns what she is, develops an interest in vampires, begins researching, compiling information. He then discovers our faux Balthasar, and proposes an arrangement to him."

"It's been a long con," I said. "And Reed is very, very patient."

"All right," my grandfather said. "Research, possibly the ledgers, would have given him Balthasar's history and enough about Ethan's to fill in the gaps. But how did he match the face? The voice? He'd have needed help."

Ethan nodded. "You're right. The 'Balthasar' we've been dealing with is a Very Strong Psych. The extent to which he can psychically manipulate—that's a level of vampire strength I've never seen, but it's not an impossible level. But that only explains part of it. It wouldn't explain his voice . . ."

Ethan looked away, nodded, considered. His gaze went distant, picking apart some faded memory. "It is the same. Precisely the same. The intonation. The intermingling of French." He looked up at me, at Catcher. "How could he have done that? How could he have matched it so precisely?"

"It's possible to emulate a person with magic." Catcher didn't sound thrilled about the possibility that that was what had happened. "It's in the same chapter as making a familiar, and equally as dark."

Mallory had reincarnated Ethan in an attempt to make him a familiar for her magical use. She hadn't entirely succeeded, but that magic, the darkness of it, had nearly sent her over the edge.

"So Reed's got this faux Balthasar, and a sorcerer to remake him?" Ethan asked, anger only just banked. Sorcerers, to his mind, caused trouble in Chicago nearly as frequently as vampires, even though there were fewer of them.

"The sorcerer would need an actual piece of Balthasar. A lock of hair, a bit of skin—"

"A tissue sample from the Memento Mori?"

We all looked at Jeff.

"They may have been torturers," Jeff said. "But remember

they were also scientists, at least to their minds. They collected samples. They ran experiments. If the ledgers survived, why not the samples?"

"So it was magic," I said, thinking not just of the tricks "Balthasar" had done on Michigan Avenue, but the entirety of his "visit" to Chicago. "I mean, there was preparation, sure. He'd have done his research, his homework, read the ledgers, learned about the man. But it was mostly magic, and he was the prestige."

"It was a *con*," Ethan countered, and looked at Catcher. "Can you talk to your Order contacts? Find out if there are any rumblings about a sorcerer in Reed's employ?"

Catcher nodded. "We can do that. Mallory's forensic skills could also help there."

I wondered if they could help with something else. I looked at Catcher. "I used to be immune to glamour, or at least a lot less sensitive to it. But after Balthasar attacked me, something changed. Everything affects me now. We weren't sure how it was possible—but maybe the magic had something to do with it. Maybe that's why it affected me."

Ethan and Catcher looked at each other, expressions considering.

"Magic and vampirism can do weird things to each other," Catcher said. "As we've seen. It's certainly possible."

I nodded.

"So if we've got all this right," my grandfather said, "and we've got a sorcerer helping another vampire play Balthasar, where's the *real* Balthasar?"

"According to Maguire," I said, "faux Balthasar knew real Balthasar from their Memento Mori incarceration. That means real Balthasar survived the attack by Persephone's family. And since Luc and Jeff managed to confirm some of what faux Balthasar told us about the rest of the real Balthasar's history, he survived the Memento Mori, too. But we'll have to go back to the timeline, those sources, to narrow it down any further than that."

Ethan nodded, then offered a hand, pulled me to my feet. "For now, we need to get back to the House, get ready for the Investiture."

"What's the dress code?" Jeff asked.

I hadn't known the Ombuddies had been officially invited, but I was glad of it. It would be good to have friends nearby.

"Black tie," Ethan said. "We're putting on a show, after all."

We returned to the House to find paparazzi outside, lining up for tomorrow's Investiture.

"Nick moved quickly," I said.

"As did Helen," Ethan said as vendors moved supplies through a checkpoint set up at the gate, carrying boxes of flowers, wineglasses, champagne.

"She's efficient," I agreed.

We walked inside, found the foyer absent of supplicants, the check-in table temporarily gone. If Balthasar took the bait and decided to cause trouble, they'd be in the line of fire. It was best to keep the House closed to anyone who didn't already need to be there.

We walked together to the Ops Room, found Luc reviewing a security plan with Keiji. Luc had been smiling, but his expression grew serious at the sight of Ethan.

"He's not Balthasar."

"He is not," Ethan said. "Although he did substantial work in preparing for the role. The Ombuddies suspect Reed engaged a powerful sorcerer and used tissue samples from the Memento Mori to emulate Balthasar."

"Oh, good," Luc said blandly. "Jeff's looking for the stand-in?"

Ethan nodded. "He wanted to use his own equipment. Would you please ask the Librarian to contact him about assisting?"

Luc nodded. "Roger that."

Ethan gestured to the House plan on the screen. "How is Investiture planning proceeding?"

"Good," Luc said. "Helps that we have the temps. We'll have people stationed along the perimeter. They'll watch and alert us if they see him, but they will not engage. We'll leave that to the two of you." He cleared his throat dramatically, looked at Ethan. "Unless of course you want to sit this one out for your own safety."

"No," was Ethan's immediate response. "This is personal, and I will handle it personally."

Luc nodded. "You're the boss. Mallory will have to drop the wards, of course, to let him into the House."

"She'll appreciate that," I said. "They're apparently exhausting to maintain."

"And she's invited," Ethan said. "She and Catcher both, so they can provide magical backup in the event he decides to utilize his cache of magic. I'm going upstairs to check in with Morgan and Scott. Morgan wants to send the Navarre vampires back."

Luc nodded. "We'll tell Chuck, keep going on Investiture prep."

Ethan nodded. "Join us upstairs when you're ready. I'd like to go over the plan with the team."

"I'll walk you out," I said when Ethan moved for the door.

We walked into the hallway, and I let the office door close behind us. "I think it's my turn to ask if you're all right," I said quietly.

"I let him into my House. I believed him. After all the years we'd been together, all the things I'd seen, I believed he was who he said he was. How did I miss that? How could I have been so stupid?"

"You didn't miss anything."

"Don't placate me, Merit."

I smiled. "I'm not placating you. You know I love to call you on your bullshit, but that's not what this is. Reed had the ledgers, and, apparently, a dark sorcerer willing to do black magic to make a vampire essentially become Balthasar. The entire exercise was designed to fool all of us, to use just enough illusion, and just enough fear, to make us believe."

I put a hand on his arm. "Maguire will soon be behind bars, and Navarre is safe again—or as safe as it's likely to be. Tomorrow night, we deal with Balthasar. And we end this."

"I end this," Ethan said, with conviction that chilled me to the bone.

I was mature enough to admit we weren't on the best of terms, but this was a crucial time, and sometimes one had to face one's fear.

So when I had a moment to get away, I walked upstairs to Helen's office, passed the closed door of Ethan's office, and rapped knuckles on the door. She looked up, face utterly blank.

"Yes, Merit?"

"I'll need a dress for the Investiture."

"Ethan has already spoken to me," she began, but I shook my head.

"Not black," I said. "Not black and not demure. I need something more. Something different."

Her eyebrows lifted. "For what purpose?"

I took a step toward her desk. "For the purpose of baiting this man pretending to be Balthasar, this man who wants to take the House from Ethan. Look, Helen, I know we haven't gotten along very well since—well, since the beginning."

Her expression stayed impressively blank.

"But let's put that aside. This man is a threat to Ethan, and I will not let anyone—or anything—hurt him. I need a dress," I said again. "A dress that will draw the man's attention, keep him focused on me. Because if he's focused on me . . ."

"He won't be focused on Ethan," she finished. She closed the binder on the desk in front of her, clasped her hands on the desktop, and looked me over from head to toe in a heavy and uncomfortable silence. She didn't need to say anything to make clear she was cataloging every curve and plane.

"Red," she finally said, lifting her gaze to my face again. "With some movement, and sufficient décolletage to keep his attention."

I could not have in a million years have imagined Helen referring to my décolletage, and I broke into a brilliant smile. I guess protecting Ethan brought out the best in her, too.

"You have a concealable weapon?"

Also technically a vampire no-no. The question didn't bother me, as I was used to my dagger, and relied on it often. But Helen was usually a rule stickler. Maybe I hadn't been giving her enough credit.

"Yes. Dagger and thigh holster."

She nodded, opened the binder again, began writing. "Heels. Support garments. You'll have to work on your walk," she said, looking up at me again. "You walk like a student. Possibly his Sentinel, but not his queen."

Nope. I had been giving her *exactly* enough credit. But me and my ego weren't the point.

I walked to her office door, closed it, looked back. "Show me."

I emerged from her office an hour later. An *hour* later, and in between had had to field several messages from Luc and Ethan wondering where I was. The answer, at least, was honest enough. PARTY PREP WITH HELEN. I AM SOCIAL CHAIR, AFTER ALL.

I didn't mention that she'd strapped me into heels, had me walk back and forth across her office until she was satisfied my posture was acceptable, my speed was appropriate, and my expression held just the right amount of "confident demureness." Her phrase, not mine.

"The grass will be soft," she'd said. "You'll want to stick to the sidewalks or the hard floor under the tent."

Or I could just take the damn things off and throw them at Balthasar, I thought, but wisely kept the thought to myself.

When the practice session was over, I gave the shoes back to her and walked down to Ethan's office. The door was open, representatives from the other Houses already there: Scott and Jonah, Morgan, Ethan, Luc, and Malik.

"This room is decidedly lacking in chicks," I said, practicing the walk as I moved to the conference table and joined the rest of them. I did not trip over the edge of the expensive antique rug, so I considered that a victory.

"I don't disagree in principle," Ethan said, "but the chicks are working while we run our mouths, so there's a current dearth."

I nodded at Scott and Morgan, then at Jonah, who I still wasn't entirely sure how to deal with. I carried my RG coin in my pocket just as I wore my Cadogan medal around my neck. Maybe that's what it would come down to: the choice between them. That certainly seemed to be the point of Jonah's hands-off approach: making me choose.

"We were discussing Balthasar," Ethan said, and I nodded, coming back to the present again.

"You don't think the plan should change because he's actually an imposter?" Scott asked.

"I do not," Ethan said. "He doesn't know that we know. And, more important, he seems quite committed to playing this role, to seeing it through. I say we give him that opportunity."

"I agree," I said. "It wouldn't surprise me to learn that he'd convinced himself he is Balthasar."

"Really?" Scott asked.

"Really. He was in my head. The only person he wants to be more than Balthasar is, possibly, Ethan." And that sparked an idea. "That raises an interesting possibility, a way we can increase the odds he shows up for a confrontation."

All eyes turned to me, but I looked at Ethan.

"We could break up."

Ethan's eyes turned to glassy green fire. "Excuse me?"

"We let it leak that we've broken up. We act like we've broken up. This Balthasar is committed to besting you, and he sees me as the chit. He's tried to use me to get to you before. I don't think he'd be able to resist the opportunity to try to get to me. I may not know Balthasar—not really—but I know the actor."

That reminder left the room in silence.

"It's not a bad plan," Jonah said. "Fireworks between you two will increase media coverage, and give him even more reason to show up."

"He did arrange for reporters and cameras when he first showed up for the reunion," I pointed out. "He loves a good show.

You could give the scoop to Nick. He'd probably be willing to boost the signal. It's a little gossipy for him, but he likes the supernatural beat."

Ethan stared at me, drummed his fingers on the table. He was as alpha as they came, and he was serious enough about us that he'd planned to propose. It couldn't have been comfortable to consider announcing to the public and press that our relationship had ended.

"It's not a bad plan. I'll talk to Nick."

There was a knock on the door, and Kelley walked in with a tablet. "I've got security plans for the Investiture, if you'd like to review them."

The Masters did, so they gathered around the tablet and got to the nuts and bolts of it.

Two hours of security detailing and ceremonial adjustments later, the sun was nearly on the rise again and the Masters were ready to depart.

To make our artificial breakup seem more realistic, I opted to sleep in my old room. Since we hadn't had an Initiate class this year, it hadn't yet been filled by another vampire. The room was small and clean, with a simple bed and bureau, a small bathroom. Nothing like Ethan's apartments, but cozy in its own way.

I lay down on the small bed, one arm behind my head, staring at the ceiling. It was weird to be here alone, to sleep without Ethan's body and heartbeat beside me, and I felt oddly self-conscious attempting to fall asleep. The sounds were different, the smells, the feel of sheets and blankets beneath me. And I was pretty sure Ethan had better-quality linens.

I stared into darkness, waiting for the sun to rise, for sleep to overpower me.

Good night, Sentinel.

His voice sounded a little lonely, which made me smile, if sadistically. It was good to know I wasn't the only one wanting.

Good night, Sullivan. In my absence, do try to keep your hands to yourself.

It was the first moderately suggestive thing I'd said to him since Balthasar. I think we both felt better afterward.

CHAPTER TWENTY-FOUR

LADY IN RED

The next evening, the energy and excitement in the House was palpable. The drama notwithstanding, the Investiture was an important ceremony. Ethan, Scott, and Morgan would be officially recognized as AAM members, and a new era for American vampires would begin.

There was a knock at the door. I threw off the covers, opened it, found a small tray outside the door bearing a bottle of blood, a Diet Coke, a muffin, and a two-inch-high pile of bacon. I might have been in a different room, and no longer—at least temporarily—Ethan's significant other, but Margot hadn't forgotten me.

Still, he'd become such a fixture in my life that it was odd to wake without Ethan beside me. "Balthasar" needed to show his lying and impostering ass tonight, because I wanted my Darth Sullivan back.

I checked my phone, found a dozen messages from family members, friends, and supernaturals with sympathies for the breakup. News, apparently, spread very fast. None of them were from folks in the House, so at least they'd gotten the word out. I'd have to make a lot of calls when the charade was over.

There was no message from Luc, so I showered and dressed in jeans and a Cadogan T-shirt—I'd be changing clothes soon enough anyway—and headed downstairs to the Ops Room.

Lindsey and Luc were at the conference table when I walked in. Luc was already in a tux, Lindsey in a sleek, sleeveless column of black silk that fell to her ankles.

"You both look amazing."

They looked up, glanced at me. "I think you're underdressed, Sentinel." Luc tapped his watch. "Party starts in an hour."

"I'm doing my Sentinel duty and checking in with you first."

"You're avoiding Helen." Lindsey smirked. "Which I get. 'Cause she scares the shit out of me."

"Helen's a peach," Luc said. "But that's neither here nor there."

"Let's get to what is. Any sign of Balthasar?"

"No," Luc said. "We put human guards on the condo, and he hasn't returned. The account manager was fired for speaking with us, so that's a no-go." He frowned, said almost to himself, "I should talk to Ethan about getting him some money or a stipend or something." Then he shook his head. "We'll deal with that later. Point is, no sign of Balthasar yet, but the news reports are building up this breakup thing pretty heavily."

"I'm devastated by it," I said.

"You look it," Lindsey said. "You could always give Morgan another try."

I gave her a flat look. "Been there, done that, DNF."

There was a knock at the office door. We glanced back, found Jeff Christopher in the doorway in a very striking tuxedo. It draped his lean frame perfectly, and he'd slicked back his brown hair, which sharpened his features. He looked a little older, and a little more dangerous.

"Young Mr. Christopher," Luc said, holding out a hand for him. "You look very official, sir."

"Very handsome," I agreed. I leaned over, pressed a kiss to his cheek.

"I'm sorry to hear about you and Ethan," he said.

Since we hadn't told all the guards about our plan, only the necessary few, Jeff was playing his part.

"Thank you. But I'd rather not talk about it."

He nodded solemnly. "Of course. If you need to vent, I'm here."

"I appreciate that. What brings you downstairs?"

"Balthasar, actually."

Luc went on immediate alert. "You've seen him?"

"No, but I think we figured out who he is. I'm sorry I didn't call sooner, but we—"

"Whoa," Luc said, holding up a hand, lips curving into a grin. "You think you found him?"

Jeff nodded. "The Librarian and me, after we started scanning the pages ourselves. He found Balthasar. I found two more names: Carlisle Foster and Julien Burrows. Carlisle's dead. He became a spy for the British during World War Two, was discovered and executed. Julien, on the other hand, has disappeared."

I felt the warmth of rising adrenaline. "Disappeared?"

"The ledgers say he escaped after a fight with the human who'd been left to guard him. The guard said Burrows, and I'm quoting, 'invaded his dreams.' There's no trace of him after that, at least under that name."

The warmth turned into a full-on fire. I squeezed Jeff's arm.

"That is good work, Jeff. Really good work. Can we connect him to Reed?"

"Not yet. But I'll keep looking. And Catcher's still looking for a sorcerer."

Jeff's phone began to buzz, and he pulled it out, took a look. "It's Chuck," he said, waggling the phone. "I'm going to head back upstairs."

"We'll see you," Luc said. "And really well done. I'll communicate your findings to the team."

Jeff nodded, then grinned at me. "Save me a dance."

"I'll do what I can," I said, and he winked and headed out.

"That's a spot of good news," Luc said. "And it's not the only one: Reed held up his end of the bargain, signed all the transfer papers during business hours today. Navarre is in the clear, at least with respect to anything it owed the Circle."

"Morgan must be relieved."

"Probably would be, except he's still got Irina to deal with. Word on the street is she's gunning for his job."

That made me sit up a bit straighter. "She's challenged him?"

"Not outright, but it could be coming. Do I think he has a unique chance to get his House in order given the circumstances? Yes. But he's got to take advantage of that, got to see it that way. Time will tell if he can do it."

Time would inevitably tell. "Ethan okay?"

"He's nervous. But security's in place and your grandfather and the CPD are in the loop. We'll all have earpieces, even the sorcerers, so we can stay in touch. We're recommending you and Ethan not contact each other telepathically until he's in our grasp. Whoever this guy is, he's a powerful, powerful psych. Could sense it, get spooked. And we don't want that. It's taken too much to get this thing planned. And now, thank God, there's nothing else to do but see it play out."

He crossed his hands over his stomach, grinned at me. "And, hopefully, watch you bring in an award-winning performance playing the vampire spurned."

"I was in several musicals," I said, rising from my chair. "Hopefully, it'll all come back to me."

"*Newsies* doesn't count," Lindsey said.

I thought about correcting her—clarifying that I hadn't been in *Newsies*, had only been obsessed with it—but decided it wouldn't help my case. Instead I looked at Luc in sympathy. "Don't we have a rule about no snark on an op?"

He lifted a shoulder. "She scored a pretty good hit with *Newsies*. I'm going to give her that one," he said, exchanged a high five with his girlfriend.

I rose, pointed accusatory fingers at both of them. "You two keep at it. I'm going to see a woman about a dress."

This wasn't just a party, so it wasn't just party preparation. It was an op, and since Helen provided the dress, she intended to oversee the dressing, too.

So for the second time in a week, I was made into something glamorous.

I was shuffled into the dressing room attached to the House's ballroom, closed off just for these purposes, where a staff of four humans hurried to turn me into a Sentinel Fit for a Ball, rather than the scrubby fighter Helen apparently seemed to think I usually was. I sat in a barber-style chair in a red bustier and matching panties, discomfitingly purchased by Helen while they swirled around me. The primpers—two men and two women—were also eager to talk about me and Ethan and the Breakup That Shook Chicago.

"It was so wrong of him to dump you," said a thin and tattooed man with a heavy beard and thick waves of dark hair, currently applying dark shadow and liner to my lids, cat's-eye-style.

Play the part, I told myself. "It was out of the blue," I agreed quietly, trying to stay still and keep the pointier ends of his tools from puncturing my eyeballs.

"You will make him so jealous," said a petite woman with a curling iron as long as her arm that smelled of heat and hair spray.

"That would be a bonus," I agreed, doing my best to offer an envious pout.

"Your dress is fabulous," said another woman, an adorable brunette with a butterfly clip in her hair and as many tattoos as the bearded man. "They're giving it a final steam."

"I haven't seen it yet."

"You'll love it."

"Very dramatic," said the tiny woman, clipping a curl into place while she worked on another section of my hair. "You're my first vampire. It's not really that different from doing a human, I guess."

"No," I said, staring at myself in the mirror when she moved away.

My eyes were darkly lined and shadowed, my cheekbones highlighted, my lips full and crimson. The bustier pushed up my not terribly impressive cleavage; stilettos with thin red straps that matched the dress showed off my quite impressive legs. My hair was dark and glossy, and as the hairdresser began unfastening the clips, it fell in large, loose waves around my shoulders.

This was to my prep work for Reed's gala what fast food was to the prix fixe at Alinea, Chicago's fanciest restaurant. Not really in the same stratosphere.

My bangs were tucked, the waves texturized and fluffed, and a faintly floral perfume was dabbed along my neck and ears. And the bearded man shooed the others away, moved toward me with a giant brush dusted with faintly shimmering powder the color of candlelight.

"Final step," he said, and began dusting my face, neck, torso, cleavage, which began to shimmer beneath the bulbs of the room.

"Just a hint of glow," he said. "We want vampire glamour, not Miami Beach glitter."

"Very nice."

We turned, found Helen behind us, arms crossed, the hanging dress in her hands. She gave me a businesslike appraisal, then nodded.

"I believe we're ready," she said, and handed the dress to me.

It was featherlight, panels of amazingly detailed floral lace and fluid organza, all in a deep crimson. The bodice was a deep-cut V of lace over a virtually invisible tulle panel, the arms bare but for a few bouquets of the same lace. The waist was narrow, the crimson organza over silk dropping straight through the hips and flowing at the knees in several fluid layers, the lace panels showing plenty of skin at the hips and thighs.

I let her help me pull it on, and when we'd managed to ensure that everything was nipped and tucked in all the right places, I checked the mirror.

For Reed's party, I'd looked wealthy and glamorous in my demure black gown.

Tonight, I looked sexy and dangerous. It took a moment of staring for me to grapple with that, accept that the striking and seductive woman reflected back was actually me.

"That," Helen said, "is a Sentinel of this House."

And it had only taken humans, a vampire, and a year to get me there.

Helen pressed diamonds into my ears and ensured that the thigh holster was snug and secure.

"One more thing," she said.

"No more diamonds."

She gave me a bland look, offered an earpiece.

"Ah," I said, and fitted it into my ear. "Test," I said quietly.

"You're live, Sentinel," Kelley said back to me, stationed in the Ops Room. "What's your ETA?"

"Four minutes. I'm about to walk downstairs."

"Roger that. I'm going to cue Ethan looking very, very jealous."

That sounded more fun than it should have.

The House's large backyard had been turned into an homage to spring. White canopies fluttered over tall urns of white flowers, and a string quartet played music on the back patio. A tent was set up near the square French garden, the water gurgling beautifully in the background. White paper lanterns created a stunning glow, adding to the ethereal look and the sense of rebirth. The event was about a fresh start for the Houses, but it was also about a fresh start for Ethan, a break from his past, or at least from a monster who'd attempted to assimilate it.

I'd always wanted to make a delicious entry, an adolescent dream of walking into the room and having all heads turn toward me.

Tonight, I wasn't an awkward teenager, but an adult. I wasn't trying to get the curly-haired quiz bowl captain to notice me—I was baiting an old, powerful vampire. And I wasn't walking into a gymnasium or cafeteria decorated with glitter and paper to look like Paris or Rome, but a majestic white garden full of fragrant flowers, and vampires in glamorous dress.

I imagined Helen was behind me critiquing every motion and

Ethan's life was on the line, and took the demilune stairs from the patio to sidewalk. I was the only one, at least as far as I could tell, in red, and stood out among the Cadogan black and demure dresses. There was absolutely nothing demure about my dress, my expression, or now that I thought about it, the walk Helen had taught me.

Heads turned as I took the paved path toward the tent. I surveyed the crowd with an even stare, met Helen's gaze, watched as her satisfied smile spread and she inclined her head in approval. I could hear the whispers around me, the questions and comments of vampires in demure gowns and tuxedos, wondering at the Sentinel in red who'd stepped into their midst.

They probably believed I looked like a woman begging for a man's attention. Good, since that was exactly what I'd been trying to do. And if our luck held, he'd show.

I searched for Ethan, found him near a table beneath the canvas, champagne flute in hand. His tuxedo was trim and immaculately tailored, his hair pulled back in a short queue. He looked absolutely magnificent, like a wicked angel hoping to sway a human or two to his very convincing side.

His gaze raked my body like a spurned lover, and I swallowed back a bolt of lust. I wasn't supposed to be lusting for Ethan, or at least giving in to it. We'd broken up.

He gave me a rough perusal before looking away, turning to the woman who stood before him, a brunette with a glossy bob of dark hair, her curvy body tucked into a sleeveless black dress with a flared skirt and black Mary Jane–style shoes with stiletto heels. His hand was on her nipped-in waist, and jealousy stronger than any I'd ever known bolted through me.

If she didn't have a hand on his arm, and I wasn't filled with a completely irrational bout of jealousy, I'd have appreciated how gorgeous she looked, and how perfect his snub had been.

I reminded myself to compliment her later. As for now, I gave her a scathing look before turning away, giving my back to both of them . . . and laying into Luc.

"Margot?" I whispered. "He invited *Margot* as his date to the Investiture? She's *my* chef."

Luc guffawed through the earpiece. "She's the *House's* chef, Sentinel, and she was Ethan's chef first, in any case. And he knew you'd get a kick out of that. And it makes the performance so much more real."

"You look amazing in that dress, but you're turning absolutely green."

I turned to find Mallory and Catcher behind me, both wearing amused expressions. Mallory's dress was Grecian in style, a long skirt of draped fabric gathered in gold clips at the shoulders and a thin gold belt around the waist, The fabric was vibrantly blue, which matched hair that curled around her head in a loose updo, a gold-ribboned headband holding it in place. At least I wasn't the only one wearing color.

Catcher wore a black suit over a white button-down, no tie, the top button unfastened. He looked sexy and a little rough around the edges, like a race car driver.

"I'm not jealous. I'm envious. There's a difference."

"You know he can hear everything you're saying right now, right, Sentinel?" Luc asked with no little amusement. "He has an earpiece, too."

When Ethan grinned down at Margot, a smile probably meant for me, I didn't much care. "Then he'll hear me warn him: Touch her again and lose a finger," I said sweetly.

Mallory grinned. "Merit doesn't like other people touching her things."

"Any sign of Balthasar?" I asked.

"Not yet," Catcher said.

"Damn," Mallory intoned, amazement in her voice. "Are there any ugly vampires?"

I glanced in the direction of her dreamy smile, found Jonah walking toward us, eyes on me. His auburn hair gleamed like bronze, highlighting his blue eyes, and in his dark tux, he looked like an Armani runway model.

"Get out of my dreams," Lindsey sang into my ear, "and into my car."

"There's a lot of male sexualizing going on right now," Luc said. "And it's making me uncomfortable."

"Snark is allowed on an op," I reminded him.

"Check out Mallory's boobs again," Lindsey said to him. "You'll feel better."

Mallory grinned, wiggled her shoulders for effect. She was in a good mood, which made me hopeful she'd talked to Catcher and resolved her doubts. But we'd get to that later.

"Focus," I said. Since Jonah kept his gaze on me as he approached, I kept my gaze on him.

"Hello," he said, eyes dipping to take in the gown, the lace, the skin. "You look nice."

"Thanks. So do you."

I felt the burst of Ethan's magic across the tent. Party guests noticed, too, and began whispering, just as if we'd actually broken up. The ruse had played pretty well.

"If you touch her," said a familiar voice in my earpiece, "you'll lose something more precious than a finger."

"Take a breath, Sullivan," Jonah intoned, his gaze on me. He slid his hands into his pockets, and I braced myself for the worst, for him to ask me to return the saints' medal he'd given me to mark my RG membership.

But his tone was utterly bland. "Any sign of Balthasar yet?"

I surmised he was still angry, whether at me, the RG, or the circumstances.

Since I was utterly in the right, I kept my tone flat and business-like. "Not yet. But we believe he's a vampire by the name of Julien Burrows who once knew Balthasar. Like Balthasar, he was imprisoned by the Memento Mori, but he escaped and disappeared."

"That's new."

"Hot off the presses," I said. "Jeff found the link a little while ago."

"The Masters are here," Ethan said through the earpiece. "Let's begin the ceremony and see if that draws him out."

They gathered on a dais at the end of the tent—three Master vampires in tuxedoes, all of them handsome beyond any human measure or level of appropriateness.

"Ladies and gentlemen," Ethan said, "thank you for joining us here tonight. We come to begin a new tradition, to celebrate the Investiture of the Chicago Masters into the American Assembly of Masters."

"Hear, hear!" shouted voices across the crowd of vampires, who filtered into the tent to hear the ceremony. None of them were Balthasar.

"Just as our American forefathers did nearly three hundred years ago, we have relieved ourselves of interests that didn't align with our own, men and women who sought to keep their power intact at all costs and to the detriment of the American Houses. Tonight, we celebrate the beginning of a new era." Ethan raised his glass of champagne. "To Cadogan, to Grey, to Navarre!"

"To Cadogan, to Grey, to Navarre!" they repeated, and clapped wildly for their Masters while I scanned the crowd for danger.

"Anything, Sentinel?" asked Luc through the earpiece.

"Nothing at all," I responded, covering the answer with my champagne glass. "Maybe the ceremony's too ceremonial. Maybe he's biding his time." But for what?

Ethan handed the microphone to Scott. "We have vowed," Scott said, "to protect the vampires of our Houses, to support their happiness, their freedom. We reiterate those vows here, and now, and pledge that our membership in the Assembly is intended solely to foster those goals. We pledge to reject any action, any resolution, that would harm our vampires. We pledge to keep our vampires' interests at the forefront of our minds in all decisions."

Scott passed the microphone to Morgan. "We take these vows here, before you whom we serve, before the Novitiates we have made, before our colleagues and friends"—he looked at Scott and Ethan—"before the other Masters with whom we share this city, because if we cannot hold the city safe, we have failed not just our vampires but each other."

Morgan and Ethan shared a long and intense look before Morgan turned to the crowd once again. "We make these vows to you, our Novitiates, tonight. May our Houses eternally prosper, may we eternally serve, and may our vampires enjoy eternally good health."

"Hear, hear," Ethan said, and the vampires burst into applause again.

And still there was no sign of Balthasar.

Another hour passed, and I was getting more nervous. Mallory, Catcher, Jonah, and I noshed on puffs of this and slivers of that, and scanned the crowd surreptitiously for some sign of him. But he wasn't there. And maybe he wouldn't be.

I sighed. "Maybe he isn't coming. Maybe this was too obvious, too much a trap." Maybe, I feared, I'd gotten it wrong from the beginning, and this wasn't the way to do it. Maybe we'd have to call him out.

"Some ops require patience," Catcher said, and I looked at him.

"You've been talking to my grandfather, haven't you?"

"I work with him. When am I not talking to your grandfather?"

A valid point.

I stood up. "I'm going to take a stroll around the grounds. If he's here, or watching, maybe that will pull him out."

"Be careful," Jonah said. "Luc, you got eyes?"

"All cameras on and functioning. I don't see him anywhere out there, but that doesn't mean he's not in a shadow we can't reach. Watch yourself, Sentinel."

"I will," I promised, and played the role. I imagined myself a spurned woman forced to watch her lover dance, smile, chat with another, a woman who wanted space from the betrayal, the emotions.

I kept my chin lifted, but sadness in my eyes, and slid a final glance at Ethan as I stepped out of the tent and onto one of the paths that wound through the lawn. I crossed my arms as if chilled, as if vulnerable, while the music faded behind me.

It had been the perfect ploy.

As I reached the side of the House, and before I could call up a dramatic tear, *he* stepped out of the shadows, looking discomfortingly handsome in a lean black tuxedo, dark hair falling across his face. "You are quite a sight, *chérie*."

And now it was my turn. I pushed down fear and revulsion, the panic that snatched at my chest with skeletal hands, and I made my voice breathless. The raven bracelet kept his glamour at bay, but he didn't need to know that. And I could still feel it swirling around me, so it wasn't hard to feign vulnerability.

"What are you doing here?"

"I am watching his cruelty, and thinking of you. Does it pain you to watch your lover touch another woman? To know that you've lost him?"

I looked away. "I don't care what he does."

"Oh, *chérie*, I can see the pain in your eyes." The man who would be Balthasar moved a step closer, the magic stronger, vibrating around me as it tried to penetrate my defenses. And the figurative probably wasn't far from the literal there.

I caught the scent of bay rum, felt my gorge rise at the memory of his hands on my body, pushed it down again.

"Would it pain him, do you think, to watch me touch you?"

He took a step forward, lifted his hand to my face. I let my eyes go soft, let him caress the backs of his fingers against my cheek, and worked not to show my disgust.

"You are agreeable tonight. Perhaps because he's left you. Because you're available to me." He stepped forward, his body against mine, obviously aroused, his lips against my cheek. "Will you cry out my name?"

And that, as they said, was enough of that. "Which name is that? Did you mean Julien or Balthasar?"

He froze, hot magic prickling around me. I'd have sworn I felt it surge forward, and be battered back by an answering wave. His magic taking the offensive; the apotrope's magic pushing it into retreat.

Slowly, he lifted his gaze to mine, his eyes boiling quicksilver. "My name is Balthasar."

"No, it isn't. It's Julien Burrows. You knew Balthasar. Were imprisoned with him." I looked at the scars at his neck. "Were probably tortured beside him. But you aren't Balthasar."

Before I could move back, he knotted his fingers into my hair.

"My name is Balthasar. Say it!" he said, jerking my head back. "Say it!"

He sounded earnest. Maybe he thought the pretense was necessary if he wanted to take Cadogan House. Or maybe that was just the magic, slowly transforming whatever might have been left of the man into the one he sought to emulate.

Whether lie or delusion, I was done being a pawn. "You are *not* Balthasar."

He yanked my hair again, reared back to slap me with his free hand. I blocked the shot with my forearm, and he dropped my hair in surprise. We broke apart, but I'd snagged the raven bracelet on his jacket. It broke open and fell to the ground.

No longer dammed, his magic spilled across me like dark wine, and suddenly the air was too thick to breathe. I hit the ground on my knees, sucking in air as his magic, angry and biting, spun around me like a typhoon. He wanted me under his control, imprisoned by his magic, a pawn he could use.

My instinct was to fight, to strike out and strike back, to push his magic back with magic of my own, however poor an opponent it would have been. And then I remembered what Lindsey had reminded me.

"You're a rock in the current," I heard her say, either from memory or through the earpiece I still wore. "Let his magic flow around you. It doesn't penetrate, doesn't affect you, just moves like the breeze."

There on the ground, mud seeping through the knees of my dress, I closed my eyes and let my breath come softly, in and out.

His magic advanced again, determined to cow me, control me. I acknowledged his magic, took its measure. It was hot, biting, and remarkably insistent. Rejection made him push harder, but I made no answer. I was sweating with the effort of not responding, ignoring every instinct to fight against the glamour that sluiced over me like suffocating water, that sought to convince and compel.

Like a breeze, I said to myself. *Like a breeze.* Maybe I was no longer immune to glamour, but I was still stubborn. Those words became my mantra, and I repeated them over and over as the barrage continued.

As suddenly as it had begun, the magic dissipated. In apparent shock that he hadn't managed to move me, Julien had dropped the glamour, stepped back.

I opened my eyes again, breathed deeply, and found his magic had fouled the air with bitterness.

"Bitch," he said, chest heaving from the effort. "You bitch. I own you, just like I own him."

"I'm not a bitch for saying no, Julien. You're just an asshole."

Fury rolled across his face. "I am *Balthasar*."

"You are Julien Burrows."

We both glanced back, found Ethan behind us. His expression was utterly blank, but his body was primed and ready for battle.

"You bastard," Julien said.

"I'm not," Ethan said. "And as Merit explained, we already know who you are. We know the Circle is paying for you to be here. We know about the Memento Mori, your time with them. And we know about Reed."

To his credit, Julien took a step back, breathed deeply, and reassessed. He'd been discovered, his lies realized, and he looked to be considering his next steps.

"He talked about you often," Julien said. "How he loved you. How you were his proudest creation. How you'd betrayed him. He knew that—that you'd betrayed him. That you'd given him up to the relatives of the woman he'd fucked." His smile was reptilian. "He never said her name. Just called her 'the girl.' She was human," he said, as if the implication was obvious—that, her being human, her name wasn't worth remembering.

"But he mentioned you frequently," Julien continued. "Your betrayal. His capture and torture. The fact that Cadogan House should have been his. That it certainly shouldn't have been held by a deceiver. So I'll do what you failed to do—protect your Master—and I'll take it back for him."

"You won't," Ethan said, then casually removed his jacket, tossed it aside, began to roll up his sleeves. "But would you like to try it?"

"I have power you can't imagine."

"I look forward to seeing it."

Julien belted out his glamour again, its claws snatching like rabid animals. Catcher and *Canon* were fond of repeating that vampires didn't really make magic, we only spilled it. It was just a byproduct of who and what we were. Glamour, by that theory, was a fluke.

But this was no fluke. It was powerful and unrelenting, and it demanded an answer.

Julien might have managed to glamour Ethan the first time around, but this time Ethan had known it was coming, and he was prepared. And he wasn't exactly a psychic slouch. His expression was mild, but he let his own glamour spread, clean and bright and sharp as newly honed steel.

Their magicks mixed, mingled, flowed through each other like two storms meeting, growing as their energies collided, burst, spilled tingling ions into the air. Julien growled in frustration, screamed as his magic erupted forward again. Sweat beaded across Ethan's face, but he pushed back with his own glamour, a swell that flooded forward over Julien's and slowed its surge.

They pushed their magicks back and forth until their clothes were damp with effort, until their faces streamed with sweat, until the air vibrated with power, drawing a crowd that gathered on the edges of the carefully sculpted grounds to watch the battle.

No, vampire magic was no fluke, and these men were masters of the craft.

A fountain of sparks followed another volley, and Ethan paused to wipe sweat from his brow.

"I believe we've reached a stalemate," Ethan said. "If you really want to fight me, you'll have to fight me with muscle, not show."

"I resent that remark," Catcher muttered through the earpiece.

"Fine by me," Julien said, and pulled off his jacket, tossed it aside. "I will destroy you with my own bare hands."

Ethan's answering smile was fierce. "You're certainly welcome to try."

They faced each other, Julien's chill against Ethan's fire.

Julien ran forward like a raging animal, aiming low for Ethan's waist and torso, clearly intent on throwing him to the ground. But he'd foreshadowed the move, giving Ethan time to prepare. Ethan set his feet, spread his weight, and when Julien hit him, redirected the force upward, throwing Julien's body over his head.

Julien managed to land on his feet, looked back at Ethan with silvered eyes and gleaming fangs. He used his superspeed and rushed forward, a blur of black silk and wool. And then the sound of flesh and flesh connecting, and Ethan's answering grunt.

His head snapped back from the force of Julien's blow, blood spraying through the air.

I jumped to my feet, lurching forward until Jeff's voice resonated in my ear.

"This is his fight, Merit."

I looked up, found his face in the crowd, his expression solemn and somehow older than his years. "He fights for his honor," he said, "and for yours. Let him fight it on his own."

Ethan spat blood, wiped a smear of it from his face, and stared Julien down with swirling silver eyes.

This, I realized, was the closure he hadn't gotten. The fight he'd never been able to have with Balthasar, might never get to. At least he'd get closure here.

I nodded to Jeff, took a step backward. Sometimes I had to let Ethan fight his own battles.

Julien had gotten in a shot and didn't intend to lose the momentum. He spun into a kick that would have connected with Ethan's kidney. Ethan blocked it with a hand strike, offered his own side kick. It connected, and Julien grunted, stumbled. He righted himself, tried a front strike that Ethan neatly blocked. And then it was one strike after another, both of them moving quickly, the pace quickening with each blow.

Ethan moved forward with an uppercut that connected with Julien's jaw and sent him sprawling to the ground.

Julien shook his head, slowly climbed to his feet again.

"You should have stayed down," Ethan said, hands on his hips.

"Because you're getting tired?" Julien said, spitting blood.

"No." Ethan smiled, with fangs. "Because Merit gets the final shot. And she's a better fighter than I am."

While Julien looked on, Ethan walked toward me, pressing the back of his hand to his bleeding lip.

I still goggled at the compliment. "I'm a better fighter than you?"

"Well, in fairness, I did train you. I've tried to soften him up a bit," he said, his eyes brighter than I'd seen them in weeks, the monkey nearly off his back.

I grinned back. "I appreciate that. But I'll probably ruin my dress."

"I'd expect nothing less, Sentinel. We've started insuring them." He winked at me, then gestured grandly toward Julien, let me step past him.

I put a hand on my hip, faced my opponent, who looked back at me with obvious derision. He thought Ethan was making a strategic mistake.

"Does he let you finish all his battles?"

"Only the easy ones," I said, and didn't delay the inevitable. I hitched up my skirt—this one being a little more flexible than the last—and kicked up and out. He was fast enough to block it, to grab my leg and twist, trying to send me off-balance.

But I'd already played that game once this week and wasn't about to lose points to that technique a second time. I shifted my weight to the leg he held, used his grip for balance, and spun around, executing an airborne parallel kick with my free leg. He'd lifted an arm to block, but missed, and I connected with his left side. He stumbled forward, leered back at me when he'd righted himself.

"One lucky shot," he said, and sped toward me. He jabbed, and I dodged the shot, his fist glancing off my shoulder, but with enough force to still make it sing. He'd left his torso open, and I punched him in the stomach. He grunted, staggered, came back again.

I'd give him strong and tenacious. But any asshole could be strong. His next shot was a right cross. His speed hadn't diminished, but he favored the side I'd kicked, and he telegraphed the move. I grabbed his wrist, swung it down, using the leverage to force him to the ground.

I stepped over him, planted a foot on his neck. "When a woman says no, she means it, you raging sack of crap."

"Fuck you."

"I already declined that very unattractive offer," I said, and pressed a little harder. Jacobs and his men had already moved into the crowd, so my time was nearly up. Might as well use it for something good. "Where's Balthasar?"

When he didn't immediately answer, I pushed harder on his windpipe. "Where. Is. Balthasar?"

"Dead. He's dead. He died at the Geneva safe house." That was the one Luc hadn't been able to reach.

Ethan's relief peppered the air.

I lifted my foot. Julien's hand rushed to his throat, massaged.

"Elaborate," I ordered.

"They thought he'd been rehabilitated." He coughed, and his voice was hoarse. "They were wrong. He killed a human girl who'd delivered supplies to the house. The safe house couldn't protect him; he was staked. There's a marker for him at Plainpalais Cemetery."

That was verifiable information. So I took a step back and swept dirt from my dress as Julien coughed.

I looked up, nodded at Jacobs. "It appears Mr. Burrows has fallen, Detective. I believe you can handle him from here?"

"You'd be right about that," Jacobs said, stepping forward. "And given his psychic propensities, we'll make sure he's in a magically appropriate space. Julien Burrows," he said as the uniforms hauled him to his feet, "you're under arrest for three counts of sexual assault, one count of attempted sexual assault, trespassing . . ."

"You son of a bitch!" Julien screamed. "Deceiver! *Deceiver!*"

The screaming and recitation of charges faded away as the cops and suspect moved around the House toward their waiting transportation.

I walked toward Ethan, took in the torn shirt spotted with blood, the bruise under his cheek, the blood on his face. "You kind of look like a disaster."

After a moment's hesitation, Ethan burst into laughter.

"Are you all right?"

"At the moment, Sentinel, I'm not. But I've got you and my House, and I will be."

CHAPTER TWENTY-FIVE

AVOWAL

I t was done. With three more phone calls to Switzerland and Ethan's excellent French, we verified Balthasar's ignoble end. He'd used "Bernard" as his alias in order to distance himself from activities in London and any lingering members of the Memento Mori. Julien had stuck to the truth about much of Balthasar's history, which Ethan verified with the safe house's archivist.

And with that, the ghost who'd haunted our dreams—literally and figuratively—was finally gone. Yes, there was still Reed and his sorcerer to deal with. But this threat, at least, had been neutralized.

Most of the vampires had left the party, returned to their Houses. Our group—our Cadogan and Ombuddy family—still sat at a table beneath the tent looking utterly relaxed and sipping the rest of the champagne.

"What's the saying?" Ethan asked. "You don't have to go home, but you can't stay here?" But he grinned at them, accepted the glass of champagne that Luc offered.

"We were just saying how gorgeous the garden looked," Jeff

said, "and how you'd probably agree to let them use it for their wedding."

Since nobody at the table looked surprised, Mallory and Catcher must have shared the nuptial news. "I don't want any fuss."

"It wouldn't be any fuss at all," Luc said. "Right, hoss?"

"Of course not. I actually already offered her the garden, if I recall."

"He did," Mallory said, reaching out to pat his arm. "It was a very nice offer."

"And it still stands." Ethan grinned. "Hell, we're all dressed in pretty clothes, and the garden will hardly get any better than this. We could just do it now."

He'd meant it as a joke, but a weighty silence fell as Mallory and Catcher looked at each other.

"We couldn't," Mallory said. "Could we?"

Catcher scratched the back of his neck, looked at Mallory. "I don't know why we wouldn't, actually. There's never going to be a perfect time. Isn't that the point of love, or marriage, in the first place? Recognizing that perfection is irrelevant? That imperfection is sometimes kind of perfect?"

Mallory pressed her lips together, trying to will back tears.

"Oh my God, are you two seriously about to get *married*?" Lindsey drummed her feet on the ground like an excited child.

Catcher didn't take his eyes off Mallory, but reached out and squeezed her hand. "I kinda think we are, yeah."

Ethan looked at the group. "Anybody licensed to perform a ceremony?"

Grinning, Jeff raised a hand. "Actually, I am. River nymphs," he explained with a shrug, and I was momentarily bummed I hadn't been invited to that particular wedding. The nymphs knew how to party. "Do you have a license?"

Mallory nodded. "I got it yesterday."

"Then we're good," Jeff said.

"Oh my God," Mallory said, her excitement rising, her eyes glowing with love and happiness. "Oh my God." She slapped Catcher's arm. "We're going to get married."

"It does look like that."

There was no regret in his eyes. No remorse. No hesitation. Just happiness, and maybe a bright edge of nerves.

Good, I thought with a grin. *Those nerves will keep him honest.*

Ethan nodded. "That takes care of the officiate. What else?"

"If we're doing this," I said, "we're doing it right. We need the traditional things—something old, new, borrowed, blue."

I looked around, grabbed the pocket square from Ethan's jacket, pressed it into Mallory's hand. "Blue," I said, and Mallory's eyes filled with tears of shock and surprise. She squeezed her fingers around it.

"Thank you," she mouthed.

"Borrowed," my grandfather said, pulling a watch from his pocket and extending it to Catcher. "My father gave it to me, and I'd be honored for you to carry it."

Obviously swamped with emotion, Catcher wrapped his arms around my grandfather, squeezed. "That is . . . that is just excellent, Chuck."

"Damn it," I murmured, knuckling my own tears away. "I didn't want to cry any more this week."

"I don't think we're going to be able to avoid it," Lindsey said, putting her arms through mine and Mallory's, linking us together. "We are going to be mewling like kittens before the night's up."

"And then Mallory will be mewling like a kitten for entirely different reasons."

We all looked back at Jeff, found his eyebrows winging up and down in amusement. "No? Too soon?"

"For the officiate, yes," I said.

"We need old and new," my grandfather said, avoiding the by-play.

"I believe I count as old," Ethan said. *"Technically."*

Mallory and I exchanged a look.

"Four centuries is probably as good as you're going to get," I said.

"Then we'll check that box," she said. "New?"

"I got this," Jeff said, squinting as he patted down his pockets. After several groping seconds, he pulled out a small green key-chain with a single key attached. It was a square of green rubber, "JQ" embossed in lime letters.

"New Jakob's Quest swag came out this week," he said, passing it over to Mallory with a sheepish grin.

"That'll do," Mallory said kindly. "Thank you very much."

Jeff nodded. "You're welcome. And I think that's it. New, borrowed, blue, vampire."

Ethan grinned. "Shall we get arranged?"

Mallory looked at me, squealed. "I'm getting married! Holy shit, holy shit, holy shit!"

"I think you are," I said. "But you didn't get a proper bachelorette party."

"Are you kidding me?" Mal whirled a finger in the air, gesturing to the tent and surroundings. "This was exactly as kick-ass as a bachelorette party needs to be. Food, drinks, vampire excitement. Sullivan knows how to throw a party."

"I do," Sullivan agreed.

"Bouquet!" Jeff said, then dashed over to a peony bush,

snapped off an early white bloom nearly as big as a salad plate, and carried it back to Mallory. "Milady."

She took it, sniffing the bloom's frilled petals, and nodded. "Thanks."

"Actually," I said, glancing between Catcher and Mallory, "there is just one more thing."

Before anyone could argue, I grabbed Catcher's arm, dragged him a few yards away to the other side of a hydrangea border that hadn't yet bloomed.

"What the hell are you doing?" he asked when I pulled him to a stop.

I fixed on my most powerful and predatory expression. "Mallory's parents aren't here, but I am. You want to marry her, you'll need my permission."

"You cannot be serious."

"I am as serious as it comes. Are you marrying her because you want back in the Order?"

For a moment, he stared me down in hard silence. "If you were a man, I'd punch you in the face."

I lifted my eyebrows expectantly. "You haven't answered the question."

When Catcher realized I was serious, he relented, sighed hard. "Of course I'm not. The timing is convenient, yeah. But the marriage is love. Her and me." He shook his head. "I nearly lost her once. I won't lose her again."

When his eyes went misty, I looked away. He wouldn't have wanted to be caught with tears in his eyes, and he'd have gotten me started again, too. And besides, he'd answered my question. It wasn't just about the Order for Catcher. By the look in his eyes—the clear adoration—that had only been an issue of timing.

The ball of concern in my gut unknotted, and I smiled at him. "Okay, then."

"I should still punch you."

"Considering the present company, I don't recommend it." I slipped an arm through his. "Let's go get you hitched."

Everything all right? Ethan asked with some amusement when we joined them again.

Just making sure we're all on the same page.

I assume, since he's still breathing, that we are.

You'd be correct.

We scooted around so Mallory and Catcher stood facing each other, Jeff in front of them, the rest of us in the audience. We were an odd group, some of us newly acquainted, some of us friends for a very long time. And what better reason to come together than love?

Jeff cleared his throat, looked around, and when he got a nod from Catcher, began to speak.

"Friends, family, vampires. We are gathered on this really odd night to witness the marriage of Catcher Eustice Bell—"

My eyes brightened. "Your middle name is 'Eustice'?"

"It's a family name," Catcher said. "Shut your piehole. Keep going, Jeff."

"Catcher *Eustice* Bell," Jeff said again, with a wink for me, "and Mallory Delancey Carmichael."

He looked back at Catcher. "Catcher, do you take Mallory to be your lawfully wedded wife, to have and to hold from this day forward, for better or for worse, for richer or for poorer, as long as you both shall live, including accidental or intentional immortality?"

Catcher ignored the supernatural smart-assery, reached out, and squeezed Mallory's hand. "I do."

Jeff smiled, turned to Mallory. "And do you, Mallory Delancey Carmichael, take Catcher to be your lawfully wedded husband, to have and to hold from this day forward, for better or for worse, for richer or for poorer, as long as you both shall live, including accidental or intentional immortality?"

Mallory shifted her gaze to Catcher, looked at him with love and awe and humility that made my tears start all over again. "I do."

Jeff nodded, gestured toward them. "There don't appear to be many dry eyes right now, but just to make certain everyone's appropriately emotional, would you like to address each other, offer some vows?"

Catcher scratched absently at his neck, and I waited for his gruff refusal. But instead he nodded deeply. "Yeah, actually, I would."

"Me, too," Mallory said. She handed me the peony, and they took each other's hands, turned to face each other.

For a moment, they said nothing. They stood with love between them, in a silence that spoke volumes more than words ever could.

I ignored the tears that fell now, let them slide down my cheeks.

"We've had some tough times, kid," he said, and a warm chuckle spread through the crowd. "I know, understatement. So they were the toughest times. Times when we didn't know which way was up, or who we were individually—or together. I let you down. Jesus, did I let you down. I let my own petty bullshit blind me, let it keep me from seeing you for who you were, and who you were becoming. And that's on me, and it will be forever.

"But it didn't matter that I'd let you down, because you were strong enough for both of us. You put in the effort. You did the work, even when it was humiliating. Hell, you did the work because it was humiliating, and you started from scratch. And that meant a lot. 'Cause yeah, you did it for you, so you could find yourself again. But I think you also did it for us."

Tears spilled over Mallory's lashes as she nodded.

"I love you," he said. "I don't like to talk about feelings, primarily because I have testicles, and I know how ridiculous this sounds, but I think I've known I loved you since the first time I saw you, right before I kicked Merit's ass for the first time at the gym.

"Since that moment, I never stopped loving you. I was afraid for a while, sure, but I never stopped. And I won't. For better or worse, I won't ever stop."

"Well said," Ethan remarked, and we all applauded the speech before turning our eyes to Mallory.

"I haven't known much of family," she said. "A bit here and there, but not in the way most people do. That bothered me for a really long time, and I searched for it for a really long time. And then I made a new kind of family." She glanced at me. "I met Merit, and we had some wonderful times."

I smiled back at her.

"And then I met Catcher, and we had some wonderful times. But something was still off, inside me." She frowned. "I screwed up pretty monumentally, mostly because I mistook power for comfort. I was looking for peace, to fill that well inside me that hadn't ever really been full before, and I thought magic was the way to do it." She looked around at all of us. "I don't know if I've ever said that to you all, but I think it's important that I say it now. I thought I needed to fill that empty space. But the more I filled it with magic, the darker and emptier it became."

Tears slipped to fall down her cheeks. "I betrayed a lot of people in that time, a lot of trust." She shook her head, smiled a little. "But you people were stubborn, and you wouldn't let me go. You just kept interfering, trying to pull me away from it. And eventually, you did."

She looked back at Catcher. "That darkness is still there. That emptiness. It's like a well in the plane of my soul. But I've learned, I guess, that *I* have to fill that up. That it's my responsibility to do that. So, I guess I wanted to explain that to you all, to let you know that I'm working on it."

She shook her head again as if to clear it, raised her gaze to Catcher. "Of all the supernatural bombs dropped on me that very first week, you were easily the biggest. Pain-in-the-ass sorcerer, grumpy most of the time, addicted to *Lifetime*. But you loved me, even with the well, even with the darkness. And you didn't give up, even when you could have walked away. And that means more to me than you will ever know." She sniffed. "I love you, Catcher Eustice Bell."

Catcher's eyes, suddenly red-rimmed, bloomed with tears. "I love you, Mallory Delancey Carmichael."

Jeff cleared his throat. "In that case, I think it's time to say that by the power vested in me, I now pronounce you husband and wife! You can kiss the bride!"

As we erupted with applause, Catcher drew Mallory toward him, cupped her face in his hands, and kissed her so furiously even I blushed. When he finally drew back, Mallory's cheeks were pink and flushed, her eyes glazed, a glow of happiness around her.

Love wasn't perfection. It wasn't always roses and candy. Hell, it wasn't even *mostly* roses and candy. Sometimes it was battling back fear that loomed like a leviathan, trying to find a way through misery, being grateful to have a companion who knew your strengths and weaknesses, and loved you not just in spite of them, but because of them.

Love was acceptance. Love was bravery. Love was sticking it out.

One day, Ethan said silently, squeezing my hand, promising me what was to come.

When the time is right, I said, and squeezed back, the agreement between us reached.

When the time is right, he agreed, and pressed a kiss to my temple.

Still in Catcher's embrace, Mallory smiled at me, pointed to the peony in my hand. "You know, Mer, you're holding the bouquet. I think that means you're next."

And perhaps sooner rather than later, Ethan said with a chuckle.

When Catcher and Mallory dashed off to their make-do honeymoon, and the rest of the guests had left, Ethan and I walked inside again.

He wanted to check his messages, determine if there was any other business he'd need to attend to before, we'd decided, we'd take the rest of the night off for an evening of pizza and movies in our apartments. Nothing sounded better.

At least until Ethan's office door closed, and the lock slipped into place with a quick snap of metal.

I looked up from my seat on the couch, found him staring at me. His jacket was off, his shirt unbuttoned at the top, hands on his lean hips.

"Sullivan?"

"Sentinel." He strode forward. "I believe we have some unfinished business."

We did. And with Julien Burrows behind us, the threat of him gone, the desire I'd banked came rushing back. I rose from the sofa, walked toward him.

"You are the most desirable creature I have ever seen."

"You aren't seeing what I'm seeing," I said. The glamour, the magic of the evening, the defeat of Julien Burrows and the ghost of Balthasar had given me a buzz of power and confidence. I decided to use it to advantage.

"Take your shirt off."

He arched an eyebrow. "Are you giving me orders, Sentinel?"

I met his gaze with my own, and when he saw that I wouldn't back down, he moistened his lip. Given his obvious and growing arousal, he wasn't opposed to the idea.

"Very well, then."

He stepped out of his shoes, kicked them away. Then he unhooked one button, then the next, each revealing another inch of his flat and solid abdomen. When the shirt was open, he slid it off his shoulders, and his eyes darkened to the color of a deep forest.

"Next?" he asked.

My heart was thudding in my ears as I watched him watch me, but I managed a word. "Belt."

"As you wish." He unhooked it, slid it through the loops with a snap of sound, looped the black leather around his hand in a manner that was equally arousing. It was a hint of experiences we hadn't shared. But if his knowing gaze was any indication, that wouldn't be the case forever.

"You look intrigued, Sentinel."

"How could I not be?"

"Indeed."

"Pants."

His eyebrow arched. "You're fully clothed. That would leave me utterly naked."

"And in your office. Where I plan to seduce you well and thoroughly. I gave you an order, Sullivan."

His body flushed with desire, eyes hooded with anticipation as he unbuttoned, unzipped, and let the pants fall to the floor. Beneath, he wore boxer briefs, the rigid line of his arousal obvious beneath them.

This time, I wet my lips.

He walked toward me. "I believe it's time to claim what's mine." He reached me and, before I could object, lifted me into the air and crossed the room. He sat me atop the conference table, stood between my knees, and captured my mouth with a brutal kiss.

His hands slid down my body, cupping my breasts, inciting the fire in my core. His hands found the dress's zipper, and it fell away, revealing the red bustier. He took only a moment to appreciate it before ripping it away. His eyes flashed silver before he found them with teeth and tongue until my head dropped back, the pulse in my ears like a timpani drum.

He pulled the rest of the fabric away, stripping me of sense and leaving me breathless and naked. And when we faced each other, naked and vulnerable, he cupped my face in his hands and kissed me deeply.

"Lie back," he said, and guided my head back to the tabletop, the polished wood cool beneath feverish and heated skin.

He slid down my body, using hands and lips and teeth to drive me to the brink.

When his fangs grazed the inside of my thigh, my head shot up. But the sight of him between my thighs, eyes silver and fangs bared, silvered my eyes.

Timing is everything, he said silently.

When he bit, fangs piercing tender skin, it was like gold rushed through my veins—hot and metallic and precious. Pleasure overtook me, blinded me, had me crying out his name.

And then he stood again, and his hand was above my heart, tracing a path to my abdomen. "You are so beautiful."

I opened my eyes, looked up at him, blond and muscled, his eyes silvered, his mouth swollen. "You are the sexiest thing I've ever seen in my entire life. Will ever see, probably."

"Correct," he said, and joined our bodies with a powerful thrust that arched my back. "As you're mine, and mine alone."

"Ethan," I said, and he anchored our hips together. Thrust again, and again, until he'd blocked out all sensations other than the union of our bodies, the arch of his body over mine.

I opened my eyes. "Call me," I said, and his eyes went dark.

"You don't need to prove anything to me."

I didn't. But if I was destined to be a vampire, I was entitled to know what other vampires knew. To feel what other vampires felt, and not because of violation or threat. Because, as Lindsey had discussed, of trust, and love, and connection.

I lifted a hand to his face, smiled as wickedly as I could. "I'm not proving anything. I'm taking what I'm owed."

His eyes flashed with desire.

"I want that between us, Ethan."

He nodded. "Very well, then. Close your eyes, Sentinel."

At first, he only said my name. *Merit*, the word a soft embrace. He was, I knew, acclimating me to the sensation, preparing me for what was next.

And it was something entirely new . . . and entirely different.

He said my name again. *Merit.* But this time, it wasn't just sound, but a calling. It was as if his voice were a light in the darkness, the bright world that waited at the end of a passageway. There would be no loneliness for me. No more isolation. Because he had created me, this Master of vampires, and made me something wonderful and magical and immortal.

I felt my lips part, felt sound escape them. He answered with a driving thrust that echoed through me like the *thrum* of a bowstring.

He called my name each time he drove into me, so that every part of my body seemed in synchronicity with his.

"I love you," I said breathlessly, my body taut with anticipation. "God, I love you. I love you."

I love you, he said to me, without sound, but no less meaningful. *Merit,* he said again, calling my body home, sending me over the edge. Pleasure sparked through me like a live wire. I lost my breath on a gasp, my body bowing like the crest of a wave, the entire universe and its history in my mind.

And Ethan in my heart.

"I don't suppose," I said after some long minutes had passed, when he lay beside me on the conference table, breathing in tatters, "that you'd like to tell me about that nickname you had for me."

Ethan chuckled. "And ruin the mood? No, Sentinel. I don't believe I do."

He rose, covered my body with his. "And I've ways of making you forget the very question."

I let him prove that.

EPILOGUE

———— ✦⤞✦⤝✦ ————

He messaged me just after midnight, asked for a meeting. And when I walked into Dirigible Donuts, a late-night favorite in the Loop, Morgan Greer sat at a small metal table, a foam cup of black coffee in front of him.

He looked up at the sound of the bell on the door, and the young man behind the counter smiled, but the look didn't reach his weary eyes. "Welcome to Dirigible Donuts. How can I help you?"

His voice was monotone, and just as tired.

I grabbed and paid for a bottle of water, sat down in the aluminum chair across from Morgan.

He smiled nervously, scratched a hand through his hair. He looked tired. That didn't detract from his handsomeness—it sharpened the edges in a pretty nice way, actually.

"Thanks for coming."

I nodded. "I'm not really sure why I'm here."

"I guess I wanted to talk through some things." He paused. "I think you got to know me, Mer. For a little while, anyway. Before things got complicated. Before all this—the drama, the spectacle. I'm not perfect. I'm not aiming to be. But I'd like to be better than I was."

"I can't give you redemption."

"I know."

"Celina changed everything, Morgan. Hopefully, they've realized by now the amenities will have to change. Belts will have to be tightened. But even beyond that, this isn't the Chicago she ruled two years ago. She changed the landscape, with other Navarre vampires beside her."

"I know," he said. "I think one of the reasons they loved her is that she kept them in the dark. Everything was wonderful—even when it wasn't—because she didn't tell them the truth. Because she sold them a very complicated lie about who they were and what the world believed of them.

"They may not want to hear the truth," he admitted. "And they may not let me back in because of it." He paused, seemed to firm his determination. "If that's what it comes to, so be it. But I can't do this anymore. Trying to play her, to cajole people I don't agree with. If they want someone else as Master, they should have it. I want to run the House differently. Not like Celina, not like Cadogan. Like me. Like Navarre."

With those four words, he sounded more like the Morgan I'd known before he bore that mantle of authority. He'd still been rash even then. Jealous and a little prickly, especially about me and Ethan. But he'd also been happy. And I hadn't seen him happy in a very long time.

"If worse comes to worst," he said, "I'll go my own way. Go Rogue, maybe hook up with your grandfather again."

I blinked. "My grandfather? What do you mean?"

He grinned at me. "Didn't you know? When he started out, I was the vampire who gave him information about the Houses."

My eyes widened with shock . . . and appreciation. "That was *you*? You were reporting to the Ombudsman's office while standing Second to Celina? Did you have a death wish?"

Morgan laughed full out, so that even the clerk, now wiping down a counter probably sticky with powdered sugar and stained with coffee, smiled a little.

"Maybe I was doomed from the beginning," he said. "Maybe there was no way I could have held the House."

"You hold it," I reminded him. "And you've held it since she died. Cadogan and Navarre may never be best friends. But there's got to be a middle ground between friends and enemies, or for Navarre vampires, between narcissism and self-abnegation."

Wasn't that, after all, precisely what Ethan had done? He'd avoided the worst of Balthasar's selfishness, but was confident enough to make his own way in the world. To pick a route and undertake it, and damn those who disagreed. They could captain their own ships.

"I'm sure there is," Morgan said. "The question is, will they go for it?" He took a sip of his coffee, glanced at me over the rim with amusement in his eyes. "You interested in becoming Second of a new Navarre House?"

There was literally zero chance I'd leave Cadogan House, much less for Navarre. It was an impossibility.

But still . . . there was something in his question that intrigued me.

I frowned down at the table, trying to unpack *why* it was interesting. Why the thought of standing Second was something I couldn't just dismiss.

I let myself imagine what might have happened if Morgan had asked the same question when he originally got the House, before I'd been committed to Ethan.

If he'd asked, and I'd said yes, I'd be second-in-command of the oldest vampire House in the country, a House established the same year the U.S. Constitution had been ratified. (Joshua Merit could choke on that.) I could admit it—the possibility of helping lead a House was attractive.

And if we were playing out this alternative history, I'd have become a kind of enemy to Ethan just as he'd been wooing me with seductive promises (and, admittedly, the occasional back-slide into haughty arrogance). I imagined furtive glances at meetings between Cadogan and Navarre staff, a stolen kiss in the Navarre garden, a brush of fingers beneath the conference table, a pilfered night in the stacks of the Cadogan library.

"You're awfully quiet over there."

I looked up at him, grinned. "Just thinking about history. Morgan, you need a Navarre vampire. You need one of your own, someone you respect, someone of the same blood. Someone who can challenge you when necessary, but present a united front when you face the enemy."

"If it were that simple, I'd have done it by now."

"You'll find someone," I assured him. "You'll find someone, and they'll help you build the House."

Morgan nodded, took the final sip of his coffee, three-pointed the empty cup into a nearby trash can.

"Come on," he said, standing up. "I'll buy you a donut."

Now, that was an offer I could accept.

I walked back into the House, only mildly embarrassed that I'd chased two donuts with a bottle of blood and seriously considered stopping by Portillo's for a cake shake. I managed to overcome the temptation, not in part because of the memories of our Mallo-cake Massacre. I still bore the mental scars.

I walked into the House, found Helen straightening the foyer table in preparation for the next night's supplicants.

She looked up, stood up. "Oh, that's convenient."

I closed the door, too high on sugar to be bothered with what I expected would be an insult. "Is it?"

She nodded, picked up a brown paper package, extended it. "A CPD officer left these for you."

I took the package, felt nothing ticking, no sense of metal or weaponry. "Who?"

"It's not my business," she said haughtily, as if managing my incoming mail—limited though it was—was too much of a burden. "It was left with the guards. They're hardly going to interrogate an officer."

Must have been from Detective Jacobs or my grandfather, although it was an odd way to get something to me.

"Okay, then," I said, and started for the stairs. "Good night."

A glance down the hallway said Ethan was still in his office—the door was open, the light on. So I took my package to his office, found him sitting in one of the club chairs with a bottle of long-neck blood in one hand and a book in the other.

I paused in the doorway, smiled at him. "Now, that's a sexy picture."

He glanced up, smiled. "Hello, Sentinel. How was your meeting?"

"Morgan's going to give Navarre House another try. And I got a donut."

"Only one?"

He knew me too well.

"What's in the package?"

I glanced down at it. "I'm not sure. Helen said a CPD officer left it for me."

Ethan took the final drink of blood, put the bottle and book on the coffee table. "From your grandfather?"

"I don't know. It's a little weird," I admitted, and sat down in the chair beside him, put the package on the table in front of us. It was tied with twine horizontally and vertically, as a Christmas gift might have been wrapped with ribbon. I untied it, slipped the tape around the paper with a fingernail, and drew open the edges.

Ethan's magic spiked beside me.

Six leather-bound books, the same size as the one I'd seen in "Balthasar's" room the night he'd attacked me. These had covers of taupe leather with burgundy spines, well-worn with age. A grinning skull was embossed in the cover above the letters "M.M."

"The Memento Mori's ledgers," I said, opening the cover of the top book delicately with a fingertip, and a piece of thick cardstock fell to the floor.

THE GAME IS AFOOT, it read. MAY THE BEST WIN. AND IN THE MEANTIME, A TOKEN OF APPRECIATION FOR OUR FIRST ROUND. I BELIEVE YOU'LL FIND THESE INTERESTING READING.

The card was signed, in bold slashes, "AR."

So Adrien Reed had come full circle. A few weeks ago, he'd drawn us into his world with a note from one of his players. And now he reminded us that he held the trump card—a card he'd gotten a member of the Chicago Police Department to deliver to our House. But he hadn't just held the card; he'd stacked the entire deck.

"Ethan," I said quietly after a moment, not sure what else to say.

But Ethan Sullivan was rarely at a loss for words. "Every move he makes," he said, quietly and carefully, "is another bit of evidence against him, and it brings us one step closer to his downfall."

He pulled me into his arms, his breath warm against my cheek. "Let us be still, Sentinel. And let us help him toward defeat."

Chloe Neill was born and raised in the South, but now makes her home in the Midwest – just close enough to Cadogan House and St. Sophia's to keep an eye on things. When not transcribing Merit's and Lily's adventures, she bakes, works, and scours the Internet for good recipes and great graphic design. Chloe also maintains her sanity by spending time with her boys – her favorite landscape photographer (her husband) and their dogs, Baxter and Scout (both she and the photographer understand the dogs are in charge).

Visit her on the web at:

www.chloeneill.com
www.facebook.com/authorchloeneill
www.twitter.com/chloeneill

Love 😀 Funny and ❤ Romantic novels?
Then why not discover

IMMORTALITY'S BITE

Blind dates can be murder – or at least that's how Sarah Dearly's turned out. Her dates 'love bites' turn her into a vampire and make her a target for a zealous group of vampire hunters. Lucky for her she's stumbled onto an unlikely saviour – a suicidal vampire who just might have found his reason to live: her.